## Praise for Louis Paul Boon

One of the few truly magnificent novels in Dutch language literature. A masterpiece. —*De Volkskrant*

The most powerful epic to come out of Flanders this century. —*Elsevier*

Even now that experimental writing is commonplace, it has lost none of its freshness and vitality. —*The Times Literary Supplement*

One long, exuberant flow of language. If Boon cannot get the whole world into a book, he does manage to encompass much of it. —*The Nation*

## Other Books by Louis Paul Boon in English Translation

*My Little War*

*Summer in Termuren*

# *Chapel Road*

Louis Paul Boon

Translated from the Flemish by Adrienne Dixon

Introduction by Chad W. Post

DALKEY ARCHIVE PRESS

Dallas, TX / Rochester, NY

Deep Vellum | Dalkey Archive Press
3000 Commerce Street, Dallas, Texas 75226
www.dalkeyarchive.com

Deep Vellum is a 501c3 nonprofit literary arts organization founded in 2013 with the mission to bring the world into conversation through literature.



Originally published in Flemish as *De Kapellekensbaan* by De Arbeiderspers, Amsterdam, Netherlands, 1953

First Dalkey Archive Press Edition, 2003
First Dalkey Archive Essentials Edition, 2025


Support for this publication has been provided in part by grants from the National Endowment for the Arts, the Texas Commission on the Arts, the City of Dallas Office of Arts and Culture, the Communities Foundation of Texas, and the Addy Foundation.

Library of Congress Cataloging-in-Publication Data:
Names: Boon, Louis Paul author | Dixon, Adrienne translator
Title: Chapel road / Louis Paul Boon ; translated from the Flemish by Adrienne Dixon.
Other titles: Kapellekensbaan. English
Description: Dallas, TX : Dalkey Archive Press, 2025. | Series: Dalkey Archive essentials
Identifiers: LCCN 2025010262 (print) | LCCN 2025010263 (ebook) | ISBN 9781628975192 trade paperback | ISBN 9781628975444 ebook
Subjects: LCGFT: Experimental fiction | Novels
Classification: LCC PT6407.B57 K313 2025 (print) | LCC PT6407.B57 (ebook) | DDC 839.313/62--dc23/eng/20250508
LC record available at https://lccn.loc.gov/2025010262
LC ebook record available at https://lccn.loc.gov/2025010263

Cover art and design by Justin Childress
Interior design and typeset by Kaija Straumanis
Printed in the United States of America

## ON *CHAPEL ROAD* BEING A DALKEY "ESSENTIAL"

Debating what makes a Dalkey book a Dalkey Book is a philosophical exercise that's two parts silly and one part a pathway to an academic career. So, three parts silly.

John would often say, "A Dalkey Book is a book that Dalkey publishes," sometimes replacing that second "Dalkey" with an "I," a truism that's nearly impossible to argue with—especially since there are a thousand titles (and only a few people—if any—who have read them all) to support your argument as to what constitutes the quintessential Dalkey book.

But there's something useful to categorizing Dalkey Archive's backlist and pulling out and observing the tricks and techniques, the approaches that rhizomatically connect great works of literature across time and space, eventually giving rise, when seen from above, to an implied literary tradition both invented and fostered by the press's list. There are many routes by which to traverse any finite and constructed tradition such as Dalkey's, detours and digressions to distract, trails veering off to books of all kinds—some fun, some extremely serious, some duds, some life-changing. In my opinion, at least, one firm path running through the forest of Dalkey backlist leads to work exemplifying a heightened awareness of the influence of form. A sort of impossible object that can observe itself coming into existence. For these works, the old adage holds true: it's not the story itself that makes a classic, but the way that story is told. Bonus points to Dalkey Archive's best books, which accomplish this with complexity and self-awareness.

*

As a guideline on how to write an introduction for a classic, underappreciated work, I can call to mind several others in which the Introduction Writer, writing about the book being reprinted, a book that usually has fallen out of favor, but had, back in a sepia-toned past, a great impact on the Introduction Writer's formative years, a book the new youth should also be formed by, and as such, in one of those sort of very good, solid, dependable introductions, this Introduction Writer will recount the first time they encountered the book, lingering on its feel or smell, the particular bookstore in which they first uncovered this gem; the professor who recommended this book in an offhand way, oblivious to the impact it would have on the Introduction Writer's life; the Introduction Writer's romantic entanglements at the time, an ex-girlfriend, the one who got away after gifting the book. An origin story that rightly balances serendipity and fate in a way that's both nostalgic and contemporary.

So here's my version: I found the Twayne Publishers 1972 edition of *Chapel Road* by Louis Paul Boon—the first ever English translation of the book you have in your hands, reader (another sort of statement that a lot introductions include, possibly because they want to make sure you notice the beautiful new cover of the product you purchased)—right outside my office door in Dalkey's headquarters in Funks Grove, Illinois on a shelf marked: "Netherlands."

This was the same day that John and I found out the Dutch Foundation for Literature was sponsoring us to spend a week in Amsterdam learning about the literary scene: authors old and new, translated and not, with the goal of producing a Dutch Literature Series. At the time, I knew of Harry Mulisch (*The Assault* is tight, brilliant) thanks to my bookselling experiences, but, like most Americans in their mid-twenties, nothing else. Which is why I turned to John's extensive library and found . . . a Flemish masterpiece.

Now I'm not going to pretend that I understood the nuanced difference between Flemish and Dutch at the time, but I did know that, from the opening paragraph alone, Dalkey Archive was going to reissue this book:

> *Chapel Road* which is the book about the childhood of ondine, who was born in the year 1800-and-something . . . who fell in love with mr achilles derenancourt, director of the spinning mill 'the filature', but who will at the end of the book marry poor oscarke . . . about her brother valeer-traleer, with his monstrous head wobbling through life this way and that . . . and about mr brys who was one of the first socialists without knowing it . . . about her father, vapeur, who wanted to save the world with his godless machine, and about all the things which I can't quite recall now, but which try to draw a rough sketch of the laborious RISE OF SOCIALISM, and of the decline of the bourgeoisie which got knocked down by two world wars and collapsed. But between and besides this it is also a book set in a much later time, in our own time of today: whereas ondineke lived in the year 1800-and-something, msieu colson of the ministry, johan janssens the journalist, tippetotje the painter, mr pots and professor spothuyzen—and you yourself, boon—live today, in search of the values which really count, in search of something which will check the DECLINE OF SOCIALISM. But . . . heaven help us if it isn't going to be more than that: it is a pool, a sea, a chaos: it is the book of all that can be heard and seen in chapel road, from the year 1800-and-something until today.

I don't know what makes a Dalkey Novel a Dalkey novel, but this sure is an impressive way to start one.

*

A common trope among Dalkey's most beloved books is a character within the book writing a book. Flann O'Brien's *At Swim-Two-Birds* is a novel about a young man writing a novel within which a novel is being written and the characters have to write their way out. It's a form Gilbert Sorrentino plays with in *Mulligan Stew*, his novel of poorly written chapters that pays homage to *At Swim-Two-Birds* while innovating on the trick. Most of Dumitru Tsepeneag's intricately structured books are about writing the struggles of writing a novel. *The Making of Americans* is incredibly aware of itself as an attempt to write a novel. Coover's *A Night at the Movies*. All of Barth. The number of examples in the back catalogue are too many to list here. Especially when you include not just the books with the narrator explicitly writing a book inside the book, but books that puzzle themselves out as they go.

This sort of play, in which a novel is aware of its construction in progress, dates back to the Greeks, runs through Joyce and *Tristram Shandy* (the book I'm going to likely fail to convince you is most closely aligned with *Chapel Road*) and the work of all the authors named above, is, to a lot of people who fall into the orbit of Dalkey Archive's backlist, incredibly fun and rewarding to encounter in all its iterations from across the globe.

*

I'm cheating in that last little riff. In an attempt to make you a Louis Paul Boon fan, I gave you my backstory of picking that book up off the shelf and finding the sublime in the opening paragraph, then immediately tied this to the Grand Tradition of Innovative Literature and subtly implied that if you're hip, if you're a literary reader, a "Dalkey Reader," you'll love this sort of meta shit. Which isn't a given: most books written in this self-aware style are boring flops. Failed experiments. It's a risk trying to write an intro in the vein of the book's own style, especially when choosing One Big Idea affirming *Chapel Road*'s space in the Dalkey Essential Series—a truly self-indulgent gesture, given that I came up with the idea of the Essentials and decide what gets included. Especially since there are other, equally valid Big Ideas on which to frame this same argument, such as how the best Dalkey Books are voice driven, or how "Big & European" is a defining feature of Dalkey's backlist.

But maybe, just maybe, that flaw is what points to what works so well in the titles of this sort that Dalkey publishes: they're self-aware of their own shortcomings.

But before we get to that, first, a bit about *Chapel Road*.

*

Even though Flemish isn't Dutch, and two different governmental organizations fund the two literary traditions, John and I were able to visit Antwerp (dreary, gray) on our Amsterdam trip. We visited the Louis Paul Boon Center, where we learned about the author's porn habit and the untranslated sequel to *Chapel Road* entitled *Summer in Termuren*, which we immediately acquired and had translated. John also loved that opening paragraph, and our joint enthusiasm made Louis Paul Boon a Dalkey Author since he was published by Dalkey.

Also on this trip we discovered Paul Verhaegen's *Omega Minor*, an incredible Pynchonian novel set in the 1990s but about World War II and loaded with all the requisite Nazis, theoretical physics, and the self-awareness to qualify as a "Dalkey Book" of the formally innovative variety.

Also, another Flemish book.

Dalkey has yet to publish a Dutch book.

*

*Chapel Road* is exactly the book it says it is. In it, l.p. boon is writing a book called "Chapel Road" about ondine, a young woman growing up in the shifting times when industrialists and the wealthy ruled everything, and the little man had to organize for their rights. But that book is constantly interrupted by all of boon's friends who come to check in on him, shoot the shit, criticize his novel, gossip, and complain about the tide shifting away from socially-conscious policies and toward more capitalist-driven ones.

I should note here that my lack of capital letters in the previous paragraph is intentional and mirrors the book itself. Throughout *Chapel Road*, Boon's eschews most capitalization and his punctuation is haphazard. In proofing this newly typeset version—the one in your hands: this intro is aware of being an intro—there were a number of instances where I'm not sure if a particular quirk was intentional or if someone at Twayne just dropped the ball. I left those in, since they haven't bothered anyone in the fifty-plus years the book has been in print, and, on a good night, I can read meaning in the extra space between "ha" and "!" as a textual way of playing up the joy in the exclamation—"ha!" Instead of just "ha!" it comes off as two beats, a joy that bounces over the little blank space to be both a "ha" and a "!"

So we've got boon's book, the "Chapel Road" inside *Chapel Road*, and the interruptions, which are equally important and account for about the same number of pages in this hefty novel. And then we have the third part: johan janssens's newspaper columns, mostly about Reynard the Fox and Isengrum the Wolf. He retells these fables to critique the current situation, but even outside of that context—don't worry, the history isn't daunting in this book—these are entertaining interludes. Which is key, since although Boon (and boon) writes with the lightness that Calvino describes in his *Six Memos for the Next Millennium*, there's some heavy shit depicted in this novel—especially in depicting ondine's social situation.

One scene in particular—no spoilers—deserves a totally different introduction that examines this book from a more feminist perspective. Or at least one more historically grounded and coming at the text from a sociological vein. A bit of a teaser for you.

But that's the sort of analysis you get in the next reissue of *Chapel Road*; in this one you just get structure.

*

And we'll end with that structure, and the awareness of it on both Boon and boon's part. But first, I have to pick up that earlier thread about the best of these books being aware of themselves and their shortcomings. That's prevalent throughout *Chapel Road*, both from the shit-shooting friends who tell boon to write different, or with more detail, or why doesn't he do this?, and from boon himself, who includes chapters he immediately wants to abandon, playing out his initial statement that this book's shape, its structure, is "a pool, a sea, a chaos."

As I was saying, this book starts by stating what it's going to be and then tries to get its engine going through a series of fits and starts. The first half-dozen pages are l.p. boon telling us what the novel is that he's going to be writing, until he finally gets into it with a handful of sections that lay out the situation in which ondine finds herself and of which, when we, the readers, alongside l.p. boon's friends, who are also readers (and/or listeners), finish that depiction of what he's going to do, we get this:

> As far as I can make out, says the music master, all the people you write about are abnormal: you pick hundreds of little facts from normal life but you mix them unrecognizably into a teeming mass and then you push this mass on to some non-existent plane.

Which, in an academic setting, is one of those moments in which a "book teaches you how to read it." *Expect interruption and interrogation of what you just read.* The text isn't sacred; it's a text that's observing how it tries to say something it believes is important.

And then we get to page 33 and johan janssens makes a very metatextual gesture by physically pointing to a printed (maybe) critique of a book we're watching try to come into existence:

> But johan janssensn interrupts you now by asking whether he wasn't talking about something altogether different, about the drama reaching its climax? Haha, and with a great gesture he reaches into his inside pocket and conjures out of it a weekly journal . . . the illustrated art review . . . and moving his index finger down the columns he says: wouldn't it be better to torment yourself with this here: although the writer of ondineke of termuren has remarkable talent, he lacks a sense of drama and he speaks flemish in such a way that his pathos seems nothing but feverish ranting . . . Then he folds the journal up and says: well, here you are, letting your heroine think and thinking yourself whether she's thinking about the right thing and there they're saying not only that your pathos is feverish ranting, but also that you've got no sense of drama . . .

But as I was saying, it's not just boon's friends who interrupt his flow and invade it with their ideas; he's just as prone to do it to himself by imagining a chapter that will never be written:

> This is the end of the chapter 'middle class recipes', but something seems to be missing: it should really have been written quite differently, more stress should have been laid on the incomprehensible desire to keep up appearances against all better knowledge. But if this had been stressed more, then the title should have been altered too . . . for instance: the proletariat of the middle class . . . yes, that would have been something.

*

All of this is fun, a special mix of criticism of art and culture and entertainment, and I hope by now you're on board enough to dip your toe, cautiously, into this book that I assume you've already bought—not for this introduction, dear god not for this, but because of that flashy new cover I keep drawing your attention to, and the cultural weight it has by being an "Essential" Dalkey book, a concept both nascent and eternal, one that hopefully this introduction helps clarify, a bit, right now in fact, as we bring in the drawings.

> yes, but how are you going to get Line and Construction and everything else in all that? Ha, and the musical eyes begin to sparkle with joy, because you're asking precisely what he expected, and he finds a stick and draws his plan in the earth:

> : verse top of hamlet the 2nd
> : thread of the story, hamlet the 1st.
> : foundation of my study: the search for the core leading to death.

> And you look and nod, but frowning, because it's just as if you'd seen that outline somewhere else . . . but where . . . ? and thinking feverishly, you look for it much too far away, because it's close at hand: you write and write, and your book lies there like a pool, like

something leading nowhere . . . but thinking feverishly you see that it really is your outline:

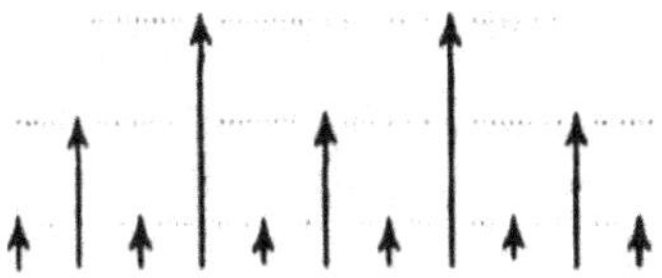

top: ondineke
thread: the world of today
basic theme: the cancer gnawing at our civilization.

*

Pulling from the meta-inventiveness of *Tristram Shandy*, these drawings point to the formation of the book and its awareness of how it is being put together. Boon is offering a roadmap to how he's going to construct this book and providing a pattern that he's definitely *not* going to follow in a strict way. But he's letting you in. He's letting you observe how a narrative—about a young woman striving, about societies inequities, about *life* itself—only gains shape as it is built. As the chaos becomes a pool becomes a sea.

There are few readerly encounters more exciting than witnessing someone brilliant, who, in what feels like real time, builds out a multi-leveled world.

*

Before I get out of here I want to recommend, wholeheartedly, Annie van den Oever's study of Boon, *Life Itself: Louis Paul Boon as Innovator of the Novel* for a much more nuanced evaluation of his work, along with the biographical information that fleshes out of one of Flanders's greatest writers.

I also want to assure you that the other books of Boon's that Dalkey has published—*Summer in Termuren* and *My Little War*—are as "Essential" as *Chapel Road.* Either one of those could be the inspiration for this introduction, but sometimes it's that first experience, that first glimpse into a writer's world that grabs you, transforms your reading life, converts you into a lifelong fan, and leaves you eager to sing the praises of this singular work to anyone who will listen:

> *Chapel Road* which is the book about the childhood of ondine, who was born in the year 1800-and-something . . . who fell in love with mr achilles derenancourt, director of the spinning mill 'the filature', but who will at the end of the book marry poor oscarke . . .

—Chad W. Post
2025

# Chapel
# Road

which is the book about the childhood of ondine, who was born in the year 1800-and-something . . . who fell in love with mr achilles derenancourt, director of the spinning mill 'the filature', but who will at the end of the book marry poor oscarke . . . about her brother valeer-traleer, with his monstrous head wobbling through life this way and that . . . and about mr brys who was one of the first socialists without knowing it . . . about her father, vapeur, who wanted to save the world with his godless machine, and about all the things which I can't quite recall now, but which try to draw a rough sketch of the laborious RISE OF SOCIALISM, and of the decline of the bourgeoisie which got knocked down by two world wars and collapsed. But between and besides this it is also a book set in a much later time, in our own time of today: whereas ondineke lived in the year 1800-and-something, msieu colson of the ministry, johan janssens the journalist, tippetotje the painter, mr pots and professor spothuyzen—and you yourself, boon—live today, in search of the values which really count, in search of something which will check the DECLINE OF SOCIALISM. But . . . heaven help us if it isn't going to be more than that: it is a pool, a sea, a chaos: it is the book of all that can be heard and seen in chapel road, from the year 1800-and-something until today.

# HERE BEGINS THE FIRST CHAPTER: SPRING IN TERMUREN

## A LINE THROUGH EVERYTHING

From your open attic window you can see no-man's wood being painted red by the sinking sun, and you hear msieu colson of the ministry's melancholy sheep bleating one last time before it disappears behind the stable door: and then you push your papers aside and go downstairs, just when the music master opens the door and together with his pretty wife lucette lets a little of that late red sunshine enter. He shakes his head in his music master's way and you hear him say:

I suppose you've been poring over your papers up there in your attic, writing about the world-of-today; well, I've misunderstood so many books already and I know that all there is to say has already been said; I'm not even talking now of ecclesiastes, of the faust-writers or the mad actor of hamlet . . . no, please, don't interrupt me, let me go on; do you really think that up in that attic of yours you're going to gather greater wisdom than lao tse, or can you be more surrealist-erotic-simple-minded than the songs of maldoror? Will you sound human depths and heights more deeply and more highly than the demons in the brothers karamazov, will you chase time outside time and space more ferociously than proust, or will you whip life within time and space more grimly than in the voyage au bout de la nuit? Will you be any better in depicting modern derailed man-in-a-crooked-society in his true condition of living and thinking animal than lady chatterley's lover? Can you play with words more soberly than lenin, more naturalistically than zola, more symbolically than the bible? Can you possibly be more solemn and more infallible than the pope in rome, more fabulously immoral than the arabian nights, more heavenly than the imitation of christ, more subtle and more cunning than the reynard of william-who-created-madoc; more tragi-rustic than nivardus' isengrinus? And can you be more modernly mangily unbelieving than tropic of capricorn? or more romantically miserable than the sprawl of suburbia?

And when you hear the music master fall silent and see him press his lips together, you reply: maybe it *is* impossible to say anything new and better, but the dust of time falls on everything that has been written and so I think it's right if every ten years someone else draws a line through all those old things and describes the world-of-today in different words.

## ATLANTIC ATOMIC

While johan janssens, poet and journalist, is walking towards you, his bare feet in slippers, saying pff instead of good morning and while the music master replies that there's going to be a storm, looking more at the impassive eyes of his pretty wife lucette than at the sky which is a sky far away in the distance—you ask them what they'd like, they've just had something about world literature, will it be the same again?

When I sum up what has been said, says johan janssens in his best journalist's style, I have to agree with the music master when he says that there's no more to be said, and yet I can't disagree with you when you say that it should all be repeated every 10 years in different words. Ha, and if I'm right it comes down to this, that the form should change, because man's increasing intelligence and lasting stupidity, as well as his faith in and his heretical doubt about the future, were exactly the same in antiquity as in our civilization today. But someone has to pour new wine into old vessels, if I may express myself thus in my capacity as a poet—so that anyone who gets drunk on it may understand that not only the magician's world of atlantic has perished, but that the jobless world of atomic follows it closely . . . hey, here I turn pale and startle and laugh at my own spirituality . . . I quickly start talking about something else; all right, the form: if we want to repeat what the music master said, we'll have to look for a different form, but which? for instance a novel into which you pour everything higgledy-piggledy, plouf, like a tub of mortar falling from a scaffold, & besides this, your hesitations and doubts about the purpose and the use of the novel, & besides and above all this, something you might call the journey from nihilism to realism—return trip, 3rd class—because today there's still hope that something will come of this world but tomorrow this hope will be shattered . . . and apart from this you could still make marginal comments, record brain waves, useless descriptions, sublimated, erotic dreams and even newspaper cuttings . . .

In other words, something like we're doing now, you say . . . and johan janssens, the music master and msieu colson of the ministry look at you with gaping mouths.

## PATCHWORK

In the mild evening-with-a-little-rain, johan janssens talks in his capacity as a poet of his doubts about the novel. But when he wants to say quite seriously that he's fed up with the novel, he discovers that he's fed up with the expression itself—to be fed up, and he demands a session in camera, to replace that expression by another one . . . and as the pretty lucette learnt later from her music master, johan janssens told them that he's making up a list of expressions which aren't mentioned in any dictionary and that he will publish this list in louis paul boon's 1st underground novel, the moment the last reader has dropped dead—of which note is taken . . .

And when your own wife and the pretty lucette have returned, he continues his discourse, that he's fed up (winking to all sides) with struggling through one respectable novel after another, because if you compare the novel with Life you see that it isn't much more than patchwork, and that it has a more than striking resemblance to the antics of a clown running after a tight-rope dancer high up in the big top, wobbling and consciously making crazy gestures, but who could slip all of a sudden . . .

And when johan janssens in his capacity as a poet takes a short breath, the music master raises his head and says that this kind of rambling talk isn't leading anywhere. But johan janssens has got his breath back and continues his discourse against the novel; but in the meanwhile the clown is still moving about on the tight-rope up there, weeping comically, but suddenly slipping and risking his life . . . for although it's his job to give a parody of an acrobat, he risks his life just the same as the acrobat who walked in front of him . . . and fidgeting with his trousers which are falling, he asks the audience below whether anyone can lend him a safety pin, but when he turns about in all directions, the audience notices a giant safety pin on the clown's back. Then johan janssens sits down and the music master adds that if you write 1000 pages you've distorted and twisted 1000 small truths, put them in a bag, shaken them about and tipped them out in a jumble. The 1000 small truths form together the 1000-fold big lie, the parody on life, the clown from the circus, the fish on the land, exclaims johan janssens in his poet's capacity and he knocks his glass over.

## NEITHER GOD NOR DEMOCRACY

You've knocked a glass over and broken it, your wife says to johan janssens, poet and journalist . . . but he sits there in his capacity as a journalist and he doesn't hear very well on that side: he taps on the floor with his feet and drums with his hand on the table; beats . . . no drums . . . the song of the rum-ti-dum novel, rum-ti-dum, rum-ti-dum the—novel, rum-ti-dum, so that the pretty lucette holds her hands to her little ears. Shaking his head he tells her that she can uncover those lovely pink ears because he's got something interesting to say: only in my capacity as a Poet do I discover that everyone lives for himself and believes in nothing; take my colleague, the poet johan brams, he tells me that he only lives for himself and has become cynical and doesn't believe in anything any more. And he tells me about the little man who was arrested and sentenced because he went over to the wrong side in the war, because he was hungry, but the great nazi generals said on the radio that basically they had never had anything in common with hitler. And he also thinks, my colleague johan brams, that we're back in '36 and that the world is moving towards an era of total destruction . . . and then there's another interesting thing, which I can't remember now. And in my capacity as a journalist I go and see professor spothuyzen in the same road, who teaches at the university and is one of the 7 intelligent people of belgium; I feel very small and stupid beside him, because he's got heine and goethe and dostoievsky in his head and comprehends the world and yet he simply plays in the village band like any ordinary bloke . . . and he tells me, hell, I don't believe in anything any more, I'm becoming so cynical that I'm surprised at myself. And I ask him what he thinks his opinion is, why the whole world is becoming cynical and believes neither in god nor in democracy nor in dog's balls—pardon me—and he reflects and tells me what he thinks about it and I'm staggered; it's such a tiny little thought it almost pushes me over on my backside. And in the evening I ask someone about this question too, again in my capacity as a journalist, someone who knows what's what and who walks around with feelers on his head and always lands on his feet whichever way fate swings him—and he was as pleased as punch because he was allowed to walk up with me, johan janssens, poet and journalist—and he answers me about this question and once again it was such a tiny thought it could have pushed me over on my backside, so that was 2 times that I fell on my backside, but of course, I didn't, I'd rather go home to my wife . . .

But the pretty lucette sits there again with her hands on her bare pink ears and your wife says: talking of falling down, are you going to pay for the glass you knocked over?

## MALAISE

It's Saturday evening and fine weather as johan janssens, poet and journalist, walks behind the music master and his pretty wife lucette and catches up with them on the way to your house. And with a glance sideways at pretty lucette's bare pink ears johan janssens says:

I was talking about faith and cynicism yesterday and I told you I'd forgotten something—it's always like that: the things that most need to be said are soonest forgotten and I get quite upset when I think of all the great things that might have been said down the centuries if they hadn't been forgotten by accident—ha, but you'd only just gone and I remembered, my colleague johan brams told me there's a general malaise, no one believes in anything any more or starts on any great work, rich people don't build workmen's cottages any more but buy themselves a row of cars and the poor who haven't got the money to build themselves a little cottage, crowd together in single rooms or in council prefabs—temporary, temporary, like everything is temporary, god and people and the world and the atomic age and the art of the novel—and the building trade lies still. No one bothers any more to read a book and the publishers reject manuscripts, good ones and bad ones, profound ones and slapdash ones . . . and when a profound book is a good book in my eyes the reverse is almost true in the desperate eyes of a publisher . . . and not a single great writer has the courage to depict this age in an unparalleled work. Ha! and that's because together with the aforementioned rich, who no longer build houses and with the poor who make the best of it in one room or who herd together even more temporarily in slum dwellings, and with the stagnant building trade and with the publisher who rejects manuscripts . . . he can't be bothered any more to start on a great work: the world is going to the dogs anyway. Ha . . . the music master wanted to say . . . but johan janssens interrupts him in his capacity as a journalist and says that he also met andré, the theosophist and medical student, and asked him whether he had discovered anything like a general malaise, but that andré replied with an innocent look: no, because they're still giving lectures at the university.

Ha . . . the music master wants to say again . . . but his pretty wife lucette laughs at johan janssens' words and meanwhile they've arrived at your house and when they enter they see you standing there with a sheet of paper in your hand: the INTRODUCTION TO YOUR NEW NOVEL.

## LITTLE ONDINE AMIDST STEEL AND GLASS

Be serious now, because although novels are no longer written nowadays, the writer of this outline wanted to present something which would embrace Life in its Entirety . . . but you see that right from the start he's got to use words that are too big, with capital letters . . . and it is to be expected, humanly speaking, that he will fail when it comes to the novel itself. He will gloss over this and expand a bit too much there and so it will become a sea, a lake, leading nowhere: but there remains the small consolation that he will be a master of detail. *He wants to write a novel with as its so-called heroine the little ondine—for amidst doubt and fear and the last hope of the last mohicans, amidst steel and glass and concrete, amidst bureaucracy and nuclear fission and the stagnant building trade, this little girl will be something refreshing, pleasing . . . but besides being the novel of little ondine it must also be the novel of her sweetheart and husband, oscar—ondine and little oscar, two o's which must be brought together by coincidence, to unwind the bobbin of their lives together, while the one will never understand anything about the other, although they will cherish the same misconceptions about everything—but god help me if it won't be* more *than that: it must also be the novel of socialism, from its beginning till the present day, and at the same time the novel of the lower class which was knocked on the head by 2 world wars, trampled in the dust, all the time saving and starving, and yet trying to keep up appearances. Oh, he would talk about vapeur with his godless machine, and about valeer-traleer with his cut-off finger and his monster's head wobbling bulbously this way and that through life . . .*

Alas . . . you've only got half way through your outline when your wife says, shaking her head: that's much too much. There can never be too much of a good thing, says johan janssens poetically, but journalistically he adds: however, lack of space prevents us . . . And the music master puts his hand up and says: excesses are odious. And msieu colson of the ministry, who never says much, says: you, mister music master, you think so because you're a man of few words.

## A MISTAKE AND A WARNING

Look, you go to a meeting where our future civilization—the one after the nuclear fission civilization—is described and promised, and you're happy like a child with santa claus, but on the way home your shoelace breaks and you swear goddamn here and goddamn there. This doesn't mean that santa claus . . . I beg your pardon, our future civilization—won't come, but it does mean that one will always have to reckon with breaking shoelaces. And so you also have to remember that you can read out the synopsis of your novel—even if it's only half the synopsis—and people pooh-pooh it and say it's too much . . . excesses are odious . . . and novel or no novel they switch on the radio and listen to the weather forecast: moderate wind force three . . . yes, but you don't therefore shut yourself up in bitterness, you also listen to the weather forecast and conclude: all is normal, and you buttonhole msieu colson of the ministry, although he never says anything and never reads a novel: *in my novel, you say, there will also be a mr brys who spoke in rhymes and was the first socialist without knowing it, and jeannine who was such a nice girl, but oh, so bloody stupid, and malvine with the squint—oh yes, and there'll be a bit about spiritualism too—don't faint, msieu colson of the ministry, and there'll even be some things in it which I can't mention to any serious person—and marvelous, touching, subtle things which are overlooked by everybody, as is always the case. And somewhere in the middle of the novel there's suddenly talk of a child, without the reader having been told that it was going to come.*

And msieu colson of the ministry, who never speaks, says: I shake my head, because your book will be a world, will be 100 worlds, but of course you'll have to admit that all these things are 1 big lie, from beginning to end: for instance, you could say that you're surprised at your own imagination which makes you think it all up, and that if anyone wants to sue you, you'll bash his brains in, because you are . . . it doesn't matter—but forewarned is forearmed.

## CHAPEL ROAD

There's been a bit of rain over rabbit hill and over no-man's wood but the sun is coming out and everything becomes much more beautiful: and you read the 1st page of the outline of your rum-ti-dum novel, which is the setting of the scene in 7 words: *the muddy chapel road wound towards the hamlet of termuren along the endless wall of the weaving mill 'the labor', and along the brushwood of rabbit hill, which was the last remaining bit of wasteland in the grounds of the derenancourts' castle. It was lonely there. Will o' the wisps, which are the souls of still-born children, swarmed above the shrubs in the dark. The cloven-hooved devil ambushed the late factory girls as they struggled through the mud on the dark path, and one of them, the loveliest ever to bloom in anyone's lifetime, had been raped there. A shame it was, to be so beautiful and to be maimed so pitifully by the devil's horns: And a nightwatchman who said he'd discovered footprints leading to the castle was dismissed from his job, because in all probability he'd been drunk again. And besides, the most clinching proof, that same week the dreaded smallpox broke out: the people of termuren silently and solemnly crossed themselves that evening.*

You give a little cough and put your paper in the folder in which you will keep the story of little ondine, while msieu colson of the ministry waits in silence, looking at the music master who's shaking his head: *you're talking there of rabbit hill, I can see it from here, and of no-man's wood, I can smell it through the open window, but you turn the ugly rich man's house on rabbit hill into a castle where a mr derenancourt, unknown to me, is supposed to live.* I don't see why; why don't you write about things the way they are, why do you mix it all up, making a hotchpotch of familiar names and unknown people and things, you're getting me confused. *And then you talk about will o' the wisps and about the devil who's supposed to have raped the prettiest girl—ouf—how romantic! and you make the nightwatchman who found a trail leading to the castle get the sack, and then smallpox breaks out and the people of termuren—a beautiful name—slowly and silently cross themselves.* But it seems to me that things are complicated enough in this world without someone shaking them about in a fantastic book till they can't be recognized and then pushing them back into a bygone time of devils and smallpox, let's say 1800-and-something. Shouldn't the novelist who's stuck to the present with his nerves and his blood and his sperm—excuse me—describe the present, instead of venturing out on the path of 1800-and-something with a stable lantern? Msieu colson of the ministry nods and agrees with the music master. *Even so, it was very nice, he says, that description of chapel road.*

## THE HEROINE BETWEEN 2 MILLS

Everybody laughs because msieu colson of the ministry says that so convincingly; you too, and after the description of the setting you try to introduce your heroine: *among the people of termuren, by chapel road, lived little ondine, who would probably grow up to be a beautiful woman, but unaware of this she went about on her clogs wearing her brown hair in 2 stiff pigtails on her back, and very selfishly considered the world of termuren to be hers alone. But the beginning of the long wall of the weaving mill 'the labor' she thought of as the beginning of a different world . . . and the grey rainy sky, against which the smoking chimneys of the spinning mill 'the filature' were outlined, was to her the sky of the filature. She felt as if her world was pressed between on the one side the endless fields where a late peasant went bent over his fallow land and on the other side the smoking, stinking town where the people of termuren went to work in the derenancourt mill. The first time she heard people talk of god, who was almighty, she thought they meant mr derenancourt of the castle, who lived on rabbit hill in the summer and in the mill town with its smoking chimneys in the winter. When the workers of the spinning mill came home along chapel road, little ondine saw them fighting with those of the weaving mill 'the labor', who lived in the first dirty houses behind no-man's wood: termuren was encyclical because mr derenancourt was, and the first dirty houses were libertine because the owner of the labor was: none of them had the vote, though . . . something ondineke didn't know yet at the time.*

Msieu colson of the ministry wakes up with a start at these last words about the vote. Perhaps, he says, the music master will say what he always says, but when you say that the people of termuren quarreled and yet didn't have the vote, I'd like to add that right now in the ministry . . . and msieu colson of the ministry does the exact opposite of what you wanted to do: he brings things from the past forward to the present. Ha, you see, just what I wanted to say, says johan janssens, poet and journalist: in my capacity as a journalist I would avoid all this poetical business: 'she thought', 'she felt', 'it was to her' . . . and I'd far sooner compose a novel straight from newspaper cuttings, from 1800-and-something to the present day. I would give information about the franchise, about accidents in the spinning mill 'the filature', about mr derenancourt in his castle on rabbit hill, about a child burnt or a tree blown down by the first dirty houses behind no-man's wood: that would be some novel, my journalist's heart would beat in it . . . I must control myself, or I'll start talking in my capacity as a poet.

## A LITTLE HUMAN BUNDLE

It seems there is a fair by the first dirty houses behind no-man's wood, in the darkening sunday evening. And the unwelcome drizzle that slavers against your windows must be equally unwelcome as it soaks the canvas on the horse-drawn round-about and the shooting tent. An evening when the world wonders whether it's worth bothering to go on turning. But the music master and his pretty wife lucette have managed to get to your house, they say there are few people about in the street. Only a few dead persons must have passed us. You put their slobber-wet raincoats away, close the door and say: as it's a lost evening anyway, *I'll read you a bit from the life of little ondine, the brat who's been stealing my life for years now, and refuses to be molded into a respectable heroine.* The pretty lucette and your wife start to drivel about the way things are and how expensive life is and about a lipstick called rouge atomic, and the music master braces himself in order not to fall asleep: *little ondine was still too naive to see the world of termuren in its true perspective. She was self-centered, and jealously guarded .all her impulses and impressions, storing them deep down in herself, without thinking any more about them. She drew the world into herself, a distorted world, it's true, a little-ondine-world, with her back to the long wall of the weaving mill 'the labor' and the dirty houses behind no-man's wood. And so to her the low houses of termuren seemed even lower, and the fields around, with the black figure of a peasant bent over the earth, even more endless. On the door of the house where ondine lived with her mother zulma and her father carolus, was a notice: here are kept the keys of the chapel of our lady of termuren; and so little ondine felt more important than the other girls who played in the mud or the dust of termuren, or hung from the iron bar by the level crossing, turning round and round, showing their dirty bare buttocks . . . but she thought it was a dreadful injustice that there was no notice on their door: here are kept the keys of the bar by the level crossing. And in order to show her annoyance about this—what won't children do—she fetched her little brother, who had a soft, shapeless body and a monstrous head, and who lay in a box on wooden wheels. He was four years old and all he was able to do was to raise his monstrous head a few inches from the red cloth he was lying on. He was called valeer, but what was the use of giving a name to such a shapeless human bundle. And now she dumbfounded the others by rolling the box along the railway and crossing the track at a savage bolt, in front of the shrieking, approaching train. The wooden wheels jolted across the rails and the head in the box jolted too. Someone screamed, a woman stood as if struck by god's hand, but little ondine doubled up with laughter on the other side.*

## 1800-AND-SOMETHING

*Little ondine took everything she had for granted but she moped over everything she didn't have. And as termuren, squeezed between rabbit hill with mr derenancourt's castle and no-man's wood with the first dirty houses and the smoking chimneys of the 2 mills . . . was a very poor hamlet, she moped almost all day long. It was in the time before the other war, when people plodded along in hunger and want, like rabbits, at noon they'd eat hash and in the evening mash. It was in the days when people had an immense respect drummed into them, from early childhood, for the priest of termuren and for mr derenancourt in his castle. Little ondine began to notice that the world in which she lived wasn't hers alone after all, but that she was tolerated in it, on condition that she politely said goodday to the priest . . . It was almost unbelievable, when after all she kept the keys to the chapel! Her father crawled, her mother humbly bowed down to the ground if a gentleman entered the house, and ondine . . . what was it they demanded of her? that she should sweep the floor with her 2 brown pigtails? This doesn't mean that she rebelled, far from it, but she couldn't possibly believe that she belonged to those who have to obey. She thought she was born to walk around with a sulking pout, like the old lady of the castle . . . she thought she was born to receive obedience and to give orders. And that the opposite seemed to be true, was something she laughed at secretly: tomorrow someone would come and tell her that there had been a mistake. She bowed lower than anyone, as if trying to do what she's been thinking: to bow so low that her pigtails would fall across her shoulders and sweep the sand on the floor. But the smile didn't leave her mouth: you see, I'm looking forward to Tomorrow.*

*She might easily grow up to be not only a beautiful woman but also a sensible woman. On the other side of the railway there was her uncle's shop-cum-inn, where there was nothing but a paraffin drum and a sack of salt and a few racks of clogs. She thought it was funny that people needed so little: some salt to sprinkle on the potatoes and a little paraffin in the lamp, when they're darning their work clothes. But more important was the bad gin which was served in the kitchen at the back. Her uncle was foreman at the spinning mill, and because he wore a beard people in termuren called him christ, when he couldn't hear it . . . but even so they were obliged to drink themselves tipsy on his gin and to sing the praises of mr derenancourt, or else be dismissed from the mill. And one day little ondine heard them calling her father by a nickname too, they called him carolus to his face but vapeur behind his back. She was angry, because he didn't know everything, she rattled the chapel keys and to our lady of termuren she said that a stop should be put to her father's unheard-of stupidity. Otherwise people will think we're just poor and ignorant, no better than the rest.*

## ONDINE AND HER CRAZY MOTHER

*When you picture little ondine to yourself, it's clear that her mother must be crazy zulma, the one about whom they said in termuren: 'when she was young, she could only count on her fingers, anything above that she used to call as big as the sky, and listen to this: she went to confirmation class for her first communion and didn't even ask please could she go to the toilet, she did it where she sat.' And because christ was her brother they let her become a maid at the castle on rabbit hill, with the old mrs derenancourt, but once behind the castle gates she wasn't allowed out any more, old mr derenancourt had it told that she had become . . . no, not simple . . . but mentally ill. Naturally, the people of termuren didn't understand it, what had things come to if you weren't allowed to call a loony a loony, but mentally ill? And suddenly she came back, for good, from within the castle gates, and she sat whole evenings by the stove in christ's house, listening to everything with a quiet and stupid and really rather frightened smile. She laughed with the others when that madman vapeur arrived in termuren, but she cried when one night the libertines painted the front of the house with blue dye, and a foreman from the labor shouted that a little senator lay buried in the woods on rabbit hill. But maybe that wasn't true at all, maybe that foreman of the labor had shouted it only because he hated the foreman of the filature. But to his surprise he got the sack, it was said that he wasn't a very good foreman; he drank and he'd kick 9-year old children when they fell asleep at work. Yet he couldn't quite understand it, he got drunk and stood by the gate of the labor shouting that he was going to find the grave in the castle woods. They came to drag him away and put him in the cell and there he bawled and sang that all rich men were bastards and that they were all hand in glove no matter what party they belonged to. When ondine first heard this she understood only that all the poor were stupid and the rich clever and it made her very pleased. Stupid woman, she said, when she saw her mother sitting by the window, looking out, and bursting into a crazy laugh now and again. Oh, she laughed at anything, at a leaf that fluttered from a tree on to the chapel, at a train shrieking past the level crossing. And if vapeur came in to see what was so funny, there was nothing, and zulma would look at him in surprise that he came to look out of the window. Yes, little ondine felt an ever growing contempt for her father because he had married a loony. Loony, she said, and gave her mother a boiling hot cup of coffee and watched her burning her fingers. And although she did it again the next day, zulma never learnt that something could be hot. But when she offered her mother a glowing piece of coal from the stove, zulma looked at her daughter and wept, so that ondine was ashamed.*

## PERPETUUM MOBILE

*Little ondine's father, then, was called carolus, nick-named vapeur; the only one who wasn't born in the hamlet of termuren, and when he got a bit tipsy, he'd say he came from brussels. Termuren couldn't forgive him this. And another thing they couldn't forgive him was that he didn't go to work in 'the filature', but swore by heaven and earth that he was different, that he belonged to the middle class. There had always been only gentlemen and workers, but now with this madman in their midst a 3rd category was born, something mongrel, unfamiliar. They had lured him into christ's inn, had made him drunk and made him talk like they do in brussels. And he, the madman, had jabbered a language they didn't understand. That's french, he said, but one day everybody will speak the same language, god created confusion of tongues amongst men, but science will bring us a new language. And because they didn't understand him he jabbered that imaginary language, zio-zio-zito, and also he started to do conjuring tricks, flung a franc away and wanted to bring it back from the nose of one of the peasants, but he was too sozzled, the trick failed and the franc fell out of his sleeve. He said he was an expert furniture maker, but after he'd made a heavy, clumsy chair for one and a pig's trough for another, and it was clear that he did indeed know what he was doing, the orders ceased to come in. But it probably didn't bother him. All he did in those days was work a bit on the land behind his house, and keep himself busy in the cold work shed with something he called a perpetuum mobile. But as they didn't understand the word—as with the universal language—he said it was going to be something with steam, with vapeur. Then they roared with laughter at that madman. Of course, he must have felt incredibly lonely in termuren, but did this mean he had to drink himself into a stupor? The end way that they saw his search for what they didn't understand, not only as ridiculous, but also as evil, and talked to the priest about it. The priest wanted to admonish him to stop this absurd searching. Well, said vapeur, maybe you'd like me to work in the filature, like all the other blockheads, and maybe you'll say that as I know something about machines I might even become a foreman. But I don't want to become a foreman, I like sitting in my shed looking for something that can't be found. And you like being the laughing stock of termuren, said the priest. And you of the people at the castle on rabbit hill, scoffed vapeur. At that moment little ondine could have been proud of him, but she was angry because he wouldn't conform to the laws from above and when he was in one of his moods she tried with her weak little fingers to destroy his work. She reproached him with 'vapeur' and with that word she flung her hatred at him because he wasn't a gentleman or a worker, but just as crazy as her mother. But he wasn't crazy; no matter how drunk he was he knew what his daughter was driving at and he silently went to the shed to sleep off his liquor in the shadow of his perpetuum mobile.*

## ABNORMALITIES

As far as I can make out, says the music master, all the people you write about are abnormal: you pick hundreds of little facts from normal life but you mix them unrecognizably into a teeming mass and then you push this mass on to some non-existent plane. Let me express myself more clearly: those hundreds of little facts from normal life in your hands become stones with which you build up an abnormal world. None of your characters are normal and not a single event has a recognizable setting either in the present or in the past.

Oh, be quiet, music master, you say . . . you make me think of those solemn, knowall, never erring modern critics: it's all very well for them to say that an author writing about life must weigh this and think of that, and must add a pinch of pepper and salt, nutmeg and cinnamon . . . no, sorry, I'm wrong, that's an omelet recipe . . . and these critics can more or less be compared with the tragic case of a baby being thrown away by mistake and the afterbirth put in the cradle. But the most tragic of all is that they have come to see this error as the normal situation and want to press their inadequate grocer's mentality on the conceiving, pregnant and birthgiving writer. And don't come and tell me 'you always write about abnormalities and call them normal', because where is the boundary separating the normal from the abnormal? Look at the masters bosch and breughel and goya, how they blurred the respectable and very bourgeois normal lines with their brush strokes, so where do you get the wretched courage to put that line back on their paintings with a piece of chalk? And listen to what a well-known psychiatrist said to me: every human being is abnormal, but the majority don't show it sufficiently to lock them up in a mental institution. And besides, surely the best way to depict normality is by way of what is abnormal? And can't one give a perfect picture of the Existing world by means of a fantastic world? But the music master, who is ensnared in what is allowed and what still isn't allowed, mocks: if you can do anything you like and write anything you like, you'll end up thinking that the most fantastic is the most realistic.

## WHERE HAS LIFE GONE?

At your front door there is a breath of a summer evening and as johan janssens puts his foot on your doorstep, he starts off by saying: don't talk about your novel tonight, and let's rather look at things the way they are . . . because I don't suppose you sit there writing all alone high up in a cotton cloud in a cardboard world . . . a novelist ought to be a journalist like me, and realize that he can be paid for filling a newspaper, but not for producing a novel, no matter how great . . . and then he'd have to assimilate that realization in his writing . . . *for instance, I assume that little ondine crossed the railway with a wooden cart, so many years ago,* but who cares about that now? Rather add to your book things from reality, for instance that your servant johan janssens had to go and see the editor yesterday because they were on the telephone all the time: why he hadn't turned up yet to receive a kick in his journalistic behind. And add this as well: that I ordered an orange juice in a café before catching a train over there by the first dirty houses, and 2 men were having a pint and took advantage when the proprietress had gone to the kitchen to change her dress: they finished their pint and beat it without paying . . . and the woman came rushing back in worn combinations, shouting and railing at the 2 men who were already on the level crossing by termuren, and by the light of the open door I could see her fat, matronly buttocks and belly, right through her worn combinations—oh, thou felicien rops—but when I arrived at the editor's office they told me once again that my work was no good, because everything I wrote wasn't the same as what others wrote . . . vive l'originalité, but not too much . . . but the worst was that I came to the appalling discovery that I wasn't a marxist like the others, but on the contrary an anarchist, a nihilist, a dirtyist, and that I ought to be forbidden to have any contact with people, except with the girls in their summer dresses in brussels . . . and even then only from afar, because if they come too near to me I see wrinkles or a wart or a pimple or something else looking like disease and telling me of their approaching death. And add finally that as I was going home on the train I saw a picture of life: in the first carriage the white collar proletariat carrying brief-cases and speaking beautiful flemish to ladies in transparent flower dresses, then in the 2nd carriage the proletariat of working class girls with coarser faces and coarser cotton dresses, and then in the 3rd carriage the proletariat of an old uncle with pustules on his face and matrons with sagging tits in their jackets, collapsing under a sack of potatoes. And when you've added all this you will at least have written something which is the other side of the medal of the novel: Life.

## DARK TIMES

Today, says johan janssens, I wrote a column in the paper about reynard the fox, under the heading: 'Dark Times': this is from reynard the fox who comes to us from the dark, wooded times of the middle ages, when counties were wild and vast, and cathedrals with their stone tracery and their scupper holes reached up towards heaven, when the castle lords were encyclicalists and returned from their robber crusades, went baptized to mass and prayers, but could burn down farms with impunity, could swoop down on the cow and the peasant's savings like vultures, and throw themselves on the women like wild bulls. Oh, what a wonderful time that was, when the feudal lords couldn't even write their own names but had traps and torture chambers in their fortified castles on rabbit hill, and a fool with bells and minstrels who licked the hands of those who hit them in order to glorify in verse the deeds of their lords . . . oh, what a time that was, when you couldn't go five steps but you came across an abbey inside whose walls they were eating and drinking till they burst, and where in order to kill time they described in fat volumes the life of saint bimbombarus, decorating it with multicolored pictures . . . and when the fat priest or the parson of termuren obliged you to go on a pilgrimage to places in spain, on your bare feet and with a fool's cap on your head and when you came back you found—oh, wonderful language of reynard's—that he had whored my dame and done a filthy shame to my children, whom he bepissed so that two of them have missed ever since their eyesight . . . *at least mr derenancourt wasn't so minded* . . . and people sprinkled pious latin texts and holy water on one another, but they brought you to the stake if by mistake you said that the earth moves round the sun. And also, it was the time when villagers and fools were still like in breughel . . . although he came much later, he had only a glimpse of them but painted them: stupid and poor and ugly and thin from fasting and praying, and from over-eating and getting drunk 1 day a year at the fair, but all the other days of the year of our lord something or other, to live in fear of devils and ghosts and will o' the wisps . . . while there were no other devils than the ones from the monasteries and the castle on rabbit hill, and no other ghosts than the plague and famine and smallpox which mowed them down like dung-flies and no other will o' the wisp than that of the most wretched ignorance.

Johan janssens is silent, he puts his papers in their cover, next to your papers, in poetic isolation . . . and the others say that it's good and that he ought to go on, and shouldn't take any notice of the rubbish the editor sees fit to say about it . . . the music master raises his hand and wants to say something formidable, for instance that it is a wonderful contribution, that it gives the novel-ti-dum perspective . . . and all the time the pretty lucette just sits there, shaking her head in silence.

## A MIRACLE HAS HAPPENED

*If little ondine lived a life apart, this was really only inwardly so; outwardly she remained vapeur's ondineke, who picked her nose and couldn't find words to express the questions that rose in her . . . today about this and that and tomorrow about something else. She frightened her crazy mother by throwing stones against the door from outside, or by running into the kitchen shrieking, with the red cloth on her head, the red cloth in which that impossible little brother of hers was usually lying. All she gained was that her mother became as nervous as a frightened bird in a cage, running wildly up against the walls and clutching the curtains in her fear, tearing them and breaking everything that came into her hands. And when her father, vapeur, came out of the workshed, ondine cried and shouted out bits from holy scripture: about jesus who had scolded the devils and said: 'hold thy peace, and come out of him'. And she thought that her father would tell her to stop it . . . dear little ondine . . . but he didn't, he leafed silently in her bible and read the passage about the unclean spirits, and for a long, long time he stood looking at ondine, as if empty of thought. Then he threw the book aside and shook his head. Finally he looked at valeer, that little clump of brother, who lay in his wooden box and had lost his cloth. Where was it? Little ondine was still wearing it on her head.*

*There were extremes in her. There were days when she sulked so much and worked herself into such a state, that she beat on the walls in fury. She would kick her wooden clogs against valeer's cot till they broke, and called: lazybones, when are you going to get up and learn to walk? After a night's deep sleep her fury was gone, she plaited her hair and wondered whether anything terrible had happened. What if she had cursed, what if she had kicked against the wooden box? It was only in order to make her mother into a proper person and valeer into a decent christian. She pushed the cart into the chapel, took valeer out and stood in front of the image: now I want to make him into a real person, now I want to make him walk. Valeer wobbled on his limp legs and capsized, hitting his huge head on the paving stones: ondine raged with fury, she kept putting him back on his legs and he kept falling, till he was blue, till his whole head was 1 large lump. Damn, damn, she said.*

*It was on st ursula's day when the miracle happened to valeer. Termuren was deserted because it was the patron day of spinners and weavers and everybody was dressed up in his best trousers and cleanest shirt and they'd all gone to the filature to form a procession: mr derenancourt of termuren castle, and of the filature, had specially come from brussels although the senate was in session, and led them to mass. And that morning, at the very hour when mass was in progress, the miracle happened to valeer: look, he stood up and didn't fall. He held on to the chairs and his head lolled about fearfully. Little ondine was quite scared, she quickly put him back in his box and didn't breathe a word about it to anyone. And in the evening she watched vapeur feeding him his hash, and putting him on the table to clean out his box. Without realizing, thought ondine. And strangely, it gave her no pleasure; on the contrary, it scared her. And yet she couldn't wait to repeat the miracle, every day at noon, as if they were acting a play: valeer walked better and better.*

## SAINT VALEER

*Little ondine read holy scripture as if it was her story: she fasted, she hit herself across the legs with a piece of string, she strapped herself to her bed at night. But she searched for something more gruesome, like driving a nail through her hand or putting her feet in boiling water. Nothing came of it though, because the others, too, began to notice that valeer was trying to get out of the box and walk, and so it became something quite ordinary, without the faintest tinge of holiness. Little ondine got cross with everybody, she pulled valeer away from them, she pushed him along the railroad and drummed it into him with hands and feet that a miracle had happened to him. In her zeal she didn't see that although valeer was beginning to walk, he wasn't beginning to think: far from it. And so her words were lost in the wind: she might just as well tell a dog that a miracle had happened to it. She saw to it that he didn't behave like an animal. And also, leading him by the hand, she looked around grimly to see whether anyone in termuren was laughing at him, but a moment later she'd hit him because he wanted to bend down and pick up a rotten apple from the gutter. Maybe she wanted to make a stone statue of him, a saint who never needed to shit. She walked on and on along the railway till she found a spot where the broom was in flower, and there, in that godforsaken loneliness, she made him a crown of yellow flowers: he walked on his feeble legs, buried under it, and kicked and cried. In her ecstasy little ondine didn't notice it, she fell on her knees: holy valeer, to whom a miracle has happened, pray for me.*

*In order to go to that spot, she always had to pass the inn by the level crossing, 'christ's place', and it always so happened that christ's wife saw them and called: ondineke, come and play with your cousin for a while! Little ondine looked in disgust at her cousin, the girl with the wispy hair and the fish eyes, how could she let a creature like that be a witness to her adoration of valeer? But it seemed that valeer himself was attracted to their cousin, every time ondine wanted to slink past unnoticed, he stayed behind at the corner, stubborn donkey that he was. He wouldn't come to the place with the flowering broom any more, all that yellow round his head frightened him. He hooked his little fingers round the doorstep of the inn and ondine had to pull him away with force, sometimes till he bled. And when nothing availed he'd say: pee, pee; then she had to undo her saint's pants. It disgusted her, most of all because it had to be just there: she beat valeer although he hadn't finished his little job yet, she kicked him and when he choked in his tears and almost suffocated, she grabbed him and hurried away. Then, on her favorite spot, she crawled about on her knees, imploring him never in his life to go with other people again; she imagined a life with him alone, she imagined a termuren on a never ending sunday morning, where the broom flowered and where you would never meet the priest or a farmer or their cousin and her mother. That night she dreamt that they got drowned together. For a few days she was speechless and when a train thundered past their favorite spot, she put her hand to her thumping heart in fright.*

## PARODY

Like someone who laughs in his sleeve—if it wasn't such a painfully serious matter—and like a beggar who says: may god reward you, but thinks: goddammit, only 10 centimes . . . this william who made madoc and who had all the animals called together one fine day, had more arrows to his bow than valentine-from-the-store has dead flies in her cake stand . . . he cocked his hat at a slant with the plume at the back and stuck his pen forward like a sword, and so he imitated the knight in his fortified castle at termuren, having brought in the loot and the un-clothed daughters of the poor peasants, and having drawn the bridge, and listening to stories of chivalry, set to rhyme and rhythm—he sat on his horse and drew his sword—of which you've seen a new, improved version during the nazi occupation . . . and william did as if everything was very serious, and as if he didn't in the least mean to poke fun at anything or anybody; what do you think, honored sir captain one-eye, and count and prince-bishop of lippeloo to lotelippe, if I talk about a wolf who has himself tonsured and introduces himself to the abbot in order to catch his sheep and eat them raw, I don't mean to make fun of monks or ultra-red marxists at all, who preach the gospel—farmer look after your geese—but I'm making fun of a dumb animal; let the poor have a laugh too, once in a while. And then it must be added that this william probably wasn't just someone who wanted to crush the grubs of injustice and lies and hypocrisy, but he must have been a human being like you and me; someone who's always in conflict with someone else, if it isn't the one, it's the other, and who would in the long run wipe his arse with belgium and would go and live in erembodeghem; that's reynard, and if you won't believe it you needn't, because nothing that's ever been written is gospel truth. But if you do read this, villagers and fools, don't start behaving like ravens who croak and screech and make everything black, snow in the winter and corn in the summer, but learn from this that in these days, in spite of all the fine sounding slogans, only 'swindle the peasant' reigns supreme, and drinking and whoring have become the highest good after god, king and democracy . . . so that for a poor, small, down-trodden and swindled man there's not much more left than to dig himself a burrow with 7 exits, taking care of his wife and his children and himself, because he will have realized that they are the only true religion and the only true fatherland. Be yourself, but learn from this that ideals go to pot through your fault and mine, but most of all through the fault of those who invented idealism in order to make some money out of it. Johan janssens.

## THE GHOST OF HUMAN TRICKERY

It needs a lot of doing for msieu colson of the ministry to say something . . . his steadfast presence is more one of silence . . . but today you see from his face that his brain—or is it his courage—is crammed full of words: I had a little bother with the outside wall of my house and my new neighbor wouldn't cooperate and so I asked my boss for time off and I went to see mr pots the solicitor and mr pots got his big lawbooks out and gave me some information and told me his life history at the same time: one brother of his is a lawyer in spa and he's rich, and his other brother is a lawyer in ostend and he's rich too, and he himself is a lawyer in this miserable provincial dump with 2 factories, the filature and the labor, and he's poor . . . poor and unknown, in spite of his masterful speeches, because he belongs to the generally despised brotherhood of our friend johan janssens: the ultra-marxists; he is truly the advocate of the poor, a romantic, honorary title . . . but the world no longer needs romanticism, except on the eve of an election. And all those poor sods with their dirty caps and sores on their faces come to his waiting room carrying the ultra-marxist paper conspicuously in their pockets, in order to get service for free: but don't ask them where for instance the office of the brotherhood is, or the ultra-marxist monastery; they never have known and never will, because it doesn't interest them at the moment: because it doesn't interest them in the least . . . only one thing interests them at the moment: to get service for free, to spoof a credulous and well-meaning man. That's what mr pots told me, and at once the ghost of human trickery loomed up in front of me . . . I fled and I daren't go back for any more advice from mr pots' fat lawbooks. And so msieu colson of the ministry has poured out his heart and his bottled-up words, and sinks back into his steadfast but silent presence.

## YOUR INTEREST LIES IN A POEM

The rain and the wind are beating against your window and you want to read out a new poem *about little ondine and her 1st love,* but msieu colson of the ministry prevents you with an unexpected Stop . . . like at the unguarded level crossing at termuren. Stop . . . and you're already thinking of death and danger and prison, but it's only in order to make you do all your purchases in the *au bon marché*. Stop with your poem *about ondine and her 1st love*, are you writing about termuren and the world today simply in order to strengthen your position? And you stare at msieu colson of the ministry, not understanding, with your wretched poem . . . but he's said his bit, Boum, and for the rest he's silent like a dead plaice in the fish market. But then you see where the shoe pinches, when johan janssens, poet and journalist, nods his head and says: I've just been telling msieu colson of the ministry how things stand these days: the workers and a new society and a more just world, o god almighty, they've all become hollow slogans; they're still used but no one believes them any more; it is perhaps possible that christ and marx have brought the world a step forward, but when you look around this is very questionable, and so I said to msieu colson of the ministry, that if I'm the editor of a paper, they can send me a poem all about neglecting the human personality and about serving the masses, but they're angry, and won't play the game if the poem isn't published at once; and encyclical poets are busy about god, but they won't have anything to do with god either from nearby or from afar, and others write about a new society but only believe in themselves and in their own poems: if there was to be a religion or a party with a cat's tail as its symbol and figurehead, they would write: o cat's tail this and o cat's tail that. Msieu colson of the ministry interrupts johan janssens and asks: and this poem *about ondine's 1st love*, are you going to try to make sure that that's published, so as to strengthen your position?

## THE OLD HUNCHBACK SPEAKS

In chapel road the music master and his pretty wife lucette meet the old hunchback, and the old hunchback says to them:

I've heard that they're writing about termuren in the year 1800 and something, and I'd like to read it, but I can't read, you know how it was in the old days . . . although in the old days I'm talking about, that's many many years ago, termuren was quite different from what you might imagine. You could hear the clogs clattering and the rosaries rattling and you could smell strong gin and smoky oil lamps and the toilets of the mills: that was termuren. And don't you think that mr derennecour of the castle and the spinning mill lived amongst all this like god in france; no, he was an animal like all the rest. Listen to this, once he'd forgotten his cigars and the coachman who's dead now had to go to the store to get a cigar but in the store, of course, they hadn't got a cent change and the coachman said, leave it, it's for you know who . . . but mr derennecour asked for his one cent change and went to the store himself: or did you think I'm rich! And at first, when his spinning mill was only small, he stood at the gate himself and he beat everyone who was late, ha, ha, and I was late, I was wearing a new blue smock and slipped past him into the mill and hung my smock on another hook and mr derennecour came to look for me and beat the others, ha! And talking of the mill, in the month of may we had to read our paternosters and on st ursula's day we had to go to mass in rows of 4, like in the army, it was just like a tape worm the way we walked there and mr derennecour was the head, but the nicest was all the kiddies, they weren't ten years old yet, specially the little girls, they were like angels, going up to pray for the prosperity of the mill . . . and naturally we had to work overtime in the evening to make up for lost time, and it didn't matter if the angels fell asleep, christ with the beard, the foreman, went round to kick them awake. And I was talking about the toilets, well, one day there was something new, a health committee, it consisted of the brother of mr derennecour's uncle and glemasson's daughter, and they were relatives . . . that daughter was a handsome female, but flatfooted, so they said, I never saw it, she always used to wear skirts down to the ground . . . and so the committee came, as I told you, and all the children, who weren't supposed to work so late, were pushed into the toilets, but one began to cry and the committee heard it and mr derennecour got her out and said: what's this, why are you hiding in there, you should be home with your mummy and you should have been in bed long ago . . . you see what children are like, she must have stayed on purpose, so she could pinch something!

And when the pretty lucette asks how it is he has remembered all this, the old hunchback says: ha, that's because in my time we had nothing else to talk about.

## HER FIRST LOVE

*Just as there were days when little ondine felt drawn towards her holy brother like a magnet, there were also days when she had a horror of him . . . precisely the things which made her so happy yesterday, disgusted her today. She avoided him, left him to himself, and said: I can't look after him for ever and ever amen. Although she felt it was something quite different: she forgot him because maybe she wanted to. She would leave the hot road by the railway and sought the shade of the castle drive . . . she'd pick a bunch of flowers on the way, far too many, and drop them one by one, imagining that they might grow roots, to mark the way along which she—saint ondine—had walked. But a moment later she'd forgotten her saintliness and climbed on the low wall of the castle park and clutched the spikes of the fence. There she saw how mr derenancourt lived, smoked his cigar, gave orders to his gardener . . . never was that cigar big enough, never did he give his orders loudly enough. But he wore a cap, she could hardly forgive him this: she would much rather have seen him in a helmet covered with colored plumes. One Saturday, when it was drizzling, the 2 little boys of the castle came running out into the garden and she saw the elder one admonishing the younger one with his finger raised. Oh, our lord jesus christ of termuren, only he could understand what ondine felt and longed for at that moment, or could understand why she thought: am I going to forget this Saturday morning and this garden and the drizzle and that raised finger like so many other things? In the meanwhile she saw herself admonishing valeer, also with one finger raised. She couldn't wait to tell someone about this, which she herself hadn't really understood, a friend, fat liza who spoke through her nose . . . although there was nothing to tell, after all, nothing had happened! Strangely enough, however, fat liza did understand her, she went straight to the fence with ondine, to look at the deserted garden. That's where they were standing, little ondine pointed. He's your sweetheart, said liza with slow, nasal sounds. Ondine looked at her in surprise and almost with excitement . . . my sweetheart, my sweetheart, it sang inside her. Don't tell anyone else about it, I'll look at you and I'll put my finger up and then we'll both know what that means. And if this secret brought its worries, and made their lives more grown up, it made them happy because of this, they would no longer have been able to live so innocently, like yesterday and the day before.*

*But there was something else which made a tremendous impression on little ondine: those 2 boys had been wearing leather jackets, she had never seen such coats before. She thought of asking our lady of termuren for one, for her brother valeer. Coming out of school she saw her brother playing with the other children: they were all his age and yet he was the most stupid, the clumsiest . . . they were playing hide and seek and when he stood with his head on his arms by the shed door, all the children went away to play somewhere else. And just at the moment when ondine began to pray, could she please have a leather coat, her cousin, the dirty witch, turned up and bumped the patiently waiting valeer with his head against the door. He bled and cried. Little ondine wanted to curse, but no sound came from her tight throat, she shook her clenched fists and kicked her clogs against the wall till they broke. Then she fell. Her father had to come and prise her fists open with force.*

## THE CRIME

*Little ondine dreamt that night—our lady of termuren showed valeer to her in a coat shining with gold—and when she woke up she lay tossing and turning in bed, unable to go back to sleep: she prayed and begged that it might be true, please. Her brother valeer was asleep beside her, she crouched down on her bare knees with her hands folded and falling asleep again she dreamt something different, that she had her cousin in her hands and throttled her. And when the next morning she went to the chapel, swaying between hope that the leather jacket would be there and fear that she would drop dead if she had been deceived, she hardly dared to look: the statue was there, the leather jacket was not. If her disappointment had been less great, she might have been able to cry, but not now; she cursed and demanded a new miracle there and then. Turning round she saw the offertory box: there was the money for the leather jacket, there was the money of the communion of saints to which valeer belonged. She took her clog and thumped on the iron plate which was set in the wall, but it made a dreadful noise and she only managed to knock a dent in it: then she went to fetch her father's pliers and wrenched the offertory box open. She carried the pliers back and counted the money in the lavatory. All by herself she walked down chapel road, to the town, following the long wall of 'the labor'. At the gate stood mr gourmonprez, the libertine; she thought he looked like a gentleman even so, a blush came to her cheeks and after she'd made a deep bow and said: 'good-morning mr gourmonprez, the libertine of the labor', she hurried away on her clogs, in the direction of the town. She had never been there. It frightened her, it was so large, all streets and shops and people. And when she had humbly greeted a priest—good-morning mr priest from the town—she saw that he didn't even know her name: so he was not all-knowing . . . and the way he walked there, his heel showing under his cassock: he'd got a hole in his black stockings! And so frantic did she become in her blind fear of the largeness of it all, that she entered a greengrocer's and asked for a leather coat there: she looked in panic at the leeks and the carrots and heard laughter. She cried. And when she finally saw a shop with a sort of raincoat hanging on a dummy, she hardly dared go in. She showed the money which had become warm in her hands, and heard the lady say that it was nothing but a few miserable cents. Little ondine fled and was unspeakably sad, no, unspeakably bitter: she bought a doll in a bazaar. She ignored the suspicious looks at the money, she could have murdered those madams in the shops. With two hands she put a turret of cents on the counter, but to her amazement, which turned to dismay, they pushed some back to her: what should she do with the change? She clutched the box with the doll under her arm and on the lonely road to termuren she threw the remaining money into the ditch. Beyond the trees were the chapel and the level crossing of termuren. She walked towards it, but it seemed as if something was wrong: as if termuren had become smaller. How silly was that white-red board with the diagonal cross and the words 'take care' . . . ha ha, for a train that hobbled past 2 times a day. Hobbled, yes, it didn't rush, it didn't speed by ferociously, like lightning. And then the chapel, and the field with a peasant bent over his rake, it was enough to make one laugh. It was enough to make one cry, so small it was. Silently she gave the doll to valeer, he clutched it and pressed it to his heart. The doll had the same flaxen hair as their cousin, he thought it was her. Ondine showed him it way a doll that could sleep, look—nighty-ni, and valeer repeated it and put his finger into the sleeping eye and there was no longer an eye, there was a black hole. And in spite of her crazy mother who sat there staring at her with fixed eyes, little ondine began to curse again, she snatched the doll and broke it against the wall. When she saw the scattered fragments she cursed even louder with fury and regret, and also because of something which reminded her of the dream in which she drowned herself with valeer. Valeer cried and called: nighty-ni. Her crazy mother laughed herself into a fit.*

## THE TAIL OF THE CRIME

*Now little ondine had to think of how to wipe out the traces of the crime, but she postponed it, she walked round the chapel looking at the grey sky above the town, at the smoking chimneys beyond the first dirty houses. She also went to look for the money she'd thrown into the ditch but she couldn't find it anywhere. Then she gathered all her courage and entered the chapel . . . perhaps a thief will come and break into the offertory box, she thought . . . and at last an old, stupid termuren woman entered, and little ondine, who had imagined it a hundred times to herself, how it would happen, began to sob and cry. But, strangely, real tears joined the crocodile tears: tears of a sudden regret that she was the way she was. The woman walked out and told everyone that the offertory box had been broken into: it was lucky they hadn't done anything to vapeur's little ondine, who was crying beside it. Little ondine didn't understand this last bit, yet she exploited it: they've broken into the offertory box and they've done something to me . . . although she hadn't the faintest idea what they could have done to her . . . but yet she had to go here and there, even to mr derenancourt's castle. It didn't worry her that the whole affair became more and more complicated, on the contrary, she was very curious how it would end, she was mad with pride because they wanted to ask her things at the castle: and most of all she longed to see the 2 boys of the castle again: the eldest, achilles, would probably be admonishing his brother again. She saw him sitting over by the pond and went up to him, 'he's my sweetheart, my sweetheart', she thought, but she didn't know what to say or do. She was flushed and happy and realized vaguely that someone, a lady, was calling her. And then mr derenancourt of the castle himself came up and asked her to tell him all about it. She repeated the same story . . . crying, because all the people at the castle spoke a language she didn't understand . . . and it was as if she was almost pleased that something had been done to her. He looked at her in silence, she had to come to town with him, where she hardly recognized the streets and the shops. The police asked her what the man looked like, whether he was tall or short. And she replied that he wasn't tall and not short either, not thin and not fat, but she thought he had a wart on his left cheek . . . ha ha, like her mother . . . and she gave the most beautiful description they could have wished: he had pushed a pair of pliers into the slot and twisted it . . . but what he'd done to her . . . I'm not going to tell, she said. And because she saw a thin man smirking, she smirked too; she was almost 11 and would soon go to first communion; she suspected at once that it must have been something wicked, about what the priest had said in confirmation class: that little girls mustn't look between their legs. It gave her a headache and she forgot to look for her money on the way home, in the ditch by chapel road.*

*But there was a tail: that foreman, who'd been dismissed from the labor some years ago, for saying that all rich people were scoundrels . . . and who had come upon bad times, as they say . . . he answered little ondine's description: he wasn't tall or fat, and he had, well, not exactly a wart, but something or other on his cheek, a scratch . . . perhaps that little girl thought a scratch was a wart. Did she recognize this man as the man who was in the chapel, if so, swear it . . . I swear by god . . . and she had to raise 2 fingers. Then it went round like wild fire that the libertines of the weaving mill 'the labor' had broken into termuren chapel, had destroyed the images, had stolen the offertory money and raped a little girl at prayer. The libertines replied you'd better go and look in the lavatories of the encyclicalists' spinning mill, and see what is done there to children. Little ondine only heard vaguely about this fight, high above her head: she walked home along the muddy chapel road and as she walked by the ditch she suddenly saw something: it was her money. She thought it strange that all the time she'd looked for it much further on . . . and the thought that you can think you've thrown away something here whereas actually it is a long way ahead; this thought she found it worth remembering all her life.*

## DRAMA HAS GOT LOST

You told us, says johan janssens, *about little ondine that she had broken into the offertory box in the chapel, and spent the money and thrown the rest away in the ditch by chapel road, you also told us that someone else was arrested after her accusation . . . someone who had done something to her, she said . . . and in the end, afterwards, or is it afterwards in the end . . . ? that she found her money in the ditch at a completely different place than she had imagined: and she found this something worth remembering all her life.* I shudder as I sum this up—is man shrewder and more savage than an animal in the jungle, that he can kick another into a pit which he has first told him to dig and that afterwards he can only think of where he found a few cents change. How much more must *you* have shuddered, as a writer so seemingly unmoved, when this drama was being unraveled! You interrupt johan janssens . . . although in fact he'd finished and interrupting is therefore only a manner of speaking . . . and you say that as a writer you may have led the drama to its climax but that as a professional you torment yourself wondering *whether according to the laws governing human emotions, ondine wouldn't have worried far more about the question: that something had been done to her; how old is she exactly? and at that age would she worry about the one rather than the other . . . ?* But johan janssens interrupts you now by asking whether he wasn't talking about something altogether different, about the drama reaching its climax? Haha, and with a great gesture he reaches into his inside pocket and conjures out of it a weekly journal . . . the illustrated art review . . . and moving his index finger down the columns he says: wouldn't it be better to torment yourself with this here: although the writer of ondineke of termuren has remarkable talent, he lacks a sense of drama and he speaks flemish in such a way that his pathos seems nothing but feverish ranting . . . Then he folds the journal up and says: well, here you are, letting your heroine think and thinking yourself whether she's thinking about the right thing and there they're saying not only that your pathos is feverish ranting, but also that you've got no sense of drama . . .

But at that moment the door opens and msieu colson of the ministry enters and hears the last word and asks in surprise: drama, what on earth is that?

## DUBO DUBON DUBONNET*

Is it saturday again, and bad weather? and the wind says hoo-hoo and all your friends, who are your heroes, or is it the other way round? . . . sit by the stove sipping the hot coffee which your wife has served with her lovely bare arms; and they've all got something to say about bad marriages and the Downfall with a capital D, which is the outcome of an excessively transcendentally orientated christian life, plus 2 wars, plus the fear of another one: from high to low, man drinks and visits whores while his wife has a child by a german or a canadian or the holy ghost, and in café matisse . . . over at the

* the question of dubonnet will be repeated somewhere in reynard the fox; we hope the reader doesn't mind . . . but if he does, too bad, that's his business.

1st dirty houses . . . she simply shits in her pants. And all at once it's quiet in your house and in the silence you hear the radio singing away tirelessly, inanely: je n'aime que vou-ou-ous. All right, and all your heroes burst out laughing . . . but doesn't this prove that everybody knows very well that the holy images have long since been eaten away by rot? . . . but that even so everyone closes his eyes from fear, from a sense of self-preservation, from the law of live-longest and they all bum fresh candles, for ever more? And msieu colson of the ministry puts his cup down and says—to your wife: could I have another cup, please . . . and to you: and this explains why the church found it necessary to have notices stuck in the windows: go to mass; 6 days you work for your encyclical boss but the 7th day must be for the encyclical god of the encyclical boss. But people know that in that case there's not 1 day for themselves and they do want one day for themselves; they want to do as little as possible and get as much reward as possible. And the next day, there was a new notice: it's time! A man walking to catch a train and a man walking to mass. And the next day another new notice: sun sunday sunday mass, like dubo dubon dubonnet. And the next day: well, there wasn't a notice any more, and it was no longer necessary to run yourself off your feet for a dubonnet mass: the elections were over and the encyclicalist bosses were in the government. And this would have been the end of it if johan janssens hadn't added: they want to do as little as possible and earn as much as possible, you say, but they have to, or else they'd have nothing for dinner except raw boiled potatoes . . . but mr pots comes to me and says that a meeting of ultra-marxist intellectuals must be called urgently and that he's already written 600 invitations, and then, at the meeting were present: mr pots, who was to address the meeting, and I, johan janssens, who was to report it.

## FOR A WAGE INCREASE

When it's all saints over no-man's wood and all saints at the first dirty houses of the town of the 2 mills, johan janssens watches you at the back of your garden, choosing a spot where you might one day plant a cherry tree. You ask him where *he* would plant one and he replies:

I won't answer, mr writer, because I think you're indulging in the small pleasures of life, they only keep up appearances; they're a deviation, and therefore a derailment of the real meaning of life. And he raises a prophetic finger because you're not impressed and merely scrape some earth from your spade: sooner or later you will say to me that I, johan janssens, poet and journalist, am a defeatist, but that isn't so; I only condemn the false appearance of things and I scratch out fine words like you scrape the earth from your spade . . . although people may shout till they're blue in the face when I say this . . . and I look at things realistically, you might say that the papers publish articles about art and literature in order to emancipate the small man, as they say, or to bring art nearer the people . . . and in your best moments you're taken in by this yourself . . . but you realize that they're only doing it because the other papers do it, and they think they'll catch a certain kind of people with it: and you look at all those pages of newspaper-spiritual life on thursdays, composed by poets and journalists johan janssens, johan brams and johan darrieux, plus the inevitable dr k. k. kakkerman, and you get something like this: we give you some spiritual life here, but it doesn't interest us very much that the small man this and that . . . maybe it would be better if we earned a bit more and had a bit more time to think, and for next week we hope we'll find something else to fill the pages with. But the public . . . oh, the public . . . what kind of a word is that . . . ? the public never protests, they just swallow, and always applaud so that on both sides appearances are saved. But now reverse the coin, dear me, what, for instance, does my newspaper want? to know how long I've worked on an article, and whether I haven't cheated by 5 minutes: that's the mentality of the worker who has stamped his card all his life at the door of the labor, and who has now by accident become the director of the newspaper factory: not spiritual values are of importance but the daily wage. Fangogh, fannostayen and picazzo by daily wage. And the prime minister and the minister of education of art of reconstruction of supplies walk in procession with the chief editor, but also with fangogh and johan janssens, all together behind a banner we demand this we demand that WE DEMAND A WAGE INCREASE . . . and in the big square the prime minister says that there can be no wage increase and all the people who have walked behind the banner with fangogh and johan janssens applaud. And in the meanwhile—yes, in the meanwhile the writers are not writing with grim determination but they stand around in their gardens looking for a spot to plant a cherry tree, that's to say, they're yielding to false appearances, that's to say, they're enjoying the small pleasures of a small life.

## MR POTS WRITES A LETTER

With his eyes to the ground msieu colson of the ministry walks towards the 1st dirty houses of the town of the 2 mills, beyond the ugly big house on rabbit hill, and there he bumps into johan janssens who's also walking with his eyes on the ground. Bang. And out of the collision there may spring a spark and johan janssens says: msieu colson of the ministry, you told me about the desperate—or is it embittered—mr pots who had discovered that his so-called idealism only exists in order to diddle somebody more easily . . . well now, maybe because he became embittered himself, he wrote me a letter, triggered off by some nonsense in one of my newspaper columns . . . about reynard's bitterness, and he explains to me what bitterness is: an illness. And he also explains to me how to knock a novel together: you just read a book by a french doctor about biology and all the rest . . . and you add a bit of imagination, he says, or rather, he writes . . . that's how you knock a novel together, yours fraternally, pots. And now, msieu colson of the ministry, I wouldn't be a poet if I hadn't looked for something quite different behind those dumb, reticent words, and I wouldn't be a journalist if my curiosity hadn't made me hurry as fast as I could to go and see him and ask him: why do you write about bitterness being an illness and the novel being nonsense, according to you, mr pots? But god almighty, msieu colson of the ministry, you can listen to a man pouring out his heart at the moment he's changing moods like a snake changes his skin, but you can't peel the skin off him once he's changed and has become hard as a rock again: I gave him my card, johan janssens, poet and journalist, and he practically threw me out: because he's come to goodness knows what conclusion, maybe that he and the new society have nothing in common, and that since he's got nothing to do with it he's got nothing to do with me either, nor with bitterness, nor with the novel . . . and meanwhile he sits there with all his fat books around him and I ask him man to man why he wants to have no more to do with the brotherhood and the new society and he holds his ruler to his mouth as if it's his finger and replies: you're young, hear and see and draw your own conclusion. How can I hear and see and draw a conclusion if no one will tell me anything, I ask . . . but his love of all loves comes between us and pushes me outside . . . but with the doorknob in my hand I say, well, I'm sorry, mr pots, and he calls from behind the closed door: yes that's right, mrrrr pots, and no longer a fraternal pots because that's all finished.

And msieu colson of the ministry looks very sadly at johan janssens; there are saviors from the right and saviors from the left and little msieu colson, the mister potses and the johan janssens get squashed between all those saviors.

## THE UNIFORM OF THE POOR

*And then suddenly little ondine had no longer any time for the things which had till then filled her young life: she was going to her first communion. And because the priest of termuren had said that she knew her religion like no other, she became at once a saint and looked up at him with her big grey eyes, as if to show him . . . but he wasn't at all impressed, it was all the same to him whether it was ondineke or anyone else: in a moment he'd fill his pipe and forget all about her, maybe there would be meat with his potatoes for lunch, and that's what he thought about. She felt as if she was growing high above him, he was only a priest but she was a saint. She felt a shivery warmth somewhere inside her, but when she thought it was in her heart, she felt it in the top of her head, or going down her spine . . . but when she, so to speak, listened to her spine, she felt it in her tummy: it made her feel weak, sinful and happy. She sat there as if she was going to die in that sinful happiness and suddenly she wondered whether her mother . . . who sat there dying all day long . . . might have the same feeling; but she dismissed the thought at once, she wouldn't or couldn't believe that things which she experienced, could also be experienced by others.*

*Her schoolfriends liza and maria were also going to their first communion and after that they'd start work in the spinning mill; they talked of nothing else but the filature, there are boys there, it will be fun . . . oh, it looked as if the priest was simply going to hand them over from the communion rail to the filature, in procession. That didn't matter; maybe it made ondine smirk, the way she also smirked at the children who were dressed by the poor fund . . . dressed by the dean, said the ignorant folk of termuren . . . and she looked at the poorest children who were put apart in a corner, and 'when the greatest day in their lives had come'—day of precious blessing, day so wondrous sweet and glad—as a poetaster priest had said, they went in their shapeless jute clothes which the clergy had donated to them. Stinking clothes, too . . . they hung round their thin shoulders as a symbol of misery. And ondine discovered the strangest thing: not only army uniforms were made in the libertine mill the labor, but also the holy communion clothes donated by the dean; so that in a way they were a uniform too, the uniform of poverty. And when the others came to tell her what lovely things they were going to wear . . . well, mine will be much nicer, because we belong to the middle class, she said. She was thinking of that old illusion that she really belonged to the people of the castle . . . but she daren't utter it, it was as if it had been someone Else's dream . . . and also, a shock went through her when the word 'dream' came to her mind . . . an unspeakable pain settled everywhere in her body. It made her tired. And then suddenly the lady from the castle stepped across their worn doorstep and said, well, let's fit you for your dress, shall we. Ondineke's heart beat faster: so it wasn't a dream, it was the truth! The truth, she belonged to the people of the castle. It made her still. First she was tired and now she was still . . . so that no one could notice how she was swayed this way and that in these days. And then came the dress: it was . . . a dress from the dean's poor fund . . . although they'd taken her measurements and it didn't hang from her shoulders like the uniform of poverty, it was still woven from the same coarse jute . . . it stank . . . she could smell it if she as much as bent her head to her shoulder. Oh, ondine's holy communion—the greatest day of her life . . . day of precious blessing . . . and her grief, her misery, were not lessened by the fact that she was the best catechism pupil, that she approached the bishop first and he tapped on her cheek with 2 fingers: it hurt her, he had hit her bleeding heart. She went back to her chair through the empty nave of the church and anyone, who wanted could see her clothes from the poor-fund.*

## REYNARD OR ISENGRINUS?

There you sit with your head bent over the white paper and as usual you're pondering as you write, about our not quite atomised but already split world . . . and at that moment the front door swings open and slams shut again and together with a little november draught, transient and fleeting, your counterpart enters: poet and journalist johan janssens: how are you, how's work? Well, says johan janssens, maybe somewhere in this rotten world some idiot is busy writing The novel, and even if the world explodes behind his back, he'll go on writing without looking up . . . what's his name, that famous man, he's dead now and already forgotten, he went on writing a story when his city was being liberated and the germans were leaving with promises that they'd come back with new weapons and the english entered with their tanks covered with flowers, and in his street there lay a dead partisan, and the dome of the palace of justice was burning like a torch in the middle of the slums . . . but I can't do that, I can start a novel but when I hear there are flying saucers over the U. N. I've got to change my novel and when I see what happens behind our lady of fatima the ending's got to be altered as well . . . that's to say the ending of my novel. I run around like a spinning top and my heart beats like mad and I decide once again to smoke less and the only thing I'm capable of doing would be to rewrite Reynard the fox . . . if it wasn't for the fact that my version would be chucked on a heap with all the others . . . and if it wasn't for the fact, also, that william who made madoc and ran amok with his time, and nivardus as well, knew how the land lay and knew who were the goodies and who were the baddies, who was the hero and who the coward, who was noble and who reynard . . . But today you don't even know that any more: I don't even know who I am myself and what I am . . . today I think I'm reynard who's played a dirty trick on the whole world by pretending that he doesn't hear or see what goes on behind his back . . . one person says that his work is unbalanced and confused and another that it's too pessimistic and another . . . well, anyway, they grin. But the next day I think I'm far more like isengrinus who comes out of the battle swindled and cheated, with a torn skin and a hungry stomach, when I've done . . . all I can say is that I'm not a woman . . . and that's my answer to your question how are you and how's your work? how can I know who I am and how my work is? If I don't even know whether I'm reynard or isengrinus.

And johan janssens, poet and journalist, has gone out into the road leaving you alone with the wind and weather of november, of sadness and fleetingness . . . and with your closely written pages . . . for do you need to know which you are, swindler or swindled, in order to go on writing?

## THE CHASE BEGINS

I johan janssens who might possibly be a distant relation of william williams who made madoc and who ran amok with his time, had better listen to my wife who's telling me how *she* would write a novel, and that the nicest books are the ones that have a different beginning and ending every evening . . . that's how it is with the novel of reynard the fox and isengrinus the wolf who have wandered through the countryside of flanders, the vineyards of france and the borders of the rhine in order to bring a little hard sunshine to the cracked lips and the broken teeth of the small, swindled folk. And when one little swindled man . . . oh, what am I saying . . . if one william williams begins one fine spring day, the other johan janssens begins on the day that peace was announced for the umpteenth time, the day when reynard and isengrinus, squinting with hunger and bent with fatigue, met the count and prince-bishop, the king and emperor and pope of all the wild animals: captain one-eye, whose wisdom rested in his claws. And to make a long story short: what shall we do about this business, so that you can establish your fame and pocket the profits? asked one-eye, looking at reynard. My fame, thought reynard, who knew very well that this meant: catch it and bring it to me—as had happened yesterday, today, and would in the future—and reynard remembered a cow somewhere in the field and began to reflect on his fingernails how he might foil the farmer who kept watch over it. But thanks be to god, the farmer had fallen asleep under the tree by the brook in the field and reynard climbed up the tree with his behind in the foliage—dirty fellow he always was—to do right above the face of that farmer something you mustn't describe but which breughel did paint, to the chagrin of those who only shit sugar. Ouf, the farmer woke up with a start and wiped the evil-smelling pulp from his face; he quickly bent over the brook to wash and wash, until reynard jumped on his back and pushed him under water, singing requiem in pace stupid yokel you are amen. But this had taken too much time for captain one-eye so that reynard had to apologize and say he'd promised his wife he'd come home alive that night, so he'd had to drown the farmer first. Don't argue about that farmer, said isengrinus, he's dead and he's given us thereby a useful lesson that everyone gets what he deserves in life: he the brook and we his fatted cow. johan janssens.

## THE KIND OF WHICH THE WORLD TAKES NO NOTICE

*Just as little ondine had thought: from the communion rail to the lavatories of the filature, so it happened, to the other children . . . but for her the days passed in waiting for what might come: she went to see liza and asked her what it was like at the filature . . . but liza hadn't got much to say: she worked there but she was still the same liza as at school: one who went through life with blind eyes and if she notices anything she'd forgotten it the next moment. Little ondine waited in suspense . . . but her mother sat staring out of the window—and the older ondine became the less she understood her mother: was she backward or only lazy or completely nuts? . . . her father made a clothes stand here and repaired a door there, always hurriedly. Nothing happened to her: would she have to walk around idly for ever? as if she didn't belong to the poor or the rich, but to a group of which the world took no notice: the middle class. A middle class which ate mash, and was proud and went hungry: it made her feel desperate, she walked about the house as if it was a prison . . . . and she thought: my mother is crazy and so is my father and our valeer is abnormal . . . and I . . . I? She cried, she thought it was because she had to live in a madhouse. Yes, she had such silly thoughts that she didn't understand herself any more and got everything confused: it was a whirlpool of thoughts in which she was sure she'd get lost. She heard and saw and tried to understand: she didn't understand much; she slept a lot. And when she looked at the things that happened around her, she yawned.*

*When suddenly one day the lady from termuren castle came to their house again, she didn't care; it was probably only to play another dirty trick on her . . .*

*to take her measurements and put another jute dress on her . . . to lead her up a mountain to make her believe she was I don't know what, and then to kick her down and let everyone look at her, in the dean's regiment. It couldn't hurt her any more, she was too numbed by all the beatings she'd had. The lady said to her mother that she'd come from the castle to ask if ondine wasn't going to school any more? Her mother was silent. Her father came out of the work shed and muttered that god knew what kind of tricks these were, because it was all very well: we shall look after little ondine . . . but he'd have to open his money box and foot the bill. And if little ondine hadn't been so naively, so endlessly sad at this time, her eleventh year, she would have been angry with her father who had no respect for the higher things of life . . . who had the gross temerity to tell the lady the truth: that he would have to fork out, what else could he think? So that's settled, said the lady . . . ondine nodded . . . she knew the lady was only a governess, a servant, a girl whose job it was to teach the two boys of the castle manners: she didn't have to be taught any manners, she knew them all by herself. The lady said that she'd have to be at madame berthe's school at 8 o'clock the next morning, you know where it is? I'll find it, said little ondine . . . and she went in her jute dress, thinking, let them all have another good laugh.*

## EVERYONE HIS DUE

If everyone has his due, the devil has nix; this was the wisdom which the toothless old woman, looking like a foetus, has stored and remembered so many hundreds of years after reynard the fox—she had forgotten who the devil was and who reynard was she never even knew—but the saying itself she'd stuffed away behind her dull eyes, the way only an old woman who's resumed the looks of a foetus, can stuff things away, from rusty safety pins to age-old wisdom. This thought, that the devil has nix, also hovered around reynard's sly fox's head and isengrinus' greedy wolf's head and the masterful head of the noble one-eye, petrified in his almighty power, and they were all three of them standing at one end of the drowned farmer's field, assessing the loot. Divide and let justice and equality reign, said one-eye . . . and isengrinus hastened to let his expert eyes move across the bull, the heifer and the calf*, and said he would carry out this duty for 2 reasons: the biggest was that he would do it for one-eye's sake and the little tiny reason which came a long way behind was that he was a bit hungry . . . and he divided the loot in 3 equal shares, the 1st share being the bull and the heifer for one-eye, the 2nd share the calf, which would be for himself, and the 3rd share, nothing, which would be reynard's . . . but one-eye shook his head at such irritating stupidity and gave isengrinus such a smack on his crazy greedy head that the skin hung down in shreds. You divide it, said the almighty . . . and reynard heaped the 3 parts on top of each other and said that the bull would be for one-eye, the beautiful fat heifer for the one-eye-ess, and the tender calf for baby one-eye . . . and as far as they were concerned, the clumsy yokels reynard and isengrinus, they would find their bait elsewhere. I recognize your feeling for true equality, liberty and brotherhood-in-christ-and-in-democracy, dear reynard, said one-eye. But the fox replied at once that he had only just discovered this feeling in himself: when I look at the purple crown which raises isengrinus to the dignity of a cardinal, and at the decoration on his eye, which makes him look like a man who's celebrating 25 years' servility at the spinning mill . . . receiving a tin watch to be reminded that one mustn't be half a minute late for work and that every tick-tock is a golden coin to be kept in mr derenancourt's safe . . . but perhaps reynard didn't mention this last bit, because one-eye deigned to give a faint smile—and isengrinus smiled too, although his wounds hurt—and one-eye said: go in peace, and if you find something useful, take it, but be careful you don't get prosecuted and have to come and tell me about it. Then he left, with dignity and loaded with loot, watched by reynard and isengrinus who were still squinting with hunger and bent down with fatigue. We'll kill him and burn his house down, reynard incited isengrinus, . . . but they didn't kill him, because between dreams and actions there are laws standing in the way and practical objections and also a wistfulness which no one can explain, and in any case the one didn't trust the other, as is forever the case with small folk, even today.

* In the previous reynard-story there was only talk of a cow. It's possible, of course, that now this cow has turned into a bull, a heifer or a calf. j.j.

## OUR LORD OF TERMUREN SPEAKS FRENCH

*No, ondineke's resentment wasn't all that great . . . because she still had a side-thought: the road between the 2 extremes, between termuren and the town . . . which used to seem so endless . . . was now only 10 minutes' walk. This thought was correct, but it looked as if she would always and everywhere overlook the important things and would always remain bogged down in trivialities. Madame berthe kept school in an upstairs room, there were about 12 girls, all of them middle class, but it was of no importance . . . it didn't have the slightest influence on her life that the girls had to crawl up the stairs on their knees when madame berthe had scrubbed the stairs . . . when one of them, clambering up, let a fart, the others laughed, ondine too . . . but not at the fart, goodness no, she couldn't laugh at anything so silly. But because it was all the same again in life: the way they were crawling up the stairs and got holes in their stockings, it was enough to make you laugh and weep at the same time. It was enough to make you laugh and weep that just she would be punished and had to sit in the wardrobe . . . and as she was a new girl, they forgot about her . . . she fell asleep and didn't come home . . . and vapeur, her father, was worried and thought she might have been molested by the devil in chapel road . . . so he went to look for her in the dark, and came to ask madame berthe in the town of the 2 mills . . . and they found her in the wardrobe and madame berthe exhausted herself in a thousand apologies . . . but vapeur said it was nothing, and started to drivel about his invention, the perpetual motion machine, till madame berthe almost fell asleep and waltzed him outside . . . and with his face against the closed door he still went on talking . . . and when they got home that brother of hers, valeer, had burnt his toes on the stove and had cried himself to sleep. It was all so ridiculously small, there was nothing in life worth bending down so low for that your pigtails swept the floor.*

*Only the fact that she learnt french, it surprised her, as if she was discovering a new country, as if she'd been given the key, not of a mean little chapel, but of the magic world of the great: she spoke nothing else with her middle class friends, monique and marie-thérèse . . . ., at termuren the girls were called liza or maria and gerda, but even so, everything else remained the same: madame berthe still said you mustn't look between your legs, but in french, and that god saw us, but in french, and that mr derenancourt was counsellor to the king . . . all, all in french.*

*She read it aloud at mass, and although they were used to hearing gentlefolk speak it, the people of termuren laughed at her . . . because if it was the gentlemen's right to walk around the mill and to look at a worker and tell him things to his face which he didn't understand . . . things which might mean his death: that he was ill and too slow and that he was going to be dismissed . . . this surely wasn't permitted to vapeur's little ondine, who crossed herself in that language: as if our lord of termuren talked french!*

## I AM BETTER THAN THE OTHERS

*When ondine crossed herself in french, this was the beginning of a time in which she lived a holier life than ever . . . it was a new religion, it was no longer the god of the nuns at the center, but her god: dieu. She couldn't bear it that anyone was holier than she; a thin termuren woman, withered from reading litanies and making pilgrimages for tom dick and harry, always for a few coppers . . . not worth mentioning . . . and who lived in a cottage which had once been painted on canvas by a painter because it was so pretty with the sagging windows and the sunflowers by the hedge, only it was a pity that you could see the chimneys of the filature . . . so they hadn't been painted in . . . well then, this thin old woman who had a fit every other day and said that our lord had appeared to her, this woman was so hated by ondine that she could have murdered her: at nightfall she used to sneak around the cottage to see how she could bait the old woman, maybe by cutting the sunflowers or shitting on the floor. No, something more cruel. And also she couldn't bear to hear her father swear, when he hit his finger . . . or that her mother, zulma, who hadn't got much idea of what was right or wrong, went into the garden and peed with her skirts held high: she exaggerated all these daily things into an irredeemable thought in her head: only in order to have the pleasant feeling that everybody was bad except she.*

*And not only was everyone bad in her eyes, but everything also began to look very small to her: it started with chapel road, and now followed mr derenancourt's castle . . . she used to think of it as a palace, with halls and halls and more halls; but now when she looked at it in passing it could hardly be called a castle; a villa, yes, that was a more suitable name. And that this wilderness with here and there a tree was called a 'wood' . . . and that beside the devil a new and more dreadful person had arrived, the tall woman, ondine merely sniggered at it. Behind the wall of the labor there was a field by the canal, a little shoe factory, a hatmaker's shop, but that was already part of the town . . ., there it was: a far too small provincial town council and sham magistrates and a burgomaster encyclical for ever and ever amen. Outwardly nothing of this was visible, the chimneys of the libertine labor and of the encyclical mill the filature went on vomiting their smoke upon the town, and the police went on treading the beat in their faded and frayed uniforms, guarding the money and goods of mr derenancourt of the filature and mr gourmonprez of the labor; ondineke saw a thing or two . . . but naturally, she didn't understand all that much, she stuck to her idea: I am the best and the world is no larger than it is.*

## IT IS DIFFICULT TO ASSESS

It's Sunday evening and your friends—your heroes—sit by the stove and the music master puts his hand in his pocket . . . but it comes back empty . . . and he says: I was going to say, shall we buy a bottle together, but I just remembered I've got to buy a book tomorrow and it's either the one or the other, either a book or a bottle . . . oh, hell, let it be a bottle. And while the pretty lucette and your wife go out to get a bottle from the store of the bottle-woman with her washed-out face . . . like a blue apron which has to be kept clean too long . . . johan janssens tries . . . he wouldn't be a journalist if he didn't . . . to assess the situation.

you, music master, you don't earn much by teaching, just like our writer here earns practically nothing at all by writing and I don't earn much by supplying the paper with johan janssens' remarks: those people who still think, weigh, ponder, take decisions freely, break down society and try to rebuild the world, these people are left to themselves by the state and the community. But the people who don't think and who are resigned to being relatives of machines, those who keep the card-index and mass-produce the blueprints . . . that is to say, those who are a tiny cog, a nut, a bolt or a spring in a machine moving into an abyss, they are seen as something useful which has to be more or less well paid. Now there are 2 ways of doing something about this: a good one and a bad one . . . the good one: to realize that those who try to stop the machine are also useful to it and therefore also have to be properly paid . . . the bad one: to pity the thinkers, the ponderers, the weighers, and say that they too have to be assimilated, that is, have to become a nut or a bolt or a spring, and to pay them more or less adequately only then. You look, for instance, how the editor of my paper offends my soul by controlling my reflections according to their length, and by telling me that I must be in the office all day in order to assist others on top of what I do already. If they want to measure spiritual values with a watch in their hand, that is, if they want to know how long it takes me to write a piece, while they can't understand that I might write my best piece in 2 minutes and take 2 weeks over an equally good piece: as music master you may give your pupils an opportunity to invent a new theory of relativity, you may, like me, johan janssens, admonish this world which is splitting in 2, and you may, as a writer, sit in your study and write in 10 days a book which will last 100 years . . . those who run into the abyss with the machine and receive a more or less exaggerated wage for doing so, get their chronometer out and say: what goes on there is difficult to assess.

## MR BRYS IS NOT VERY WISE

*So to ondineke the world was no larger than it was . . . but it was big enough to wander around in, after school . . . not in order to see and understand everything, but in order to be seen, to show others that she and her friends belonged to the middle class and understood the french shop signs: monique was the worst: she persuaded ondine to wait at the gate of the boys' school, for her sweetheart . . . he was only 14 and she had told him to become a doctor so that he could examine her body. Ondine was curious to see him but he was disappointing: he had spiky hair and was shy, and all he could do was shout something to another boy, an equally big idiot, who was also walking with his sweetheart, and he swung his satchel so as to scare them. Oh, ondine belonged to the middle class, it was true, but she didn't like those 14 year old middle class schoolboys, she liked that other boy, the eldest from termuren castle . . . she would never marry anyone but him . . . and she said: I've got a sweetheart too, I pass by the castle park every night and he waits for me there. And when monique asked: and what does he do to you then? . . . she replied: I'm not going to tell you . . . No, she wasn't going to tell, she carried such lies inside her as if they had really, really happened.*

*But most of all, at the time when clerks and office workers were on their way to work, they would set out to amaze the people in the shopping streets in town, with their french and their middle class education . . . monique introduced ondine to her uncle, little mr brys, the bookkeeper at the spinning mill . . . he took little tripping steps and wore a pince-nez, but he was very funny and spoke in rhymes: hello monique my dear, I'm glad to see you here. He also made a rhyme on ondine, and they laughed, but they were sorry it wasn't a french rhyme. Although he did know french rhymes too; he was very learned, but no braggart and as he'd been married for years but had no children he loved all children and also all those who were deprived . . . but platonically, like our lord . . . blessed are the poor . . . but without doing too much to remove the poverty. But no, that isn't just, to say that, he wanted to start evening classes for the workers at the filature . . . they couldn't even write their own names but had to sign with a cross. And then in new street, a busy shopping street, a spinner passed them on his wooden clogs and called: Hello mr brys! . . . and mr brys called back, very loudly: oh hello jef, aren't you coming to the evening class? Oh, you can just imagine how monique and ondine stood there with their middle class education . . . monique said: I'll never go to new street again, if my uncle shouts out to mill hands in clogs . . . and ondine said: your uncle talks in rhymes, but I'll tell you one too, your uncle mr brys, he isn't very wise.*

## MIDDLE CLASS RECIPES

*This was the end of the story of mr brys for ondine: monique told her the next day at school that she was going to avoid new street at the times when mr brys went there like our lord to meet the poor; either you belong to the middle class or you don't; and then she came to school with something to pin on her blouse, it was glittering and very smart: a jewel. But the next day marie-thérèse, the other girl, had an even lovelier thing to pin on her blouse: an even costlier jewel. And ondineke? Yes, there she was, she also belonged to the bourgeoisie, but didn't have a brooch; if the middle class mothers were trying to ruin each other, ondine had to rely on herself; she had to choose between being outshone or, as before, to take her father's pliers to the offertory box, but she didn't do that, she was too shrewd to play the same trick twice. She climbed on a chair and looked for her father's money, which lay on top of the cupboard: she bought herself a brooch, at the Saturday market, from the bran-tub. For 25 centimes you could rummage in the bran and dig out something . . . monique and marie-thérèse doubled up with laughter: oh o, they're bran-tub jewels! They're not, shouted ondine, terribly taken aback that they'd discovered the truth so easily . . . and she swore . . . the word had slipped out before she realized. Naturally, that wasn't middle class either and so it was goodbye to walking arm in arm with the others through the shopping streets. And in order to revenge herself on those ladies-never-shit, she spent all the money she'd pinched from her father, a powder compact and a case with mirror and comb and a handbag, but she hadn't got enough for that so she had to pinch some more: she felt as if she'd die of anger and regret if she wasn't able to buy all those things. But most difficult of all was to smuggle it into the house unnoticed; and to hide it in the attic in a box behind a crate of rusty locks and keys; when she wanted to deck herself out with her treasures she dragged the crate of old iron on to the trapdoor and strutted about the attic like a lady.*

*But after french, cookery was the most distinguished and the most middle class thing she learnt at madame berthe's. She had a special exercise book for recipes and there was mention of cauliflower with egg sauce, of salad and strawberries and ice-cream, of things she had to look up in a dictionary and of which . . . no matter in which shop in this small provincial town of the 2 mills . . . no one had ever heard. Ondine came home with these recipes, but couldn't find artichokes at termuren . . . and they didn't have a teaspoon or no one knew what cornflour was. She cooked up something that looked a bit like it, but it didn't taste like anything and was no food for her father who was out at the farthest corner of termuren helping a farmer, building a stable out of tree trunks.*

This is the end of the chapter 'middle class recipes', but something seems to be missing: it should really have been written quite differently, more stress should have been laid on the incomprehensible desire to keep up appearances against all better knowledge. But if this had been stressed more, then the title should have been altered too . . . for instance: the proletariat of the middle class . . . yes, that would have been something.

## THE PEPPERPOT APPEARS

*The way it was in termuren, today some sunshine and tomorrow rain and wind, that's how it was with little ondine: young though she was, she withdrew in herself, she had moods and whims, she'd pout and cry at nothing: something in her body began to ripen, she didn't know what. Suddenly in the middle of the night she heard the girls at school say things which shocked her . . . words which tore something, broke something. And yet she saw at the same time other pictures, spring clouds, smooth trunks of fruit trees and such masses of flowering broom that all that yellow really frightened her . . . and meanwhile she thought of endless grey rain drizzling down, desolately, it all became strangely intermingled, in this devastation, in the endless succession of rain and sun, of life and death, of budding flowers and withering branches . . . in all this lay her nameless melancholy. There was also something irrepressible about it: she dreamt she was clinging to the mane of a runaway horse, whose hooves kicked the mud of chapel road high up in the sky . . . crushing playing children to pulp . . . what did it matter? she clung to its mane and swayed to and fro blissfully; she was tossed about, her legs wide apart, her hair flying loose. And when she woke up it was no longer a dream, but something she had experienced long ago and had since forgotten: it was the revelation of what she daren't admit to herself: that another life existed, wilder, more untamable, a life which couldn't be expressed in 1 or 2 words . . . or if it could, she wouldn't dare, but began to pray devoutly. It gripped her when she saw people being uninhibited, doing what she herself would have liked to do . . . although she inwardly shouted that it wasn't true; people who, to talk in the words of her dream again, held on to the horse's mane and said: let things go the way they may, goddammit . . . Sometimes she grew cold, sometimes she was flushed . . . and the skin of her breast hurt so much that she fell ill for two whole days; the sight of the pepperpot pissing behind the inn by the level crossing . . . with his back to the hedge, nauseated her so profoundly that it put her off her food . . . never, never would she eat again. And indeed, when vapeur gave her her porridge, she smelt again the pepperpot with his back to the inn, she smelt the lavatories of the filature, although she'd never been there . . . tears streamed down her cheeks, she dropped her spoon weakly: I shall never be able to eat again, she thought . . . But the next day it was beans with a bit of bacon, and she ate till she couldn't even yawn.*

## THE VOID GAPES AT YOU

*You see, that's how it goes: you write a novel about 100 lives, in which ondineke of termuren takes shape: the music master inspects her spirit and the painter who came to live in termuren last week, tippetotje, she inspects her body and msieu colson of the ministry inspects her emotions . . . saying that she shouldn't drive it too far, now that she's entering Those years* . . . and johan janssens, poet and journalist, inspects the rest, which comprises all sorts of things: you work you build you think you live: but suddenly: how is it possible, all your heroes withdraw—no, they wither, they disappear into the Void and you stay behind alone and see only emptiness gaping at you. You commute every day to brussels, on the train, with msieu colson of the ministry, you have worked with johan janssens on the paper, you have read and misread many books with the music master and you have asked the four corners of the world when you might have ½ hour off, and be alone . . . and ½ hour comes when your work is no longer so pressing and you are alone, but you see only the void gaping at you. *Because it's not worth the bother to go on working on the history of that urchin ondine* and it's too much trouble to lie down in the grass and look at the clouds; because you've been watching the clouds pass by since the other war and in the meanwhile another war has already been and now there's talk of yet another one and the clouds go on passing by, unperturbed: and you're afraid that suddenly they will all have gone past and that you'll lie there in the grass and be alone and only see emptiness gaping at you. And when you're lying there thinking, you suddenly have a thought which might become a wonderful poem, a story, a painting; a wall as high as the sky . . . no, a wall infinitely higher than a wall as high as the sky . . . and the clouds drifting by and finding their way barred and waiting there patiently with their stupid, vacant cloud-souls . . . but while you write down the title: 'a trick played on the universe', something deep down in you asks why this has all got to be put down on paper and whether you're not being guided by an illusion when you think you've got a Duty . . . towards future generations . . . not to let a single thought get lost: because you see, books and writers drift past like the clouds, and you always see new books and new writers coming, just as there are always new clouds: you stare at your paper with the title: 'a trick played on the universe' and you're alone and see only the void gaping at you:

And you hurry to your little garden and dig a hole and put 5 dead sticks in it which will come to life in the summer and be fangogh yellow: you stamp the earth down and fill the hole and think: in the summer, that will be a lovely sight!

## END OF THE SUNFLOWER CULT

While you're crouching at the back of the garden, tippetotje suddenly turns up; *the painter of the level crossing, of the sheets of concrete by the weaving mill, and of ondineke of termuren who . . . without anyone knowing and without being spied on by the pepperpot . . . goes for a swim in the brook by the castle . . . she stands still with her slip in her hand;* that is if you want to believe tippetotje's painting. And you tell tippetotje that you were thinking of planting a cherry tree . . . they're so pretty in the spring when they're in blossom . . . but in life things are just the same as in your work: you think and choose and deliberate, because once it's been planted or written it can't be changed; and there's no point in saying: I would rather have had that other cherry tree. And in order to apologize for the doubts in your work . . . because tippetotje is laughing at you . . . you add that everyone is not like her, *simply putting ondineke of termuren by the brook and painting her in her lovely bare body: I torment myself thinking whether she wouldn't instead have been looking at the brook from behind the bushes, thinking . . . yes, I wonder what she would have been thinking?* And again, as an apology for your doubts about the cherry tree, you add that you've stuck 5 dead sticks in the ground which will come to life and will grow into some sort of sunflower and that they were sold to you as fangogh yellow . . . because fangogh is fashionable as a spicy decoration . . . sunflowers have been planted and the minister of culture related a few episodes from fangogh's activities amongst the miners, and the influence of these activities on the development of sunflower-painting; the director-general of the ministerial department for the better understanding of artists who have died in poverty, then gave a vote of thanks on behalf of the numerous personalities present; the golden book was signed and an official banquet held . . .

But tippetotje goes on laughing and says that if she were some fangogh or other, she'd quietly shoot the ravens in dr gachet's garden: the personalities will sign the golden book and the writers will wait in their gardens till a bit of fangogh yellow opens out . . . but also, if she were to put her cut-off ear in a parcel on my doorstep, not only would the sunflower cult wither, but the writers would wither too, haha . . . because even 2nd hand bookshops are closing down, they sell up, or suddenly vanish . . . I thought there was one left behind the trulleberg, but the other day I discovered it's been converted into a garage, and even in the palace of fine arts the bookshop has been turned into a cloakroom . . . and in spite of signing the golden book and giving the official banquet: the end of the sunflower cult and of the art of printing are here. And tippetotje leaves me, mockingly, but when she has gone I reflect that her words were really my own thoughts, inspired by fangogh yellow: you'd do much better running a business selling fangogh yellow than painting or writing about sunflowers and *about ondineke of termuren.*

## THE WILL OF OUR UNCONSCIOUS WILL BE DONE

*But it wasn't only ondine . . . that brother of hers too, valeer, as he grew older, could scarcely be kept away from their cousin with the wispy hair and the dirty bubbles under her nose . . . and the worst: she hardly ever wore pants: what kind of mother have you got, said ondine. And one day she found that those two had crept into the attic to do god knows what: maybe things ondine herself dreamt about . . . no, the blood didn't rush to her head, it drained away from it, she turned as white as a lamb. She wanted to open the trapdoor with a bang, and surprise the 2 . . . but however dim valeer usually was, this time he'd used the same trick as ondine: he'd pushed the crate with old iron over it. Open up, called ondine. She heard them laughing above her head, so it wasn't the crate, they themselves were sitting on the door, and this made her even more furious, the discovery that others were craftier than she. She thumped savagely on the door . . . and as there was nothing else she could do, she thumped at it with her head: the children simply laughed at her, her head ached, she sat down on the ladder, powerless, she had to vomit. Then the thought ripened in her that she should kill him, it couldn't be that her holy brother would live and die like this. Her day passed in blindness and sometimes it was as if objects which always stayed in the same place, started to move of their own accord: the table, for instance, suddenly pushed itself away from under her elbow, a long way . . . and came back at once; she had to go and stand by the back door for a while with her head on the cool stones. She saw a knife. Someone had been shaving wood and had forgotten it . . . it was like god's finger: she hid it under her skirt, it hung from the cord which held her pants up. And when she lay in bed she was still looking around with rigid doll's eyes, the knife had become warm on her body . . . she thought: in a little while, when it's quiet. She heard sounds nearby and far, which she had never heard before: a train was rumbling past, a long, long train . . . it's a goods train, she thought. She clutched the knife as if she was going to cut right through the oak door of the chapel. But valeer had guessed: when she bent over him he looked at her with big, frightened eyes . . . ondine couldn't bear to see it, she began to pray aloud as she stabbed. And valeer, who saw the knife coming down, hadn't even got the strength to jump aside . . . maybe he didn't think of it that he might escape his fate . . . but in a mad impulse of self-defense he clutched the hot blade—yes, it was hot . . . and for that very reason he clutched it more tightly. He cried. Ondine prayed: thy kingdom come, thy will be done . . . she shouted the words, trying to wrench the knife from his hands. And meanwhile she heard her mother zulma, in the next room, joining in the prayer: and forgive us our sins, amen.*

## FACTORY GIRLS HAVE SWEETHEARTS

*The end of this story was that one of valeer's fingers had come off. Their father vapeur had torn the blood-stained sheet to shreds . . . it was ruined anyway, and had wrapped them round his son's hand into a large, white club; it became a red club; no doctor came and no one asked any questions. Vapeur stood in his workshed and reflected that he hadn't asked his children anything; he went to the kitchen where they were, but stared in front of him with the doorknob in his hand—at a lump of plaster which was about to fall from the wall, and then he went back to his shed. And when they went to sleep at night, ondine and valeer, side by side in the same bed, there was something under her . . . she fumbled . . . nausea throbbed from down in her toes to her brown pigtails: she flung the finger out of the bed as if it was a strange animal, a worm. Then she managed to laugh hysterically, shrilly, till the madness had gone and hot tears began to flow. That which had started to ripen within her, bewildered and dismayed her more acutely every day: in these nights of restless sleep she no longer clung to the mane of a horse, but she was with the pepperpot who was peeing with his back to the hedge . . . she knew, but she didn't want to know . . . she held her arms crossed over her breast, in order to conceal something she didn't want to see . . . she loathed her brother when she thought of him sleeping near her at night, and even more when she remembered she'd once asked him not to play with their cousin but always to stay with her: she hated him and she was sorry he'd only lost a finger. And when one day she heard that people in termuren had chased him for a joke, like a dog, to see his big head wobble on his shoulders, she felt as if she'd have a fit of fury . . . not in anger with those who slapped their thighs with laughter . . . but because of valeer himself, the ass, who would never learn anything, with his balloon on his shoulders. She ran, but something at the place where she usually crossed her arms, shook gently as she ran, and somebody called: what have you got there, ondine? She thought she'd sink into the ground; swine, she said. But at home she asked herself, what have you got there? And she laughed sneeringly at the world, at herself, at god who had made her the way she was. Yet, that same evening she saw liza and the other girls, coming home from the filature . . . their hair was covered with tufts from the spinnery—there was a crowd of them and they were laughing: their voices had become husky and they thought nothing of it to say: 'kiss my cunt, at night-fall in chapel road . . . they were talking about their sweethearts, but because ondine was coming near, liza said to one of the others: it's not true, he did ask me, but I pushed him away. And when they were alone by the chapel, ondine asked: what did he ask you? Well, said liza, they laugh at you when you don't have a sweetheart, but they laugh even harder when you've seen too much of your sweetheart and you get caught.*

## THE PICTORIAL ELEMENT IN LITERATURE

Look, says johan janssens, I've written in the paper about goya and breughel and bosch, about picasso and renoir and magritte, about louis paul boon and about children's drawings and for a long time I've been thinking of writing about the pictorial element in literature, and by god, someone's beaten me to it . . . he unfolds the paper and reads:

how many writers, for instance, understand the essence and the soul of the pictorial element in literature? They are tied to their own artistic expression; the story, and they look for a story everywhere else: they ask of a painting that it shall be a colored illustration, because the pictorial element is to them a dead letter . . . naturally, you can recognize this lack in their work, because they do take account of sound and rhythm, but not of line and color, which should form part of their prose too. *Now suppose you were to write a story about factory girls, who return home in the late evening, in rainy weather along a country road . . . as it's raining you would say that the road is muddy, and in describing the setting you'd make it look like this: factory girls walking along the muddy chapel road at nightfall, in the rain. Perhaps that road leads past the long, high wall of the weaving mill, the labor* . . . and look at the words high wall, which form a repetition of the same i—and a—picture as in the word nightfall . . . you see, I say picture, not sound, and you then get a grey picture with nothing but dull colors: evening rain mud long wall weaving mill labor factory girls. To the writer something like this is sufficient, he has created an atmosphere and a setting and has set the story in motion. But if he realized the value of the pictorial element in art, then he would add a color to these grey tones which would give a bit of a blaze . . . a red tone, say, would make the other, grey tones look even more somber, it would make them run backwards and so evoke unsuspected depths. And also because he, being a painter, loves color simply for its own sake, and because this warm tone in the middle of the others shows his love of painting for its own sake. Well now, in order to get this red color *he could make one of the girls laugh, in the dark, in the rain* . . . the word 'laugh' would immediately achieve the purpose . . . but from a literary point of view it would be no good . . . laughing doesn't go with this story and the dark opening of the first sentence is broken by it . . . *imagine now that one of the girls curses and says: kiss my cunt* . . . then the grey tones would vanish at once and make room for the shrill red tone of the taboo word. The 2 fold purpose is then achieved: as a painting it is complete and in a literary sense it is correct, and it deepens the grey atmosphere of homeward bound factory girls.

Johan janssens folds the paper, he's sorry he was too late, and says that surely the writer of this piece must have been someone who knows chapel road and the weaving mill . . . and because he sees a grimace on your face, he says: ha, I see!

## THERE'S PLENTY OF FAT LEFT ON THE STRING

So there they stood: isengrinus, whose only thought was that his wounds hurt and that he was still hungry, and reynard, who, on the contrary, had remembered that once again he'd have to go home to his wife and children with empty hands . . . and was also wondering why there need be a lord and master, if all could be their own lord and master and could divide things . . . that is to say, the loot . . . according to a higher law of justice? In the land of the blind, one-eye is captain and master, agreed isengrinus, who remembered this saying thanks to his shuttered eye. Let us unite, said reynard, and they stood there and proclaimed some republic or other . . . the one of the Negation of existing things . . . but all the while isengrinus thought of his hunger: right, let us unite . . . he grabbed reynard and was going to eat him up. However, reynard had envisaged quite a different kind of unity, but no matter what he said, that this wasn't the way to reach their common goal . . . and that they shouldn't go forward inside one another but beside one another . . . his lofty words were wind in a bottle and he had to bring other, more edible arguments forward. Glory be to the young republic, he saw a farmer walking in a field, with a big side of pork on his back . . . but isengrinus remembered too well the hard sticks with which farmers batter your back: you go, and I will do the reviewing, he said. And so he only watched as reynard lay down in a hollow road, in the path of the farmer. Hey there, a half dead fox, the farmer exclaimed: that will be a lovely collar for my new coat . . . and he hurried towards reynard, who limped a bit further, so that the farmer ran a bit faster, so that reynard limped a bit faster still. In brief: the farmer put down his side of pork in order to make one last jump: but general isengrinus, who had followed the events from afar, quickly picked up the meat and made off with it, straight to his lair . . . and then reynard stopped his crazy limping game so that the farmer tore his hair from his head because he had to choose between nothing and nix; between his fur which was running away and his meat which had gone. But isengrinus had already forgotten the community of the republic and had bolted the door and hung the meat up in the hearth to dry . . . and to reynard, who drummed on the door and raged that he wanted his share, he called: what do you mean, your share . . . didn't I get this meat in exchange for a good review? I'm not one of your poets who can live on good reviews, retorted reynard; I have a wife and a child and I've got worries in my head. And when he heard the wolf's wife say that there was nothing left but the string from which the meat had been hanging . . . give it to reynard, it's nice and it's got plenty of fat on it . . . he shouted he didn't need a piece of string, as he wasn't going to hang himself yet: on the contrary, I'm thinking of going on a pilgrimage against dishonest friends. You do that, answered that dirty witch hersinde, you go to our lady of termuren and confess that you incited my husband to do away with one-eye and we will commend you to god in our prayers. And I will commend you to the devil, thought reynard, who went home and scorched his shins by the stove and ate his heart out. johan janssens.

## A PITY THIS AND A PITY THAT

*Ugh, how nauseating was life to ondine . . . and at home by the stove, in the deadly quiet of termuren, alone with zulma, she reproached her mother that it was a sin to marry and lie in bed with a man; the craziest things she reproached her mother with, the most unutterable words came out of her mouth . . . but it was as if she wasn't saying those words herself, but somebody else inside her; she only needed to open her mouth to hear all these words jumble out . . . and to hear all the things about which she had dreamt at night but daren't think of in the day, pouring out like water bursting through a dyke. She was a vessel, she didn't know what was in it; she listened to herself, pale and with open mouth. But one day when it rained and rained, her crazy mother zulma showed signs of restlessness, she suddenly got up from her chair and walked slowly and menacingly towards ondine: she said that ondine was a devil: you reproach me with all sorts of things that aren't true, that something happened to me up at termuren castle, that . . . that . . . She got confused in her words and stammered that it wasn't true that she slept with a man, that carolus hadn't touched her since valeer was born . . . and you, you're a devil, she screamed. So that ondine was mad with fear for several days, it was as if not her mother, but the whole world had shouted devil at her; she began to believe it; she walked around in the rain, she went along the railway where the broom had flowered, but where there were now only wet, bare branches . . . and at the place where she used to adore her holy brother valeer, she now crouched down to shit . . . I shit on it, she said, I shit on the world . . . she wiped herself clean with the wet grass and went back, past the cottage which had once been painted on canvas by a painter; she looked at it, and really, it was picturesque, even now with the autumn coming; there was a dead elder tree and here and there hung a dead flower . . . a pity you could see the chimneys of the filature. But then that was so with everything: everything ondine had ever experienced might have been beautiful, but this was a pity and that . . . in her honor a miracle had happened, but it was a pity she was a devil . . . a pity that she had sat down to shit on the holy place where the broom had flowered, and a feeling of despair grew in her, so deep, so abysmal.*

## HISTORY OF THE PEPPERPOT

Msieu colson of the ministry says to you: you sit there in the cotton clouds of a cardboard novel world and write *about ondineke of termuren*, but in the meanwhile I had my rotten legs firmly on the ground and saw the following: the history of the so-called pepperpot who also works in the ministry and who studied to be a priest in earlier days but let his tonsure grow, he joins in the procession of our lady of fatima with a burning candle in his hand and he says that you can have a sinful desire even by looking at a flower . . . you can imagine the way things are with him . . . he goes absolutely berserk when his encyclical blood gets hot; his wife is always pregnant and he sings exasperating little songs: who would go hungry for one extra mouth . . . but as soon as the office closes he goes to the outskirts of the city, to jump suddenly from behind a corner when a girl passes by, or to stand by a hedge . . . I, msieu colson of the ministry dare not describe it all, it's too indecent, but you dare . . . and when a girl recognizes him: isn't that what's his name, the pepperpot? then he goes to the police to declare on his word of honor that that girl has offended his honor. And if a mother goes to school with her daughter to give an explanation of this pepperpot business, then she's hardly said two words and the nuns interrupt her saying that it's nothing but slander and that they don't want to hear anything about mr pepperpot . . . because he's so courteous, he always takes his hat off so politely, saying good-morning, reverend sisters, and carrying a burning candle behind fatima. Ah, but I, msieu colson of the ministry wouldn't tell you all this if the pepperpot hadn't written to my boss that you have written a bad book and that I'm a friend of yours: now I must explain that my boss and I are good friends, from back in the war when he used to come to our house to listen to the English radio . . . you remember, on the 1500 meter band, turlelut, turlelut . . . but now my boss doesn't come to our house any more, he prefers to go and see the pepperpot.

You put your pen down and shake your head, but msieu colson of the ministry puts a threatening index finger on your nearly filled sheet of paper, and adds: and do you know what I think? that all those young women and girls *are pleased that there are pepperpots walking about, because there's not an evening goes by when he's not up to his tricks . . . and this has been going on for years . . . and yet there's never been a single one who's brought a charge, it's always: he did . . . one evening . . . and then they're indignant or pretend they are . . . And msieu colson of the ministry looks indignant because you say: well, there's no need to exaggerate, because I've already written about how ondine of termuren met the pepperpot . . . and she* was *indignant.*

## SHOW US YOUR FINGER, VALEER

*Little ondine walked round the cottage of the thin old woman of termuren, with a hard, cruel smile on her mouth: she was thinking of killing the pig with the 2 safety pins which held her pants up, and to throw it into the trough . . . she was just about to open the stable door when the woman came outside: ondine startled so violently that all she could do was walk away on legs as limp as rags . . . her pants slipped down, she was still holding the 2 safety pins. She felt sorry for her-*

*self, she wanted to pat herself on the shoulder and ask: dear ondineke, what wrong have they done to you? She leant against the whitewashed wall by the ladder to the attic and became furious because a lump of tears wouldn't come out of her throat . . . she wanted to rub her eyes . . . and then she saw she was still holding the 2 safety pins in her hand: she started to scratch in the plaster, on the wall . . . more and more fiercely, more and more furiously . . . in the end she held the pins as if they were daggers . . . she stabbed, she thought it was someone, a person, all people; she murdered them all, the cowards, the scoundrels, who . . . who . . . won't they let me have my due. Although she wasn't sure what was her due: wasn't it simply the awareness that the world was too large and she was too small; that termuren and the nearby town and everything else within her horizon could never be arranged the way she wanted. Yes, that she would never be the master of people and their wishes? that she could never chase vapeur, her father, to the mill and knock some sense into valeer and order the priest to preach that anyone who sleeps with a man will go to hell? Then she locked herself up in the attic with her treasures, the glittering brooch to pin to her blouse, the case with the comb and the pocket mirror, and the leather handbag . . . naturally, it wasn't enough to rule the world with, but yet, it was a start: she secretly longed to show these treasures to the world . . . to the world which for the time being was valeer with his cut-off finger, and their cousin, for these 2 were inseparable . . . she'd have to show both of them, or no one. But when she did show them, they remained unimpressed, they were thinking of themselves; a case with a pocket mirror meant nothing to valeer, who had no imagination, and a brooch on a blouse meant nothing as yet to their cousin, she was too young: she looked at it with her lightless eyes and said to valeer: shall we go now? They clambered down the ladder and returned to their own world. Ondine suddenly saw it: everyone had his own world which he thought the most important: she felt like kicking the case with the comb . . . she was about to do it . . . but it was too lovely, she hesitated, and all she did was stroke it. It's not worth the trouble, she said. Through the attic window she saw their cousin and valeer walking past the chapel; another girl joined them and their cousin said: show us your finger, valeer. Oh, it made ondine feel suddenly so empty and weak: that she should accidentally see someone showing off something of which she had been the cause! She suspected that their cousin said it many times during a day . . . that she said it whenever they met anyone, maybe even a dog or a tree: show us your finger, valeer. And he, stupid and sheepish, obligingly stuck out his hand . . . damn, why didn't I kill him, thought ondine.*

## THE 5 FINGERS

You let your letters slide into the letterbox by the 1st dirty houses and as you're doing so you think 3 different things which you've often thought but always forget again . . . 1st thing: that they told you when you were still a child who believed everything, that you had to shout very loudly into the opening of the letterbox: a letter to brussels! and that after all these years you still want to shout that. 2nd thing: that a writer should have the right not to answer a single letter, because you write enough in the daytime without having to keep up with your correspondence in the evening . . . 3rd thing: that they might add another letterbox to the one by the 1st dirty houses, nearer chapel road. And thinking this, you return on the other side of the brook by the castle, and you see johan janssens, poet and journalist, in lively conversation with tippetotje the painter and you hear him say that he too knows something about painting because he writes about it in the paper: as I said, I didn't only write about goya and breughel and bosch, but I also explained in minute detail what impressionism and expressionism and surrealism are. And by the way, he says, I wrote about expressionism that you first feel a certain hesitation because something which is dormant in all people wants to resist and wants to go back to the ordinary, safe world where A HAND IS A HAND WITH 5 FINGERS and where the eyes are on either side of the nose and not in the nose or behind the ears . . . because one wants firm ground under one's feet and not the abyss, which you, tippetotje, would open for us if you painted in the expressionist way . . . that's why we are only very slowly beginning to realize that this expressionistic foot, however strange, is a masterpiece of draughtsmanship . . . and then we discover for the 1st time in our lives an arm, a hand, a penis . . . and then, instead of coming to terms with that special world of the painter, we discover with amazement and dismay that this world is only too familiar to us; we discover that it is actually Our world but that we never wanted to see it like that.

You see, continues johan janssens . . . to tippetotje, who isn't listening any more but goes on painting the winter landscape and the 1st dirty houses . . . you see, says johan janssens, without losing courage . . . to you, so that you can't do anything else but listen . . . you see, and just after I'd written about that safe world where a hand is a hand with 5 fingers, that same day in the evening edition . . . would you believe the coincidence . . . my other colleague, expressionist non-expert johan van boebaerderococo, wrote an article in the New Times about you, the writer of ondine of termuren, and he said that if mr boon wants to become a writer of stature he will first have to learn how the FIVE FINGERS OF A HAND can be clenched into a fist. Haha . . . tippetotje bursts out laughing and johan janssens bursts out in a double laugh because someone laughs at his joke. And you?

## BURNING CANDLES

*Would things have improved for ondine if she'd stabbed her brother valeer to death? The fact that he existed and was a thorn in her flesh . . . that wasn't the root of her wretchedness, the source of it was her own nature, perhaps that sinful nest she came from, or something inside her which craved for satisfaction. From her own unrest she looked at her father's peacefulness: he was deeply absorbed in a book about steam engines, and didn't know yet that yesterday she'd torn a page from it to take to the bog: he muttered word after word and followed the rhythm of the sentences with a raised finger as if to imprint them for ever on his memory. She sniggered aloud at his peacefulness, in a termuren where most parents never saw their children during the week: leaving for the spinning mill in the dark and coming home again in the dark along chapel road and all they had seen in the day was a dumb mill . . . and as hardly a single one of them was able to read a word, they lay down and slept, went to mass and got drunk in the café of christ, the bearded foreman; they wandered around in eternal darkness. She sniggered at his peacefulness over his open book, even more so since the priest had preached that all evil came from so-called science and progress. But she also sniggered at the priest who flung something into everyone's face in turn . . . everyone, but never the gentlemen; this evening it was vapeur with his book about steam engines, and the next evening the girls of the filature: the light of the candles danced to and fro, shining on the fluff in their hair, because no matter how they combed and combed, the fluff from the mills never came out again. They listened with bent heads and felt guilty . . . yes, it was true, they were sinful and bad, they thought of it with shame that they cursed for no reason and said kiss my things; and the other day the priest had said that it was better to tie a big stone round the neck of a young whore and throw her deep into the river dendre, rather than that she should bring forth a child of sin . . . he had barely said these words when one girl fell down from her chair, screaming, and pulling down two more chairs in her fall. Ondine stayed with her, out of curiosity, in the dark porch where the flickering candle might go out any moment, she heard the others going away into the dark evening: they were no longer so noisy, but away in the distance, swallowed by the dark, she heard them laughing again, hoarsely, sinfully. It was liza who had fallen from her chair, she heard the laughter and said: where does it get him that sermon, except that tomorrow the others will make fun of me and scream and throw the chairs about, but maybe they've just been a bit luckier than me . . . honestly, I only let him once, I may drop dead if it isn't true.*

## THE BOOK-MIRROR

A lot of trouble and misery must have gone through chapel road in the course of time . . . you see snow or sunshine on it and think only of its beauty, of tippetotje the painter, of johan janssens in his capacity as a poet, but today there's neither sun nor snow, but it's wet and chilly and dark and goddammit, there's a black shower hanging over there. Tippetotje the painter hurries home with all her luggage: folding easel and canvas, and huddled in her collar she almost knocks over johan janssens who almost knocks her over: that shower is coming this way, says tippetotje.

Johan janssens nods: of course it's coming this way, it's hanging over my heart and my soul and my penis . . . now that we're walking alone in this beastly weather, tippetotje, may I pour my heart out; in the paper you've always got to watch your words so . . . the cloud hangs round my penis which has crept into a corner like a crying child: because all day long I've been writing little columns for the paper—not about reynard the fox, and not about chapel road, but something to the taste of the editor, something I signed with the pseudonym book-mirror, because I didn't want to call it 'another owl'.

And I wrote about the great ideas of our great journals . . . no comment . . . and in the meanwhile I was thinking that all these journals asked me to send them my great ideas . . . oh, dammit, tippetotje, let me curse from the bottom of my heart since we're alone anyway: let them look between their legs, there hangs another great Idea. I have no great ideas, I only write the way you paint, and I only know that people, with here and there an exception, are stupid and selfish . . . that in their journals they write white on the first page and black on the next . . . but they expect a decent article from me: 'an accusation of the proletariat against the trusts' . . . with clumsy words and a few grammatical mistakes—that improves the tone, the working class boy who's become poet and journalist, but I'm not allowed to say anything that is true, or my contributions are . . . not rejected, no . . . but *not* published. And I know for a fact that they use big words in their journals only in order to conceal the emptiness of their puffed-up heads, like 'the components of a microcosmic perception or conception of the physical and psychological reality of life which moves and affects' . . . but not one of them can write something solid, can bring a bit of order to the chaos; all they think about is to see their stupid little names in print: pascalius prostituanus . . . or no, I forgot his title: dr. pascalius prostituanus. And because I knock my head against all the walls, in the office that is, because it rains angry letters to the editor about my work, because a certain little clique from the ultra-marxist world are hugger-muggering, that's why I succumb, tippetotje, and I write owlish columns: the book-mirror.

Tippetotje looks up at the sky which is one sky and says: it might even pass, that cloud.

## POOR BABY JESUS OF TERMUREN

*Ondine too went to confession and accused herself of sins . . . but she accused mainly her father vapeur, that he was trying to invent a devilish machine . . . and she accused her mother zulma. because she was crazy, one who hadn't been afraid of it in her youth and had had a child from mr derenancourt of the castle: the priest said that such a thing was impossible, that one shouldn't slander, and also, he asked, where was that child then? Ondine thought of the foreman of the weaving mill . . . where he might be now . . . who had alleged that there was a little grave in the woods by the castle: but it was so mysteriously half-dark in the confession box that she was driven into saying things which perplexed herself: I am that child of the castle. She listened in dismay at her own words, she practiced silence, and made a firm resolution never to sin again and not to speak a single word all her life: as she didn't speak, however, she had more opportunity to think, she looked around in her little world and everything piled up inside her like a mountain . . . her eyes, which used to be wide and large, narrowed, and looked at everything mockingly: it was as if she found Life not worth wasting any words on. So it seemed. In reality all those unuttered words mounted up inside her unbearably . . . all her unuttered thoughts crammed beside one another, and the things which made her laugh but at which she kept a straight face, filled her to the point of bursting; she'd suddenly break out in laughter; she laughed and cried at the same time; she was afraid she would become like her crazy mother zulma. Idiot that I am, she thought, idiot, don't I understand that a sermon is a shoe that fits everybody . . . that they preach about greed and avarice, that everybody meets something on his way, good and evil, but mostly misfortune, and they say of the one that it's his punishment and of the other that god is putting him to the test; well then, how can you know whether someone is good or bad. And something within her began to itch . . . to walk into a house, any house . . . and then to chatter and chatter about everything, about her happiness and sadness and her restlessness: she went to see liza who had had her baby and who looked happy, although her breast was sore and was beginning to fester: a child with a child. Ondine laughed at that too, although she felt no joy . . . liza looked more like our lady of termuren than like a whore . . . it might be the baby jesus lying on her lap, a baby jesus with wrinkly hands and a head swollen from the forceps: ondine smiled, although she had to fight against her hatred. And suddenly, as if the devil whispered in her ear, she remembered that our lady wasn't married either, when she had her child . . . and her whole religion seemed so pointless at that moment that she had to start thinking another thought at once, to fill the gaping abyss: it is permitted to saints and gentlefolk to cross the small boundaries between good and evil, but not to us, people of termuren.*

## CROSSED BOUNDARIES

Every day I read the paper on the train from brussels to the town of the 2 mills, says msieu colson of the ministry and if I were to read that some people are allowed to cross our sexual boundaries, then that wouldn't surprise me in the least . . . just look at the commercial travelers, I don't think there's a single one amongst them who doesn't see life through sexual glasses . . . listen to them on the train, talking about Lassies, as they say. And look at jaspers, the commercial traveler, the way he looked at the girl with the fat behind, the one who lives in the caravan which has been standing at the other side of no-man's wood for the last few days, where the poor from the 1st dirty houses come to throw their tins and pots . . . and as she was scrubbing the steps of the caravan, she was bending over so much that you could see the beginning of her pink behind and jaspers simply changed into another pepperpot who studied to be a priest once but who now works at the ministry: he wanted to blush and laugh but instead he went white and swore, more at her, over there, than at me: dammit, I could bite that pink behind. And maybe msieu colson would have liked to add a thing or two, but tippetotje the painter gets hold of a button on his jacket with one hand, holding her sketch book in the other: where did you say there's a caravan where a girl with a fat behind scrubs her pink . . . I mean, the steps? Msieu colson puts his jacket straight and watches tippetotje disappear, shaking his head; then he goes on talking about the crossed sexual boundaries: that these commercial travelers are always on the road and in stations and on trams and trains and always see legs and parts of buttocks and parts of breasts . . . and so they walk around with all sorts of fantasies in their heads . . . and yet, wherever they go, they're received without friendship, and get the devil and his mother flung in their faces . . . and in order to get a bit of balance they try to take the opportunity and wipe out a rebuff here with a sadistic victory there. But this way they slowly slide into a pit without realizing that in the long run they'll know no other life than one between the buttocks of the lassies, as they say.

And when the others have gone, you call msieu colson of the ministry back and you ask him what he meant by all this: I only wanted to tell you that it's permitted to everyone . . . on condition that you manage to conceal it properly . . . and that you don't tie a noose round your neck.

## THE GENTLEMEN ARE COMING!

*Although ondine had consciously deceived herself, had tied a noose round her own neck and had mocked at others . . . had occupied herself with other people so as not to have to think about herself . . . she understood, deep down, that she belonged to the class of serfs: no matter how she pretended to herself that she was a child from the castle, her life would pass in serving and obeying, unless she crawled and slandered, flattering the ones above her and kicking the ones beneath her. Every morning anew she was pulled as if by a magnet to the center of her world: the castle, and she went into the wood where it was quiet and where a longing arose in her for forbidden things . . . one day she saw the 2 young gentlemen of the castle in a canoe on the brook which was covered with green duckweed: she imagined that in that canoe they were discussing things which touched the core of Life, the things about which she too had thought and thought till her mind was blunt, without ever seeing clearly . . . oh, she saw only the eyes of the older boy, achilles, eyes bigger than his face, bigger than the world in which she wanted to lose herself. She heard him saying that he thought everything was sad: look at love, I think people talk too much nonsense, twisting words, but no one dares mention the one thing that matters . . . and he did mention it, but in french . . . it was a word ondine knew because she'd seen her schoolfriend monique write it down in the sand, very quickly, and wipe it out again. It makes you shudder how stupid and small and cowardly people are, said achilles, and he forgot to paddle, but he didn't get an answer: his brother, norbert, was only 17, but already felt tired and old. When ondine wasn't in the wood, but in the field by the railway, she saw achilles again, with the other rich boys: they liked wandering about the neglected park, and maybe they thought that the fields around termuren were part of the park, and they shot with their carbines at anything they saw stirring among the trees . . . but what they liked best was to put their carbines in a corner of a peasant inn and seduce the daughters: norbert was never there, he was a dreamer, he couldn't bear to see dead animals and blood, and pretended to be ill, so that he could stay in bed and amuse himself with his own flesh. The other gentlemen went from village to village and suddenly discovered the inn of christ, the foreman at the filature . . . but they didn't want the beer that the poor drank, they ordered special barrels . . . and if they forgot a mug or two, the poor would soon finish it off. Oh, when the gentlemen were around, ondine noticed that shutters would be closed very early and that young girls were kept at home . . . because late at night, when the carriages were waiting for them, the gentlemen might break any window, and spoil any girl who might stray from her mother's apron strings: yes, they had no trouble with these girls, who had never seen anything except the lavatories of the filature and had never heard anything except sermons and benedictions, and that idleness is the devil's head-rest . . . and now the devils themselves came and made them drunk with beer, the only time in their lives that they had a chance to drink it.*

## DAY OF DEJECTION

On this miserable day you walk to the 1st dirty houses, because you feel the need to escape from people and things, for just 5 minutes, and although the caravan and the girl with the fat behind left the brook by the castle long ago, and jaspers' commercial traveler's blood is being made to run faster god knows where . . . although they've gone, the caravan and the girl with the fat behind, you sit down, dejected, in the trampled grass, by the tins and pots that were left behind and you pour out your heart in 1 breath: I sit here and I don't live and I don't write and don't think and I only am dejected . . . where are you and where is msieu colson of the ministry, where johan janssens the journalist and where tippetotje the painter, where professor spothuyzen and ondineke of termuren? They're ghosts, girl with the fat behind, they are ghosts that don't exist. And you yourself, who don't read this novel about chapel road and who are yet a character in it, you don't know yourself that you exist . . . you don't exist and that's why I'm dejected: the beautiful people about whom I write don't exist and I've written about the ugly people around me till I'm sick and tired, and that's why I feel dejected. The things around me become too hard and too sharp, too biting; it's all steel and concrete and glass and split atoms and my wife has got trouble with her nerves again—that's the illness of modern mankind, girl with the fat behind, the illness you don't know, because you fart on the world and laugh, and vanish . . . in the old days they used to have smallpox in termuren, now they've got nerves, and the one is the one and the other is the other, and that's why I feel dejected. In the old days they used to have smallpox and lived in poverty: and now they've got nerves and they still live in poverty: today, girl with the fat behind, is the 3rd time in my life that I'm without cigarettes, and that's why I'm dejected. And in the meanwhile the world, that big atom, splits into ideologies, but there's no change in rococo literature, it goes on like a never-ending pot-pourri; in gilt chairs they talk about it with a Capital letter, and in the weekend supplement they write about it, because everyone knows all about it and says his little bit . . . like parrots, they twitter and twitter . . . while the real value can only be measured, girl with the fat behind, by my wife, who as a result of it all got the modern disease of the modern world: nerves, and behind the mirrors of her eyes she feels the regret that I'm incapable of getting some sinecure and that's why I feel dejected. Because I go on walking with my eyes open and I only make enemies: this is an s. o. s., a last cry of distress, girl with the fat behind, in your rolling caravan. And wherever it is that you're scrubbing the steps and making jaspers' blood run wild: don't ever learn to read or write, or see the world with my eyes, but go on signing your name with a cross and say as you always do: I'll draw a nice wind-mill for you. You will draw a nice wind-mill, heroine from my writings, and I shall go back to my papers and go on writing without cigarettes . . . and maybe I shall overcome my dejection.

## REYNARD'S DREAM

It was all very well to say that reynard sat by the fire burning his shins and eating his heart out: that was a good ending to a story. But in the meanwhile life must go on, with hermeline cooking meat and buying butter and paying the rent and the water rates and the electricity. His experience with one-eye, who granted him the right to hunt but demanded the loot for himself . . . and his experience with isengrinus who gave him much praise but wrung the neck of the community of saints and nihilists, and ate them . . . plus the dead farmer who was still lying in the ditch by chapel road, and on his conscience he could write fascinating stories about all this, but his hungry children were gnawing the tail from his behind, it was no use winding pretty words around that sober fact: I've been diddled once again . . . that was the end of his evening prayer. And after racking his brain the whole night, lying now on this side, now on that, he fell asleep in the morning and dreamt a confused hotchpotch in which the priests of rabbit hill had turned into surrealist wooden figures . . . after they had proclaimed him, reynard, to be chairman of the republic of Negation. After this, they had pulled a red cloak riddled with holes over his head so that he suffocated in the white collar: dreams are froth but if you shit in your bed you'll find it is the truth . . . and when reynard woke with a start be found hermeline laughing beside him; she prodded him and said: you were shouting out loud: I'm finished and done for! But he couldn't laugh, the resentment at yet another day of god knows what adventures drove him close to the warm body of his wife to whom he could confess his dream . . . and although his blood beat a little faster because of the beauty of her eyes, which stared at him in alarm, his brain had to accept her explanation of the dream: the red, tom cloak was his own skin and the white collar which choked him was the teeth of all those who were ready to shout 'long live reynard' and eat him up forthwith. But it's nothing, said hermeline, I know a magic potion which will enable you always to say yes, while you might as well mean no . . . to weep with everyone with one eye and mock them with the other . . . and to swear by god and all his saints with your mouth, but never to put it down in writing. Reynard swallowed the potion and went out into the road, after having put the identity card and his certificate of good behavior and civil loyalty and trade registry number in his pocket . . . and the first one he saw was the crow, who was sitting all by himself in a tree, scratching himself. He quickly lay down, spread his arms, closed his eyes, and stuck his tongue out of his mouth . . . and the crow, who thought that there was yet another fox who'd been murdered, swallowed his spittle and dived straight down. But reynard with his magic potion, which made him close one eye like a corpse but leave the other one open like the crack of the chapel door at termuren, jumped up and grabbed him. And without a boo or a baa and without even crossing himself, he ate his breakfast: that wasn't a bad start to the day in his new life. johan janssens.

## WOUNDED I AM WITHIN

*She couldn't sleep, ondineke, when she knew that achilles was amusing himself with others at night. She secretly got dressed and slipped out: she laughed when she saw all those tipsy girls, hardly able to stand straight on their legs and being sick in the ditch. She stood in the darkness, by the inn, staring her eyes out at the anointed ones with their fur coats, their carriages and their grand horses. They didn't see her, but if they had looked into that dark corner, they would have found an ondine who no longer hid her heart under her crossed arms, but an ondine who excitedly held her little breasts in her hands as if she was offering them to the gentlemen in their carriages. The gentlemen are coming, she sang. It was a song of joy . . . no, it went deeper even: it was a prayer. The priest said it from the pulpit, he muttered it while holding up the host, he said it as he turned and made the sign of the cross over the people of termuren. ite missa est, the gentlemen are coming this evening! And ondine hurried outside, hours too early, to hear the dull thump of hooves on the muddy road and the clanging bells; achilles once got out of the carriage with another gentleman whose eyes burnt—yes, they burnt towards ondine—and although her longing really went out to achilles, to his eyes as large as the world, the burning eyes of the other one stirred her too: it was the 1st time she had been noticed by a man, although she wasn't much more than a child yet, with silly little pigtails on her back. It shook her deeply, in fact it wounded her . . . she would have wished to die from this wound. And since the others took no notice of her—that child over there—and moreover spoke french, in the firm conviction that then they could say whatever they liked, she heard that he was the son of mr gourmonprez the libertine: workers at the libertine weaving mill had fought against workers at the encyclical spinning mill, so that some lay half dead in the road . . . girls from termuren had been excommunicated and had been refused absolution because they'd been lying in the bushes with men of the labor late at night; and now ondine learnt that the sons of the labor and the filature were friends and that they called each other by their first names: he was called ludovic.*

## ITS SPRINGTIME

*He was called ludovic . . . ondine tasted the name like wine, and vaguely remembered the time when she was sorry she wasn't a boy so that she could be a server in church; now she served holy mass to the rich men's sons. And suddenly she'd forgotten how she had struggled not to have to look him in the eyes: she noticed that they said something or other about her, while mr achilles was examining her with a smile: she was ashamed because they inspected her body like an animal . . . and yet, mr achilles beckoned her and she came nearer, hesitantly, she stood there confused and with beating heart amongst them, she didn't understand their french, she tried to remember what a particular word meant, she searched and searched her brain but didn't find it, and meanwhile they had already said a lot of other words. Mr achilles held her by her pigtails although he hadn't been the first one to notice her, but as if he saw and understood that her whole heart burst out in flames for him . . . oh, how she lo-o-oved him, ever since the days when he had laughed at her from behind the castle gates. And yet, now the other one, ludovic, seemed to have a right to her, because he had noticed her first: she was sorry, and looking at him with feverish, glowing eyes, she would have liked to call out, with a dry mouth: it's him here, with his beautiful eyes, he may take me. And when they let her go, she started to run, at once, to let her thumping heart calm down somewhere in a forgotten corner: it had been so overwhelming that she thought she'd never be able to have another adventure, but the days passed, the impressions faded, and something in her asked for newer, more violent impressions . . . a dry field, a parched desert was begging for torrents of rain; she walked along chapel road, or in the fields along the railway; round her neck the glass beads and on her arm the leather handbag which had been hidden in the attic for so long, and she almost wept when she couldn't find the gentlemen anywhere. When she was with them, she had looked tiny, tucked away, she was so young and small, but her love was greater than everything and flared up so high that she wanted to tear herself open: to let him drink of my blood, she thought. She was tired and weak as she walked home past the 1st dirty houses behind no-man's wood, and in the late Sunday afternoon when everyone had gone out somewhere to find what hadn't been given to them, she crept into the attic to see where mr ludovic had touched her: it was the 1st time she dared look at her own body: this is where they touched me, she thought, because she thought of them both, she couldn't imagine mr ludovic of the labor without mr achilles of the filature.*

## THE BEAUTIFUL AND THE SUBLIME

The meeting is complete again and msieu colson of the ministry is joking that those that are absent must raise their hand . . . but the music master can't laugh at this, he's got other cobwebs in his head: you wrote there, he says, *that ondine looked at her own body for the 1st time and said: this is where they touched me* . . . well now, if you ask me; I've got something against that kind of prose; soon you'll be no better than tippetotje's paintings and when I go outside I think that the first woman I come across will be walking about stark naked . . . write some more beautiful, more exalted prose. The music master's words hurt you *like the barbed wire round the castle woods: because in order to draw ondineke after life,* you wrote with mariake's photograph by your side—which made your wife a bit cross—you wrote down everything that happened to jeannineke . . . and you were thinking of writing a separate piece about all jeannineke's adventures, but what will the music master think of that! Johan janssens nods and says: all right, the experiences of all the mariakes and jeanninekes and therefore also of *ondineke, the heroine of your novel,* EXIST, . . . but look at yourself, writer, when you were walking in the city with me yesterday, you laughed when you looked at the kiosks where they sell those magazines that have a lovely girl on the cover: and there in the midst of all those fantastic beauties there was a dark hole where the woman of the kiosk sat, selling the magazines: a very ugly woman, wiping a few centimes with her black fingers from a white newspaper into her dirty lap. And because you were laughing, I laughed too, naturally, . . . but in fact I thought it was rather sad, because reality is never just what the books and religion and the parties and the ads try to make us believe . . . and that's why it's good that you stress this in your writing . . . but if I remember well, I remember that you never write much else than what's ugly and mean, thoroughly wicked and dirty, and I'm not asking you like the music master here to write something more beautiful and sublime, but I'm asking when, if ever, the beautiful and the sublime will appear in your writings? Where are they?

You bow your head in silence and you wonder; where indeed?

And you make a firm resolution to better your life and also to write down all the things you find beautiful, but meanwhile you're asking yourself whether you haven't in fact begun to find all the ugly things beautiful?

## THE UMPTEENTH MASK

While you're writing about 'the beautiful and the sublime' someone rings the bell solemnly and when your wife answers the door it's professor spothuyzen . . . why the honor? . . . and he sees you bent over the beautiful and the sublime and calls out: let them go to the devil, those novelists, I'm not interested in their lies any more, today at this hour they're in a particular mood . . . let's say mood a.z. 4007 . . . and they start writing a novel. But tomorrow and the day after and the whole year round they struggle through all the other possible and impossible moods, but they're obliged for the sake of their hero to adjust themselves to mood a.z. 4007, and so they create the ridiculous illusion that they're an immutable god, eternal and unchanging. As a man of learning I ask of a writer to prove beyond doubt that he's an ordinary human being, who has seen something tragic happening today, but who will go to bed all the same and go to sleep and even snore a little . . . or who had heard a good joke today and laughed heartily, but who can yet have a sleepless night haunted by ghosts: someone who proves, in his writing, that he's an ordinary human being with ordinary complexes . . . because I can't believe that an ordinary man in a normal world can wish to bury himself in an unreal world of paper shadow figures. I ask a writer to show me in his work what erotic deviations gnaw at his heart and mind—because, again, a normal human being lives and doesn't look back, but in the twisted labyrinth of a sick brain eros inevitably plays a role of fantasy—but away with him if he puts on a mask and begins to write about 'the beautiful and the sublime'. And professor spothuyzen looks at you and asks: writer, what can you say to this in defense? And you reply: professor spothuyzen, please take into account that I'm not a member of the society of men of letters and so I can't be placed in the category of what you like to call: crazy poets and abnormal writers . . . but that my indecent dreams stem from a decent life like everyone else's, with this difference that with you and with others these dreams sink back again into the deep well of your unconscious, but with me, a piece of writing paper is stuck in between. And if you ask me to show you that I'm abnormal and know that I'm abnormal, and therefore very dangerous—since I know that art of putting on 100 masks and leading the innocent reader up the garden path—if you ask that of me, you'd better start analyzing my dreams and my stories yourself. But professor spothuyzen reads 'the beautiful and the sublime' and replies with a bitter grimace: you already had 99 masks concealing your abnormal personality, but this frankness here is your hundredth mask. He slams the front door and is gone.

## PIGTAILS

*Ondineke walked about in silence, but it was no religious mania, it was the mystery of love, making her speechless . . . she thought everyone could see how much she loved mr achilles—loved? . . . no, more accurately, how her body yearned for fulfilment. She walked past the cottages by the chapel and heard someone opening a door, and her instinct told her that somebody wanted to talk to her, perhaps about the gentlemen who had touched her, and that they would see the glow in her eyes: ondine! someone called . . . But her instinct had cheated her, because it was only to ask her if her father could repair a dovecot. She looked at the man; he was thin, a little stooping, and he wore moustaches which drooped as lifelessly as everything else on his body: she had to laugh at it inwardly: you won't rise above these people if you don't use your brain, she thought. And with ill-concealed pleasure it occurred to her that not only his shoulders and moustaches, his head and his arms drooped, but that between his legs it would be just the same. She asked him in french, but he didn't understand: surely now he'd think that she was just like her mother, and he'd go and tell everybody that vapeur's ondine was crazy: she's talking french to us now. You've got to repair a dovecot, she said to her father and then fell back into silence; she picked up her french books and studied and studied . . . and suddenly she remembered another period of silence, although that had been out of penance, out of piety . . . but when she thought about it carefully, she had to admit that this time too it was piety, only with a different heaven and a different god . . . or no, it was still the same god, the one of the encyclicals and the libertines, of the rich, who made a poor man work 10 or 12 hours for a pittance and who said that laziness is the devil's head-rest: the difference was not in god but in ondine who had become more practical in the application of what she had been taught . . . it wasn't by praying and fasting that you could gain heaven, but by learning french and loving the gentlemen and by letting them touch your breasts. And whereas she used to feel ashamed of their cousin who didn't wear knickers and walked around with a snotty nose, she now began to be proud of her: her cousin lived in the house where the gentlemen came to amuse themselves; her cousin was the daughter of christ who way foreman at the filature. She began to visit their cousin, first she only dropped in for a moment, but soon she stayed for hours and hours without anyone remarking on it. As their cousin was still a child and played with a box full of rags, ondine had to resume the thread of her 13 years and get her old rag doll out of the corner: she played on the floor of the inn, squatting. But on Sunday when the gentlemen were about to arrive, her calculations misfired: their cousin had to go to bed and she was sent home; she stood in her night-dress crying with anger and disappointment. But as soon as her brother valeer was asleep she got out of bed, listened to her parents' breathing and got dressed downstairs. Then suddenly she decided to comb out her pigtails into a fan of brown hair: it was unbelievable how grown-up and beautiful she was with her hair hanging loose. She hung around outside the inn, listening to them talking, cursing, laughing, such a long time that all of a sudden she stood in the light of the open door and the gentlemen came out: mr ludovic found her there and called to mr achilles: look who's here! They examined her from all sides and couldn't make out in what way she had changed; it's her pigtails, laughed mr ludovic and he kissed her because she was such a good girl, waiting for them like that . . . mr achilles didn't kiss her . . . he probably daren't, thought ondineke.*

## IN CONNECTION WITH THIS AND THAT

Johan janssens, poet and journalist, says: in connection with what we said the other day about the beautiful and the sublime and where it's gone . . . and also in connection with the mariakes and jeanninekes about whom you're making a study . . . *and again, in connection with this last story about ondineke, in which she combed out her pigtails into a brown fan* . . . plus, in connection with the promise I made, to read you a piece from an eye-witness report which was rejected by the editor because it was in the middle of the election campaign . . . in connection with all this I'll read out a piece from this report, and it's called: bobine:

When it is about 11 o'clock, the last dance in Van Dyck's hall is made to last a bit longer, and the girls dance a little more stubbornly, already with their coats on and looking in their purse for their tram ticket; tomorrow they'll be standing in nestor martin's again and at lunch time talk about how they had ever such a nice time last night. And when they leave the dance hall and walk down the narrow steep wooden stairs, there's the negro with his aniseed-balls and the fat tit, calling out and rolling his eyes, grabbing at legs on the stairs. They hit out at him and the aniseed-balls bounce on the floor, but he doesn't care, he pushes them back into their paper bags with his black hands. And then the girls hurry to the tram stop where they stand shivering in the cold evening. Evening over brussels. But there are some who look for a café where there's more dancing, always dancing, while someone sits asleep on a platform pulling at an accordion, and another, with his face painted white so as to look funny, drumming on a row of bottles—but when he pauses for a moment he looks into the café, his hand resting on his hip, and he's forgotten he's painted his face white. And sometimes there is amongst the dancing girls a child with the eyes of an angel and the legs of a filmstar and a mouth which makes the thermos-flask on the piano, the negro with the aniseed-balls and the white-painted man on the platform gasp for breath—oh god, it isn't right to let such children loose in the jungle of brussels—and the searching pimp who no longer dares look other than georg grosz drew him; not ugly but with his eyes set too close together like the faithless lover in the cinema and with his genitals showing right through his clothes; he dances with her and promises her heaven knows what and makes her a little tipsy—taxi—and when the grey morning surprises her, she thinks of her mother's house where she won't be allowed to go back, but that's nothing, he knows of another house where she'll be happy and earn a lot of money doing very little, only by being nice. For the rest all remains the same, everyone has to make sure he earns his bread and can pay his taxes. And anyway, the girl who was too pretty to be at large in brussels is bound to see her mother again some time. In Van Dyck's dance hall, in the bobino and at spillemaecker's no one notices that one girl has left and a new one has joined.

## CATCH THE THIEF!

That wonderful trick should really have yielded a bit more than those few measly crow's feathers, but ah well, thought reynard, perhaps many crow's feathers equal one side of pork. And if he hadn't known that bitterness is an illness like all others, he might have been resentful of isengrinus who had relieved himself on reynard's soul . . . now he only sneered . . . and when he came within sight of his uncle's house he put on the looks of someone who returns, fasting, from a pilgrimage to our lady of termuren . . . and the 1st person he set his soulful eyes on was the wolf's wife, knowing full well that women are sensitive to the lovely eyes of a melancholy youth: ooy—ooy, Reynard dear, what's the matter? and she got out of bed, quickly arranged her hair, and slowly started to fry some kidneys for the starving reynard . . . not a lot, because pity was cheaper . . . however, seeing the stolen meat there, grinning at him piggishly from the hearth, he didn't really fancy the kidneys. Do you know, uncle, it's dangerous having that pork hanging there, you know what people are like these days! Pshaw, said isengrinus with a churlish face, all I know is that many can see it but few will taste it. How do you mean, asked reynard, but he knew . . . and suppose a pilgrim to termuren asks you for a bite? Free to ask, free to refuse, hersinde snapped, because she was a witch, really, she might have been touched one moment but all the other 59 moments she was what she'd always been: a greedy, grasping female. Reynard politely took his tail in his hands; thanked her lavishly for the none too lavish kidneys and in the doorway he said: if I were you I'd take that meat from the hearth and tell everybody that you've been robbed. And night had scarcely fallen when he crawled cautiously onto the roof and made off with the meat: his uncle's, in joint ownership with reynard . . . And when day came, what was this? 'My' pork, which I righteously stole from reynard who stole it from a farmer who stole it from a pig! . . . And the wolf's voice climbed higher and higher on the scale up to the highest rung and then tumbled down . . . my pORk! It sounded funny and all his children burst out laughing, but they at once got a drubbing from hersinde who picked up the snapped thread of her husband's voice and screamed: catch the thief! Then reynard entered and asked his lovely aunt what was the matter: oh my boy, said the wolf, our pork which I'd hung up to dry there to share it out equally afterwards, you know, it's been stolen. Reynard nodded and said: it's not bad like that, only, you ought to shout a bit louder. But . . . said the wolf and stopped in despair . . . But . . . and he pulled himself together. But it's TRUE, it really HAS been stolen. Reynard said with a laugh: ha, that's better, that's the stuff, but really, you don't need to try and convince ME, I know very well that some people moan who have nothing to moan about . . . but if I'd been in your place I wouldn't have made such a big hole in the roof, now you'll even have to get a plasterer in. But the wolf said bitterly—because it wasn't to him that mr pots had said that bitterness is an illness like all others—if I knew who'd let me in for this I'd make him sorry for it. Perhaps it was the President of our Republic, suggested reynard and went home, laughing, where the smell of roast pork caressed his nose and his palate. johan janssens.

## CURLS

*Ondineke heard christ say the next Sunday that they'd have to clear away their dolls and go to sleep . . . but she'd only just got home when there was a knock at the door: the gentlemen had come to fetch her back; they didn't know she'd been sent home and vapeur, her father, silently watched them undoing his daughter's hair, combing it and tying a ribbon round it, and taking her along to the inn: there was nothing he could do . . . and anyway, he was too overwhelmed to say anything. In the café she had to sit on mr ludovic's knee and drink wine: it was as if now for the 1st time she really went to communion. Slowly she began to know them; they had been unapproachable gods before, whom she'd seen from afar, from behind the castle railings, or through the carriage windows. Now she felt their hands and drank from the glass to which they had first put their lips. She listened to their conversation and marveled to discover that they thought and said what she also thought but had never dared to say . . . that they rolled with laughter at things which had amused her secretly, because she had to conceal her laughter for the sake of the poor, stupid people who would have run to tell the priest in no time. Amongst them there was a certain mr glemasson who had a huge belly and 3 chins and who had to lean backwards because of that belly and those chins, and who said to his manservant: bring me a mirror because I haven't seen my tool for 7 days; he was the brother of miss glemasson with the fiat feet, who was on the health committee at the spinning mill; he had a short, dry laugh and was fond of breaking humble people: he'd go into a shop where they sold pins and thread, would buy 100 francs worth, and put in an order running into thousands which had to be delivered during the next week, so that the little shopkeeper didn't know where he was, saw his trade getting much too large and went completely round the bend; and then mr glemasson came and crawled on the wife and even crawled on the poor man's daughter and ruined the little man himself after having lured him into a brothel and made him squander all the money he'd earned . . . and if the poor devil then knocked his head against the wall in despair, then mr glemasson gave a short, dry laugh. This joke was told in the café by the level crossing, while ondineke was sitting on their knees: she laughed too, but wasn't content with the joke alone, she wanted to know names. Mr ludovic told her that it was a little shop by the station, boone, who had a pretty blonde for a wife; ondineke looked in admiration at mr glemasson who told her he was sorry he wasn't a feudal lord: because it might sound incredible, but he had a fool. And if he said to his fool: make me laugh, then the fool had to think up something that would have made other people weep. Make me laugh, said glemasson, and his fool suggested to undress ondine, turn the light off and smear shoepolish all over her in the dark; ondine felt that something was going to happen to her; she pressed close against mr ludovic and begged him not to let them make fun of her. Ludovic, however, thought it was a splendid joke, but then someone grabbed her in the dark and pulled her away . . . they fled outside and in the sparse moonlight she saw that it was mr achilles embracing her—she laughed and cried and kissed him; oh, she said, why didn't YOU take me on your knee, you don't know how I love you, love you. And the whole evening she sat on his knee like a small, frightened child, not daring to look the others in the eyes.*

## THE GRAND WORLD

The music master has hardly sat down when his pretty wife lucette starts talking to your wife about nylon stockings and yet another kind of lipstick called rouge atomic and the music master interrupts her to say that this would make a very nice ad: the world explodes but instead of arms and legs it's red lips that are shattered about . . . but she hasn't heard him and goes on, to your wife, about that new lipstick, rouge atomic, and about mariake whom she met this morning: mariake was only about 12 when she started painting her lips and she couldn't sit down without showing her panties to the world and she couldn't stand straight or it had to be in a filmstar's pose: conclusion: I, lucette, was very curious to see what would become of her. And now mariake is 16 and learns haute couture from a lady who belongs to the aristocracy and I ask her out of politeness, how are you, mariake? And she answers politely, in the usual way; very well, thank you, I'm learning haute couture from a lady who belongs to the aristocracy . . . and suddenly, god, it startled me, she starts to sob her heart out and she tells me a story she can't bear to keep to herself any longer—oh, some story—that haute couture lady buys her models in paris, 30,000 francs for one dress, and there's only 1 made and sold of each one after it's been launched in the grand world of the rich in brussels. Every other week that lady would hold a fashion show—very privately—of negligees and slips and pants of real silk in costly transparent lace and tulle . . . yards and yards of material around the legs and trailing on the floor but the body almost naked so that you could just about see their thing. That was in the war and the tulle came from america, said mariake; yes, can you work that one out, how tulle could come from america in the war; maybe it came through portugal, or maybe it fell out of the sky, maybe it didn't come from america at all. And then who'd come to the show; they were all decrepit old gentlemen, you imagine, with children of 14, or should I say, children of 13? with breasts still looking like young plums and a thing with the first young down showing on it, and in the presence of these gentlemen they'd stand there stark naked smoking a cigarette while they were trying on a slip . . . you think of that . . . a slip costing 40,000 francs and mariake who's 16 having to try it on . . . oh, and they smelt of some strange oil they rubbed all over themselves; they were 14 but without that oil they already smelt, of er . . . mariake didn't know what of and at least that was a good thing that she didn't. And one day she said to her madame that she didn't really like being present on those occasions: I don't really like it, madame. And her madame said to her; but this is nothing, you'll see a lot more in life. And now . . .

And the pretty lucette is silent when she sees the music master and you and everybody looking at her in expectation. And so her story ends very beautifully, with a question: and now?

## THE BOY FROM THE DEVIL ROOM

*But something surprised ondine: that she didn't hate mr ludovic for that dirty joke they wanted to play on her . . . on the contrary, he remained to her number 1, who had shaken awake the sleeping woman in her and had drawn the others' attention to her beauty. And he could cover her with shoe-polish, he could cut her body and soul in half, he remained the one who had taken and initiated her in the mysteries of love. Mr achilles, however . . . she didn't really know, but . . . She loved them both. And love seemed to her to be the Word that should not be taken in vain; if she uttered the word god that didn't mean heaven and earth, because one had to flee from the bodily pleasures and fight desperately against all sorts of demons . . . but if she uttered the word love then this meant Everything, it was the magic word connecting heaven and earth with each other. She heard that liza was married and lived at her mother's and she hurried there to compare her feelings with liza's: to see whether she too danced about the house even though everything was put in her way and was thrown in front of her feet . . . whether she too answered with a smile even though they had talked to her humiliatingly and contemptuously . . . whether she too, amidst the grim and gloomy words of this world, heard only that one word, that one name. But love . . . ondine soon saw that to liza it meant little else than the obligation to lie in a bed; naturally, a patient wife didn't protest against her husband's pleasures, but she didn't get much out of it, usually it hurt, inside her, and then . . . she had other worries in her head. The boy she was married to, he'd been in the devil room first, and now he'd changed over to the courtyard, to push carts or carry bales of cotton thread; it was cold there in rain and wind, last week there had even been snow—indeed, ondine remembered ludovic talking about it last week, he wanted to take her out one day if it went on snowing, in a sleigh, out into Tralfene woods—so it was cold for him there on the floor of the filature; he hadn't got warm underwear because they couldn't afford it yet . . . nevertheless liza didn't feel like the most miserable woman on earth, as ondine would have done in the same circumstances: she kept gazing at liza and something in that face made her sad: when you listened to liza now, did she in any way differ from the other women in termuren? And yet, it wasn't that she spoke like the other termuren women that made ondine so sad, with the same husky sound of making herself understood at the filature above the din of the mills; it was the laugh . . . she remembered too vividly the little liza who'd been at school with her, and who'd felt childishly happy because 'the wicked are punished and the good are rewarded', but who hadn't been able to remember a letter as big as a house—yesterday she was an ordinary termuren child and now she'd become an ordinary termuren woman . . . but she did laugh, showing a broken front tooth. Yes, that was it. That broken tooth made everything so hopeless; tomorrow this child of liza's wouldn't be able to remember a single question from the catechism and it would get pushed down by a man wading through the snow in the courtyard at the filature and it would lose a front tooth. She didn't talk about achilles; she went away with the thought: that if she wanted to keep her happiness and her love, she mustn't come near pettiness and misery any more.*

## IN DECEMBER

Now it's december and the rain pelts down or the snow whirls or the wind says hoo-hoo in your garden and you look at the 7 black branches on your cherry tree and think of the Fool who crawls into bed in his overcoat in such weather; it is strange that there are people whom you can't imagine without the sun and others not without the wetness and the snow of december; the snow whirls round the fool or the wind says hoo-hoo; his life is a life of bad weather. And looking at the black branches of your cherry tree you say: you're just like the Fool, you . . . And the soul of the cherry tree, which becomes the soul of the Fool, begins to speak and says: why I was thrown out of my parents' home and how I scraped a living those first days, is of no importance now, but at night I slept in half-finished houses or in a railway car in the shunting yard or in a moving van outside a house in the suburbs . . . and one early morning that moving van drove off to brussels with me and that's where I was dropped . . . I'd never seen brussels . . . it was snowing, because it was december, and I soon got myself a corner in the 3rd class waiting room at north station, I carried a suitcase for a chinaman and got 10 francs and came back whistling and as I was kicking the dirty snow I hit on a wallet full of banknotes and a visiting card: I went there and the gentleman in his dressing gown answers the door himself, and gives me 2 francs and the advice to buy myself a rope because I must be a fool to come and return a thing like that—so a fool I was—and I, the fool, became dishwasher in a fish and chips shop on the nord—ever seen the lamp-lit window of a fish and chip shop in brussels when the snow is whirling outside? and then I work in a rolling mill . . . and I become redundant and I pinch copper wire at night with a chap who's been dismissed from the mill too and with the money I go to charleroi and live respectably, but I still keep longing for brussels, the lamp, . . . and I, the fool, the moth . . . and I find work, board and lodging as a coachman, and high on the box of my carriage I always find time to read a newspaper: I save up a bit of money and buy myself a book sometimes . . . I go to lectures and meetings and soon I talk in esperanto about social change with my new mates . . . I help organize a transport strike and again I'm out in the street with my feet in the december mud and snow . . . a drunken widow with 6 kids takes me in and I start a small business and earn money but she spends it all on drink . . . and one day I see one of my very first friends at north station and he treats me till we can't stand on our legs and in order to get some more money we give an old woman a bash over the head and with the contents of her purse—12 francs and a key—we run till we get to st gilles prison: with the german invasion they let me out but soon I was put on the boat to jersey and the boat was machinegunned so I walked all the way back to brussels, soaked to the skin, and went back to the widow, where I still am; her oldest is about 15, and me, the fool, I've never been used to much, I'm glad if I can sometimes peep between her legs.

Then the soul of the fool in the cherry tree is silent, but the rain clatters and the wind says hoo-hoo in this month of december.

## THE GENTLEMEN'S DEVIL ROOM

*The world was a house, thought ondine . . . in the drawing-room lived the gentlemen and in the shed by the dustbin lived the people of termuren . . . or no, termuren itself was the dustbin and her place wasn't there: she was allowed to sit in the drawingroom next to mr achilles—or if need be next to mr ludovic, because it looked as if he still had a right to her—to forget the stench of the dustbin. She did sit on mr ludovic's knees, but she couldn't, no she couldn't stop looking at mr achilles: only to smile at him now and then, to wink at him and know he was still there. She always liked him to be present when the others were kissing her, as if he was a comrade who could understand that she had to be fondled by everyone . . . a brother who wasn't jealous and who could bear the thought that her passion was satisfied by others but who appreciated something different in her, something hidden deeper down, of which the others understood nothing: a secret, a bond of their souls perhaps. Sometimes christ left the counter to sit next to mr achilles . . . the others were drunk and tried to amuse themselves with the craziest whims, bringing a pig into the café and making it drunk, paying small children to do dirty things or to make them say the most appalling swearwords . . . mr achilles kept his head, he only went pale when he drank, he went out to vomit and came back to listen to christ; it was about the mill, there were malcontents who weren't afraid of going to hell but talked about demanding their rights. Well, demanding is a strong word, said achilles: I saw them, the poor sods, stammering for a bit of wage increase. They will unite and become powerful, said christ, and his beard seemed to stand up as if to confirm this prophecy . . . but mr achilles shook his head in disbelief . . . they'll never do that, they're too stupid. Ondine slipped down from somebody's knees to join them: she thought it was ridiculous to have to hear that this dismissed mill foreman, after all those years, was still wagging his ranting tongue . . . she thought it was a priceless joke that that sucker boone who lived by the station had opened a kind of thieves' kitchen where all the malcontents gathered. But that's not the worst, said christ, the worst was that the rot had even got into the office of the filature: with this bookkeeper, a man of over 60, who said it was true that people suffered hunger and that there should be something like a sick fund for instance, and that it wasn't only a matter of the poor not having the vote. The bookkeeper at the filature? asked ondine . . . a man of over 60? Well, that must be mr brys, monique's uncle . . . sure, she said, mr brys isn't wise, he speaks in rhymes. And she gratefully took the opportunity to tell them what she'd been thinking, that the world was a house with a drawing room, with carpets and lovely vases, and with a coal-shed where the dirty washing was thrown in a basket and where the dustbin was and the lavatory: and now this mr brys was so crazy that he wanted to bring the dustbin into the drawing room! She wanted to give the impression that she knew all about what happened in the filature and in termuren and in the whole world. She pondered and bit her nails and then suggested they give that mr brys promotion and then lure him into a brothel one day, just like mr glemasson had done with boone, . . . and then he'd forget soon enough that people should be in a sick fund; mr achilles looked at her in surprise and kissed her as if she had said something far too sensible for a girl of her age. And at that moment ondine knew what it was that attracted them to each other: it was her mind, her spirit, she had a soul, and the others hadn't understood this. They stood around her, trying to make her look ridiculous, they were nothing but a mob, thinking of their own amusement, but with no inkling of the problems and the ideas that existed in the world: it would be better if you agreed on politics, said ondine.*

## WITHOUT HEAD OR TAIL

This title only serves to lead the rare reader onto a wrong track, because it's a story which johan janssens would like to write for the paper with the title: 'the grand world once again' . . . in case they have the guts to publish such stories . . . well then, to give an account of what happened: johan janssens comes in with a mournful face but with a twinkle in his eye which contradicts his mournfulness: I'd like to write a story for the paper which could be presented as a fairy tale but of course, I must use more serious words than you do . . . because no matter how you twist and turn it, it always boils down to yet another social joke, like in chaplin's gold rush, where the man with the frozen foot says that nature can sometimes be just . . . hey, now I see I should start my story with chaplin's words, because nature was once just, in the 1st dirty houses behind no-man's wood: drunken hortense lives there, who says that writers are dirty men, because that report in the paper . . . of the girl who was too pretty to be at large in brussels and would never see her mother again . . . well, what does that mean, hey? And then she tells me that it's a good thing that writers never come as far as the 1st dirty houses because once upon a time dirty jeannette lived there, who quarreled with her husband, and he shouted out loud at her: it's your damned fault I've got sores on my flute, you filthy whore. And while drunken hortense is telling me all this, I remember her pretty daughter and I ask: how's your daughter, your jeannine? And hortense talks and talks about jeannine who grew up in this filthy slum; she was a blonde and 14 years old and very very pretty—you see, how I can put it as if it were a fairy tale!—and once a week she threw her satchel in a corner and rushed to her dreamworld, brussels, to dance her shoes to pieces . . . as she grew older she became prettier and blonder and stayed in brussels more and more till finally she only wrote a letter home now and again. And drunken hortense shows me these letters . . . all with a crown at the top, she says proudly . . . and indeed, they're all on writing paper with the crown of some baron or other, which jeannine uses to write to her drunken mother . . . and hortense shows me photos from nice and monte carlo, from paris and lucerne, from naples and tunis . . . o la la, she says, that's not for the likes of you, when you see the photographs of jeannine in her ski-suit, in her bathing suit, in her fur coat and in her evening dress with her back naked down to her behind, on which I so often smacked her by god. And hortense tells you in ecstasy how jeannine wrote to her that she should come and stay with her, jeannine, as she was quite near, in ostend: and I went to see her in ostend, she lived in a castle and 2 man-servants in long white stockings stood at the foot of the stairs and took me up to our jeannine; she had pearls round her bare neck and I asked: are they real? and she said yes, they're real. And she drove me round in a car, I'd never seen a car like that before, and she took me into a fur shop and bought me a coat, but what can I do with a coat like that? And I told her so too, I said, jeannine, I said, if you want to do something for your mum; you buy me a good bottle, I said.

## THE GODS

*It would be better if you agreed on politics, said ondine . . . but the way she sat there with flaming eyes and streaming hair: it was impossible for them to keep a straight face: they thought of that joke again, to put her in her naked skin and smear shoe-polish all over her . . . mr glemasson's fool went around plotting and in order to distract her attention they threw up all sorts of objections; what they'd do with mr ludovic, for instance, who wasn't for nothing the son of mr gourmonprez of the labor . . . and therefore a freemason . . . and therefore one of the leaders of the school-struggle . . . and therefore of the opinion that children don't need catechism lessons in order to come to work in the labor, since god doesn't exist anyway. Then the tears came to ondine's eyes: and suppose god doesn't exist, she said, crestfallen, that's no reason to tell the people of termuren so, if they don't have a heaven in the hereafter I can well believe they want to unite so as to get away from the dustbin. Mr ludovic looked at the fool behind her, who gave him a sign to go on talking . . . so he explained to her that the libertines were for freedom . . . laisser faire laisser alter . . . and she thought that was splendid: it was wonderful to sit on his knees and let things be . . . and also it would have been wonderful to sit next to achilles and to know that all the same there was a god who had created everything the way it had to be. And just when she wanted to say: you both want the same thing; they switched the light off and started to pull her pants down from her struggling thighs. It couldn't go unnoticed in termuren that the gentlemen went on gallivanting till 3 or 4 o'clock in the morning with that girl of vapeur; neither she herself, nor the gentlemen, dreamt of hiding it . . . but termuren's hatred didn't go out to the gentlemen, but to vapeur's daughter whom they allowed to be in their company. In I respect the people were pleased: it couldn't be that ondine would go unpunished: today or tomorrow something was going to happen, they were already wringing their hands with glee. Ondine, however, knew how incredibly cowardly they were: no one would ever dare make her a direct reproach: the priest had told her that they'd asked him to preach a sermon about those drunken parties at which ondine was present . . . and then he asked her why they didn't go to another village where no one knew them? Couldn't you suggest that to them, miss ondine? Ondine was silent and defied all termuren by sitting in the front row at church and saying her prayers in french. She nodded to the priest, very condescendingly, as if he hadn't asked her, begged her, anything . . . as if she knew nothing about it that this evening there'd be merry-making again in the café by the level crossing. And the priest, well, yes, he nodded at her too, and everyone saw it; he raised his hat and was silent . . . and mr achilles, who was an encyclical, and mr ludovic who was a freemason, with miss ondine in their midst, they were the gods.*

## REVERSE EXPLORATION

You put your pen down and look through the window at the house opposite, the house of danckaert the nouveau riche, and you're musing, how this house has changed in appearance . . . for just as everything changes in appearance, the chapters from your life, the chapters from your novel, the chapters from the dead lives of houses change as well: first there was a poor dirty house with an archway where henriette used to live—people used to call her henriette from the gateway—she lived there with all her lovers and with her husband's father who'd been her lover too, but who'd become too old, while her husband always had to earn his bread—and the bread of henriette and her lovers—in foreign parts; he broke his loins harvesting in france or went down the coalmines in wallonia or he worked under a rain of bombs in germany, and now he works on reconstruction in the ardennes, although there is no reconstruction in the ardennes. And henriette's husband's old father—that's to say henriette's old lover—always sat in a rickety chair in the shabby gateway against the weathered, cancerous facade while the children walked in and out, playing cat-on-the-blue-stone, or sat down to shit or pee by the side wall; because the house next door jutted out a little at the back, forming a suitable leper's corner where the children tucked up their blue, yellow and red dresses, baring the white patch of their vest and pants and the pink patch of their buttocks. Behind it there was the dirty grey wall and high above, the even dirtier and greyer clouds raced past . . . and how often haven't you said, looking up from some chapter or other from some novel or other: when this book is finished I will NEVER write any more, but I'm going to paint that lepers' corner.

But just as the chapters come to an end, and you start hesitantly like a cat with a mouse on yet another chapter, so a new chapter also started for the house opposite: henriette left and went to live in mijlbeek, somewhere in a street with another dirty house with another lepers' corner, and danckaert the nouveau riche came in her place: he had a lot of money and had to show this to everybody, and so—to your infinite regret—he had the facade covered with something they call simile paste . . . different, more modern windows were put in, which didn't reflect the sun and the rain so beautifully as the old, badly founded glass . . . and a real oak door was put in, shining with varnish . . . and in the simile facade a white enamel plate was fixed: danckaert-verlack.

And every time you put your pen down to look outside, waves of regret rise up inside you, with ever increasing passion . . . but one morning—he had a new servant girl—the door opened and somebody started to scrub the alley by the side of the house, o god almighty, you've never seen such a lovely girl in all your life—and every time you put down your pen to look out of the window she's there, scrubbing the alley and cleaning the windows, with her buttocks and her breasts and the red ribbon in her dark hair, enough to make every passer-by hold his breath and invent god knows what to be able to stay and watch. And then you think: when my book is finished I'll NEVER write anything again, but I'll paint that parvenue facade with the girl who sometimes shows you her smile and her breasts and sometimes half of her lovely pink behind.

## HAMLET THE SECOND

The music master comes into your garden while you're busy putting various dead things in the ground . . . which, how is it possible . . . will give you jasmine in the spring and asters in the autumn . . . and he smiles, at your courage always to start anew, planting and writing, when you never know beforehand whether anything will come of it, and whether it's worth the trouble: you, who dare make the reverse exploration, he says with a significant smile. And he adds: and talking about those reverse explorations, I've just read you Part 1, spring in termuren, and I also made a little private exploration: don't you think you should have drawn a stronger and more beautiful and especially a more visible line in it? And don't you think you should have given it a stronger and especially a more balanced construction? And finally, wouldn't you think that you should at least know what's going to be the main theme and what the ground theme and what the side themes and after that, the various additional supporting themes? Look at me, for instance, I've been wanting to publish a collection of poems for years, with the title hamlet the 2nd but in these poems I make a study of hamlet the 1st, of what I think Shakespeare meant: that man, bending over his inner mind, has to bend forever lower, deeper and deeper, into a bottomless pit, in which the core must be hidden . . . but having found that inner core, he has found death . . . and that in death there may be an even deeper core. But in order to spin out this thought, I'd have to demonstrate the story of hamlet the 1st visually . . . and finally there are my own poems, I should almost forget them, haha. And while the music master laughs self-confidently, you straighten yourself by those dead bushes and sticks which are to become jasmine and asters, and you ask: yes, but how are you going to get Line and Construction and everything else in all that? Ha, and the musical eyes begin to sparkle with joy, because you're asking precisely what he expected, and he finds a stick and draws his plan in the earth:

: verse top of hamlet the 2nd
: thread of the story, hamlet the 1st.
: foundation of my study: the search for the core leading to death.

And you look and nod, but frowning, because it's just as if you'd seen that outline somewhere else . . . but where . . .? and thinking feverishly, you look for it much too far away, because it's close at hand: you write and write, and your book lies there like a pool, like something leading nowhere . . . but thinking feverishly you see that it really is your outline:

top: ondineke
thread: the world of today
basic theme: the cancer gnawing at our civilization.

And you give the music master and yourself a tap on the head and say: hey, by god, maybe that's the plan of your hamlet, but isn't it even more the plan of our book about chapel road?

## YET ANOTHER REVERSE EXPLORATION

There is johan janssens, poet and journalist, watching you and nodding: yes, your 1st chapter is now lying in the straw and you make a reverse exploration . . . you look at all that's been written so far and at all that still has to be written if you go on having enough courage and strength. But forgive me, I don't know where you have discovered this idea of a reverse exploration but I saw it being applied for the first time when I was a poor private in the army, exercising in the field . . . we lay in the grass with our heads on our packs, looking at the clouds or at the worms which came crawling out of the ground under the warmth of our bodies, while the officers were exploring the field from the direction where the imaginary enemy was supposed to see it—exploration in reverse—so that we could start the attack afterwards . . . 2 wars and twice the poor little belgians had to make a hasty retreat and yet they never taught the soldiers to retreat according to plan, but always only the attack . . . so that we, who had to make the attack later, would make use of the tiniest bush, the smallest hollow in the field. And you interrupt johan janssens by asking in dismay whether he thinks that you consider the imaginary readers of the book about chapel road—with which you play like a cat with a mouse—to be enemies, for whom you should make a reverse exploration, and have to make use of the smallest cover? But johan janssens doesn't hear you, he's living in his army-memories, and he continues: and in the field our lieutenant said we had to remember if there was ever going to be a war, that the smallest blade of grass could save your life . . . he repeated it all the time with his fire-eater's voice so that in the end it was engraved on our brain . . . as we ran and fell down and jumped up . . . crawling around on our elbows and knees: the smallest blade of grass can save your life . . . we laughed at it then, we repeated it as we were lying on our sack in the barracks or eating our soup or fumbling under the skirts of the servant girls in the dance halls in xyz street . . . but later we gratefully remembered it when it was really war and all the officers left us in the lurch: the smallest blade of grass actually did save our lives then. But in the chapter when we were still laughing at it, we were lying in the field while the reverse exploration was being made . . . we didn't see the point of it, we ate a piece of cake or drank a bottle of lemonade from the barrows which had followed us—they were small, mean traders, those men with their barrows, they used god and the holy ghost to knock money out of our pockets, they displayed doughnuts filled with cream and covered with chocolate and they brought their daughter or if they hadn't got a daughter, another young girl; every soldier would go and pee somewhere near the barrow with his face and his things towards the girl and the girl watched smilingly: she mustered those things with a smile, and sold doughnuts and bottles of lemonade; oh, what a lot of bottles of lemonade she must have sold and what a lot of peeing things she must have seen every year . . . so that she, in her turn, also made a reverse exploration of the field and became the queen of the tilting-ground.

## THE QUEEN OF TERMUREN

*Ondine had become proud, and strutted around as if she was the queen of termuren: too surprised even to get angry, she could look at someone who had passed her without saying: good morning, miss ondine. And now that she had risen to the highest peak, now that reality had become more beautiful than her dreams, she sometimes had moods of false generosity: she had been a poor little girl who had looked upwards with longing, who had lied and cheated in order to get up there . . . now she looked down from her heights and longed to enter those little houses and to strew around so many benefactions that the people would never forget her in their prayers . . . and please also protect miss ondine who has been so good to us, amen. This was romanticism, she knew it, she laughed at herSELF, but life was what one made it; the only thing that really counted in life was to be crafty and to make sure you didn't get caught, but this became so common, so stupidly ordinary, that she romanticized it with benevolent self-deceit . . .*

*in the 3rd cottage behind the chapel lived maria, whose father had died of tuberculosis . . . and maria's story was just right: now that her father was dead she and her mother had to take care of all the younger little brats; she sewed men's shirts for a shop in town, 30 centimes for 2 dozen, while the kids cried themselves to sleep . . . and as romantic poverty has it, they starved with hunger and froze with cold, while maria worked herself blind, sewing by a flickering light . . . the truth was, however, that maria, carrying her bundle of shirts, had been*

*molested in chapel road by a man from the labor . . . someone she could now no longer do without . . . someone who drank and with whom she drank . . . and as it was a kind of gin which had the advantage of being cheap because it was adulterated with wood spirits, it had the disadvantage of burning their stomach and slowly making them blind, making them crawl into bed in order to make more brats who most certainly would never learn a single catechism question—he died of his stomach and she went blind, very slowly, so that it never occurred to her that drink was the cause, but she would have sworn it was a fire on her eyes—why didn't ondine know all this? Well, she simply wanted this romanticism; blind and deaf to the reality of life, she longed to be adored as the benefactress and queen of termuren: she went to see maria, who sang as she was darning the socks by touch . . . you're still singing, said ondine . . . and maria replied that the poor sing in poverty as well as in wealth. Ondine brought her all sorts of things which her family could very well have used at home, but which she took away, giving rein to her pride: the next day she went there again, to receive her first portion of gratitude; maria was just taking the ash tray out, to tip the ashes behind the chapel . . . it wasn't allowed, but who could forbid her? The policeman in charge of termuren had to take off his jacket and work in the castle gardens. Maria was singing again, Ondine said good morning and waited for her blessing, but maria scarcely took the trouble to strain her worn eyes to see who was there, and then she simply said: hello, ondineke of vapeur . . . and went into the house, closing the door behind her, and went on singing as if . . . as if goddammit I hadn't given her any bread or stockings, cursed ondine.*

## STILL LIFE WITH CLOGS

*Ondine turned away from blind maria in fury, to cool her vexation elsewhere . . . but where? At home, where she'd sit moping and feeling defeated? At home, where she would wage a battle against her own misplaced sense of romanticism?*

*She stood there and thought . . . she thought till the earth had gone round at least 7 times, and got herself all worked up; one moment she raged and the next moment she felt defeated. And suddenly :\he had to laugh because she saw herself quarrelling with herself, once again: and then she swept all those useless cobwebs in a corner of her mind and light-heartedly began to cultivate new, different cobwebs. New cobwebs indeed, because sunday crawled past termuren without the gentlemen showing up. It was torture, it was unbearable, the way her restlessness grew, especially because she stood by the door with a ribbon in her hair, and opposite, the people of termuren sat on their doorsteps. She tried to look indifferent, she tried to whistle a tune like a man; she leant in the doorway and looked at the world as with the eyes of someone with too much time: she noticed a brick beside her in which letters had been scratched . . . the first letters of their names: ondine and valeer bosmans . . . the v was the best . . . and she remembered having done it herself, with her vicious fingers which could never remain still; and suddenly she saw how low down it was, how small she must have been then. Oh, and then, she couldn't say in what way the evening was folding down on the little world of termuren . . . so slowly . . . so far removed from the time when she still was little ondineke, but it wasn't that she suddenly started feeling very sad, it was much deeper, unfathomably deeper . . . I'll try to explain it to achilles, she thought; and she wondered in despair why they hadn't come; Sunday would soon be over! But after that sunday yet another sunday went by and still she had to explain how evening had fallen . . . but there was always more to tell, always something different, so that she forgot the previous thought together with the following one . . . she had to explain the sadness she had felt, the first week, and she had to tell him how furious she had become, after a time, I know you come out of your own free will, and stay away of your own free will, I do understand that you want to enjoy yourself . . . that you come to a village and break all the windows and spoil all the girls . . . and when there aren't any more windows and no more girls you go to another village; but surely you don't take me for a window? And she tried to enter into their thought: would it be possible to look at ondine as a very ordinary fish in the kettle, as a window that must be broken, as a vagina that has to be opened? No, no, ondine is more than that. She has a brain, too. She understands the right proportions, she's one of us. She's one of them . . . and yet they didn't come. And she* *remembered a sermon by the priest which had made the blockheads of termuren laugh: about a false prophet who had said that he would go to the mountain if the mountain wouldn't come to him . . . but there wasn't anything to laugh at . . . if the gentlemen don't come to me, I must go to the gentlemen, she thought . . . But alas, alas: she couldn't go because she was wearing clogs . . . like everyone else at termuren, where one shouldn't give offence by wearing leather shoes: she left her clogs by the back door for days without touching them . . . or sometimes she came in and saw valeer's clogs, her father's and her mother's and all the clogs of all the poor together: and hers were standing amongst them as an eternal mistake: she made herself stumble so that she could kick her feet in savage fury, so that the clogs were flung against the walls. But fury? No, it was masochistic pleasure.*

## TIPPETOTJE'S REVERSE EXPLORATION

Oh, says tippetotje, if you think about it carefully, you see that reverse explorations are being made all the time in life . . . you'd almost say that life is a chain of reverse explorations . . . for instance, when you've been to the lavatory, who would dare to say with his hand on his heart that it never occurs to him to have a look at what lies there behind him? I remember the days when I, tippetotje the painter, was friendly with a glazier who was working somewhere on a roof in the center of the town of the 2 mills: below him was one huge labyrinth of roofs and alleys, sheds, outside toilets, coalsheds and courtyards . . . yes, a narrow wedge like this between 3 high walls they call a courtyard, and the missus in one of these courtyards went to the lavatory and didn't realize that 2 glaziers were sitting on a roof somewhere and when she had finished and had wiped her bottom with solemn ritual, she made a reverse exploration, she stuck up her colossal behind and put her face into the lavatory pan. And although you laugh at tippetotje's story, you do realize that the heart of the matter really is like that, and you nod. And then tippetotje asks whether you don't make a reverse exploration too, after you've riveted your wife with your nail? the old god and the young democracy and the evolution of things—and also the Negation of things—and also your work; there was no sense in it any more, because inside you a thousand tiny worms were burrowing more and more urgently, shouting more and more loudly to be let out . . . and then, they've had their way, they've been poured out and lie in a rolled up cloth . . . and while the sweat which broke out begins to feel clammy and is drying up painfully, you feel that you've still got a heart which is going on beating and that you've still got brains which are going on working like a bird trap . . . and you begin to make a reverse exploration: what are you doing here, why were your work, the new democracy, the coming Things, suddenly of no importance just now? And how should you restore your equilibrium, how can you find everything again, pretending you hadn't . . . just now . . . well, eh, betrayed them? And it's the same with my paintings, with your books; we haven't the courage to go on with them, because we stick to our view that a writer, a painter, is a person who can't find his equilibrium in the world as it is around him, and who therefore enters a fantasy world, to his own taste and size: but being a writer you're also a man and when a man is hungry or thirsty or has to shit or feels his rod swell when the servant girl of danckaert the nouveau riche is cleaning the windows, then the writer has to stop working . . . and when the man has eaten or drunk or done a shit or has thrown his sperm into a corner, then the writer goes on writing where he left off . . . as if nothing had happened . . . and when I, tippetotje, make the reverse exploration of your first chapter, I see cardboard screens between which the heroes walk who have learnt their part by rote, but between the wings I notice the bare walls where the actors have hurriedly relieved themselves.

## JOURNEY FROM NIHILISM TO REALISM

It's sunday afternoon and you hear a sparrow twittering in the garden that these are the beautiful hours when you're allowed to put half a foot in the golden age—no, it's even more beautiful in french: l'age d'or—which man still has to conquer: and you think of writing it down . . . but johan janssens the journalist pushes the front door open and that's the end of your meditation about things the way you always meditate about them: johan janssens sits down beside you and tells you the following: yesterday I was writing an editorial based on a news item: a Chinese statesman says he has the discouraging impression that the world is heading in the wrong direction . . .

that he, having reached the evening and the twilight in his life, realizes that his energies are fading, and that he feels gripped by a tremendous longing to see the world finally on the road to peace and prosperity . . . and that in the course of his long life he has often noticed how much people tend to give priority to their political ideas rather than to their more obvious interests . . . and that this is a universal phenomenon . . . and that, at the stage we've arrived at now, every serious human being has to pause and wonder where we're going: he will see that we are in an era of spiritual decadence. And sitting beside you, who are after all writing a book about chapel road, I, johan janssens, would add that this Chinese states-man, however sensible he may be, confused one thing with another thing: he didn't distinguish between politics and party interest, which shifts unnoticeably from party interest to personal interest . . . because, look at the socialist and the ultra-socialist parties for which some people slave their guts out, for which the little militant is canvassing in rain and wind, for which I write till my fingers are stiff with cramp . . . and all those sacrifices, this courage and cramp in the fingers are useless, because their politics swing further and further from party interest to personal interest. And sitting next to you, who are busy writing it all down in your book, I have to add one last thing: that above all parties there should be a party of the honest . . . a world-union of the Honest . . . that's to say, as far as I'm concerned, socialists or communists or anarchist-syndicalists or trotskyists may be whatever they like, but the very honest ones of all these parties—who are now being pushed in a corner by those who know how to work with their elbows, and shout out their lies and dangerous thoughts—that those very honest people then, would have to wring the neck of their foolish idealism, and become more practical and ask each other to what purpose they let themselves be pushed into a corner by the stinking mass? And having asked that question, they would each have to return to their own clique, party, religion, philosophy . . . not in order to found something new or something Different . . . because all the novelties and differences crowd each other out and make the chaos even more chaotic . . . but in order to throttle the careerists, the dangerously ambitious, in their own ranks and at last take over the leadership themselves.

## A WHEELBARROW, HAHA!

*One day ondine said she'd rather die than go on living unappreciated, forgotten, and the next day she thought of going to see the gentlemen, one sunday . . . wherever they might be . . . she'd walk into the café where they were and push some silly goat from their knees and scratch her eyes out. And another day again she thought she'd take her revenge by never going outside again, never speaking again:—never-to-speak-again became a regular theme in her life—never to look at anyone but only to take a breath of air in the evening, in the garden, where her father had stuck a few crooked brussels sprout plants in the ground: but it was impossible to forget the gentlemen. If she went somewhere where no one had ever heard of mr achilles or seen him, it was incredible, but somebody would start talking about him. In the days before she longed for him like a . . . like a . . . whatever it was, when she didn't have such a raging hunger for him yet, no one knew him, no one ever mentioned his name. And now that she wanted to forget him, even the smallest child knew all about him . . . knew things that she had never even suspected, she, who had sat on his knees! and had been cuddled by him! But she pretended indifference . . . she said: oh yes, mr achilles, I know him . . . and she quickly began to talk about his friend, mr ludovic, because she found it less painful to speak of him. But there was always news about mr ludovic too: he was often at nieuwkercken, a hamlet far from termuren, almost right on the other side of the town of the 2 mills; the gourmonprez family had a villa there, a castle . . . he lived there with the proprietress of an inn, a very good-looking woman, he'd gone to live at the castle with her for 3 months . . . it was said that they'd been seen walking naked in the park . . . and now that she was like this, he'd sent her back to her husband, like a shovel, like a wheelbarrow which one wishes to borrow and returns when it's damaged, haha. Ondine had to tear herself away from these stories, her heart bled, and in the silence of the night she suddenly woke and felt fragments of these stories sticking in her like clamps: a hot woman . . . they say they were seen naked in the park . . . and that he . . . o dear god, tear these pictures out of my head, tear, tear . . , that he crept on her like a dog . . . o god, tear harder, tear harder, these pictures are wedged inside me like barbed hooks . . . a wheelbarrow which he returned because it was damaged . . . ha . . . HA. And she woke up the others, shouting suddenly: stop it! What d'you mean, stop it . . . ? I didn't do anything, said valeer.*

## THE MURDERERS ARE COMING!

*In order to fill her cup, ondine went to see liza again . . . she seemed to want to fill her cup . . . hadn't she said herself that one should never look at misery from close-by? She seemed to have forgotten this, she found liza with yet a new baby, and with yet another tooth gone but it didn't horrify her so much now; misery seemed to be just like everything else: if you saw enough of it, you got used to it; as long as you first persuaded yourself that all was as it should be, you could look at the worst misery with a clear conscience. The boy whom liza had married had just been allowed to leave the courtyard of the filature, and start cleaning the machinery, but had fallen ill . . . and now one couldn't possibly expect the filature to wait for him to get better, someone else would take his place, and he'd have to start from the beginning again: whenever there was a glimmer of hope, it was snuffed out again; however, there was no lack of hope, mr brys had been to see them and had asked how they lived, where they slept, what they ate and how much cash they had; she'd been ashamed to tell him everything and yet she'd had to laugh, because cash, well, they didn't have any. Ondine became impatient, she wanted to know what exactly mr brys had asked and said and written down, literally; but how could liza have remembered? . . . she had other worries in her head, she said again. It's a pity you didn't answer that when we were at confirmation class, replied ondine. Then they both laughed. She tried to remember: mr brys had asked what she'd do if her husband remained ill? . . . well, what could she say to that? He'd talked of a fund, a sick fund . . . In england people put money together to pay a doctor if anyone was ill . . . and in england there were evening classes . . . and in england there was a trade union too; liza said that surely he couldn't expect everybody in termuren to move to england; no, mr brys had said, but we'll start a union here and we'll let your husband be in it too. And what else? Nothing else . . . but it was more than enough for ondine: don't let your husband join it, she said, because mr brys is crazy, today or tomorrow they'll give him the sack and then you've lost the money you put in that union of his . . . and besides, it's only riff-raff that joins it, thieves, layabouts, malcontents . . . and besides, it's against the law and it could easily be that they'll put your husband in the nick. And with that she went home, leaving liza worrying. She knew quite well that there was no law forbidding it . . . mr ludovic had told her this that last time, when after endless arguing she had had the nerve to go to a furnished room with him . . . because even in bed she still went on talking about god and the world and people. But . . . that furnished room by the station, how long ago was that? She asked herself, almost in tears, why they didn't come to termuren any more . . . soon it would all be too late . . . soon all the workers would be united and they would burn the filature and the labor down and they'd murder the lot of them, mr achilles and mr ludovic, without distinction.*

## WHAT DID I WANT TO TELL HIM?

*When ondine couldn't stand it any more, she took some money from the canvas purse on the cupboard . . . it wasn't theft, the money was there and it was just as much her property as her father's: otherwise it would only have been used for heaven knows what trifles, to buy rubbish for his perpetual motion machine . . . while now it was going to be used to conquer her place in life, the eternal, ceaseless perpetual motion machine. She went to town and bought herself a pair of shoes, heavy, solid ones, and as she was in town anyway, she went to have a look at the house of the derenancourts: it was even bigger, more impressive than the castle at termuren; it frightened her. From far away it had been easy to think: I'm going to their house in town and I'll ask for mr achilles . . . but now, when she saw that door with the two freestone pillars beside it, it wasn't easy to do. And yet she couldn't come away from there, she thought, maybe he'll come outside while I'm here. But it became afternoon, it became dusk . . . She felt neither hunger nor fatigue, but she got a head-ache from waiting such an incredibly long time. Once the door opened, but it wasn't him, it was his father, whose cigar could never be big enough. No, it wasn't easy to show the mistake to the world: she saw now how hard a struggle it would be; much too hard for such a little girl, she thought; it's as if god had forgotten he performed a miracle for me. And when darkness fell, she sat down on the freestone block by the door, because her feet hurt, and fell asleep on the spot . . . because suddenly she dreamt that the carriages were arriving at termuren and . . . she looked with surprise into the dark street and heard indeed a carriage: mr achilles got out and was surprised to find her there: she let herself be cuddled, hardly feeling it, she way so exhausted from sleeping on that freestone block. They got into the carriage again, she told him everything she had thought and felt and experienced, those last days, all jumbled up. She cried. And she also knew she was forgetting something, something very important, which she ought to tell him but which with the best will in the world she couldn't remember. Can you stop thinking of ludovic then, even though he was the first one to pick you up, he asked. Actually, he asked it in quite different, nastier words, which she tried to ignore: I've come to give myself to you, she said, but it isn't true what you say . . . he's touched me, yes, you've seen that often enough . . . but not the other thing. He wouldn't believe it . . . I'm still a virgin, she said. He reminded her of times when they'd all been in a heap, drunk: that doesn't mean any-thing, she said. You've been alone with him in a furnished room, he said. But she smiled, and repeated in french that she was still a virgin. Then he went almost mad. She told him how she yearned to belong to the ruling class and how she had been too intensely happy to choose I of them . . . she got confused in the end because it all became so complicated, there's something else I must tell you, she said . . . but she couldn't remember what it was. He put her down by the railway ditch, not far from the place where she had once thrown her money away . . . she didn't notice, she needed all her attention to put her clothes right. And as she was going to bed and pulled the covers over herself, she suddenly remembered what it was she'd wanted to tell him: that she had seen Evening falling over termuren.*

## ABOUT PLAICE

In books and in a man's life only those things are mentioned which stick out a bit above the rest, but that's wrong, really, because it's rather the thousand and 1 ordinary events which characterize the thousand and 1 ordinary lives. Look at reynard, you'd think that he would every day anew . . . no, no, most of his days passed in a routine, a rut, with resigning himself to circumstances: one day he might cheat someone, but the next day he would be cheated in his turn, he might pull the wool over somebody's eyes but the next day he would be the one to trot to the internal revenue . . . and as he didn't belong to one of the 27 trust families, he had to be quiet and meek. And when there were days when his wife hermeline wasn't very well, because there's always something with a wife, if it isn't children, it's nerves: and then reynard had to scrub the floor himself and make the bed, and then, there was never any money coming in, because he couldn't do anything in the way of buying and selling: only the anti-socials could still do any trade, and unite into a new, now illegal guild of black marketeers. But it's time we started on the umpteenth symphony of ludwig von reynarde, when he slammed the front door with a curse and walked down chapel road; he listened to the world, his world, and heard a cart rattling in the distance. And leaving useless descriptions aside, they were fish sellers with their baskets full of eel and plaice . . . and also, the same as nowadays, of herring, which ought to have been dried or salted, because it was getting a bit stale and was beginning to smell. Reynard wasn't really so mad about fish, but well, winter was coming and you mustn't be too fussy . . . anyway, a good plaice fried in butter isn't bad . . . he didn't bother to think up another ruse, but as usual lay down in the middle of the road with his arms spread out like a cross, his tongue stuck out half a meter and his eyes shut. One of the black marketeers began to call out: is that a fox or a badger lying in the road? And the other one said: fox or badger, we'll put him on the cart. How much do you think his fur will fetch? Pawing the fox, the first one said: 1000 francs. But the other one replied: yes, but a real fox costs 3000 francs in the shops. Reynard let them talk; he knew that the road between talking and doing is usually blocked: he let himself be swung on the cart, yoo-hoo, and cautiously groped about to take the edge off his hunger . . . then he picked up a reed used for stringing fish on, stuck a row of eels on it and slipped down: hey, friends, I've fallen off, he called. But don't bother to help me up, I'll find a furrier's by myself. Our fox, our fox, shouted the fish-hawkers. Yes, sure, Our fox, reynard answered, running home, where he started to fry the eels at once, calling out, that is to say, reynard—: shut the door, so that no one can come in and bother us. johan janssens.

## THE WORLD A WOMAN

*Now it went like THIS every sunday: mr achilles came to fetch ondine by the bushes where the will o' the wisps lived . . . she was all quicksilver, bubbling with happiness and life, so that he forgot he was sitting beside a girl, and listened for hours to her chatter. He wanted to know everything about her childhood.*

*Her childhood? That poor chapel and those broom bushes? . . . It was hardly worth talking about, but with her sparkling imagination she yet made something of it, so that they both shook with laughter. It wasn't only gay stories, though, especially the story of valeer, when she'd gone to the broom bushes in blind fury and could have done anything there . . . smash the world to pieces. And what did you do, he asked . . . give me your hand, she said and she held his fingers in front of her eyes, as if they were a mask: I shat on it, she said . . . so softly that he didn't hear and had to ask her again. And those two began to understand each other so well that all the time she felt like confessing more: even that about the offertory money. Often it lay on her tongue, but her breath halted every time she wanted to start talking about it . . . and also, every time something interrupted her, ridiculously trivial, but breaking the atmosphere all the same. She could never quite make him out; yesterday he was like this and today like that; the people of termuren could be classified straight-away: one was a drunkard, another a lady killer, yet another a lazybones or a thoroughly good man . . . but him, here, he was too complicated. Now he was underlining words in bismarck's memoirs, and said that the world lies there for anyone to take . . . those were the only words he spoke that whole evening: hasn't he got lovely eyes, she thought. But weren't they really the eyes of a woman? When in the past she'd let herself be kissed and fondled by the others, and had suddenly thought of him . . . wondering what he would think of this now . . . strange, then she saw him smile as if he had guessed her deepest thoughts . . . as if he had felt by intuition what she had been thinking deep down: and wasn't this intuition something characteristic only of women? But she'd dismissed it then . . . only a woman herself is able to feel things by intuition, she had persuaded herself. Now he was reading bismarck and conquered the whole world, in his mind . . . he forgot her, ondine, and she discovered that he was too selfish to be really handsome. And the strange thought occurred to her that the world he wished to conquer in his innermost thought was a woman he wanted to possess sexually. She hated this world which was a woman . . . she couldn't think of anything more shameful, more monstrous. Oh, she analyzed him completely, the way he sat there . . . she began to see through him . . . and she also knew that she must never tell him anything about her discoveries because then he wouldn't want her beside him any more. Yes, there were moments when they drew apart: the next sunday she brought a book, too, her only book, her french grammar . . . but that day he hadn't brought one, and got bored to distraction, and the world—that woman who had to be conquered—was worthless: everything is nonsense, he said.*

## BOATS IN THE STORM

*I've written a poem, said achilles derenancourt with a mocking laugh . . . as if writing a poem was even greater nonsense than all other nonsense together . . . ondine read it and didn't understand it too well: it was about a woman: why should I love you if I should first learn to love myself, why should I love you if you are only a toy begging to be broken? And she suspected that it referred to her . . . is that about me, she asked . . . if it was about a woman, it would also be about you, he said, because you are a woman, but it's not about a woman, it's about the world. And as they sat there looking at each other they were like ships in a storm, like wreckage, sometimes drifting towards each other by chance, sometimes moving away; there he is again with that monstrous idea, that the world is a woman shouting out to be conquered, she thought. There she is again, jealous as a bitch because a man also wants to conquer the world, he thought. He sat in one corner of the carriage and she in the other, and she wanted to heal the estrangement between them with words . . . she wanted to carry on chattering . . . but whatever she tried to say, she had hardly begun when she found herself saying something ludovic had once said to her: that poem of yours, in which the world is a woman, I think you're wrong to think she's no more than a toy asking to be broken: the world only gives itself to him who's wise enough not to desire it. She had hardly said it when she realized that it was ludovic who had said some-thing like that . . . and she thought: oh, it was ludovic who said it, that last time when we were in that room by the station, . . . and achilles got angry and said that these were ludovic's words: words which he must have heard from my brother . . . our norbert, the crazy idiot, the mystic . . . and he only understood them half, anyway. Achilles made a movement with his hand as if to wipe out the words. That isn't true, said ondine, I thought of it myself . . . He jeered, what could she possibly think by herself, except that she had to flatter who was above her and kick who was below her: you're far too much a termuren girl, he said. She could have murdered him for this insult, if it hadn't been . . . yes, if it hadn't been for the fact that it was absolutely true what he said. So she cried. And in her tears she was so glad that she had kept the secret of her theft, that she found this great truth in herself: never be such a fool as to confide to others something which you have to conceal from yourself . . . because no matter how close you may be to someone today, tomorrow the storms will sweep you miles apart.*

## KRAMIEK RINGS

The doorbell rings and your wife looks up and says: I suppose it's another literature maniac, a fool, a pedant who never reads a book but knows all the names of all the writers and knows exactly whether they're due for honors class or for promotion A like football teams . . . someone like seeverman who said he wasn't going to buy your book before he'd read the reviews in the papers. No, that's not how he put it, before WE have read the reviews in the papers. As if personality was the last shred of a worn rag: We, the united pedants, who have no personal opinion about your books, wait till the reviews have given you at least 6 out of 10. And having said this, your wife turns her lioness' head contemptuously towards the front door, where the bell rings a second time: shall I get rid of him or do you want to see him and use him as money in the chapel road book? She opens the door and it's kramiek with a face like Strindberg but with a hand held out to you like a fish that's been dead 3 days: and he says that literature is the flag under which we die and that he writes letters of 6 pages to his girl friend, but no silly talk, only analyzing books and so on: I showed her in my last letter that your latest book is sykelogically much more profound. At that moment you give a sign to your wife that she can open the front door now and chuck him out . . . because as a hero in the chapel road book he's played more than enough of a part . . . but he sees you giving that stupid sign and stands up and holds out his dead fish and says he's got no time to stay any longer: I'll come and see you tomorrow when I shan't be so busy.

And when he's gone your wife plants herself right in front of you and your papers: let's have a straight talk, she says: why on earth do you want to go on writing if nobody who is anybody reads your books? Haven't you seen it often enough that they always confuse your books with literature . . . and that it's only pedants who read books and don't understand them . . . and don't you see that they only read your books because they try to find in them the literature they would love to have written themselves? And without even putting your pen down you answer that you won't write in order to provide the pedants with literature or in order to lead the world towards beauty and the sublime . . . but that writing is a necessity to you like for instance going to the lavatory is a necessity: suddenly you feel the urge and you have to hurry or else it's too late. But for the rest you don't look at it any more, you don't care what happens to it . . . so that you're even surprised when some magazine asks you for a contribution: it's as if they were asking for a bit of used lavatory paper. And when they don't publish it after all . . . . having read with respect, we regret . . . then that doesn't surprise you in the least: you wouldn't either in their place.

## I WILL DIVIDE MYSELF BETWEEN YOU

*Oh, mr achilles only saw ondine as a toy or maybe only as a dog, a bitch which stroked his legs and looked up at him and was faithful, and maybe he couldn't quite bear it that she had at one time had another master; maybe he was afraid that mr ludovic would come back and call: ondine! And that she'd follow him, wagging her tail. Ondine had been something new in his life: all those little secrets which she had told him, struggling with her embarrassment, it had made him even more pleased with himself, it had made him grow in his own eyes into a judge of people: only I know all these women's secrets. And now she would grow away from him; and maybe go back to ludovic, and chat about all her secrets to him? . . . and as he was disgusted by anything that had been touched by others, so he in his turn made her feel disgusted by blurting out all sorts of things about ludovic gourmonprez . . . things she didn't even know existed, which frightened her: and suddenly, in the middle of a discussion about life and love, with a smile on her lips still, she burst into tears. Naturally, this sort of thing only happened once or twice, the other days they enjoyed themselves tremendously. And inevitably there were also times when they didn't get exactly bored, but when they wanted to run, run after happiness, carefree happiness, like a couple of lunatics . . . and when they raked up the old jokes which used to make them cry with laughter but which strangely enough couldn't even make them smile now: without saying it. they were both thinking of going to find the others, wherever they might be, and to smash to pieces everything that came into their hands. Yet ludovic was the reason why they daren't mention this wish, to see the others: she thought that he would fear an encounter between her and ludovic . . . and also, she thought, yes what didn't she think? . . . And it was exactly the same with him: they thought too much, as if they had become old, bloodless people . . . they were afraid a hole would appear in time, in eternity, in everything; they were afraid of all sorts of things that made no sense at all, but which made the simplest things in the world so complicated that it gave them both a head-ache, each in a corner of the carriage. But by chance they stopped at a café one evening, lost in the fields, and god, there was the whole troupe, and of all the things they'd been meditating and pondering about, on their own, not a pin was left . . . they laughed and shouted and suddenly, how it happened they didn't know, ondineke looked up in surprise at achilles, when she saw herself sitting on both their knees . . . of achilles and ludovic together . . . and she heard herself say: I'll divide myself between you: you take this buttock and you the other one: she laughed at herself. But that was because she was drunk.*

## HISTORY OF JEANNINE, THE TEMPORARY ONE

*I just read how ondine divided her thighs between the gentlemen . . .* says tippetotje, whose voice still sounds a bit husky these carnival days . . . but if it was your intention to show that so many years ago the top layers of society were covered with mold, it would be unfair not to show that the bottom layers were just as moldy . . .

Tippetotje sits down, and there is bewilderment in her words, because in a quite different, dejected tone she adds: you see, yesterday I would have said that the top layer and the bottom layer of society really *ought* to stink, if the center of the cheese is to be tasty and wholesome . . . but today I must add in perplexity that the middle is beginning to rot and stink as well: last night I joined in the carnival to see james ensor again, and I went to have a look at all the dressed-up people by the 1st dirty houses behind the labor, and what I saw there still hits me in the stomach: they were all dressed up and had a wonderful time singing dirty songs, a competition in filth, and all the women had to take their pants off because they'd laughed so much that they'd peed, and then they had a competition to see which of the men had the biggest thing. And that was such fun that they went on right through the night: all the women had their skirts tucked up, in the café on the corner, and all the men were walking around with their things bare. And jeannine, yes, what should I call her, because you've already been talking of drunken hortense's jeannine who was too pretty to walk about in the jungle of brussels . . . but it wasn't her . . . and you said you wanted a certain jeannine to play a large part in your book, and of course it isn't her either . . . so I'll call this one jeannine the temporary one. Well then, this jeannine of mine is about 16, and she was walking around with her skirts tucked up, and when it was almost morning she suddenly walked into the café, naked, and she showed her dirty dress to everybody, singing and gabbling: look how the men have made my dress dirty with what comes out of their thing! And I, tippetotje, went home with a gnawing saw in my stomach, in my head, in my blood . . . and I was sick, to get rid of that pain at the back of my head, to forget that I'd seen that the center, the crumb of the bread, the stupidest and most honest and best of society, is also being eaten by a cancer.

## THE POET A SIGNPOST AND A PROPHET?

Johan janssens sits down with the crumpled piece of paper which he wants to read out . . . but he puts his weary hands on it and says: do you know that tippetotje said something quite baffling just now? . . . something I've touched with my own fingers, and seen with my own eyes, have heard with my own ears but have never wanted to accept with my mind? . . . she, tippetotje, went to see james ensor but what she saw was in fact a bit of the downfall of our civilization, the disease, the cancer . . . and I, johan janssens, went to flagye square in brussels, in my capacity of poet, to give a talk on the radio about the relationship between the poet and the masses . . . and when I'd finished speaking and came outside and saw the evening settling over the square, I was still a bit absorbed in my beautiful, lofty words, and then I saw between these words the downfall of our civilization: the search always to find new tricks to get money, and then to squander it again; a woman buttonholed me, supposedly to pay for the tram, and I gave her 3 francs, because she had to change trams, she said, but she went straight across to the other side of the square, in the dusk, to another passer-by. And because these things hit me in the stomach I went to a café on the corner, to the gents—doesn't it make you laugh—which was next door to the ladies—doesn't that make you laugh, too—and between these two lavatories there was a wooden partition with a hole bored in it so that the gents could have a close-up view of the ladies, with their eye on the hole. And the next morning I sit by the stove with my crumpled radio talk—the vocation of the poet in relation to the masses—with disheveled hair and trembling hands, smoking a cigarette and holding a cup of coffee, to wash away the nasty taste . . . and I see myself sitting there as an aimless wreck on the river congo . . . as a useless poet of the beautiful and the sublime in an ugly civilization which is rushing towards the abyss. And then my wife sits down next to me and I see bewilderment in her eyes: what kind of a world is this, she asks me; yesterday when you'd gone to give that radio talk I went to the front door and looked out into chapel road and there I see a mason filling that hole in the wall of the labor . . . he sees me and gets his thing out of his trousers, pretending he's going to pee, but such a huge thing I couldn't help looking at it, it's horrible to have to say it . . . but he just stood there, and he could hardly get it back into his trousers.

And johan janssens sits there in bewilderment, like tippetotje, and forgets to read out his radio talk: the Poet as a signpost and a prophet for his contemporaries.

## A THOUSAND THINGS GO UNPUNISHED

*And yet ondine wasn't so pretty: in her childhood it had looked as if she might become an unusual beauty . . . now it was clear that there was no dimple in her neck, but that its roundness suddenly swelled into the breast: wasn't that the beginning of a goitre? and her nose was a bit too sharp and too curved. And there was something about her eyes . . . although one couldn't say whether it was a defect or something striking and spicy . . . but they were too cunning. She was pleased because they'd discovered who she was. And that they dropped her at termuren in the very early monday morning . . . termuren where another week in clogs awaited her, with zulma and vapeur and valeer and the lonely forgotten our-lady in the chapel—where a swallow made its nest every summer, covering the altar with droppings—it didn't matter. She knew that the poor, ignorant yokels of termuren called her 'vapeur's bitch' . . . but if one buys happiness one's got to pay for it, how stupid of people not to understand this. The poor ignorant clods said it wouldn't last, you wait and see . . . ! As if ondine didn't know: what does last? Where's the girl who never grew old? But that 'it won't go unpunished', it made her laugh . . . thousands of things go unpunished . . . and she thought of the offertory box, her swearing in the chapel, of the muck on the holy broom bushes, yes, of valeer's cut-off finger: god knows who was allowed to commit crimes and who wasn't: all this was permitted to her because she was going to mean something in life. And if evil days came, then she'd take them, as well as the good ones: she could take them. It became one of her favorite thoughts, with which she flattered herself in rare moments of reflection. She'd sit with her hands in her lap and would suddenly get up and say: pshaw; pshaw, mr glemasson's fool was there to drive away their boredom and the sour aftertaste of their practical jokes . . . to drive them away with other, newer, even funnier jokes.*

## THE PRIVATE NATURE

Yesterday it was spring, with the roses growing shoots in the sun, and with crocuses, and today there was suddenly frost again and snow and anti-cyclones: the shoots on the rose bushes turn black and msieu colson of the ministry's nose turns blue, and so it's not surprising that his smile is frozen, as he grimly digs a piece of newspaper out of his pocket—coal would have been better—and begins to read: mr knots, ultra-marxist minister, arrived Wednesday morning at 11.30 at melsbroeck airport from the congo . . . the minister's journey was of a private nature . . . At his arrival mr knots was greeted by mr knoker, the colonial secretary, and by members of the cabinet. And msieu colson's grimness hits your eyes like the icy wind outside; oh, you writer, who stupidly and rather childishly think that the world can be subdivided into right and left, capitalists and proletariat, reactionaries and revolutionaries . . . who think that the world evolves so fast that yesterday it was here and tomorrow it will already be there . . . who don't see that everyone can be everyone's enemy, a wild animal, a secretive animal, slouching to and fro in the silence of the night, lying in ambush and walking about in clothes like a wolf in sheepskin . . . who don't realize that everyone can even find an enemy for himself inside himself, who don't suspect that everyone is a respectable citizen begetting children but at the same time a werewolf devouring children . . . and especially, who don't understand that someone can be an ultra-marxist of the extreme left and a proletarian, but that the same person can meanwhile be a minister and fly to the congo . . . and moreover, o bitter mockery, o irony, can have a private nature. And when msieu colson had finished shrieking all this at the top of his voice like the anti-cyclone moving across our region, leaving you dismayed and silent with your papers, he jeers: what's this, and you think you weren't allowed to join in because an ultra-marxist minister doesn't like the congo and the union miniere du haute katanga? No, no, that's not the reason. It's only because there's a difference between an ultra-marxist who's a minister and who has a 'private nature' . . . and a writer who may or may not be a marxist, but who never will or can have a private nature, that's to say who will never for a moment want to shut his eyes, but who will put it all in a book: my little congo.

## THE VERY FIRST SOCIALISTS

*Mr glemasson's fool suggested they all go to that chap hoone who'd opened a thieves' kitchen by the station and who'd called it 'in justice and freedom' . . . because that's where they went, the abbeladoes: the dismissed foreman from the labor, the sacked nightwatch, the so-called sailor who had always served on the great lines hamburg-new york and antwerp-riga and who always got the days of the week mixed up because he was tipsy all the time; a fellow with I hand who went pilfering on the railways and who'd lost his hand getting it jammed between the sliding doors, a student, who'd been sent away from home and dreamt of a world where everything would be 'beautiful and sublime'. And 'socialists'? No, they daren't call themselves that yet, they were* THEMSELVES *still rather frightened of the word because it meant red, fresh, steaming blood and smashed crucifixes and decapitated nuns: the student talked of organization and trade union and sick fund, and that everyone ought to have the vote . . . sometimes he stood by the gate of the labor, sometimes by the filature . . . but at the labor they laughed at him and pretended he wasn't there, they walked over him and trampled him as they poured out of the gate, and at the filature it was even worse. But the bookkeeper, the little grey man of over 60, with his pince-nez, stood beside him to protect him and to tell him that there was some truth in it: he started talking about his evening classes, because now they could only put an x when they had to sign their names. The student asked him to come and talk in their café 'justice and freedom'. . . at first he daren't . . . he said he'd founded a trade union—although that wasn't true, it was only a sick fund—he was no troublemaker but he tried to come to an agreement with the gentlemen in love and friendship, to get better conditions for the workers: I'd rather you joined my fund, he said to the student. Come and tell us about it one day, said the student. And finally mr brys went down to the café by the station and shyly gave a talk about what he called 'work in joy', for the benefit of the sailor, the fellow with 1 hand, boone and the student, and one other man who'd just joined, a knife-grinder who'd done 5 years for showing his thing to a girl under age. And as mr brys couldn't say 2 words without one of them being 'therefore', he said that therefore the spinners and the weavers should unite in a union therefore, with someone from the employers in it as well. And as there were neither spinners nor weavers nor employers present, the sailor answered in their stead: he said that he'd 'therefore' seen the whole world, and england too, and he'd had a sweetheart in manchester once who was drunk every day and that it was no better there than anywhere else, so why do you come and drivel about trade unions and work and joy? Mr brys slinked off and the student went to stand by the gate again, calling: unite, come to justice and freedom. Mr brys, in his turn, visited people in their homes and wrote down names for his sick fund: the people didn't quite understand and asked him whether they were socialists now; he needed all his powers of persuasion to get them to see what those men of justice and freedom wanted and what he wanted were two entirely different things: if you write your name down with them you're a member of the 1st socialist union and if you write your name down with me you simply belong to a sick fund. They just let him get on with it and trusted like they had always done: in god's mercy.*

## KISS THEM

*And so mr glemasson's fool came along with the proposal to have a joke with those nuts of justice and freedom: to get a whole lot of spinners and weavers drunk and let them write their names down as . . . socialists: it was a big crowd there . . . there were even policemen amongst them, disguised in blue overalls and cloth caps . . . under the leadership of a foreman of the dye house, a man so tall he had to bend down when going through a door. The little inn was chock-a-block, and boone, who wo? standing alone in the bar, lost his head . . . they were all thronging around the counter and wanted to join the trade union: write us all down as socialists! And as the 1st socialists didn't even have a members' list, he had to write them down on a paper bag . . . and then someone knocked the pencil stump out of his hand, another one let the beer keg empty on the floor and one after the other they started to break the beer mugs . . . a policeman in disguise leant against a window and pushed with his back until the glass broke: hey, boone, where's your paper bag, so I can write myself down for a new window pane . . . and they pulled the members' list out of his hands and let a policeman, who was able to write, scribble the most incredible absurdities on it. When the game was nearly at an end, the gentlemen happened to pass by with ondine in their midst, and they saw a weaver climbing on the bar and relieving himself.*

*there was 1 thing which began to be repugnant to ondine: that mr ludovic wanted to kiss her like he used to. She realized that he wanted to use her as a shovel or a frying pan, and so she held her hands in protest between her body and his: I'm not a wheelbarrow, she said. And suddenly she was the center of attention, when mr ludovic flared up that no, she wasn't a goddam wheelbarrow, she was a bag, though. She laughed at this, and at his face, screwed up with anger, the face of a small-minded person who would no longer have the right, for instance, to go to a furnished room with her. Yet she wanted to explain to him that she refused to be kissed because she wanted to mean more to him, but that was only to show the others her authority over him. He laughed: you mean you don't want to be kissed by somebody because you like him too much . . . tell that to the geese! She tried again. In order to bring clarity into her feelings she started to choose words she hardly ever used . . . but in the midst of her confused monologue she saw mocking smiles here and there . . , and interrupting her half-finished sentence she said: kiss them! She went over to mr achilles, looking contemptuously at the others. Kiss them, kiss them . . . called out mr ludovic . . . I've kissed some that didn't stink like that, do you hear!*

## EVENING AT THE CASTLE

*Only we understand each other, said ondine to mr achilles. He stroked her neck, where there was no dimple, and her nose, which was a little too sharp and curved, and he said she was his own silly little ondine, and took her home . . . she didn't know that he went straight back to the others to gloat over her 'kiss them'. He slapped himself on the thighs, roaring with laughter. If she thought she was smart and cunning, he way even more smart and cunning: he went to live at the castle—and as winter was coming and the derenancourts had gone to their house in town, the castle with its garden and pond lay deserted in their desolate, rainy mood—in the evening he sent for her and together they walked through the bedraggled park: oh, she loved this evening mood, with the dogs beside her and the raindrops falling from the weeping willows on the grass or splashing in the pond. She said, I wish I'd never have to leave this garden and never see any people, I wish I could always go on walking here. He asked why she wanted to go home every night, and she replied that he'd never asked her to stay. Well, stay then, he said. And so she stayed: it had only been a bit of banter, unreal in that atmosphere of autumn and dead leaves . . . and they had been influenced by the book he had had with him, poems, where there was mention of a sweetheart who was lying on a rug, by the open fire which was casting bizarre shadows on her body. He wanted to possess something like this too, although those 'bizarre shadows' made him laugh, and when ondine lay in front of the fire he looked in wonder at her neck, which was too round, yet he couldn't resist writing a poem in his turn, in which he confused ondine with the world which was a woman and in which he confused the world also with god. Yes, he'd looked at her neck in wonder, but in the morning he was even more surprised to find her beside him in the huge bed, small and lost, curled up under the blankets. She went home once, but only to fetch her french grammar: he had to teach her; it was incredible to see how she could remember all sorts of words and yet never managed to learn any grammatical rules. Once he was doing his utmost to drum it into her for the last time, how to form the plural in french, but she jumped up from his knees to chase the dog: she opened the french doors to the wintry garden and disappeared in the grey dusk of the vast, too vast park. Much later she came back, her hair wet with dew; she saw he way annoyed: you'll never learn french properly, he said. Although he didn't care two hoots about her french; it was really because he'd discovered that she loved the garden and the dogs and the autumn more than him . . . because she didn't love him, achilles, but mr derenancourt who lived at the castle.*

*He was a bit cool, but in bed she raised herself on her elbow and said: on forme le pluriel en adjoutant une s. Oh, really, how could you get cross with someone like that.*

## GAVE HIM A SHAVEN CROWN

At reynard's they were just sitting down to fresh eel when there were suspicious movements outside the window: it was the honorable isengrinus who'd lost his pork and had nothing between his teeth, and who was wandering around in search of reynard, so as to make him pull the chestnuts out of the fire: he'd been peering through the window for a long time, hand above his eyes, and had sniffed an unfamiliar scent: were those not pork ribs, on which his nephew and brother-in-arms was gorging himself? It gave him canine hunger and swallowing his spittle he went to the door, but unfortunately he couldn't squeeze through the letterbox. Hey, dear nephew, he called, open up, I have very important news from the king of the republic . . . that's to say . . . well, never mind, but open up. Reynard finally pulled his legs away from under the table and asked from behind the closed door who was there. Me. Yes, but who's me? It could just as well be a pork thief and a trickster. What a misunderstanding, called the wolf, it's your uncle isengrinus asking to be let in. Then reynard said he'd like to open the door, but the problem was, the Brothers were having dinner with him . . . that is, they were actually real canons from the new monastery of the scarlet-reds, sons of saint one-eye; they've granted me the forgiveness of my sins and are going to let me join their order. And when isengrinus was a bit too eager asking to be introduced, reynard called back that that couldn't be done: you're not in the right state. What d'you mean, not in the right state . . . I'm in a state of great appetite, isn't that enough? But reynard got angry and said, he was insulting the Brothers, it's the state of never eating meat again that you've got to be in. And what are those monks of yours eating then, what's that I smell through your letterbox, stinking cheese, perhaps? Reynard explained to him that it was the smell of fried eel, of which the abbot of the scarlet-reds advised always to choose the best bits . . . but he couldn't let him in, he'd have to be ordained a monk first. Ha, there I recognize them, said the wolf . . . and fresh eel, you say: is that nice? Reynard hastened to hand him a little morsel through the letter box, saying that the Brothers presented it to him, in the hope that he'd join their order . . . oh, that's quite possible, said the wolf, also in hope; give me another piece, because I feel I'm near my conversion. If you go on like this you'll be the superior of the monastery by whitsun, said reynard. The superior, asked the wolf, do you really think so? that clinches it, you can come and clip me. Not only clipping; shaving, reynard urged. All right, shaving, said the wolf quickly. Reynard went to fetch the boiling water which was meant for the washing-up: put your head through the door, uncle . . . and he poured the boiling water over isengrinus' head, who called out, dancing with pain: to hell with the tonsure, you're making it much too big. No, it's just the right size, said reynard, and now the rule is this: you must sit here on the doorstep all night in pious vigil and prayer. If I'd known, answered the wolf, you can be sure, I would never have become a friar. johan janssens.

## THE SPIRAL WITHOUT END

You wander about in termuren . . . through no-man's wood where the girl with the fat behind will probably never return . . . past the 1st dirty houses where carnival finished long ago, where a sluttish figure is doing the washing in a zinc tub and a blind finch is singing in a cage . . . *behind the brook by the castle where the pepperpot is still wandering although ondine is now much too old to go swimming there* . . . in the town of the 2 mills where it's always raining, even when the sun shines. And everywhere you feel restless, because there's tippetotje, with her talk of our degenerating civilization, which she expresses far too vividly . . . like someone who's been silent about something for too long and suddenly blurts it out in excessively sharp words which offend even himself. And there's msieu colson of the ministry with his newspaper cuttings, reading out facts which are too harsh and come too close after one another . . . like someone sitting on the outer rim of a wheel, bumping against every stone in the road, so that you, sitting on the axle, are constantly being disturbed in your reflections. And finally there are johan janssens' accounts, making you skittish, when he keeps telling you you should have been here or there, that you should become a world citizen and know what's what, so that msieu colson of the ministry pushes you too near the outer rim of the wheel and you can't let things sink into your mind properly . . . and besides, through the fault of johan janssens, you know that you're too much stuck in your own little world and you're not sufficiently a world citizen. And when after your wanderings in this little narrow world of termuren you finally go home and creep up to your study, it doesn't smell like the study of a writer ought to smell, but on the contrary, it smells of a 3rd class waiting room at 4 o'clock in the morning when the 1st train is about to leave . . . *and then the sheets of paper with the story of ondine look yellow and dusty: is THIS something alive, is this supposed to embrace the world, is this the book about chapel road which like vapeur's perpetual motion machine is to bring about a revolution in steam engines and religions and wars? And so it's not surprising that you start saying: and yet ondine wasn't so pretty as it had seemed in her childhood . . . you could see she had no dimple in her neck and that her nose was a little too sharp and curved. Neither is it surprising that in your search for what might possibly save our civilization from total destruction, you make vapeur confess that he's searching for something he knows he won't find.*

## VAPEUR'S CONFESSION

*Unforgettable were the evenings when ondine stood by the cooking range in the castle and fried and baked all the things she'd learned at madame berthe's . . . she stood there with glowing cheeks and glittering eyes, putting slices of apple on cakes . . . and in the meanwhile she talked about her struggle against mr brys and his sick fund, about the days when she stumped about in the mud of termuren, forgotten by everyone . . . I didn't deserve it, she said: I'd expected so much of life*

*. . . yes, really, and do you know how old I was when I first thought of you as my sweetheart? And as he didn't answer she turned round smiling. He'd fallen asleep in the warmth of the cooking range. Yet she wasn't annoyed, she was sensible enough to see that everyone has his own life: I'm the lady of the castle, she thought. But what use was it to be the lady of a castle if no one saw it? And by the gates, looking out into chapel road, she suddenly thought of her mother . . . she had stood there too, many years ago . . . she opened the gates and went to her parents' house where she hadn't set a foot for days: she went to the workshed and stood there with a defiant smile, watching vapeur, who at once flurried; he'd been busy with some nonsense or other: he'd put a copper cent and a piece of zinc in a cracked cup full of acid, and he probably didn't even know himself what he expected to happen. Now he clumsily knocked the cup over, the acid dripped on the floor and the cent rolled under his workbench . . . he went to look for it . . . he crouched down and groping with his hand under the bench, he seemed to be searching for words to say to ondine. The priest has been here, he said. Ondine went on looking at him with that provocative smile. The priest has been here, he repeated, and I had to tell you . . . tell you . . .And still fumbling under the bench he picked up the cent; he looked at it, wondering what it was he had to tell her. The priest had been to see them, yes, and had told vapeur to give ondine a proper talking to . . . You should do that, vapeur had answered; that's what you're a priest for . . . No, you're her father, the priest had replied. So they'd both tried to push the dirty job into the other's lap . . . and of course they'd started arguing about religious questions, about cain who found a wife in the land of nod and about where this woman had come from? The whole book of genesis is full of childish stuff about something that's much bigger than your god, vapeur had said . . . it would be much better to explain it all scientifically . . . people are still poor and ignorant now, but that won't go on for ever; one day science will give a far better explanation of everything. And naturally, the priest wanted to have the last word and left, saying no more about ondine. Now ondine was standing there . . . and what was this, was she mocking him? He looked at his hand, at the cent which was tarnished by the acid: it's all very well to laugh, he said, and he told her what was going on in that cracked cup: it's an electric cell, he whispered. And he talked about his troubles in life, about this dump here, termuren, and about his wife . . . and about her, his daughter. It*

*wasn't really an accusation, no, it was more an apology, a confession. She was a bit taken aback; she'd come to wage a fight, and so in heaven's name she merely waged a fight against the people who waited in vain for the divine punishment which would come down on vapeur's bitch . . . all the while still calling her miss ondine and asking her favors. But she looked at them with piercing eyes and asked why they were ill and always wearing patched-up clothes: have you got something on your conscience or are you too lazy at the filature, that the lord is punishing you like that? . . . and I think you poach hares at night in the castle woods; you watch it that I don't catch you out!*

## THE MORTAR OF THE GRAND WORLD

It's odd, says johan janssens, how a story affects each reader Differently . . . *the writer told us it was about vapeur's confession, and yet msieu colson of the ministry was most of all struck by ondine's words: you watch that I don't catch you out in the woods! . . . I on the other hand was more impressed by the scene by the cooking range at the castle.* But maybe that's because of a story I heard from some workmen from the 1st dirty houses who came to mend my fireplace last week: they started off by opening all the doors and then complained of the cold, and they damaged the stairs with ladders and ropes and buckets . . . but at noon they came for their coffee which had been stewing on my stove all morning and they sat around my desk eating their sandwiches. But in exchange they told me their story: they remembered that once they'd been working on a fireplace in a big hotel in brussels and that fireplace was in a livingroom . . . in the attic; question of letting as many rooms as possible . . . the tiles were painted bright red and there were some of those big beams underneath with sculptures on them . . . well, sculptures . . . and the furniture was all in keeping, and so was the fireplace, terribly smart! And the masons had to repair the chimney and do the pointing, on the roof; they'd made cement down in the courtyard where there were tubs in which leftover food was chucked . . . and he, the oldest mason, had seen stuff being tipped in there which he'd never eaten or seen anyone else eat, and I, the mason, I'm fond of a good laugh . . . that's to say, I don't mind a dirty joke when we're a bit high at carnival time . . . but one day a lady came out into the courtyard where we'd just made some new mortar and the gentlemen who came out with her got hold of her and threw her right in the mortar, it came up to her waist . . . her dress and her underwear and her stockings and shoes; it was all ruined. They were lovely, expensive things as I saw it all being thrown in a heap, and somebody was at once sent to get boxes with new shoes and stockings and underwear and a dress . . . and while that lady, she was a bit tipsy, was laughing away in the mortar, he, the oldest mason, said to himself that it wasn't right for a workman from the 1st dirty houses to have to see something like that . . . and afterwards he did a little sum on the roof and said that they'd spent more money on that lady in ½ an hour—food, drink and clothes—than he could earn on the roof in ½ a year. And the youngest mason who'd been listening in silence all that time, put his coffee mug away, with the lady who'd been thrown into the stuff still in his mind's eye . . . and when the oldest mason had finished talking he put a full stop after it: no, it's not right to see a thing like that, because then you don't feel like going back to the 1st dirty houses, for instance.

Johan janssens lit a cigarette and continued: and now maybe you were the most of all struck by that word 'for instance', the last words to come out of that mason's mouth . . . but to me the most impressive thing is that these grand people living in hotels, are not able to build and point their own chimneys: you accept that somebody can feel an abnormal desire to be thrown in the mortar, but you don't accept that a workman then has to use that same mortar, high up on the roof.

## THE UNHAPPY BEAST OF PREY

*These words—'Watch it that I don't catch you!'—were ondine's highest trumps and she carelessly threw them away . . . seemingly carelessly, because behind it she hid her listlessness, perhaps her pain: she knew that one day she'd have to lose the game, however well she was doing at the moment: the time was coming that achilles would marry, wanted to marry, and by god, not with her. Not with me, it hammered in her head, it hammered in her blood, right through her body. She walked from one end of the park to the other, no matter how far . . . she threw herself down somewhere in the wet grass and cried till her head ached . . . and then she went back to him, a little pale, but calm enough to face the situation: so he was going to marry someone from his own class, fat glemasson's sister. And unconsciously ondine's thoughts wandered around miss glemasson's long skirts, as if she was trying in her thoughts to lift those skirts up: was she flatfooted yes or no? And without realizing it, she said aloud: but her face isn't really ugly: with those big blue eyes and fair hair she's just like a doll, like an angel. Achilles understood ondine: he had met his future wife only a few times, but both their families had decided she'd one day be his wife . . . even in their childhood they'd decided this . . . and he too thought of those long skirts trailing on the ground: he took the book in which he'd been underlining a great deal of late, and he read some to her: it was german, and although she'd never learnt any german, she understood it very well: man is a beast of prey with broken teeth. He looked up. So did she. And at that moment she hated his beautiful eyes, she could have scratched out those predator's eyes, with her fingernails: I hate you, she thought, I hate you because you don't deserve to be loved by me. And her thoughts could be read so clearly on her face that he started to speak contemptuously of man's smallness: it was one of his favorite themes, that man could only think of himself, and that it was right so . . . but that he, achilles, wanted to rise above this smallness and accept also its naked truth: I have loved you, he said, because you were able to think of greater things . . . it was a bit ridiculous, your idea to unite encyclicals and libertines in one bond of rulers, but it proved that there was more in you than in all those other girls. Stop it, she called . . . and she sat there pale and trembling . . . I'll never talk about this marriage again, she thought . . . Oh, how slowly, how sluggishly did the evening pass in those impossibly big drawingrooms, how irritating and stupid were the rules of grammar: feminine and masculine . . . she always got confused, she thought masculine was feminine because in the termuren dialect a girl was called a masken. And when many, many hours seemed to have passed, in which thank god she hadn't talked about his marriage, she looked at the clock and only one hour of the long, dreary evening had gone: she picked a quarrel: she was the most unhappy girl in the whole world, she couldn't remember her french lessons and there was nobody who didn't hate her and she couldn't love a man or he picked a quarrel with her.*

## JOHAN JANSSENS, A LION MAN

With all those girls walking around in brussels, looking like flowers, says johan janssens, you can't help having erotic dreams . . . but I dreamt so erotically that even my unconscious was ashamed and daren't let me remember it the next morning: I felt something like remorse, something was gnawing at my conscience, because it seemed that in that dream I'd been unfaithful to society and to people and to my own family . . . and I looked at the shop-windows to buy a little present for my wife and child, in compensation, and yet the oppressive feeling remained that I'd gone through a strange world where primitive eroticism was born, which the negroes must still be able to remember vaguely, when they jump around naked in the jungle, to the drum of the tom tom, by the burning fires.

and suddenly a fragment from my dream came back to me: I was reading a book in which negroes were dancing at the festival of their daughters' first menstruation: the oldest negro women invited the young girls for the first time to a dance depicting the postures and gestures of coitus and they had to imitate these gestures and in the meanwhile fetch a scalding hot jug filled with boiling water from the fire . . . and dancing the coitus dance they mustn't drop this jug or spill from it . . . and then the strongest amongst the men entered the circle of dancers and they copulated . . . a pseudo-coitus, because they had to remain inside these girls all the time while the old women went on dancing, but they mustn't move inside the girls or pour out their seed . . . and in the meanwhile, in the center of the circle, there was a negro with an abnormally large monster-thing, which was like a third leg between his legs, on which he danced.

and when I arrived at the office there was a reuter report to be written up, and another fragment occurred to me, which I shan't tell you because you can read it in the paper: the dance of the lion men, the gruesome mauling of their victims . . . dar es salaam . . . the lion men, who are as much feared as the leopard men from west africa, have committed a number of horrible crimes in the region of singida in tanganyika.

and sending this report to the composing room, I, johan janssens, bent my head as if I was one of the suspects, dancing on his third leg in his dream and assisting in the festival of the first menstruation: and therefore living by the law which creates life . . . but also slouching around like a beast of prey: and thus living by the law which destroys life.

## WHAT SHALL I BE LIKE AFTER 10 YEARS

*Not a single soul can see me without hating me . . . said ondine. She added that she was lonely and that no one understood her, and with her eyes raised towards heaven she asked why she had deserved this? . . . And you, thinking of your marriage all the time, she called out . . . she walked away and locked herself in a room by herself. He banged on the door in vain; she wouldn't see him or explain to him, because everything was much too confused in her mind, much too difficult to express. And anyway, how could he have understood her? It was so remote to him, this marriage . . . everybody married, but nobody married the person he loved . . . this was as eternal and unchangeable as any natural law. And in any case, what should one do with a wife one loved? Adore her, not daring to violate her, put her on a cross, much too high? so that to her it would become a comedy, during the daytime to hang on the cross, on display, with her arms spread . . . and in the night to leave that cross secretly and to let herself be treated like a bitch in the arms of someone who loved her a little bit less . . . with her legs spread. So he thought. And anyway: love, love, he was still so far away from ever having loved anyone: he loved himself. He found it morbid, those people who suffered from altruistic feelings. And when he put his arms round ondine and ran his fingers through her brown hair—it was beautiful, really, that thick animal fur—it was more in order to soothe his despondency; he really believed it, that man is a beast of prey with broken teeth . . . he believed life had come into existence by accident . . . he believed that the human race was a link in a chain, which would drop out as soon as the time was ripe, in order to produce a different, more intelligent kind of being: and right through all these callous theories he felt cold and tried to warm himself on her love. You must never forget me, he said, and in his selfishness demanded impossible things of her: she had to laugh at it, and forgot her anger for a new feeling, yes, a feeling of contempt, which raised its horns beside her hatred. Come on, she replied, you're the one who's becoming romantic now, how could anyone think of someone all his life? . . . I loved you and yet I had to make do with ludovic . . . he took me . . . and now, what has become of him, where is he, where am I, where shall I be in 10 years? . . . and then, in your selfishness you don't even think of me: how they will mock me in termuren on your wedding day! Although she felt herself far above it . . . it yet made her bitter, it made her listless, there was nothing for it but to start throwing away her highest trump cards, recklessly.*

## THE SECOND JOURNEY FROM NIHILISM TO REALISM

It's as if a meeting of the 1st world parliament was being held—but of course, there's no question of this happening this year or in 50 years—all your heroes have gathered and in the front row sit the music master and his pretty wife lucette, plus your own wife with her nerves and her thin blood, and the others sit or stand or hang around them: tippetotje the painter, johan janssens, poet and journalist, msieu colson of the ministry and professor spothuyzen who has sent an apology and is therefore not present. You open the meeting and the 2nd journey begins: johan janssens has told us that there's too little mention of Beautiful people in your book . . . and I've been wondering for a long time whether in general I hate people or I love them, whether I write a book in order to help them or to scoff at them: and I still don't know the answer: but I have discovered that although I get angry with people who can't see the use of becoming united, I'm fed up to the teeth with people who are united. Look here, I've cut a piece of prose out of a journal of dutch ultra-scarlet writers and poets and painters and artists in general, and they assert firstly: if a human expression is to be appreciated as culturally and socially necessary, then it should in every age fulfill the *then* valid requirements about subject matter, form and content—or, may we write our book about chapel road the way we are writing it, or should we first ask whether it meets present day requirements—and secondly they allege that art has a social nature reflected in social conditions, which are based on the development of production forces, which are characterized, in a class-structured society by the irreconcilable antithesis etc etc. And now I should like these undersigned ultra-scarlet writers and artists to join us on our second journey from nihilism to realism, so that we could ask them in all honesty whether they always write and compose in order to examine whether the social conditions are based on the development of the production etceteras . . . or whether they don't, like me, write purely and simply because they like the work *itself*. For how in the world else is it possible that you come home in the evening, tired and hungry, and you've hardly said good evening or you settle down with a blank sheet of paper? . . . Maybe later it will be said that I loved people and fulfilled a social duty towards them . . . but if you cut out the desire to hear, every time again, the soft scratching of a pen and to feel in your heart the satisfaction of being creative . . . cut that out and ask yourself in all honesty if your desire to see a better world would be great enough to work, like me, night after night, at something which faces you with nothing but mountains of muck. And then I'd like to ask them whether it ever occurred to them that outside their social problems there might still be other social problems? . . . for instance the fact that society is a body and the individual is a cell and that I, a cell, can be attracted but also repelled by the other cells . . . that I, as johan janssens, can be a respectable poet and journalist during the day time but in the night a lion man bent on murder and robbery?

You are silent and look around as if you expect the ultra-marxist artists to give you an answer . . . but you only see the over-familiar faces of your heroes . . . and 1 of them replies: it's as if they were thinking of betting on a horse, with that theory, no matter what horse . . . for instance the socialist horse . . . and that for the rest they couldn't care less if they scratch out their own eyes with their own fingers.

## A SERPENT AMONGST THE FLOWERS

*Ondine stayed with achilles till the last moment: the fact that she was sensible . . . . that she behaved sensibly, so he thought . . . made it hard for him to separate from her. She suggested that they go and choose wedding presents together and to talk with a florist about the wedding bouquet: her taste wasn't actually bad, but he had to temper her: she was too fond of showy things, she was a bit bourgeois . . . He said the word casually, in an unguarded moment, and she looked at him in surprise: was it something to be contemptuous of, to be bourgeois? I belong to the bourgeoisie, her silly father had said with pride . . . and she herself, had it not always been her last defense, when nothing was of any use and everything fell away from her? And now it seemed to be something impossible, mongrel; a condition which attracted the hatred of the workers and the contempt of the rulers*

*... but it was impossible to change her personal taste, to make it more sober: it was in the blood; they entered a jeweler's and asked for bracelets: haven't you got anything more attractive, more expensive? she asked. There was nothing she could do about it, she couldn't change herself into a different person. She was shown a bracelet which was like a chain of golden disks, but it seemed to her too simple to be beautiful ... she picked out one engraved with flowers through which crawled a serpent with glittering eyes; she saw against her own arm what it would look like, and subconsciously thought of this miss glemmasson who wore the loveliest clothes that had ever been seen in this small town of the 2 mills: her father was chief shareholder of the discount and credit bank and chairman of the trade court and her grandfather used to drive in a sedan chair ... she was slim and blonde, like an angel ... no, ondine had never referred to her flat feet, however difficult, however impossibly difficult it was for her not to refer to them: she stood there with the golden snake round her arm and saw how lovely it was. It was a symbol: a slim, thin beast in gold: the image of that other woman who all her life would be wearing something which ondine had chosen in her place. And she's flat-footed! It suddenly escaped her, in despair.*

*Yes, it looked so lovely against her wrist that she hardly dared look at it, and turned her head away ... he chose the other one, the one with the golden disks ... and meanwhile she stood there with the bracelet which didn't feel cold and strange any more, as in the beginning, but had already assumed HER warmth, as if it had become part of her body, of her soul, of her deepest I: she knew she would cry when it had to go back to the window, as something which had never had anything to do with her. Mr achilles paid. He paid for two bracelets: one with disks and one with a snake crawling through engraved flowers ... and now she cried after all ... she went outside with the bracelet on, and with a veil of tears before her eyes: she didn't even see that the door had been opened and bumped her head against it. And in the carriage she heard him say that after all, she was a girl too. This made her forget all her ... yes, her contempt.*

## FOR THE DEVIL ALMIGHTY

*Mr achilles derenancourt, son of old mr derenancourt who was a senator and the owner of the spinning mill and shareholder of the discount and credit bank, married the daughter of glemmasson, who was chairman of the trade court and also chairman of the above mentioned discount and credit bank: the red velvet canopy was placed over the church porch, and on the carpet 3 priests came to meet them at the entrance, with vases of incense and holy water, as if he was our Lord coming back to earth . . . an officer of a foreign army had come to be a witness, and so many children went in front with flowers that they seemed to be walking in a gigantic bouquet, so that no one paid any attention to the bride's feet: all the people in termuren were given flute-beer to drink, 1 bottle per 3 men, and it was marvelous but sad to see them quarrelling for their ⅓ of a bottle . . . ondine stood by the church entrance, watching: mr achilles didn't see her, nor did he know that this day was the cruelest of her whole life: he was now married to fat glemmasson's sister, and glemmasson himself took over achilles' sweetheart, in a sudden gust of kindliness . . . but he was too dreadfully bitter to ondine's taste: he believed in nothing: neither in god nor his commandments, although he was an encyclical . . . are you afraid of me, he asked her . . . I am, actually, said ondine . . . and she broke off the affair. Well, the main reason that he was too fat for her, too impossible with his triple chins and his panting, as if the little train was jogging past the level crossing: he groaned whenever he was going to sit down while his fool pushed a chair under his behind. This fool was never allowed to leave him. And as mr glemmasson also thought he was the center of the world, just like mr achilles, just like herself, she looked at that fool and thought it was hopeless that this failure, too, perhaps thought of himself as le nombril du monde. She met ludovic again and threw herself in his arms; she wanted to go straight back to that furnished room, she let herself go: it was as if she wanted to hurry towards her downfall. And then for a time she became the sweetheart of achilles' brother, their norbert, who still indulged in the same whims, like pretending to be ill and lying in bed for days . . . so that he had no use for ondine or for any other ondine. And one day she saw this norbert derenancourt hastily stuffing a parcel away: she had lost everything even remotely resembling a sense of shame: she grabbed the parcel and examined, it in front of him: it was a pair of stilts and an unusually long white robe . . . she jeered bitterly and asked him if it wasn't too cold in chapel road at night to act the Tall Woman: he turned pale and demanded she should be silent: you'll tell no one, do you hear, not a soul, that you know who the devil is, or I'll kill you. She asked what with. And as he'd committed one act of folly, he committed a second one: he showed it to her, it way a steel bodkin. He stood with the bodkin in front of her and demanded she should swear 'by the devil almighty'... she swore, and left, feeling ill, although she realized that this oath was not much more than a joke... only a bit of jiggery pokery to make her scared: as if she believed that anyone could sell his soul to the devil, ha ha!*

## THE FISH HAUL WITH THE TAIL

There was a biting frost and still the wolf sat on reynard's doorstep in pious vigil and prayer, soothing the burning wounds on his poor head, and weighing the advantages of that 1 piece of eel against the disadvantage of this tonsure which the devil was scratching with his claws; and moreover my behind is getting frozen stiff on this doorstep. At that moment reynard came out to tap the praying insengrinus on the shoulder, like silent monks do, and he painted for him the picture of an uncle who was, perhaps, the most pious of all... and who yet stayed outside in the merciless cold, while inside the feast was in progress, but console yourself, because, as one saint said, the road towards recognition is sprinkled with tears... and besides, blessed are the hungry and thirsty; I shall lead you to a pond where the fattest eels jostle to be picked out of the water first. The wolf was moved by all these words and stammered: you may not be a poet, but you do say things that are really worth listening to... and together they marched quickly to the frozen brook behind the castle in which a hole had been hacked, for the people of termuren to fetch water: look, their bucket was still there. And when reynard said: you simply hold the bucket in the water till it's full of eels... isengrinus, wanting to show that he wasn't a fool, added: I should think the best way is to hang it from my tail and to sit over the hole with my behind. Reynard shook his head in amazement at his uncle's shrewdness... and you know, he laughed, I remember a piece of advice: 'hollow on hollow and all is full'; do you know what that means? No, you can't catch me, said the wolf; that's me, of course, making a miraculous haul of fish. And the 2 dirty monks laughed till they shook, although reynard did warn him all the time: don't shake so, uncle, or the fish will fall out again. So the wolf sat dead still and around both bucket and tail the icy water began to freeze and slowly turned into ice . . . he winked at reynard and whispered: they're biting, but I'll just wait a bit longer till I've got the bucket full. But soon reynard saw his uncle making fruitless attempts to haul the bucket up: reynard, help me, I think I'm too tired after sitting up praying all night, and besides, I think those eels are biting my tail off. But reynard replied: I see, you've been too greedy again. Nothing but a full bucket would do and now you can't pull it up! But at that moment baron derenancourt came out of his castle, going hunting . . . and what did he see? . . . a wolf crouching over the frozen hole in the brook? He jumped from his horse and drew his sword, to hack the wolf in 2 . . . but he slipped on the ice and skated along . . . and as he whisked by, the sword cut off part of the wolf's tail and the wolf, past caring what odd spectacle he must make, was gone from the ice in no time, far away from the dogs . . . and with one hand on his bleeding hole and the other on his blistered head, he came home to his witch, hersinde . . . who immediately started nagging him: gallivanter, gadabout; where have you been? Ssh, I've been ordained a monk, said the wolf, and when hersinde asked where might his tail be, then, he replied: have you ever seen a monk with a tail? . . . he wrapped bandages round his wound and lay down on the bed and thought: I'm beginning to think that it really is a bit reynard's fault that I always get into trouble. johan janssens.

## THE GHOST AGAINST THE WALL

*But the next evening norbert derenancourt read to ondine the story of the fox sisters from hydesville, new-york: she got frightened and daren't sit alone in her corner . . . she asked could she sit close to him, because although he was the devil himself, he was at least something she could touch, not the secretive, elusive figure that hovered behind him in the dark: she pulled his arms around her and asked if it was the devil who'd answered the sisters fox; she shuddered when she saw him shaking his head. I can't explain it to you, he said, because you'd be even more frightened. What is it then? And all she understood about it was that within a person there's another person, his double, a devil, a bestial ghost which lives on for a time after the person himself has died . . . he was very grave and looked into the darkness behind her as if there . . . But she screamed that it couldn't be true, you are . . . you are . . . she didn't know what she was going to say he was: you've had too much pleasure with yourself, she shouted. And then she ran outside, to leave chapel road behind her in one breath . . . but she heard him following her, he'd probably got his bodkin with him and would murder her . . . she panted and stumbled, her breath stuck in her side . . . she couldn't go on and leant against the wall of the labor; it was strange to think that tomorrow the girls of the filature would pass by and would find vapeur's ondineke, her belly torn open by the devil. He stood beside her and it didn't even occur to her to defend herself . . . but how terribly mistaken she was, he put a trembling hand on her arm and asked what she meant by those words. Those words ? She tried to remember . . . yes, she said, you got over-excited and yet you never touched a woman, that's going to do you no good, you take care that you don't go mad. He listened, small and frightened; all his life he had doubted . . . this . . . this . . . ondine, suppose she was right! . . . suppose that what he had seen was nothing but the product of a brain disorder! Of course he defended himself: all I've seen, others have seen too, he said . . . and what you said just now, about my lonely pleasure, it isn't true. Oh come on, don't tell me any stories, she said; I've been going with you long enough to know how things are with you. And so the roles were reversed: instead of him teaching her the occult sciences, he became her pupil in the most primitive things, in something the most wretched yokel in termuren knew all by himself: she gave him his first lesson, leaning against the cold wall of the labor, and really, it was enough to make you laugh—no, to make you weep: he'd only just started and he'd already finished. And because he stood there crying, on the same spot where he went spooking on other nights, she laughed, harshly and mercilessly.*

## LA FEMME NUE DE TER-MUREN

*De notre correspondant particulier: ter-muren est une petite ville de 2 usines labor et filature . . . la dendre y roule ses flots . . . c'est sur ses rives qu'un ouvrier de l'iusine labor décrouvrit le lundi le cadavre d'une femme entièrement nue, affreusement mutilée et dans un état de putréfaction . . . le corps ne portait aucun vêtement ni byou qui pouraient aider à l'identification de l'inconnue . . . sèule une jarretière noire à chaque jambe retenait un lambeau de bas . . . chaque articula-*

*tion était tailladée si l'assasin avait essayé de sectionner le cadavre . . . n'en a-t-il pas eu le temps?*

## THE NAKED LADY OF TERMUREN

*From our own correspondent: termuren is a small town with 2 mills, the labor and the filature . . . the dendre flows through it . . . and on its banks a laborer from the weaving mill 'the labor' found, on monday, the body of a completely naked woman, horribly mutilated and in a state of putrefaction. There was no clothing or any jewelry on the corpse which might help to identify the stranger . . . only a black suspender belt with a shred of stocking on each leg . . . every joint had been slashed as if the assassin had tried to cut the body up . . . did he not have the time ?*

## AND FOR THE REST, EVERYTHING SO-SO

*Ondine reflected that one brother lay in bed with a flat-footed woman while the other brother was spooking about in chapel road, in the shape of the Tall Woman. It was painful having to know all this and to be silent about it: they might think SHE was abnormal and put her in a madhouse, if she blabbed about it. She tried to accept things the way they were, after first having tried to forget them, with wine, and jostling and the horrible screeching of chairs being dragged across a floor—something which was like music to mr glemmasson's medieval ears. She boldly got drunk, and taught herself to understand that it would always be like that: always to gossip with the rulers without ever belonging to their ranks, to pawn her body, leaving her spirit outside it. But at night, or in the loneliness of her long walks along the railway, far beyond the broom, she rejected this recognition of the truth. She even feared the truth. And with the unfathomable grief which a 16 year old girl can feel, she said: it really is stupid of men to think that a woman is nothing but a cunt. Oh, it was sad. But . . . and she looked round as she said this 'but' . . . there used to be always something I could console myself with, what had it been? It was that she belonged to the middle class, to the bourgeoisie, and that she knew french: but it was impossible to retrieve those thoughts now, it was as if her unconscious mind wanted to forget them. And it was better so, because otherwise she would have realized that to belong to the middle class and all the other things, were nothing much, only so-so . . . like on the day when her father, for 2 weeks on end, had said that one day this month they would have fish for dinner. Fish, fish, she had cheered—and then, at noon, it was only herring.*

## HAMLETS ON THE CONVEYOR BELT

Professor spothuyzen turns up at the moment when you don't at all feel like working and working . . . because once again you are wondering what's the use of it . . . none; no one reads in your work *that* which you write, but everyone reads in it *that* which he likes to read . . . and then there's something else besides, there's more: the general despondency of people today, of which you, writer, are the seismograph, and your pen is the needle swinging backwards and forwards: the heart, which was too weak and failed, and the mind, which isn't yet or is no longer able to disentangle the thousand and one interwoven problems and to solve them one by one. And at that moment professor spothuyzen turns up, his arms and hands and eyes and mind all moving, full of electricity, letting off sparks, and he says: now that it's the easter holiday in the factory of the universal intelligence, I should like to make a quick study of hamlet: hamlet is not, as your music master alleges, inner contemplation leading to madness . . . hamlet is weighing and deliberating so many different aspects that they lead to zero, to a point in infinity: a dead point. And now, professor spothuyzen continues, I'd like to demonstrate that hamlet isn't just an arbitrary case, but rather a general problem dominating our time. Those who hear the groans of the clogged-up machine, know that something ought to be done . . . and the sensible ones among them sit down with their head in their hands and begin to think . . . but by thinking they constantly discover possible answers, and then they see that each possibility creates in its turn a new problem . . . but in the meanwhile the clogged-up machine groans even more fiercely, even more savagely, and circumstances shout out for Action, and then the fools come and act: they say: we don't know whether it's good or bad, we act, and afterwards we shall think . . . that is . . . afterwards we'll ask the sensible people to think . . . Here you interrupt professor spothuyzen because fear and despair sweep through your heart and force your mouth open: but then, in the history of our civilization, every possible action has already been taken by fools, and have the sensible people never done anything except thinking what should be done? Professor spothuyzen moves his arms and hands and mouth and eyes, which are all full of electricity, and says ironically: I don't know, I first write my argument down and I think about it later; for the moment I limit myself to looking for hamlets in history: politicians, economists, statesmen, professors . . . all those who weighed and deliberated till they reached the dead point, while circumstances were screaming, weeping for action: everywhere you find prominent men who withdrew the moment they had to take a decision . . . take for instance . . . And you, with your heavy heart and conscience, you don't hear whom and what professor spothuyzen mentions as examples: you are thinking of yourself, moving from person to person, from party to party, from philosophy to philosophy, and feeling at home nowhere . . . and you know and see that writing is no use, because while you're writing you are unable to reach The Solution.

## THE COUNTRYSIDE, BUT WITH NOT TOO MANY TREES

Between 2 april showers, the music master drops in to protest: it's not true that I said that hamlet is self-contemplation leading only to madness . . . I said that it is self-contemplation leading to madness and death . . . and for death I might just as well say the Dead point. And at the same time I take the opportunity to draw your attention to the most foolish question you ever uttered in the presence of professor spothuyzen . . . because if the wise weigh the pros and cons more than the fools, this doesn't mean that no sensible deed is Ever done . . . but it does mean that on the one hand doubt, and on the other hand the numerous foolish deeds that are committed, make the situation more and more chaotic. And talking about chaos, not only do you, writer, express the despondency of our time, but you also unconsciously give expression to the chaos . . . if I open the folder in which you keep the pages of your book about chapel road, chaos comes bursting out of it like from a drawer where cloth and pins and thread are stuffed away; I'm appalled by the mess, I'm overwhelmed by the disorder, the muddle makes me nervous: the moment I think: *now I'm about to learn something about ondine, about HER doubts, HER despondency at everything in life being only so-so* . . . at that moment you turn up with YOUR doubts and YOUR despondency and you let professor spothuyzen say that it's a general condition and a general problem of our time. If you want the chapel road book to be a work which will stand the test of time, you'll have to bring some order into it . . . and don't confuse order with form now . . . you may use a form which you've knocked up somehow, out of your disgust of everything that is tidy and established, but the eternal laws of order and intelligibility must be present in it: why for instance shouldn't the text of the various intertwining main ideas be indicated by different colors? . . . if there's talk of mr brys and the first socialists, and johan janssens with his newspaper, you could use red . . . *and when there's talk of ondineke and of the jeanninekes and the grand and the small world, and of civilization running towards the abyss, you could use brown* . . . and when there's talk of hamlet and doubt and despondency and despair, you could use ochre . . . etcetera, because there are always more colors than ideas. You may object that you can't see the use of this, because today you write the book only for yourself and for a few faithful friends . . . but the day after tomorrow or in 700 years, at least if the book hasn't exploded together with the rest of the world, it will be published and you have to come to an agreement with the potential readers and a reader is like somebody who loves to go for walks and who loves the countryside, that is, well-ordered countryside, with paths meandering through fields and an arrow at each crossroad, to Mon Repos, so that the walker, who loves the countryside, knows he won't be late for lunch . . . but he doesn't care for real countryside, which is a jungle in which he would get lost, where beasts of prey roam about and man-eating plants have their tentacles at the ready so that he would never see his mother-dear again. And when the april shower has gone and the sun has come out again, the music master hurries outside . . . to enjoy the countryside around termuren, where there aren't too many trees to block the view and stop him from finding his pretty wife lucette again.

## PERIODIC WEARINESS

*In ondineke there was something unnameable, a kind of weariness of everything which came back periodically as if it was part of the monthly thing about which she never spoke—it was always very profuse with her—but it was strange that although she hadn't been troubled with this any more of late, her restlessness had grown and was more vehement than ever: it grew into a weariness of life: oh, hell, what's that to me, she said, no matter what it was that people were talking about. It was nothing to her that mr brys had been called to mr derenancourt of the mill and that he had been told to choose between staying on as a bookkeeper and stopping his silly jabber about something he called a sick fund, or to go on making speeches but to be dismissed and wait for what else might happen . . . no, there was no mention of starving him, breaking, killing him . . . and now it was gossipped at termuren that he'd been given 14 days and that all those who'd registered as members with him had been sacked: people were excitable in those days, life was more feverish; there was laughter, swearing, crying for no reason, and also there was fear of unfamiliar things in the air . . . changes . . . maybe improvements, but of the kind which wouldn't leave the world the way they'd always known it: what sort of crazy world is this getting to be, they asked each other on the way home from the filature, late at night. Liza came and knocked at ondine's door, she stood in the doorway . . . she even addressed her respectfully as miss ondine, as if they'd never been at school together . . . she looked crestfallen and asked if miss ondine wouldn't say a word on behalf of her husband, please, because he too had been sacked . . . and yet mr brys had told them it wasn't a socialist union; but ondine shrugged her shoulders . . . she could have answered that a word on his behalf was useless because today he'd been taken back and tomorrow he'd join another union, maybe even the socialists themselves . . . but her weariness, her nausea with everything, with life, and with that stupid, cowardly liza in the doorway, and with mr brys and his rhymes . . . he could make rhymes on himself now, like: I'm mr brys, I say; worry is making my hair grey . . . nausea rose in her throat. She pushed liza outside and closed the door, and resumed the thread of her thoughts: that she could have vomited with disgust, because no one, absolutely no one was like her . . . unless it might be norbert . . . certainly, his disgust with life had driven him in an abnormal direction . . . that's to say seen from HER absolute point of view, he seemed abnormal . . . but this disgust itself, this hatred, which made him get on to a pair of stilts and drive people even crazier than they were already, she had, on close examination, to recognize as HER hatred, HER disgust.*

## TOO COMPLICATED

Would you like a piece of cake too? your wife asks msieu colson of the ministry, amidst the hubbub . . . No, thank you, I'd prefer an aspirin, says msieu colson, my head feels as if it's going to burst. And turning to you he says that the world-of-today is becoming much too complicated . . . not only in this or that journal, where in the thousand and 1 ideas of each article of each journal the world is forever being changed, reshaped, turned inside out, folded up and blown up . . . but also outside the journals, in the real world, in which we live hardly knowing why we live and in which we understand nothing whatsoever of anyone else—we don't even want to, although we can't bear it when others don't understand us. One person wants to turn left today and right tomorrow, in the morning swearing by distance and width and in the evening longing for peace and depth, and another one wants exactly the same but in the reverse order, so that they shake their heads over each other and wonder what the world is coming to with such people. In the meanwhile the masses remain the masses, with each particle keeping on its individual guard . . . and then again, an avalanche of papers engulfs the world, enfolding us, as they used to say at school, with its soft white shroud: all the time there are more and more ministries and offices and authorities . . . among which there occasionally remains a private house, with a threatening notice by the doorbell: no offices here . . . and you're overwhelmed by so much paperwork that the man who has to hand it all to you, stamping this and stapling that and putting photographs on, is run into the ground by it all . . . and everything you touch or look at has a number: like in the restaurant at the ministry, where they first give you a ticket with a number which you have to hand in, in exchange for a meal ticket with a number, and with this you sit down at a table with a number: I joked about this the other day with my boss and he felt in his pocket for his meal ticket, but all he got out was a leaf of a block calendar with telephone numbers scribbled on it . . . and he finished off, savagely, where I had started: that the world perishes under an avalanche of complexities and paperwork.

And when msieu colson of the ministry has swallowed his aspirin, he takes two newspaper cuttings about italy out of his pocket: cutting 1: a bill to forbid a novel by sartre, as an 'attack on decency', cutting 2: a bill Not to disenfranchise ladies of easy virtue, so as Not to impair their rights as citizens.

## . . . AND TOO HARD

And another thing, says msieu colson of the ministry, the same evening as when he took an aspirin . . . the world isn't only becoming too complicated, but also too hard: iron and glass and concrete and steel, between which we're obliged to let our poor, small humanity be crushed, cut in half, smashed, flattened and pulverized: look, on the wide pavement by the theatre there's a man with an instant camera—and like a real judge of people he chooses the right victims and at the moment you look at him, his victims are going to be: a woman and her son, carrying a satchel on his back . . . and as they approach, his hand goes to the shutter release, but then he notices that the woman has a deformed foot, and he stops; she won't buy a photograph. And a few moments later you see the young man who can't have been blind for long yet, because he's learning to walk with the white stick and with the new glass eyes just arrived from the factory . . . and the two friends who are with him say behind his back: you can tell he's still hesitating too much. He hears it but says nothing and walks on bravely, with his stick and his new glass eyes, to show them he'll conquer that hesitation. And what else did I see yesterday and today, will I see tomorrow and the day after? . . . this and that, it's too much for me to have the guts to write it all down, to remember, to go on looking at it: the world of today is too complicated and too hard for me, whose heart is stirred by the things my eyes see . . . and only those who have adjusted themselves to living amongst machines and farms, can keep going: for instance like creatures who are vaguely aware that they have to knock at a door before opening it, and who therefore knock before going out . . . and the rest, who have heart, eyes and some brains, will perish in the avalanche of paper and steel and glass, if we don't start finding out how a bit of humanity can be brought back into this world.

## THE ETERNAL PERPETUUM MOBILE

*Ondine's nausea grew day by day: it was as if there were lumps of phlegm in her throat . . . and deeper, much deeper, which had to be washed away with something acid; she ate hardly anything but some pickled herrings, although her breath started to smell of it, but it was the only thing she could get down. She felt an absurd longing for her childhood, for the days when she lay praying on her knees by the flowering broom . . . why? . . . well, perhaps in order to start all over again, to be different, not better or worse, but . . . yes, only to be different. And sometimes, as she was listlessly eating her mash, anger swept up in her, because of valeer, who was holding his spoon in a peculiar way in his maimed hand, staring in front of him with dumb eyes, without noticing that he spilt blobs of mash all over his jacket . . . anger swept over her, also with her mother, who became more and more simple-minded every day: she saw the time coming when they'd have to put her away. Yes, maybe that was the matter with ondine: she saw too far, too widely . . . she couldn't help it but she saw someone growing old when he was still a child. And yet, it wasn't that, it was all the result of something quite different: she felt her breasts stinging as if milk was swelling up in them . . . later she felt something stirring in her belly; in those months she anxiously avoided going out lest the neighbors suspect anything. She needn't fear her father, he noticed nothing except his perpetual motion machine; she smiled at it, that the everlasting movement should be in this house, in her belly . . . life and new life, without ever ceasing . . . and what was old and worn fell away by itself; it died and became manure for what was coming; her foolish father would never get that far; new iron would never come out of his old rust. Her mother, too, saw nothing: ondine didn't even think of hiding it from her, she pretended to be ill and walked around in her night dress till noon, and in the afternoon she'd sleep for a while in the upper room, where some onions were rotting in one corner and apples in the other . . . she'd brought water there and a blanket and a straw pallet, and looking in a cracked piece of mirror she realized wryly that this was what she would look like when she'd grown old, and hadn't got out of life what she'd asked: at such a thought her regret and anger flared up again and she told everyone in the house to go to hell . . . especially valeer she couldn't bear to hear or see; she asked him questions from the catechism, about the commandment of unchaste acts and thoughts, so that valeer turned a flaming red: she also reproached him that he always used his hand as an excuse, and that it would be better to look for a job, he'd forget his handicap then. And the fool didn't even have the courage to retort that after all, she was the cause of his handicap—god knows whether he even thought it—his head was too full of their cousin and he became mad with fear hearing ondine speaking of these things.*

## NEWSPAPER FOR SALE

With a face on which you can see neither joy nor sadness, neither regret nor satisfaction, johan janssens the journalist gives you an impassive account of his last trip to brussels, to the editor: I went to the office and saw them pouring the text into the paper as if they were tipping out a bucket, or dumping a cart of bricks: as long as the hole gets filled . . . and in the meanwhile they asked tippetotje the painter to do the lay-out, in theory, but she's not allowed to touch it, because the chief editor exists to muck about with the lay-out and to make his own lay-out instead: smack; because according to her salary, tippetotje is only an ordinary editor and he is, according to his salary, the Editor in Chief, and so he knows best. Meanwhile the paper declines in quality, merit and turnover . . . and everyone I meet asks me, just as if it was my fault, what's the matter with the paper? We buy it because we . . . yes, why do we? . . . but we feel forced to buy another paper besides, just in order to have a paper to read: here there's nothing but the driest politics in the pre-first-war style: and you go nuts even when you open it, the way everything's been poured in hotch-potch, and the news is always two days late. And because the paper is sinking, less money is put into it, and every time the money gets less, the paper sinks Deeper; and here I come to the office yesterday and I see that on the front page, next to the title, there's a huge empty space with an announcement:

like a poor small craftsman, who's fallen upon hard times and puts a yellow card in the window: foot-warmer for sale.

## BROKE

This story about your paper, says msieu colson of the ministry, has moved me more than a whole lot of pages about *ondine and the rest*: precisely because johan janssens told it so unemotionally, such things grip me, msieu colson of the ministry, because I see More in them than a small personal affair . . . I just read a book about the life and work of the german cartoonist georg grosz who said that only work which was done conscientiously and well interested him, but that great art, depicting the beauty of the world, didn't mean anything to him. Only hogarth, goya, daumier. He would have liked to be an illustrator and journalist, a craftsman, a worker working for other workers. But when the artist becomes a laborer, he enters a class and acquires the conscience of that class, he abandons all individualism and is in the service of a social doctrine opposing another social doctrine . . . grosz didn't escape this logic . . . in the first years after the 1914-1918 truce this destroyer of ideologies accepted the marxist ideology, he embraced the doctrine of the extreme left, the way he had embraced futuristic and dadaist ethics: his negation of germany was absolute: he only tried to distinguish between wolves and sheep, between a party of good and a party of evil: he drew for revolutionary papers: but the revolutionary papers of the extreme left refused those drawings . . . and therefore he published them In small propaganda organs such as 'broke' which he founded in 1919 and which had to be discontinued after the 3rd issue.

## THE DEATH CANDLE

Johan janssens continues: and in the meanwhile there are daily meetings to talk about the paper, and I go there, one day, and see them sitting there, all with yesterday's paper in their hands: the title should be a bit larger, and there should have been a line there . . . and that report was only 1 day late, we were early this time. And the main editorial was Very good, they say to editor in chief captain one-eye . . . but not a word is said about our cultural life, because I'm present . . . and when I've gone they *do* discuss our cultural life: it's no good, it's too international again, about a german cartoonist georg grosz, although nobody has ever heard of georg grosz and although there are lots of horrible things about the Worker in his drawings . . . it's as if he's taking it lightly . . . you look at this drawing of the baths in berlin, where a worker dressed in an impossible swimsuit lies in the sun reading our paper, while his wife allows a bloke with a moustache to tickle her fat behind . . . and while in the corner a little girl nulled her pants down to push a turd . . . it's just like the prose of that dreadful boon, writing that book about chapel road; what will people think of us . . . instead of writing about what's his name, the flemish journal of ultra-marxist intellectuals, to which only ph d's contribute: dr pascalius prostituaan, about 'nietzsche, a forerunner of fascism', 'd.h. lawrence, a fascist'; 'sartre, a neo-fascist', 'the party in france has made a stand against—ugh—things like georg grosz' drawings and that dreadful boon's writings'. But let's get on with the meeting, what else have we got that's no good? Here, the film page, because it's about an avant-garde film, masereel's idea, instead of writing about a film that's worth seeing: but the main editorial was very good, very dry, political, in a splendid style of before the other war . . . and the lay-out was splendid too, just like a tub of mortar chucked from a scaffold . . . proficiat! And editor in chief one-eye says: thank you. And I go to tippetotje and tell her that there's a meeting in the big office, and tippetotje asks, isn't it about yesterday's paper? . . . because they never talk about the coming issue; it's almost 6 o'clock now—and tippetotje looks at the old alarm clock, next to the broken radio—and now they still don't know what should go in today's paper . . . And in her picturesque style tippetotje says: they're holding a meeting the way neighbors keep watch by a death bed in the clammy morning hours . . . sh, it can come any moment—and they sit there with a flickering, stinking candle in their hands . . . praying and praying.

## THE DARKNESS

*Ondine closed the door so that no one could enter the house and once, when the priest knocked, she called from inside: don't come in, I've got smallpox. Smallpox?*

*The people of termuren crossed themselves when they heard The Disease mentioned. When her time had come, she locked herself in the upper room and stuck paper over the narrow window so that at every hour of the day there was twilight. It was more difficult than she had thought, she suffered monstrously and had to admonish herself in order not to faint or to start calling out; then she had something in her hands which was wet and slippery, she dare not look at it properly . . . she was close to dying, she tried to get up and staggered, her blood ebbed away: but whatever might happen, first this had to be got out of the way. It had been afternoon when she lay down and now she opened the door and saw it was completely dark . . . she was somewhat surprised . . . it was chilly outside and feeling her way along the walls she came to the toilet into which she threw the thing she hadn't seen. Now she could go back and die . . . Yet, dying, that was more easily said than done, she couldn't die . . . she raved and in her delirium she saw hall after hall, full of blood stains which had to be wiped away . . . she worked like a horse but it was all useless, for as she scrubbed, the blood kept flowing . . . she wept at her impotence, she died with pain. And when in her delirium she knew herself to be dying she saw how flickering candles were placed about her deathbed by norbert derenancourt and by fat glemmasson—how strange that these 2 extremes who never had any contact with each other, should be here together!—and she also saw how her mother, against every sane reason, was mopping with something which couldn't be measured: a rag, at first only the size of a postage stamp, but growing all the time heavier and larger.*

## KRAMIEK'S DEFINTION

Everyone is present except johan janssens who is away reporting again, this time an event on the belgian coast in april . . . there are no tourists, it looks cold, dead and deserted . . . and the waiters and bathing hut men are hibernating in the shape of masons and plumbers, and the whores in the guise of beguines trekking to early mass every morning: and you hear nothing of what the people in your house are talking about, you're listening to the running commentary of that event and you're wondering whether he, johan janssens, will write anything worth while about it . . . for at the newspaper office they're beginning to be difficult and you're afraid he won't hold out there much longer. And meanwhile you find yourself having to listen after all to the conversation in your house, because it's about the chapel road book, *about ondine who dropped her baby in the john. It's been written with far too transparent an imagination, says the music master, just as if the writer had a different meaning in mind all the time . . . a baby can also be a symbol of an ideal and so you could also throw an ideal into the john . . . and as far as the story itself is concerned, it looks to me as if the writer hadn't really got it quite under control and, hocus pocus, thought up a dream . . . just as if ondine's feverish dreams had to serve to cover up possible mistakes. And for the same reason he's strewn around far too many freaks, says msieu colson of the ministry, like those two halfwits . . . norbert, who occupies himself with ghosts and spiritualism, and fat glemmasson who is an encyclical simply and purely in order to get away with more blatant sins . . . and these two place candles round her deathbed while her dotty mother wipes away the bloodstains with a fantasy rag. And the pretty lucette blurts out: she oughtn't to have done it, ondine, throwing a child into the john! And once again it's your wife who alone happens to be standing beside you, quite symbolically, and says that she knew of a similar case which happened in her youth: but then it happened to liza who was at the convent school with me, and the nuns always held her up as an example of a saintly girl, the way she always walked demurely with her eyes cast down . . . but suddenly she turned out to be like That . . . when she was hardly 14 . . . and her whole dark double life came out into the glaring light: at night she drove off with the sons of fat glemmasson—very rich folk all of them—yes, and what's his name was there as well, one of the derenancourt sons . . . and liza's pants were later found in the car of fat glemmasson's son, after she'd gone for a drive with those 3 men . . . and it happened in the same way: she dropped it into the john, now she's been married for years to the chauffeur of fat glemmasson's son.*

There is someone in the house who considers he belongs to the company, and wherever he goes he says that he too is part of the book about chapel road . . . but he sits there and he's got nothing to do with it . . . his name is kramiek . . . but he's a nogood kramiek who always agrees with everyone and never dares say anything which might put him in opposition. But now he suddenly says something unexpectedly apt: he shakes his head when he hears that girls drop their babies in the john and he says very sadly: well, when you hear all this you see that life is like a baby's smock: too short and with shit on it.

## THE BATHROOM

You tear open the letter which has just been brought in to you and it's from tippetotje the painter: I meant to write to you long ago but I didn't because the subject would have been looked upon as something which was, politically speaking, incorrect . . . but since johan janssens is also telling you things which are politically incorrect, I can forget my objections . . . and so I have to tell you how I found right and left, and how I naturally found right and left thoughts, but that the people of right and left were the same poor devils . . . the small people still live in poverty and want, but they are resigned to their life of poverty and want . . . they still do the same as before, but they don't go to mass any more and they say of the priest that he's a black thief who beats the money out of our pockets while promising us a heaven hereafter . . .

and while the church is burning down they stand there laughing that the saints are burning too, haha. Soon we'll have to dig into our pockets again when the priest comes to the door, haha. It won't be the priest himself, but some old sod of a pauper who earns his bread working for the sick fund of the encyclicals' association, haha. No, it will be the daughters or the missus, of the encyclical bosses of the encyclical factories, and we'll have to fork out, goddammit.

and in the meanwhile, in spite of his plaster saints and his candles burning against sickness, the little man is a socialist or an ultra-marxist, but he never goes to a conference or a meeting because that politico is a red thief who beats the money out of your pockets, while promising us a heaven of social justice . . . they no longer stand there dirty and black and no longer spit out the tobacco juice from behind their filthy teeth . . . but they live in a block of workmen's dwellings built by the state, and here we've been deceived once again, because in these houses, in order to save appearances, a little room was intended as a bathroom, but they have to use it as their store room and put their coal in the zinc bath or their potatoes, or old newspapers and tax papers. These are all things which I, tippetotje, shouldn't really say, since it's not political . . . realistically, it is of course the truth, but a realistic truth isn't always a politically correct truth. Because rich people like mr derenancourt would say: you see, the working man doesn't need a bathroom with a bath, because he only uses it for storing potatoes . . . all that twaddle about social improvements isn't something the laborer himself wants, but it's been invented by people who see a livelihood in a socialist or an ultra-marxist party: to make the little man long for heaven or a bathroom is a trade like any other trade. Yours tippetotje the painter who is coming to live in termuren 1 of these days.

## ONDINE'S RETREAT

*Ondine got to her feet again, looking pale and haggard, and with the shine gone from her brown hair . . . she now had the face of a bird, and would probably never lose it again . . . her 1st walk was to the toilet but on the way there she saw nothing suspicious, nowhere a trace of anything which might give her away. She didn't understand it. She no longer thought of a miracle but called it luck . . . really called it ill-concealed whore's luck . . . while she bent over the john and noticed nothing in there either. It wasn't possible, it must be something more than luck. Then she watched her father closely, but all his attention went to 6 clumsy chairs and a table which he had to make for some peasant yokel, a fellow who worked somewhere north of brussels on a building site and who had been fobbed off with a sweetheart who had first been got drunk by mr ludovic gourmonprez . . . and the priest had come to see this fellow and had told him that mr ludovic might be a libertine but that he wasn't such a bad person, and that he would buy him a nice set of furniture if he would marry her—ondine talked of going to collect the money as soon as she was cured, and as she stressed the word 'cured' she didn't take her eyes from her father: he didn't let on anything, he was, as always, a bit sheepish and only sensible in things which were of no practical importance. And she also looked attentively at her mother, and at valeer: which of them was such a cunning devil that he could remove all those traces and yet not open his trap? Or could she have said something herself, in her confused dreams? Her mother was a bit more excited, but not much, she muttered a bit louder to herself, she listened and looked round as if someone was standing behind her and answering her. But that wasn't so bad; only ondine who had been watching her from close by for so many years, could notice it. And valeer? Apart from his cousin he knew nothing of the world: he walked beside that yellow-haired girl, with his big heavy head, they would go for walks along the railway, where the broom would soon be in flower again: it made ondine laugh; a sad, smutty little laugh.*

*She lived withdrawn . . . it was something she scoffingly called her retreat, she had no intention of giving up anything whatever; on the contrary, it was as if she wanted to get her breath back in order to jump all the more relentlessly. It started with that bill she was going to present, but what she really wanted was to see the child: yes, it had the same dark hair, and those not very big but sly eyes, the eyes of gourmonprez whom she hadn't seen again since they had let the devils loose in that furnished room . . . but otherwise everything in the little infant's features marked it as a pauper's face. It had this from its mother. And ondine wondered what on earth he could have seen in her, oh, nothing perhaps, except that she must have been sweet, fresh, and perhaps a bit bold after having had her first lessons about life in the lavatories of the mill . . . or perhaps he hadn't even seen her face properly, and she had been nothing but a vagina into which a way had to be made. Ondine put the bill down and left. No, that thing in the john . . . well now, even in my thoughts I mustn't mention it any more, she thought . . . but it would have looked quite different, anyway, how silly she had been, to imagine that all those children would look like each other. On the way back she had a feeling as if she had been somewhere very far away but where she'd found the door closed: I'm tired,*

*I'm ill, she thought. She went to bed and stayed there all day, staring at the white-washed ceiling with eyes that saw nothing . . . her belly hurt so much she couldn't tell a soul.*

## FROM NOW TILL DOOMSDAY

The elections may be slowly coming nearer, but the manifestos for and against king nobel, for or against one-eye, for or against or without democrats, they all piled up in isengrinus' letterbox, for he had no time or desire to read them, he lived from day to day and only thought of his cut-off tail, on which he had to smear ointment or put bandages. He found it quite natural that the great ones had made a fool of him in a big way but he was angry with reynard who in his turn wouldn't be made a fool of by him and who in particular cherished that crazy illusion of proclaiming the Republic of the Free, and of dividing all the spoils equally among all thieves. This reynard is becoming far too dangerous company for me, he thought, and he told that witch of his, hersinde, that she should say 'your uncle isn't in', if he knocked at any time. But when he heard someone ring he pulled the door open and saw reynard standing there . . . 'Your uncle isn't in', he was about to say, but he kept his stupid mouth shut and listened reluctantly to reynard who began to make excuses for unforgivable tricks which he had played on his own kith and kin . . . but isengrinus began to listen more attentively when he heard reynard mention something like compensation: could that be true? Certainly, said reynard, and pointed to the manifestos which were overflowing from the letterbox into the hall: you know that the old world is divided into two camps, it's a matter of dividends, of trusts and oligarchies, of uranium and world markets, which is why all the goats want to lure the black sheep to them, but in spite of each side's claim that they alone are the real democrats, and that they will save something or other—the souls of the children or the salvation of the world, the fatherland, freedom, life eternal—there is still disagreement over which of them has the right to make off with the biggest loot and who on the other hand, will have to cough up. And do you think I might . . . ? asked the wolf with eager eyes. No, said reynard, but where there is disagreement there must be an arbiter and if you would, perhaps, in exchange for a new fur . . . Understood, said the wolf, and together with reynard he went to the field where the goats lived in discord about thEIr democracy and thEIr dividends. As soon as reynard had managed to let them have his uncle act as arbiter, in exchange for the hair off their backs with which hersinde could mend the holes in his coat, isengrinus stood in the middle of the field and called out: run to me, all of you, and the first one will be allowed to impose his freedom on all the others . . . for in his curiosity to see who would be the first to arrive, it didn't occur to him to choose his words a bit more tactfully: he watched with an interested smile how reynard gave the signal, and how all the goats came storming towards him, in order to be the first to offer him the souls of the children and the salvation of the world, but they all ran equally fast, all equally keen on getting the largest share . . . and unable to check themselves at the goal they all rammed isengrinus at once, left and right, from behind and in front. For 1 brief moment the wolf remained standing, but crushed and shattered by the stampede and bleeding everywhere, he soon sank down in a heap, closed his eyes and thought: this is the day of the last judgment, I'm blowed if it isn't. johan janssens.

## NEWS FROM THE OLD HUNCHBACK

*Slowly ondine got her strength back, and she began to long for news from the outside world . . . and the old hunchback—who still walks about termuren as if he has the right to be immortal,—told her the things that were the talk of the day.*

*you know, mr brys has got the sack at the office, the fool, and he made a speech and afterwards certain people whom I won't name, went to bash his windows in and wanted to smash up his cottage—if the first socialists hadn't been there to protect him . . . and you know, people say that the student suggested to mr brys to get himself and the whole caboodle of his sick fund registered with the socialists . . . but he didn't want to, didn't dare . . . and then there's something I saw myself, the other things I only have from hearsay, mr brys came wandering along past the mill gates, musing and pondering with his eyes on the ground, and he stopped to ask the people something when they were just coming out, but they booed him and kept making a fool of him so that he couldn't possibly make himself heard . . . at the mill they all got half an afternoon off and bottles of beer, in order that they should go to the café 'justice-and-freedom' and smash the place to pieces. But the mill workers had to withdraw . . . what is that, you'll say? A drunk and a clod with 1 hand and a student with consumption, how the hell could they get the better of a mob? But you probably didn't know that the socialists had barricaded the café with more than 30 men? You see, yesterday there were only 3 of them and today there were 30 and how many will there be tomorrow? I myself didn't go with them to smash the place up, by reason of that misfortune I carry on my back, but I know it and others know it too that some of the mill . . . some of the ones that went to help do the smashing up . . . ran ahead and suddenly stood beside the socialists . . .*

*Oh, ondine was angry because they had been afraid of those 30 men. She was sorry that it had happened at a time when she had no contact with the gentlemen . . . it was as if god himself wanted everything to happen in this way . . . and so that's why she drummed it into the old hunchback and said: It seems to me you're pleased that there are thirty socialists already . . . you watch it . . . ! I'll tell mr derenancourt. And the old hunchback bent his hump meekly and was silent.*

## IN MEMORIAM LITTLE VEENMAN (1)

*Soon the broom will flower again along the railway, veenman, and while I'm reading the daily papers, on the evening train, and underline what I'll have to cut out tonight . . . because if one doesn't, veenman, one can't follow the course of events . . . and while I'm writing notes in my notebook, what human insight the closing day has given me, I feel a vague gnawing at my conscience. Because the thought of flowering broom creates another thought association; in which the heroine of this unfinished novel, ondine, is haunting me, asking me when I'll go on with the novel of her life and her time? Last year, veenman, . . . or is it 2 or 3 years ago? the broom flowered and I wrote that there's always something that's a pity in life . . . a pity this and a pity that . . . a miracle had happened to little ondine, but it was a pity she did shit on that holy spot where the broom flowered . . . and now ondine herself had begun to flower too, but she dropped her child in the lavatory . . . and now, veenman, while the train is waiting somewhere at a signal, an eternity, I remember that tomorrow and the day after are holidays so that I can throw myself on ondine with fervor . . . figuratively speaking of course, very figuratively . . . on that whore ondine who dropped her child in the lavatory and didn't have a cent's worth's regret . . . And the next day I get up very early, at about 4 in the morning, but I've hardly picked up my pen when I've got to go where she threw her baby, hurry, hurry, and while I tear off a piece of paper, veenman, and quickly, out of a wretched professional mishabit read what it says . . . goddammit . . . I don't feel like working at all and I waste the whole holiday!*

*. . . it would be wrong to conclude that there's complete stagnation in the publication of novels: on the contrary, quite a lot comes onto the market; never*

*have so many literary prizes sprouted from the ground as since the liberation, but who among the newcomers can pride himself in having anchored his name among the spirits? A kind of breach seems to have been established between reality and the creative spirit that has to embroider on it: the reports and naked documents about the horror camps are so conclusive that they block the novel's way, as it were . . . but they are insufficient: on the last evening of these 2 holidays you, veenman, come back into my life: you come in with a book I wrote, you put it on the corner of the table saying: what's his name is our greatest writer so far. I nod, because someone has got to be our greatest writer so far and I don't begrudge what's his name this . . . but the way you say it, veenman, it's as if you want to challenge me: you're not our greatest writer. It makes me laugh, because how can I explain to you that I couldn't care less? I don't write in order to be the greatest, but because I like writing, and because I may make some money out of it . . . when my wife and child have gone to bed and it becomes so still that you can hear the reading lamp hum . . . or when it's about 4 in the morning and I hear the first train whistling in the distance and think that at this moment it will be rushing past the broom which will soon be in flower . . . oh, be quiet, or ondine will raise her head again . . . and a pile of papers will be waiting for me, god, how warm it will be in my heart and what creative joy I feel when I see the pen staggering along in its hurry to keep up with the words: and I'll show what I've written to someone who LIKES to read it . . . but not to you, little veenman, because you don't understand it, you think that I . . . want to take pride in having anchored my name in your spirit . . . like in that piece of newspaper I wiped my bottom on this morning, and I start explaining to you, little veenman, that writing brings warmth and the joy of creation into my heart, but meanwhile I ask myself whether I write and write in order to pursue this joy and this warmth every day anew? . . . and you, little veenman, reply—quite rightly—that in your opinion writing must have something which could be called a Purpose, because if it doesn't have a purpose you might as well, like in your youth . . . eh, how to say it, in your wife's presence . . . indulge in something which gave just as much pleasure but which was just as useless.*

*oh, veenman, be quiet, because when you read these papers, about the stagnation in the development of the novel and the breach between the naked documents and the creative spirit which has to embroider on them . . . and when you hear yourself talking very highmindedly about a Purpose, while in the meanwhile a mean, low thought is being repressed . . . because a bare behind could also be a purpose—little veenman, you'd better be quiet.*

*yes, suddenly you turn up again in my life, little veenman: you come in and say to my wife: hello, maria, although you'd never seen her and didn't even know her name. It's just like a little veenman, she says to me; where did you pick him up?*

*little veenman, you were part of my youth, when we were still young and foolish and thought we could change the world: do you remember our home, which was at that time a monstrously ugly rat-ridden empty house? Wasn't it called the Flame, little veenman? and do you remember that one day we decided each to go out a different way but to meet at a certain pool, the donk, far from the small smelly town of the 2 mills? And then we all got there with our rucksacks and our blankets, except you. little veenman, you arrived 3 months later: you'd walked straight on and had stalked along the south coast of france.*

*and once, when we came back from some trip, we found you, little veenman, in that ugly rats' nest the Flame, and you were standing in the living room on some kind of pedestal, stockstill like a statue . . . do you remember? . . . no, we thought that maybe you were trying to be funny, and we left you alone—everyone to his fancy, said the farmer and he had the fly put in the seat of his pants—and nobody looked at you, high on your pedestal, the whole long afternoon; but you, with your buddhist theories, you remained stockstill like a statue, and late at night someone said: veenman, are you coming down or must I pull the pedestal away? and they pulled the pedestal away and you hit the ground and stayed there, and a lump began to swell on your head the size of a goose egg.*

*and then, veenman, it was tippetotje . . . tippetotje the painter who later disappeared in the brussels jungle and who returned years later, like you . . . but with a scooter and a lover, and on the ride back she forgot her lover . . . and who, on the rare occasions when she did turn up, was received with the cry: the ship of lies has arrived! . . . it was this same tippetotje who stayed in the Flame night and day and so in her own odd way she tried to be a vestal virgin guarding the Flame . . . her heart was filled with the Flame but her stomach was empty, her stomach was as empty as the head of a petty bourgeois with a bowler hat . . . and it must have penetrated even to your buddhist indifference, veenman, that tippetotje struggled day and night against the emptiness in her stomach, because one summer evening she stood in the door of the Flame and saw someone coming in the distance . . . wasn't that you, veenman, with something in your hand? and the nearer you came the more clearly tippetotje saw that you were holding something between finger and thumb, a yard in front of you . . . well, a yard is perhaps exaggerated because apart from tippetotje it wouldn't occur to anyone to ascribe arms of a yard's length to you, pompous little veenman . . . and as you came even nearer, tippetotje saw it was a dried herring which you were holding up by the tail, the way one would carry away a dead mouse . . . and you stopped right in front of her and said: tippetotje, this is for you. Thereupon you turned round and walked with your pompous little steps the same long road back.*

*and then you disappeared from my sight, veenman, I got a wife and a child and a war and a stomach complaint and suddenly you turn up with a book written by me in your hand and you lay it on the table . . . like tippetotje's dead herring . . . and say that what's his name is our greatest writer so far: and furthermore I hear that you're still clinging to your buddhist theories and behave as oddly as years ago . . . when we were still young and found odd behavior interesting . . . but now you go to cafés and you know a certain maria the jewish bar maid from the café on the corner, over by the 1st dirty houses . . . and you're looking for material for an extensive study of alchemy: I shall gratefully go through every book in which alchemists are mentioned, you say, in your usual pompous way . . . so I start looking for 'là bas' by joris carl huysmans . . . and in the meanwhile andré the theosophist has come in and hears you talking about alchemists and tries to convert you to theosophy . . . and I did find 'là bas' but you, little veenman, never came back for it.*

*since then, veenman, my wife has restless dreams; she suddenly wakes up and thinks the wall is covered with blood: oh, I saw veenman with an unrecognizable face, she says. And three weeks after that dream, veenman, we learnt that you got drowned and that you must have lain in the dendre for three weeks: your face was unrecognizable because the rats had been gnawing at it.*

*and 3 months later, veenman, goddammit . . . andré with his theosophy, who didn't remember he met you at my house and who moreover didn't know you were drowned, dragged out and buried long ago, . . . andré says to me: now I've met an interesting person who's ripe for theosophy: veenman !*

## AT THE EDGE OF THE WOOD

*Ondine went into her uncle's inn, because she knew there were people there . . . sooner or later there would be gossip about that winter she had lived at the castle and she wanted to forestall them, she wanted to take the bull by the horns herself; mr achilles is married now, she said, but god and I alone know that he wanted to do himself in; he cried and said he could never live without me. But the time of cheap drama seemed to have passed in termuren: she was out-trumped with something else: with the news that the derenancourts were going to build 4 new houses at the edge of the wood. By the wood! She breathed hard when they spoke of that place where the souls of stillborn children wandered . . . but yet she managed to smile and to say that that would be the end then of the will o' the wisps. Yet unconsciously she was moved by the news about the new houses . . . there was talk of nothing else, as if apart from the 4 houses by termuren wood there was no news in the world: so that she looked surprised when she saw a piece from a strange newspaper lying at home, and noticed that there were a thousand and 1 other things: valeer had found the piece of newspaper by the railway and was proud because he didn't understand the contents—it's french, he said with shining eyes—ondine read it, and learnt that measures were being taken against the trade unions, and yet another new demand was being resisted—something called general franchise . . . so that the sad duty had rested with our soldiers to shoot at the troublemakers. It was an encyclical newspaper. But encyclical or libertine, ondine had a premonition that the world as it had been till now was going to the dogs, that the small man would rebel against the upper classes, and since she still cherished the illusion that she too belonged to those upper classes, it seemed to her that the people were rebelling against her, vapeur's ondineke. And yet, at termuren the building of the 4 houses was more important . . . she too went along the road one day to the overgrown shrubland but all she saw was a lonely man wading through the brambles with a youth, taking measurements. Are they going to build 4 villas here? She was lucky; he was a man who felt greatly aggrieved in life because he always knew everything best but was never understood. He said he'd told the derenancourts that it would be unhealthy to live here; in this damp, rotting place, that in winter there would be nothing but mud here . . . but what can you do . . . Ondine had got tired and sat down on the bank . . . she was brooding over something, that was obvious, as she listened vaguely to the man below her, who had stopped measuring and kept on prattling compulsively. The youth also came along, looking around and picking his nose, till he suddenly saw ondine's legs, above him, and the world stood still for him.*

## IN MEMORIAM LITTLE VEENMAN (2)

*And meanwhile, little veenman, . . . now that you're drowned and they're still trying to convert you to theosophy . . . the trains still rush past the broom which will soon flower again and that cursed ondine goes on haunting me and I write about the lonely man taking measurements and feeling aggrieved because he always knew best and was never understood . . . and I add a youth to this who was able to peep under ondine's skirt and thought the world was standing still . . . and as soon as I'd described these 2 men, veenman, I realized that I had described you twice. O little veenman, o least common multiple of my youth, incredible man who does things that shouldn't be done: like reminding a respectable man of his unrespectable youth.*

*and through your mouth, which was a mere stripe, a sharp notch in a block of wood, and which has now been gnawed away by the rats . . . you pushed out words which I only half understood, but which even in their half-intelligibility would have been worth collecting and publishing as the narrations of little veenman, expressing your disgust with life. You displayed your disgust to me about the way in which your parents brought you into the world, your father making a child in his balls and your mother accepting it . . . and your disgust about the way you were left alone when you were a boy with things that . . . well, er . . . so you sat at your school desk and felt your little veenman's thing grow impossibly large and you touched it and were beaten half dead by the indignant schoolmaster while you looked horror-struck at your soiled hand . . . and afterwards, crazy with fear, you told this to your sister, slightly older, who demanded more and more impossible explanations and finally looked horror-struck at her soiled hand. And so it went on, every morning and every afternoon and every evening and every night, you got a disgust for women, who were not like the earth, waiting patiently . . . but who were scrubbing the pavement or cleaning the windows or riding past on a bicycle . . . and didn't know that you, little veenman, passed them almost in tears, with your poor veenman's thing tied to your thigh with a piece of string. And growing older, you discovered works of literature and politics . . . you discovered that people put down their ideas and strange thoughts and untamable temptations on paper . . . because seed belongs to the earth and sperm to the woman and ideas to paper, and you, little veenman, committed the brave folly of turning the world upside down, grabbing a sheet of paper each time your thing rose imploringly, and you wrote and wrote, anything that occurred to you, till your head was stiff with cramp, till your brains were stiff with cramp, till the thing ww finally exhausted and you sat there, bathing in sweat, dumb and silent. And once, some time later, you went for a walk by the dendre, with the traditional jeannine from the 1st dirty houses behind the labor . . . the dendre, little veenman, where the rats nibbled at you . . . and you managed to push her on her back and she got furious because you tried to squirt it into her like a doctor with a syringe, quickly, quickly, to have done with it, so that neither would get any fun out of it . . . and she taught you, that girl, that jeannine from the 1st dirty houses, that you first ought to make her hot.*

*and so it goes on, little veenman, your narration, in which everything went wrong, and where there was only 1 way, 1 cure, 1 remedy to clear away all that was wrong: to carry out what lenin had said about it . . . and what you, veenman, imagined according to your experience, was the application of all that lenin had said about it.*

*and later, veenman, you studied to be an architect, because even the houses in which people lived were altogether wrong . . . you had already got many ideas about future ways of living . . . but you neglected your studies to ferret in lenin, and to help distribute the newspaper in rain and wind . . . because that paper was only a tiny leaflet then, one small sheet, printed on one side only . . . and badly, too . . . and in those days you were already in conflict with the party: you'd rush outside and withdraw into your buddhist postures, but you were a moth and the party a lamp and you kept circling round it, and were taken back. And in your last days there was still Nothing Right in the world . . . but, whereas you used to say this self-consciously, knowing a remedy which rose in value as the world lost its worth . . . in later days you said it—the world, goddammit, the world—you said it in despair because to you the remedy didn't exist any more: you said lenin was dead and all that was left of him were a few plaster busts . . . standing in the kitchens of the workers like sacred hearts . . . plus a few books whose meaning had been distorted.*

*and suddenly I met little pros, veenman, another least common multiple of our youth, another bearer of the Flame, another eccentric, he tugged at the button of my raincoat and said . . . by the way, did you know . . . veenman is dead.*

*oh, veenman, you're dead, by the way . . . and little pros tells me I mustn't think that you walked into the water because you were pissed or that you drowned yourself because you were a buddhist . . . no, no, I could take it from him that you were thrown in by the dirty remnants of the dirty Black gang, from back in the war . . . because they said that during the war you made a list of all those who were seen going in and out of black houses . . . but that wasn't true, said little pros, because veenman couldn't care less who went in or out of black houses and veenman never made lists except maybe of alchemists.*

*oh, hell, veenman, suddenly the void stares at me when I think of our youth . . . of our youth and of all those who should now be between 20 and 40 . . . should be . . . but only about 5 are left . . . there's you; you're dead . . . drowned, or thrown into the water . . . let me count them all on my fingers, veenman; 2 died in spain, 2 croaked in breendonck, 1 was sentenced to death . . . it would be easier to count the ones who are left, wouldn't it . . . how is it possible? . . . I and tippetotje and little pros—and who else? . . . hello, hello, veenman, roll call of our youth . . . hello, hello, men of the Flame . . . who's still around? . . . goddammit, veenman, who's still there? . . . Liske? . . . no, liske is dead too. No one else? . . . hello, hello, our youth's being sold by auction . . . no one else? . . . sold*

*how different are the young today, veenman, they don't risk their skins any more . . . or at least not voluntarily . . . they want to face poverty and shame and slavery and bombings and nuclear fission without hesitation, without even batting an eyelid . . . but they don't want to do anything, veenman, 'for their emancipation' as we used to say a bit bombastically; they don't mind facing death and shame, as long as they can do so dancing and chewing gum . . . And do you remember, veenman, . . . but of course, you're dead; you were drowned and your face was eaten by rats, so you can't remember anything . . . but that doesn't matter, I'll remember it for you . . . do you remember, veenman, that we sat, as we were sitting in the Flame; look how rebellious the young are, and think what the next generation will be like and then one after that . . . in 3 or 4 generations the new world will be there!*

*and now . . . don't talk to me about the young generation of today, veenman, because everything has become different, everything should be started all over again . . . or nothing, everything is hopelessly lost. When I look back objectively and take stock, I see that you died in vain, were murdered in vain, hit your head on the walls in vain, let your face be eaten by rats in vain*

*because you look at kramiek, who belongs to the young of today; he says he's a Flame bearer too . . . but don't ask how . . . don't ask how . . . he's a dud, a mollycoddle, he's got feelers on his head to find out which way the wind is blowing and never says a word wrong, he never says anything about himself and can talk about everything with long, long sentences that twist and turn . . . saying everything and nothing and stating opposites twice without in fact having made a Single point*

*oh, veenman, in memoriam old boy, in memoriam, goddammit.*

## THE KEROSENE LAMP

You're taking the roll call of our youth, says tippetotje, and you're forgetting the kerosene lamp! Maybe he got his name because of his shape with his ears sticking out . . . or maybe even more because of his painful backwardness, which reminded you of the smoky paraffin lamps from past dark winter evenings in flanders, when jingling rosaries were read against stupidity and poverty, cholera and plague and famine . . . but the origins of things don't interest me, tippetotje, only the things themselves do; he was nicknamed kerosene and that was a name cut to size: just funny enough for him and also because of the picture its sound evoked: everything he said came out with stammering words which got knocked to bits against edges and corners . . . He was the son of jeannette proust, who lives in the 1st dirty houses behind the labor and came by a child in the most unfortunate way:

still a child herself, she was molested by 4 or 5 german soldiers of 14-18 and the fruit of it was: kerosene. And if only this little oil lamp had been content to shine in its own little street, he would have been the source of much stupid mirth: for instance, they would have scared the wits out of him in the café on the corner, threatening to nail his ears to the bird cage, or making him tipsy and trying to pull his pants down, encouraged by the waitress, who after all ought to know how a lamp wick works. But kerosene didn't stay in his own street, a marxist immigrant came to live somewhere in an attic room, a Flame bearer, and kerosene became his shadow, his dog . . . he was present at the stormy meetings, when we sounded the death knell over our old civilization . . . he was there when the old clothes were shed and we went naked, shitting on respectability and decency . . . he was there when we marched through the streets, not with drums or banners, but carrying the Flame . . . god the holy ghost, lenin, trotsky and wait whitman . . . naturally, among the thundering laughter, he was the only one people pointed at: look there, the new era, haha! a tiny crooked abnormal, an oil lamp with flapping ears. And then, forgive me, I don't know how it came about, we grew older, more serious, we got ourselves a household and a career, a stomach complaint and maybe a decoration, but in exchange we had to put out the Flame in our hands; one of us died of hunger and another is almost a minister. And on Sunday evening I, tippetotje, went to the station in the town of the 2 mills and what do I see, goddammit, there's kerosene lamp at the station, small and bent, and grown old under the small misery of his small life: he'd read an announcement in the paper—maybe something like this: respectable girl of very encyclical parents wishes to marry another lame duck; and he'd written and was married although his mother jeannette proust had cried till her hair fell out . . . and after the wedding kerosene and his kerosene wife went upstairs and the next morning she stood there in her combinations packing her cardboard suitcase and walked up the road to the station: she was never seen again. Oh, perhaps jeannette proust knew why she'd been tearing her hair out; he's been standing by the station for a month now, he says . . . yesterday, today, and tomorrow . . . he waits for her to come back, in her combinations and with her cardboard suitcase. Because, he says with those broken, knocked-about words which I won't try to imitate: she has no right to leave the marital house for more than 24 hours, I know that. So he knows that. I, tippetotje, know nothing except that I ought to kick myself for this story.

## THE 4 VILLAS

*Every day she went back to the wild shrub-land and watched men cutting away the bushes and starting to dig foundations . . . but as soon as evening fell, she hurried away, because, although she wasn't afraid of will o' the wisps, she didn't want to be reminded of her own hellish night . . . the lonely man who had measured everything came to tell her that he was master-mason, but didn't know yet who would be the carpenter: ondine looked at him pensively . . . yet remaining near enough reality to notice that the youth was looking at her again from below . . . but his eyes were too eager and ondine pressed her skirts against her legs: I see, so you don't know yet who'll be the carpenter, she said. And one day mr achilles came to have a look, as she had expected . . . she smiled thinly, and withdrew her hand which he held a little too long . . . because she was no longer like the others, an animal, to be stroked, to be admired, to be bought . . . she reminded him that man is a beast of prey, with broken teeth, trying to become the manager of the spinning mill, and chief shareholder of the discount and credit bank . . . lying in bed at night marking books in order to become a senator or who knows, even a minister . . . she ignored the fact that he was watching her with a somewhat mocking smile, and interrupted her saying that HE didn't wish to become this or that but that circumstances forced him. She insisted stubbornly that he was ambitious and tried to be successful in life . . . and, she said; surely you don't think I'm waiting for you here in order to spend another winter at the castle with you? No, I don't think that, he replied, I think you've come to ask me how you could earn a bit of money somehow, at these 4 villas here . . . and he laughed at her confusion . . . what do you want, he asked. Oh, it was hard, it was steel against steel, and she tried to wrap her question in a sweet smile—because hell, hell, you never got anywhere with men unless you reminded them all the time that you were wearing a skirt—and she thought with bitter self-mockery that naturally he was already coveting others, younger, and especially more naive . . . while she was only good enough to let children, like that boy down there, look under her skirt. And what she finally asked was: to be allowed to undertake the carpentry for the 4 houses—but she went home doubting whether he'd think of her again . . . of her, perhaps, of her youth, of which he'd taken the best . . . but not of ondine, the daughter of vapeur—expert carpenter.*

*She took off her bracelet which she had worn for the occasion . . . and put it back with all the other things she'd wheedled out of the gentlemen and which were of no use to her, except to remind her of the days of which she . . . you see . . . hadn't profited enough.*

## LILIES OF THE VALLEY

Now that it will soon be the 1st of may, tippetotje the painter goes to the woods beyond the castle to pick lilies of the valley and she meets msieu colson of the ministry who's on sick leave—his blood is too thin, it's down to 11—and together they walk on and meet you: are you coming to pick muguette? calls tippetotje the painter, . . . who, as you hear, comes from forest near brussels and so says it in french. And looking for muguette you tell them that veenman led you astray, even though it wasn't against your will; in fact, right at the beginning of the story a publisher asked you if you had anything for them, but afterwards you wanted to talk about 'the purpose of writing' . . . because it turned out that they had something against the manuscript . . . it was full of those . . . ugh, well . . . but you firmly refused to change or cut anything—after all, what's the use of writing something that forces a door open if by publishing it you have to scrap it, that's to say, gently close that door again? So you wrote back to them: you'd better give me the manuscript back. And suddenly they no longer had any objections, this and that . . . they bandied about big words and incomprehensible terms and wanted to start printing right away . . . but when you asked for the financial questions to be settled in a contract first, you found out that they were trying to paint you a friar* only so many copies printed and with a royalty that wasn't worth mentioning. Then you go on to tell tippetotje and msieu colson of the ministry, all the

* The non-existent reader may remember the expression 'to be fed up' . . . Well, here's another expression: 'to paint one a friar.' Such expressions will be replaced as soon as the above-mentioned non-existent reader will have reached the age of discretion and understanding.

while looking for muguette, that you went to your usual publisher with the manuscript and told her everything frankly—as no longer behooves a modern man—and your publisher replied, also with indecent frankness, well *you* can write things that others aren't allowed to write, people know you just blurt them out. But even so she pushed your manuscript aside and told you about her worries: that not a single book of yours sells well . . . the encyclical press says they're bad books and so the encyclical readers shun them like the plague . . . *like smallpox in termuren, in the old days* . . . and when you ask incredulously whether it really still exists, the . . . well, er, the inquisition? . . . she quotes an irrefutable fact, that the encyclical press had by accident reviewed a book of yours favorably, and that she was about to start a 2nd edition, but that suddenly a bishop or a cardinal—you don't quite know the distinction between those guys in uniform—wrote a circular that the book was unsuitable for encyclical readers . . . and the encyclical critic, who had made a mistake the 1st time, reviewed it a second time, unfavorably, and your publisher hasn't sold a single copy since.

## THE ORDER BOOK

*A few days later a gentleman knocked at ondine's door, he'd got the drawings of the 4 villas with him and asked for carolus bosmans . . . and ondine said: you show me those drawings. The estimate was given long ago by another carpenter, said the gentleman, but achilles made some changes at the last minute . . . I know, said ondine . . . he asked whether they could do it for that price . . . she glanced casually at the figures and although she'd never seen anything like it, she nodded: but then the gentleman disclosed something else: although the houses were going to be built on the derenancourts' land, who were, in theory, the clients, payment would be arranged as follows: listen . . . ondine listened and all she understood was that the discount and credit bank was going to give a long-term loan to the future owners, who would have to budget within this, to pay for the land, the masonry, etc . . . . and etcetera also included the carpentry, ondine gathered . . . to the contractors directly. She also understood that not only the future owners, but also the contractors, and everyone else who had anything to do with it, were going to be bamboozled . . . all except 1: the bank, young mrs derenancourt with her flat feet, who for all her angelic looks wouldn't, to put it crudely, take hold of the shitty end of the stick . . . and at the same time she was making this wilderness into a building site, 4 villas in chapel road, where no one else would go but chief clerks from the bank . . . only people who belonged to the bourgeoisie. Ondine recognized the masters from such a trick . . . she'd look out, she'd show them that other women could be crafty too . . . she signed all the documents and then went to fetch her father from the work shed: vapeur looked at all the plans and papers in surprise: these are plans for 4 villas, he said, as if the others didn't know. He also looked in the order book and said it was one of the biggest swindles he'd ever seen: the sucker who's got to do the carpentry there will be lucky! But what a start it gave him to see the book signed in his own name . . . only the c of carolus had been tampered with, but no, it wasn't a c, it was an o . . . and then he understood. Must you swear like that in front of strangers, asked ondine . . . but it didn't calm him down, on the contrary. First he asked sneeringly how they'd manage this and that but soon he forgot the actual business and dragged in all sorts of things that had nothing to do with it: if things were to go wrong she'd leave him in the lurch and would go and live at the castle again. Ondine was a match for him; she imitated his universal language: zio zio zito. The visitor looked at them as if he thought he'd got stranded in a nut house. Ondine saw it . . . she said to her father that mr achilles had arranged credit for them at a timber yard . . . and you're talking of helpers, she said; you can hire them can't you? . . . and anyway, haven't you got hands on your body? . . . and valeer, is he never going to start work?*

## THE PILGRIMAGE TO SAINT WOLFGANG*

Exalted above all strife by his inviolability, king noble of nobelgium sat high and dry but was far from happy; he was struggling with the writing of a white paper and cursed and fell fatally ill . . . and his wife told all who cared to know that there was only wine at lunch every other day, the other days they drank water like the humblest folk in termuren. This turned the scales, and the goat sapine—who was encyclical and sympathetic towards

* As this piece about reynard, contrary to custom, hasn't any obvious points of contact with what we might call . . . yes, what would we call it? . . . but draws its inspiration from local color—for instance: the king of the blacks with his white face—the reader has to be informed that the sum of the narration can be multiplied by a figure, hovering between zero and infinity, so that the narration will, after all, have points of contact with what we might call . . . yes, what would we call it?

the flemish—weepingly took her rosary and decided to go on a pilgrimage to saint wolfgang to pray for noble's illness. But she had hardly put her hat on when the billygoat bekard—who was also encyclical, but more fascist—took his coat out of the cupboard and said he was coming too . . . because out of sight out of mind, he said to his cousin the ram, who in his turn decided to come along . . . you never know what luck might come my way . . . but just to be on the safe side I'll take black sheep along who's just come back from the center for maladjusted citizens. The group was ready to leave when carcofas the donkey came to join them, because he simply loved the atmosphere of pilgrimages, he said, but no one paid any attention to that insignificant assistant priest, except sprotinus the cockerel who was coming as 5th wheel on the cart. But the only one who didn't show himself was reynard, who'd had an invitation, but thought: go to hell . . . I can always say that unfortunately I received the circular too late. Yet he was curious, and hid by the roadside where the pilgrims would pass. But he heard a rustling noise in the undergrowth and to his amazement he saw his uncle with a bandage round his head and a crutch under his arm . . . and soon they were agreed that sprotinus the cockerel would be for reynard and that gerarda the goose would dance her last dance between isengrinus' teeth; the wolf looked pensively at his crutch and said: do you think the best thing for me to do would be to throw my crutch between her legs and fall down on top of her? Reynard, however, thought it would be better to follow the pilgrims from afar and to tie a bundle of straw under the wolf's crutch so that no one would hear the tapping . . . no sooner said than done, and somewhere at an inn the procession stopped to stay the night . . . but they'd hardly sat down when the ram noticed a shadow at the window . . . the wolf was too careless again . . . and the ram shouted into the bar: you know, when we're on pilgrimage to saint Wolfgang, we must eat wolf's head if we want to earn absolution . . . and rattling with the saucepan he asked: who'd like some more wolf's head. The wolf, who was resting with his paws against the window pane, dropped his crutch in alarm and so he crashed into the room with the breaking glass. Sprotinus the cockerel flew up in a fright and hit the lamp, and at the same moment sapine the goat fell into a swoon. And although black sheep drew the rusty revolver which he had proudly carried in the war—on which you could still see the initials of soot-sheep: SS—it was no longer necessary: the donkey, who was so fond of pilgrimages, but not of this one, and who had fled upstairs in his fright, fell through the ceiling into the bar, on top of the wolf. And the wolf, who felt his crutch pressing into his body, began to scream: I'm dead, they're pushing a gun between my ribs. johan janssens.

## ON THE 1ST OF MAY

On this official holiday you're walking along chapel road together with the music master and johan janssens the poet and journalist . . . johan janssens stops for a moment to look at the long wall of the labor . . . and following his glance you see the socialist manifesto stuck on the wall: 'for peace and prosperity celebrate the 1st of may', and next to it the manifesto of the ultra-marxists 'for peace and prosperity celebrate the 1st of may' . . . and it is with bitter mockery which has to hide his despair, that he says: you'll see the Festival of Labor announced in large type in all the papers and all the columnists will tie a red ribbon to the corner of their column . . . but if I, johan janssens were to write about the 1st of may, I'd do it like this: it is the 1st of may but outside the socialist or ultra-marxist papers you notice nothing of it . . . because the 1st of may and the trade unions are official but the worker who used to wear a red flower in his buttonhole and was a little tipsy, has no longer anything to do with the 1st of may or with the trade unions . . . the 1st of may is the official festival and the trade unions are the official organizations of the respectable socialists with the prime minister as their leader and the laborer from the 1st dirty houses behind the labor knows that he mustn't grumble or strike, because the official trade unions would exclude him and rob him of his bread; koestler: who will protect the worker in a workers' state? And in the meanwhile the socialist minister of education has just got a law through that a pupil can choose between the subjects of religion and ethics . . . when the encyclical opposition stands on its hind legs and protests to the socialist prime minister . . . who gets cross at all the trouble they're making for him and with the flower of the 1st may still in his buttonhole he hands in his resignation no, he hands in the resignation of his government.

At that moment the music master, who's been listening as if it had nothing to do with him, says: this 1st of may . . . it's nothing to me . . . I'm not a social creature, I'm a music master creature . . . but I am dismayed that at this time, near the end of the 20th century, I see a socialist government fall on the 1st of may because it wants to enact the law of freedom of religion . . . because at this time, near the end of the 20th century on the official festival of the 1st of may, the encyclicals are still so powerful that they can stop a law for freedom of religion which has already been voted on, from being applied . . . and I lose my head, because I'm a freethinker, but every morning I have to start the day with my pupils who're also freethinkers, in the name of the father and the son and the holy ghost amen.

## THE SECOND OF MAY

*It became a gay time for ondine, she was more often in the town of the 2 mills than at termuren . . . she went to timber yards, to ironmongers' to buy nails, screws and hinges . . . I come with the compliments of mr achilles, she said everywhere, at every suitable and unsuitable occasion: it was a magic formula and she exploited it so much that she sometimes wondered whether someone else hadn't just said it too . . . that man over there, with the round right shoulder, hadn't he just said the same? But she never went straight home; she hung around in the market looking at the barrows where pins and cakes and cloth were sold; she stood by the entrance to the townhall where something different was going on every day . . . the day before yesterday a wedding coach driving into the courtyard, yesterday the 1st brigade coming out . . . a fire in the old church . . . and where today she saw the conscripts, with flowers on their caps, singing 'vivat leopold, let him come and kiss our balls'; she was appalled: those fellows by the station, those socialists, must have a lot of influence already, if people no longer respected the king . . . and she thought of walking past boone's café, past the 'justice and freedom' meeting hall, where the may flag was probably still hanging . . . but there she saw the cart from the timber yard; she called the driver: it was their wood he was carrying. She'd promptly forgotten boone and the socialists, climbed on the cart and was given a lift to termuren. When the timber had been unloaded, there were big piles of it, there was even wood under the trees by the chapel, and she kept having to chase the children away who clambered all over it with their dirty clogs; they climbed on top of it and kicked the others down who were trying to follow them up, or they crept into the middle, pretending it was a castle—the castle of termuren; they copied mr derenancourt or played dirty games together—ondine thought they'd gone to play somewhere else, but then she saw smoke rising from the planks: she climbed on top of the pile and saw them making a bonfire in their castle: what did they care if the whole lot got burnt and the chapel besides. She swore at them and boxed them on the ears right and left so that I was flung against a corner hitting his mouth . . . in no time he had a lip like this, his mother came to complain to ondine, patati patata, and ondine called out: if his lip's swollen, he'll have to look out he doesn't trip over it.*

*The villas grew amongst the brambles, stone after stone . . . vapeur tormented himself; the order book was never out of his hands, he'd decided not to hire any assistants but to do everything himself with valeer as his only helper. It was pathetic to see those two carrying planks, from the chapel next to their house to the site a long way further on . . . they trudged, their steps were uneven, and not far from the building site valeer began to swagger like a drunk . . . it was so pitiful that even ondine had to turn away . . . but it was even more pitiful to see him walking on the walls, when the joists were being laid: how he could keep straight, wobbling about like that, no one under-stood . . . it looked as if he hooked his toes on the walls like claws, right through his clogs; and people watched to see how he held the hammer in his maimed hand, trying in vain to drive a nail through the wood.*

## COMMENT AT THE END OF THIS CHAPTER

Hardly has the 1st of may gone, when the substitute 1st of may of the encyclicals arrives: our lord's ascension—and all the people who might have walked in the procession of the socialists and the ultra-marxists, walk in this procession, winding endlessly through all the streets of the small town of the 2 mills . . . and they're all in uniform, singing like the german soldiers used to do, and carrying a large misleading banner on which the same slogan is written as was launched by the socialists and ultra-marxists: for peace and prosperity. And you, who were writing again, writing and writing, you put your pen down and stand at the front door, looking at this endless procession . . . and you draw a line under the chapter and you don't know whether it's worth bothering to start on the next one: although you'd thought of a nice title for it: today a little sun and tomorrow some wind and some rain.

## COMMENT ABOUT THE ENDING

And then it's tippetotje the painter who presses yet another comment on you, even after the ending: this substitute 1st of may of the encyclicals, she says somewhat cynically, I looked at that too, and I saw all those young . . . young . . . yes, what shall I call them? . . . but jeannine from the 1st dirty houses was there too—in a light blouse stretching across her breasts which bobbed rhythmically up and down . . . and I thought it was a pity that it was only meat for mr derenancourt's mouth and not for mine. And that's precisely why it's wrong of you to think it isn't worth bothering to start another chapter: let the tits of the young encyclical girls dance across the finish, and simply write down the title: what was it again? . . . today a bit of rain and wind and maybe tomorrow fine weather.

# HERE BEGINS THE SECOND CHAPTER: TODAY A LITTLE SUNSHINE AND TOMORROW A LITTLE RAIN AND WIND

## IF ONLY I HAD KNOWN

Staring at the last pages of the finished chapter, the music master rests his musical head in his musical hand, and his silent face seems to say: oh well, it's been written now, it's too late to change anything . . . but I don't know, I'm sure . . . Then suddenly the words pour from his mouth: these last few pages are written much too hurriedly and rashly . . . of course it's quite true that the people of termuren WANT to be swindled, but weren't you a bit TOO pleased to use this as a nice ending to the chapter? It's a pity . . . I was talking about your book with somebody yesterday, and I must say, it's a great pity. Because that person happened to be a talented musician and he said: as far as I can gather from your description, this book looks like a symphony to me. Well, if indeed it is a symphony, in which various themes tumble about one another and run side by side, the main theme should have been underlined once again on the last page, in my opinion, with all the available instruments . . . and this hasn't been done, it's about an ordinary first of may, in which I'm not in the least interested, and so the book gives the impression that it's had a socialist sauce poured over it.

You raise your head, as if you're going to say something, but the music master gives a sign that he hasn't finished yet . . . but then johan janssens, journalist, suddenly makes a sign to him; he comes forward from the shadows and says: as far as this first of may is concerned, there are two things wrong with it; it's been looked at from too close by, with a squint at that, and it's too superficial as well . . . I know, I know, I wrote that little piece myself, but I didn't know it had to serve to pinpoint the last pages of that chapter; if I'd known, I would have written something quite different.

## A GAME LIKE ANY OTHER

It's a fact that all created things—that means, according to the bible: all things made out of nothing—end up by growing over the creator's head; so:

man has grown over god's head, and technology and economics have grown over man's head . . . and so your heroes, the music master and journalist johan janssens grow over your head. Look at what they just brought out of their quiver! Nothing less than that our book is a symphony. You reply with a protesting smile that it's just a simple game, a game like any other.

Like that man on the train the other day of whom you made a note in your notebook . . . but all you wrote down was: 'odd hat' and now you find you can't describe that hat any more because you've forgotten what was so odd about it . . . you tormented yourself with the question what he might do for a living, until he took a catalogue out of his pocket: le palais du levrier . . . and like little pros, with tight lips, he started telling you about dog racing; that it's an honest game, a game like any other . . . you looked at his hand which he had learnt to use without making it look conspicuous: a leather bag with 2 fingers and a thumb.

*It suddenly reminded you so much of ondine's brother, valeer, that you conjured him up and made him help build the 4 villas; you wrote that it was pathetic to see how he tried in vain to drive a nail through the wood with his maimed hand.* The wound also reminded you of little pros' mouth, which is a stripe, a notch cut by a sharp knife in a block of wood . . . and it reminded you of how little pros used to push words out of this groove which you only half understood, but which for all their unintelligibility would have been worth collecting and publishing as THE NAR-

RATIONS OF LITTLE PROS . . .

But while you're busy explaining all this to your heroes, msieu colson of the ministry sits up straight like a dagger: you're mistaken, at the end of the last chapter you said it was veenman who had a mouth like that, and that *his* stories were worth collecting with the title: the narrations of little veenman!

You stare at the floor, smiling timidly: of course, you did write that . . . in the piece: 'in memoriam little veenman' you borrowed little pros' mouth for a while to give it to veenman, but hell, it doesn't matter . . . and besides, it was better like that at that particular moment, so . . . now we'll give little pros his mouth back: here you are and thanks very much. Because if your book is a symphony to some people, to you it's a game, a game like any other.

## THE ANTHOLOGY (1)

It's a saturday evening in may, the silence over chapel road is only broken by the twitter of the birds in no-man's wood and by a pensive man poking his ear with his little finger, over by the 4 villas . . . and by msieu colson of the ministry who suddenly says: a symphony—an anthology, that's what it is!

And because he's silent after this, as silent as that dumb stone there, johan janssens the poet begins to explain what msieu colson really means: one evening, says johan janssens, we'd been turning the world inside out for the umpteenth time, and afterwards msieu colson drew a conclusion, as he usually does, but as I was still trying to think of some more, better arguments, it suddenly struck me that his conclusion was so true and so profound and so dead right, that I could accept it as a new Rule of life . . . and I looked at his words as they were floating in the evening sky over chapel road, and I said: we ought to write this down for the book on chapel road, msieu colson! but later, when I really wanted to write it down I'd forgotten it . . . and msieu colson had forgotten it too, because he said he'd only said it casually, only to hear his own voice in the evening air. But from that moment msieu colson always carries a notebook in his pocket and writes down anything that might be useful for the book on chapel road; anything he comes across in his humdrum civil service life, anything he sees, hears, feels, thinks, has said or left unsaid . . . for instance, about the pretty lucette, who used to live near the station in the town of the 2 mills, and who said that from her window she could see the brothel where a peasant girl got stranded by accident one day—probably because she'd heard that one could get easy, well-paid work in town—and who'd been there only 2 days when she jumped from the upstairs window into the street . . . and about his daily walk from north station to the ministry, that one day he met a postman who threw a letter into a letterbox, and then, noticing that the stamp had come off and was fluttering across the pavement . . . picked it up and threw it in the letterbox too . . . and that one day he met the legless man who lives on the pavement in a crate on wooden wheels; the women walk round him in a wide circle, on account of their short skirts . . . and that one day he saw a beggar holding out his tin mug in the rain, and the mug was half full of water; and then there were poems, tumbling from the tip of his pen into his notebook, without msieu colson of the ministry even being aware of it.

But standing in the door, in the may evening, you hear your wife calling from inside: supper is ready! . . . and because of her nerves and her thin blood you don't keep her waiting: you all go in at once . . . and johan janssens breaks his anthology in 2.

## THE ANTHOLOGY (2)

But in the house . . . which is full of vases of yellow broom . . . johan janssens continues his bisected anthology: so msieu colson wrote poems without knowing it . . . naturally, not poems like the ones that come out of the poetry factory, cut to rhyme and rhythm . . . but more like the 1 kloet made, when he was drumming on the closed shutters of the café by the 1st dirty houses, at 2 o'clock in the morning, shouting abuse at the landlord, matisse. He first shouted that matisse is an effeminate ninny whose girlish voice reminds you of a hermaphrodite and whose daughter is most certainly not his, with her thin body and bouncing, spindly legs, but with tits that dazzle all the drunks for miles around; you'd say how on earth is it possible that such a thin little body can support 2 such fantastic tits; and so there was this kloet shouting his poem at the closed shutters:

hey, so I went too far did I,
matisse?
so I'm a dizzard and a pea-merchant, am I,
matisse?
well, so are you
you're a this and a that; hey, where's my jacket?
hey, here it is
how dare you say I went too far
and where's my cap?
hey, here it is

You see, this is how msieu colson wrote his poems, one after the other . . . and when I, johan janssens, the poet, was waiting in the deserted station with him one night, we were looking at a measly bunch of people, waiting behind a barrier under the dark station roof—o, that huge, empty hall, and those 7 people behind that barrier—and I said: look, msieu colson, there's another poem for your collection . . . he answered a little hesitantly: I really ought to dedicate my poems to the writer of the chapel road book, because if it wasn't for that book I would never have thought of writing it all down.

Johan janssens is silent, but his silence is more triumphant than his words. Meanwhile msieu colson sits there quietly, he jokingly dashes away a tear and says: so I write poems that aren't poems and add them to our novel which isn't a novel . . . but an anthology.

## THE USE OF ART

So now you see that writing is useful . . . kramiek suddenly bursts out. Everyone looks in surprise at the mongrel figure who has just joined, rubbing his hands together as soon as the tiniest cloud of an easy solution appears on the horizon. So now you see that writing is useful. He explains himself by means of his hands and feet, that you had doubted the use of writing and the use of the novel, that you had expressed yourself contemptuously about that usefulness, after veenman's death, but that you can now see that there are people to whom the novel means something: for instance to the musician who compared your work with a symphony, even though he only knew it from hearsay . . . so what will he say when he actually READS it . . . and for instance to msieu colson of the ministry who wants to dedicate his poems, which aren't poems, to you and who calls them an anthology after the example of your novel . . . and for instance to me, kramiek, whose wish it is to live and die in literature . . . rubbing my hands together I, kramiek, can imagine you coming home in the evening and kicking off your shoes and throwing aside your collar and flinging yourself on ondine . . . figuratively speaking, of course, as you yourself said so beautifully . . . very figuratively speaking . . .

And as if he does it on purpose to give kramiek a stab under water and a kick in the pants, msieu colson of the ministry opens his anthology and reads out a poem: about the Use of Art: at a table in the ministry restaurant, sit 2 gentlemen, silently eating their soup, but then opposite them at the same table, there sits a very attractive lady—attractive in the eyes of the soup-eating ministry gentlemen—and they start talking and talking about something which is VERY difficult to understand: modern art. They utter words of which they haven't the faintest understanding and which, frankly, they're merely flinging against the wall. Then the lady leaves and the 2 gentlemen stop talking and finish their meal in silence, because what's the use ? The attractive lady—in the eyes of the ministry gentlemen—has gone.

When he's finished, kramiek begins to speak again, using words which he has read and properly remembered, but not understood, about the Use of Art.

## WITHOUT A SOCIALIST SAUCE . . . OR: THE MYSTERY

The broom is in flower and with a blob of chrome yellow paint next to her nose, tippetotje the painter enters indignantly: I'm angry, I'm bitter, because nobody thinks the end of the chapter is any good . . . what twaddle is this of the music master, saying that the end theme should have been something other than the 1st of may . . . has he gone deaf and blind, that he never noticed that the main theme isn't at all the 1st of may ? *The main theme is the 2nd of may, when ondine was thinking of going to have a look at the red flag which was surely hanging out at the café of the very first socialists . . . but she didn't go, she minded her own business, the timber that had arrived, from which she had to chase away the children* . . . because this is the way I understand your book: on either side of may the 1st there are 364 days when the worker is biting on his knuckles, steeped in poverty and worry, and has to bring up his kids all by himself . . . even though maybe he didn't make them himself . . . and that only on the day of our lord's ascension our little lord jesus is allowed to show himself, but for the rest of the year he has to sit like a stupid beetle in the priest's matchbox . . . and I also understand from your book that behind the changing decor of the human comedy there are always the same dirty bare walls, but that behind what was created out of Nothing, not even a dirty bare wall existed: behind everything there's the void, there's impotence, ignorance, black night, the god of the encyclicalists, the great secret . . . the everlasting question mark. I say this because I know that this is what you mean, writer . . . but to me the main motive really consists of the tits of the encyclical girls which I said were bobbing and dancing across the finish . . . because all that matters to me are the palpable things which you can see and touch, which have shape, like the flowering broom giving you the pleasure of painting with blobs of yellow . . . next to which you can paint an ondineke, lying down, with her white slip showing in the vault of her blue skirt . . . and in her slip her pink thighs . . . and between her pink thighs the everlasting secret which cannot be painted . . . and before which kramiek stands still with round eyes and a hollow head, saying: it's wonderful . . . but only licking his dirty thumb and fingers.

## THE CLAY PIPE

*So we'll be getting some money from the future owners, on the 1st of next month, will we? vapeur asked one evening . . . with a face as if it had never occurred to him that the future owners would Once have to start paying . . . actually, he was a bit frightened of it . . . he was so used to messing about in his shed for hours and hours without getting any money for it that in the end, whenever he'd repaired a chair or a cupboard, he daren't even count on being paid. Oh, just give me this or that, he'd say. And he always added the difference himself. Sometimes he'd have a drink first to give himself courage, but instead of making it easier, it got worse, because people who'd had a few trivial little boards put up, thought he was getting drunk on their money: he tormented himself with the thought that the day when he'd have to receive payment was inevitably getting nearer. You'd better go, he said suddenly one afternoon . . . at dinner time nothing had been said about it and nobody knew what he was talking about . . . at least valeer didn't . . . but ondine understood, because she'd been thinking of it too; she thought how remarkable it was that 2 people could be thinking of the same thing and strangely enough, would start talking about it at the same moment, because she'd been just about to say: those payments, I'll see to that. They were going to be the most blissful moments of her life, but she didn't intend to show this new joy to others . . . she reflected that you can taste pleasure and joy best like a sin which isn't seen . . . and also, that joy is doled out too sparsely in life, to share it lavishly with others. Yet, it became a beautiful day: they were all in agreement, even on the most improbable things about which they usually quarreled: vapeur told a moving, though puny story, from his youth . . . to which no one listened because they'd all seen or done the same . . . and valeer was allowed to go and buy himself a clay pipe in their cousin's shop, and smoke.*

## AN OLD ACQUAINTANCE

*The great day had arrived, the 1st of the month . . . and whatever ondine might have imagined it would be like . . . how she would walk past the un-finished villas, calling good-morning to her father and brother . . . it didn't turn out like that, because vapeur made a Sunday of it: I honestly couldn't work today, he said. She went to see the owners, the first I lived in pont street, not far from ondine's old school . . . she saw the girls entering and it seemed to her as if they were still the same girls as in her time . . . she even looked closely, to see if she could see herself . . . madame berthe stood in the door and looked at her, but ondine went past without a word . . . she thought, no, she didn't think anything, what was madame berthe to her, what was the whole world to her? And the owner from pont street, who was going to live in the furthest of the 4 villas, was a gentleman who dabbled in literature and wrote fairy tales; he and his wife lived with his mother and in all the years they'd lived there, his wife had quarreled with his mother every day . . . you might have thought it was about this or that in particular, but no, it was about everything . . . about an ornament his wife put here and his mother there . . . because it had always been there, hadn't it, ulrich? So ulrich was glad it was the 1st of the month and he could pay: it seemed to him that the house where he would at last live in peace had become his property by so many francs more. And the future owners of the 2nd villa were a couple living in rooms; the lady said that people of their social position had to live in a villa . . . and it was so lovely in chapel road, really the countryside. The 3rd owner lived in a house in the market square, ondine had to wait in an anteroom, just as in rich people's houses . . . but to her astonishment . . . it was monique, her former schoolmate! She hadn't changed at all, on the contrary, she came into the room wearing a night-dress printed with flowers, with a cord tied round the waist and falling open at the neck so that one wondered if she was wearing a slip underneath . . . and she wasn't ashamed! . . . ondine told her how staggered she was to meet an old friend here . . . and such a lovely dress, she said, I'd like to buy myself one like that. It struck her like lightning that she could actually buy one with the payment money. In a blind illusion of grandeur she told herself that they were big contractors: 4 villas, and this monique here, in spite of all her rich lady's airs, had to make payments for one of these little villas. She inspected the floral dress again and remarked that it was a trifle too showy, a little too bourgeois, as mr achilles would have said . . . and also . . . the way it falls open at your neck, she said, it's a bit too . . . too . . . yes, what shall I say? . . . But monique was her match, she nodded condescendingly and replied that ondine thought so because she belonged to the working class . . . the poor are easily offended by something which is quite normal to the rich . . . she was married to the chief bookkeeper at the filature, mr van wesenborgh, and she had bravely consented to live down in chapel road, pioneering and making a way through the wilderness for the other employees . . . but she'd only agreed on condition that her husband would never give her a child . . . children are so messy in the house . . . although, she knew chapel road well enough to know that it was haunted by the souls of still-born children. She laughed. Ondine's breath got caught in her throat, that throat in which there was no dimple as in other women's, and her heart began to race . . . that bookkeeper was bothering her too, she suddenly remembered mr brys, who was a relative of this lady muck. Chief bookkeeper, she had said, was it her husband then, who was a socialist? Monique, who had already opened the door to see ondine out, closed it again and explained that ondine got things confused . . . that to get things confused was something that didn't happen in the better circles . . . that it was her uncle, who had been ostracized by his family, actually . . . although he wasn't in fact a socialist; mr brys went to confession and communion every day, and his• purpose . . . or whatever he called it . . . was only to relieve the needs of the poor somewhat . . . he had started his sick fund again and it had almost 100 members . . . her husband, mr van wesenborgh, had been told by the gentlemen that her uncle would be allowed to return to the filature on condition that he and his sick fund would openly join battle with the socialist trade union . . . his family, too, would take him back then. And when she had explained everything carefully, monique pulled the door open again for ondine. Ondine remained seated, smiling. Mrs van wesenborgh stared at her in surprise. What about my money, asked ondine . . . oh yes, of course . . . she paid, but maddeningly slowly.*

## THE BEARSKIN

The music master and johan janssens, journalist, open their mouths at the same time . . . and together they say: I have . . . and after arguing who's going to let whom speak first, out of politeness, the music master says: *I have read that last piece about ondine—it's far too long and I didn't understand it . . . all those irrelevant bits, surely they could have been left out? for instance about the children at madame berthe's school or about the 1st and the 2nd and the 3rd future owners? God knows we may never see them again in your chapel road book. Seeing them again is the last thing that matters, says johan janssens, but that nothing of interest is said about them . . . All I remember of that whole long piece is that there's contemptuous talk of literature . . . the owner of the first villa, he was a gent dabbling in literature, writing fairy tales and living at his mother's house with his wife . . . but nothing is said about those fairy tales, only about the quarrels between his wife and his mother . . . oh yes, I also remember that monique wore a negligee . . . a night-dress, ondine called it . . . with gaudy flowers falling away from the neck . . .* but there's no bite in these remarks; when I was in brussels yesterday I looked at the women and at the clothes they were wearing and I made a remark that DID have bite to it, if I may say so myself: that some women may be wearing a bearskin and are still naked . . . while others might walk around stark naked and would still be wearing an impenetrable iron suit.

## THE DAUGHTER OF THE MACHINES

With a modest, and therefore engaging smile, msieu colson of the ministry comes into your garden, carrying his anthology, and sits down beside you in the shade . . . and of course the first thing he says is that it's hot, and whether you too have heard on the radium—as the old hunchback says—that there's going to be a heat wave . . . and with reference to that heat wave he starts *discussing the latest piece about ondine, which has expanded in the heat and lies there, limp and apathetic . . . and this leads him to compare your humdrum prose with johan janssens' far more impressive metaphoric style . . . you wrote that her dress fell away from her neck, while johan janssens said that the gaudy flowers on her dress fell away from her neck . . .* but—and here msieu colson opens his anthology and engagingly—but what he says about women is quite right, although incomplete, and that's why I allotted some space to another kind of woman in my anthology: the daughter of the machines:

how is it possible that so far I haven't written anything in my anthology about the man who comes to service the washing machine and the sewing machine and all the other machines in our house? Someone who's the absolute prototype of modern man, whose character is in marvelous harmony with the character of machines, and who is aware of this, and who therefore says that man really ought to stand in a field like a horse because he has become something that's made of iron and rubber and chemicals. I must also mention his distaste of any books that are novels or anthologies: what drivel, he says . . . and also his irrepressible urge to know Everything and to ask about Everything: *what law is this or that subject to? and how his daughter, who has the same big, questioning eyes and a large nobbly forehead, but who's shabbily dressed . . . but I forget, I still have to tell you of his inability, in spite of all his knowledge . . . his understanding of Everything, his insight into everything concerned with technology and chemistry and physics and biology and all the rest . . . his inability to make a decent living, in spite of all his genius and knowledge, to chase away the specter of poverty, because he only overhauls machines if there's anything he doesn't understand, and then he studies it for so many days that no one can pay him for his labor . . . but one day he was suddenly so depressed that he said: dammit, this has got to stop . . . and he put his mind to the same things as others put their minds to, he began to lie and cheat, he started buying up old broken down machines and he did them up a bit . . . as only he could do . . . and sold them as brand new and earned Gold. But nature cannot belie itself, because his daughter now, she's just the same, she stands beside him when he comes to repair our gas cooker and she holds the burner and the soldering bolt; she's thin and wispy, not attractive, only intelligent, only gifted where it concerns machines . . . daughter of the machine man, daughter of the machine itself . . . and one day she comes back to our house, alone, I open the door and see her standing there, with her little smile . . . and she's come to ask could she have another look at my wife's weaving loom please, to see how it works, how it was made, according to which laws it was built.*

## THE 4th OWNER

*There was one more person whom ondine had to go and see . . . because there were 4 villas and therefore also 4 future owners . . . and this last one lived far away in a street she had never heard of . . . she walked and walked and asked everywhere where scherreveld street was . . . it was near the cemetery, almost in the fields, in an even drearier neighborhood than termuren: it was a recently built row of laborers' dwellings, still smelling of unfinished payments: she wondered why they were moving; maybe only to dig a new pit in order to fill the old one. But all her knocking and ringing and looking through the letterbox into the cold, empty corridor, were no use: no one came to answer the door . . . she looked at her list and saw their name was schatt: treasure; a promising name. She went home, and in chapel road she remembered that she'd again forgotten to look at the socialists' café. And although in the two following months she didn't see the schatts either—the house in scherreveld street remained like a mortuary—she regularly came home with a lot of money. As they hadn't started repaying the timber yard or the ironmonger's yet, it looked as if there was no end to it . . . the money was piled up, it was even becoming ridiculous, the way it was stuffed into that humble purse on the cupboard. Until now money, to her, had only been a symbol, the outward sign of belonging to the rulers' ranks, but now money became currency, with which she could buy herself all sorts of things she coveted . . . first a night dress with strange, large flowers, very low cut at the neck, and then, yes, for years and years they'd had to go without meat; why shouldn't they, once or twice a week, open the front door and let the smell of roast meat waft into the street? It was rather late in the afternoon and in the butcher's shop there was nothing left but some mince . . . but mince was all right too . . . you had to season it with pepper and salt and a bit of onion, add an egg and some bread crumbs, and braise it in the oven: that's what it said in her old recipe book, from madame berthe's. She went home, but on the way she tasted some of it, and raw it tasted even better than it ever could with breadcrumbs and whatnot . . . she took another bite and another, and after a while she made a bargain with herself: one half for her and one half for the others at home . . . but she nibbled so much from that other half too, that it wasn't worth bothering any more, she licked the paper clean and threw it in a crumpled ball into the ditch, at the bottom of chapel road . . . she was no longer hungry and with nausea she watched the others eating their hotch potch with a scrap of bacon.*

## THE INAPPROPRIATE SPEECH

Reynard stood outside the inn and heard the wolf screaming blue murder while he was being mauled . . . but although reynard might have been his brother's keeper once, it had never been his intention to lend his legs to somebody who'd give him a kick with them in his own arse . . . he entered, amidst the confusion, and cordially shook hands with everyone: bekard and sapine the goats, carcofas the donkey, and also his uncle, with the crutch between his ribs. Good evening, my dear friends, I was in such a hurry, I'm out of breath, because unfortunately I received the invitation to the dance in noble's honor too late . . . but no one was fooled, his words were received coolly and the donkey said bluntly what the others thought: you have remarkable talent, but what you lack is a sense of drama, and in any case, the way you speak flemish, your pathos sounds like so much feverish ranting*. Thanks for the kindly interest, thought reynard, who didn't worry . . . because words were wind, which couldn't be cooked and eaten: he devoted all his attention to sprotinus the cockerel, and when the crowd left the inn, they were standing a bit at the back together, to the uneasiness of the cockerel who'd rather be in the front row. But reynard held him by one wing and discussed the essence of the novel and the freedom of verse . . . you, who are an existentialist poet, he said to the cockerel . . . and again, he halted his steps . . . and although sprotinus saw the distance between them and the other pilgrims widening, he began to recite his latest poem with 1 eye shut: oh, how often would I not, at the distant eastern front, wish to while the time in dreams, if it wasn't that I must, on the dung heap over yond, rush from one hen to the next . . . Not bad, said reynard, cocking his head, but what you lack is the true drama of closed eyes which speaks flemish and makes your pathos rant* even more. Thereupon sprotinus closed his eyes . . . but reynard had already got hold of his wings and

* the reader—if such there be—who has had the courage to read as far as this page—where does he keep getting the courage from?—will understand these words better if he remembers that an encyclicalist weekly once gave this verdict on johan janssens himself.

was about to make off without the pilgrims noticing anything; unluckily, his uncle just happened to look round and started to shout: share it! share it! So then all the others saw it too, kicked isengrinus' crutch from under his arm and began to chase reynard . . . sprotinus dangled to and fro as reynard ran, and with his heart thumping in his throat he said: tell them not to bother; I agree with your criticism and I commend my spirit into your hands. Reynard stood still and addressed his approaching enemies with the most beautiful but most inappropriate speech, for no sooner had he opened his mouth than the cockerel spread his wings and flew into a tree. Cursed be the mouth that speaks when it ought to be silent, stammered reynard, taken aback . . . and from the tree the cockerel replied: and may the devil blind him who closes his eyes when he should keep them wide open. Sprotinus would have added more, never a wise man who isn't a fool at times, but this didn't mean that reynard was like carcofas the donkey who dropped his glasses twice, tripping on the same stone, and trampled them with his own ass's feet: reynard didn't want to hear any more and hurried away from the spot where he'd been such a fool. johan janssens.

## FEAR

It is still june, but the heat wave they talked about hasn't come, there was a thunderstorm and then it started to rain and rain and it's still raining . . . tippetotje listens to the distant rumbling and says that ever since her childhood she's been afraid of thunder, although she was never afraid of being struck by lightning: she was frightened of the rumbling itself, in the same way as she was frightened by a cart dumping a heap of rubble or by a procession in the small town of the 2 mills to the sound of drums: I used to think . . . well, no, I didn't think, she says . . . but I used to have visions of terror and death . . . I didn't see my own death but that of other people . . . I saw ruins overgrown with weeds, I saw decomposing corpses, I saw skeletons in every corner, I saw the end of the world: a vision I often tried to paint, in vain—later, when I'd become a painter—but at that time I was still little tippetotje who didn't know she *had* to become a painter—and if I'd been able to paint it I would have called that vision: after the terror. Because I wasn't really afraid of what was going to come, I was afraid of what was going to stay, after it had come. Nietzsche dreams of the übermensch who will come when man has disappeared from the face of the earth . . . I tippetotje am afraid of the time in between those 2 . . . thousands of years, and maybe more, when there will be absolute silence on earth and only weeds will grow, so high, and only vermin will thrive, in teeming swarms. But as I grew older I rationalized this fear, it was something below the heart and I called it a stomach ache; I went to all the doctors and got all sorts of medicines for my stomach ache which wasn't a stomach ache but fear . . . fear of the thousands of years of absolute silence and absolute death which would reign over the world: and now I try to get rid of this by painting it out of my system, like you try to get rid of it by writing it out of your system . . . and wherever I go, wherever I open a book, I see the same thing: fear of the unnameable, looming in the air like fate . . . and we, who are inwardly forced to write about it or paint it, turn it, in spite of everything, into something with a certain beauty . . . and so it can happen that in the encyclical spectator, the fascist camp, or the scarlet debate, they find this beauty of fear eerie and condemn the Reality of fear as something they don't wish to see . . . and one might say: I don't write or I don't paint for those people any more, but if we, who are so few, are alone in feeling this fear, don't we have the duty to go on warning the others?

But as the distant rumbling of the thunder dies away, everybody answers tippetotje . . . msieu colson of the ministry and the music master, poet and journalist johan janssens, professor spothuyzen and mr pots, you yourself and even kramiek: but what is our duty? . . . to express our fear as a piece of information . . . or to bear it alone and to avoid creating a panic . . . or to resign ourselves and let the weeds grow after the terror until the über-mensch comes and finds a lone human skull? And in the silence kramiek says: just imagine it's My skull they'll find!

## VALEER'S COUSIN GETS A HEART

*Every time ondine brought home something different: paper flowers to put in a vase, a dress, an apron . . . they hadn't got enough change in the shop in the small town of the 2 mills, and she said: all right, I'll have 2 dresses then, then that'll be just right . . . she bought cocoa powder, something you couldn't buy in termuren . . . what could you buy there, apart from wooden clogs? . . . she made chocolate milk and sent valeer to fetch their cousin: I suppose you don't have this in your shop? she said. Far from having it in their shop, she'd never tasted it and asked for another cup . . . she asked did ondine drink it every day, when she used to live at the castle . . . and there was no nastiness in her question, she was so innocent that she thought she was giving ondine great pleasure by reminding her of that time . . . of a life she herself might like to lead. She was now 15, but in a short time she had got the figure of a 20 year old, especially her bosom was unbelievable, but she still had no idea that termuren boys fought with peasant boys from further up, about her; ondine said to her aunt one day what a good thing it was that the gentlemen had forgotten termuren, because they would have had to hide their daughter in the attic: I, ondine, I had enough sense not to let them come too near, and anyway, I was too encyclical, but your daughter . . . I don't know what might have happened to her. I can hardly hide her in a sack, can I, said her mother. Ondine said, yes, it would have been difficult to hide her in a sack, but surely she could be kept away from the café . . . because she always comes to us afterwards, crying when somebody has made rude remarks about her breasts. It wasn't true that she came to them to cry, but ondine had overheard valeer and their cousin whispering and had heard her say: my mother wants me to laugh when they make remarks about my heart. And what surprised their cousin most of all: that they forbade her to roam about freely with valeer, although he was the only one from whom she wouldn't have minded any remarks about her heart. She asked at home why she wasn't allowed to go and see ondine and valeer any more . . . they drink chocolate milk there . . . she was such a child still that one day she dropped in at ondine's and said: now we've got cocoa too; the traveler brought us a bag of it.*

## WHITE AND BLACK SNOW

It's still june and still raining and johan janssens, journalist, travelling home on the train from brussels, together with msieu colson of the ministry, says that according to the calendar summer starts tomorrow and that they must have made a mistake in their calculations: they tuck away the few left-over hours in each year in a leap year but who can say whether maybe they're still a bit MORE out. Who can say whether maybe the earth isn't a round ball but an egg with a fat round bottom and a large point? because if after god you've also lost faith in science, what then? . . . And with a smile which soothes his despair, like jam on a stale piece of bread, he concludes: maybe tomorrow there'll be snow in june. Msieu colson adds: there's snow already, but it's black snow, falling on your non-believing spirit . . . and talking of snow, I found something about snow in a forgotten corner of my anthology: snow in the metropolis: 2 policemen, after wading through the black slush, are standing round the coke fire . . . and what world-shaking events are they discussing? . . . one policeman says: but I told jefke and dolf . . . the other policeman nods his head, with drooping mouth, looking into the coke fire . . . yes, they told jefke and dolf and for the rest they dry their shoes which will get wet again in a minute when they walk on

johan janssens nods and nods, with drooping mouth, just like that policeman . . . and he says to the other policeman, no to msieu colson: this reminds me of what you said earlier on: black snow . . . black snow in the metropolis; when I gave a talk about the Poet-in-his-time last year, there was an audience of 12, plus a fellow who was asleep and who snored to the rhythm of my words . . . and when it was over a shabby and rather simple-minded woman came up to me . . . with high-laced shoes and a faded brown shapeless dress . . . and she explained her case to me, that she'd applied for a job on the newspaper and that they'd told her that she should first have written a book before she could write for the paper—it must have been that cynic hooizolder—and then she explained to me that she was now writing a book and would I please give my opinion on it . . . all sorts of feelings of pity came streaming through my body and I said, all right. But I knew I'd never see that book.

## I OUGHT TO HAVE A SWEETHEART

*In ondine's opinion, this traveler in cocoa was in and out of their cousin's house rather a lot . . . he really had to be in the town of the 2 mills but soon enough found his way down chapel road to termuren . . . he hardly ever had an order in Christ's shop, and ondine, who saw him at the level crossing, asked him bluntly what it was he'd lost here . . . he looked embarrassed . . . very embarrassed, when she asked him this and that; he was as transparent as glass, she'd never seen a man who was so virginal, and he a commercial traveler! He must go through life wearing blinkers, otherwise it wasn't possible . . . he'd fallen in love with their cousin's bosom, it was crystal clear . . . as soon as he entered the shop ondine stuck her nose round the door too . . . she asked him how old he thought their cousin was . . . twenty, he said . . . they laughed at him: can't you see from her face she's hardly more than a child? . . . and he, poor duffer, was ashamed again, turned flaming red and in his embarrassment he let slip that if he'd known he would have waited . . . waited, what with? . . . He was silent and hated ondine so much that he thought . . . no, it didn't come as far as a thought, he way one of those people who read books, and write poems about trees and dream about their lonely heart, who feel rather than think . . . he felt that he was made of glass and this ondine of steel; that's why he didn't really hate her: he was afraid she would break him. Yet it was useless for ondine to make scathing remarks about him to christ, because he'd enchanted the family with his naive talk; he's such a decent chap, they answered. Decent? It made ondine roar with laughter; what's the point of being decent if you get kicked around by everybody else who isn't decent . . . and anyway, decent? Wasn't it rather because he'd said, casually, that they had a large business in brussels? They replied that it was nothing but spite on her part, because she, ondine, couldn't get a sweetheart; ondine laughed again, much too loudly . . . she named all the men who had wanted to marry her . . . and out of sheer defiance she bought herself a sunshade in town, although there was only a faint wintry sunshine, alternating with blustering gusts of rain. Wasn't it the truth, the deep, deep truth, what they'd said about a sweetheart? No, she said to herself; I feel so wretched because the summer won't come and I can't stand this rain every day . . . it makes me think too much of pain and death . . . and then I think I shan't live very long, because I feel so tired and sad . . . and besides, dying itself is nothing, but dying like me, without knowing why I've lived . . . I ought to have a sweetheart, a man*

*and if at that moment she hadn't felt such a pain in her belly, she would have laughed at her more than peculiar train of thought.*

## A RESPECTABLE AGEING SOCIALIST

Johan janssens says, in his capacity as a human being: I'll tell you about a respectable, ageing socialist who, when he was still a child, lived in another small town of 2 mills, where anyone who was a socialist and joined the union, got the sack . . . and so he'd come to work at the labor in this small town of 2 mills and joined the very first socialists and helped to distribute their news sheet called justice and freedom, in the evenings . . . at first, for many years, after his day's work at the labor, and later, when they had a certain number of members paying contributions, officially, and for a hunger wage . . . gradually the party grew into a mammoth party, with a cinema and a bakery and a clinic and a library and a printing works and a co-operative, whose functionaries drove around in cars . . . but he went on distributing the news sheet, always for the same pittance . . . then finally the last war broke out, and he fled to france with the money he'd just collected with the news sheet . . . but after having escaped to france, he remembered that the money wasn't his and that justice and freedom wasn't being distributed any more . . . and so he returned, with the money, and he started delivering the news sheet again. But remember that meanwhile the world had been turned upside down: the nazis had abolished democracy and disbanded the socialist party, and filled justice and freedom with their OWN PROSE—but the respectable socialist didn't realize that on his return a new chapter had begun: he stupidly carried on with the previous chapter, distributing the nazi justice and freedom. Then the war was over and the nazi chapter closed, the world became the old world again in which the respectable socialist, to his astonishment, and dismay, was denounced as a traitor to the socialist cause . . .

johan janssens halts, in his capacity as a human being, and then continues his narrative: look, this was my introduction, now I'll tell you the real story about the respectable ageing socialist: in the evenings he sits in his living room, the radio is on and the socialist paper lies on his knees, and he says to his wife, the respectable ageing wife of a socialist—he says: our socialist prime minister, there's a great man for you . . . but why do you think he no longer wears a top hat?

## QUESTION TIME

There's johan janssens coming down chapel road, and it's only just afternoon . . . he must have caught the 12.15 from brussels, otherwise he couldn't be here yet . . . and tippetotje, who's still painting the unguarded level crossing, puts her palette down and asks: what's this, back so early, and you look like a beaten dog . . . is something the matter? Trouble with your work, with which you earn your bread and that of little jo janssens? Johan janssens stands still, not knowing where he stands . . . he looks at tippetotje's drawing, not knowing what he's looking at: his heart is 1 big wound, dammit, and he curses: I was questioned by the editor-in-chief, who asked me why I Always wrote about picasso and magritte, and I looked at him in surprise and I said I also wrote about breughel and bosch and kurt peiser and permeke! . . . but the editor-in-chief shook his head and said that They had told him that I wrote too much about picasso and magritte . . . for although they are great, I mean, well-known ultra-marxist painters, we must in the first place think of our own clique of painters and poets and sculptors, insignificant though they are, according to you . . . They don't like the work of picasso and magritte because the one is a cubist and the other a surrealist, and they don't understand it, cubism and surrealism, they paint still-lifes and landscapes in the same way as it's always been done . . . as we've always been used to it . . . so you'd better write about them and say that they're the greatest artists . . . But . . . I answered . . . But the editor-in-chief raised his hand and said: quiet. And so, I, johan janssens, was quiet. The editor-in-chief went on: we usually have committees for everything and so we'll also have a committee for the cultural page, consisting of intellectuals who are at least qualified to talk about art . . . these intellectuals will meet once a week and decide what you, johan janssens, will write or won't write. I, johan janssens, demanded that the list of intellectuals be shown to me first: and there at the top was dr pascalius prostituaan. Right. I took my month's salary in silence and I left the editor's office in silence; although my heart was 1 big wound, dammit, I thought wryly: the articles on cultural life . . . which I only manage to get done by writing till my fingers are stiff with cramp . . . and which I now may or may not be allowed to publish . . . that these articles will be passed from hand to hand, from dr to pr . . . and the one will say yes and the other no—while most of them won't dare say Anything—and so there'll be a page once a year instead of once a week.

## DEAD SOULS

*The pain which hardly ever left ondine since that night, tormented her more than anything . . . she badly needed to sow discord and strife, to pick quarrels and to wear clothes of which the others daren't dream: it was her only support in life. Meanwhile valeer walked around like a tramp in his torn, patched jacket . . . he had no time to go and see their cousin, the rafters of the villas had to be put in place because it rained and rained and rained . . . but when in the late evening there was time, he didn't go either . . . he stayed with zulma, by the stove, licking his broken fingernails and the chafed skin on his hands; everything hurt him and he was too tired even to feel hungry. And their cousin? . . . valeer must have heard something, somehow, otherwise he wouldn't sit there musing so quietly . . . or was it musing what he did? . . . he put his tormented head on the bar of the stove and fell asleep at once, exhausted from clambering and scrambling all day, and struggling against his arch-fear, up on the scaffolding. At the other side of the stove sat vapeur, thinking of his invention, he hadn't dared look at it of late, it was buried under dust . . . formerly, working on it day in, day out, he'd always been of good courage . . . tomorrow it will be finished, he used to think . . . but now, working on those 4 villas, it seemed to him as if he could see his invention in its true perspective, from a distance, and he doubted whether he, carolus hosmans, would ever be capable of finding solutions for which men had searched for centuries . . . who or what are you, anyway, he said to himself . . . are you a stupid bungler, the half-baked fool they take you for, walking around with a fixed idea, or are you really . . . a genius . . . who's going to find by intuition what all the great scholars have overlooked? He didn't know, although he did believe that maybe . . . and then he made excuses as if someone might have overheard his thoughts and would laugh at him. What I lack is knowledge, he said. I ought to look at my Mechanics, I ought to study the resistance of Materials, and things like, what do they call it, geometry of space . . . but these were things he had said ever since he was 16, and which he repeated every 3 or 4 years or so, without ever carrying them out. The evening passed in dead silence. But when ondine entered she prodded those dead souls awake and asked about their work . . . how much timber had been used now, and whether the pulley, which was hired by the day, couldn't be returned yet; now that the stairs are in, perhaps you could carry everything up, she said. Valeer gaped at her and looked at his father: his father didn't know either; the work was beyond his strength, he had to do it all by himself, really, because valeer could hardly be counted . . . valeer had had to nail some skirting boards today, the easiest job on the whole house, and when vapeur, who'd been putting in doors in the meanwhile, came to see how he was getting on, what do you think? . . . valeer had nailed them all the wrong way round. He thought ondine didn't understand a thing like this, she talked figures all the time, whereas he thought of only 1 thing: the bed on which he could finally lie down to sleep. However, ondine understood all too well, but what was life worth if she couldn't badger anyone? Nothing, she might just as well hammer a nail in the wall and hang herself.*

## EVEN AN ONDINE MAKES MISTAKES

*Vapeur's thoughts crawled around in an endless spiral . . . in the order book there was a page about glazing and in the early days he'd said: yes, that's for the glazier . . . but now that the doors and windows were in position, and no glazier had turned up from anywhere, his unrest grew: he was frightened of glass: it broke, it splintered and crashed, it cut your wrists. So there was nothing for it but to give his gain—haha, my gain, you mean my loss—to somebody else who wasn't frightened of glass. But no, surely that couldn't be so, surely a carpenter didn't take on glazing . . . or did he . . . and he daren't break away from his spiraling thoughts, for fear he might find out the truth; the truth that he'd broken and wrecked himself, had worked himself to the bone, all for nothing . . . and that wouldn't have been so bad yet, he would have given the best years of his life, to break even . . . his cruelest worry was this, that he would be out of pocket by a fantastic amount. It's all ondine's fault, that snotty-nosed brat, he defended himself . . . but would this cut any ice with a judge, to hide himself behind his daughter? Damn, damn. Shouldn't we start paying for the wood? he asked her. Yes, it was true, there had been a reminder, . . . but ondine couldn't part with the money just like that . . . the banknotes had piled up into a fat wad . . . she'd put them in a different place, because lying on the cupboard it looked like a poor man's savings, as if through years of toil and deprivation they'd managed to save a bit . . . she'd bought a little iron casket in town and now it would be a shame to empty it and pay that stupid timber yard . . . maybe next time on the first of the month she might think of it again . . . now she went on buying herself all sorts of things without worrying. And when it was the 1st of the month . . . of july, and by god, it was still raining . . . she took 1,000 francs in her hands, turned and turned the banknote, hesitating, looking about at all the lifeless things around her; and she saw herself closing the iron casket and creeping upstairs to the attic with the 1,000 francs in her hands to hide the money in a tin. When she turned round she started violently at the sight of valeer's head in the trapdoor . . . it was only then that her eyes were opened to the crime which someone else inside her head committed, and only then did her heart begin to thump: how long had he been standing there? He went straight to the tin, almost stepped on it . . . but no, he walked across it and took some tobacco leaves which were hanging there to dry. Suddenly he saw ondine . . . then it was his turn to change color, he asked her not to tell anyone about it. About what? That I took a tobacco leaf, he stammered . . . he was so small and humble, and began to explain how he'd been allowed to buy a clay pipe, but hardly ever got any tobacco. And do you stuff it into your pipe like that? asked ondine. She meant it as a joke, to make him laugh for once and to show him that she wanted to be his accomplice. But he was such a dope, he didn't understand jokes, but started giving explanations. She went into one of her rare spells of pity: every time she managed to scrape through some wickedness, she permitted herself a little pity for others, who were less crafty . . . who were less lucky. She asked him why he never went to see their cousin any more, and she was about to give him some advice . . . but he withdrew stubbornly into his dopeyness: Because! he replied evasively to all her questions. She shrugged her shoulders and went downstairs, smiling. It was stupid of her; she ought to have chased him downstairs first before going down herself. But . . . even an ondine can make mistakes.*

## DEEP RIVER

Msieu colson of the ministry comes running along, out of breath, *when the others have already heard about ondine's stupidity* . . . he says indignantly that they should first listen to his story about bessie smith . . . oh, bessie smith, he says . . . and then he doesn't know what else to say, till suddenly, in a raw, jarring voice, he wrenches a negro song out of his guts: oh what strange fruit hang from the trees in america! Kramiek bursts out laughing. Msieu colson looks at him as if about to bash his brains in: bessie smith was a negro girl whose soul was shaken to and fro like a duster, between the cotton plantations and the american suburban gasovens . . . whereas in fact her soul should have been blossoming like a wild flower in her own land: africa: and this is why she sang deep river . . . because to her the river jordan, that deep river separating the jews from the promised land, was really the atlantic ocean separating the american negroes from africa—and this is why she sang: oh what strange fruit hang from the trees in america, meaning her brothers and sisters who were lynched there . . . and this is why she sang of heaven which was promised to them, but which would probably be just like the new york trams: one compartment for whites and one for negroes. And then . . . says msieu colson, solemnly and severely . . . bessie smith was going to sing in a show one evening . . . but on the way the car overturned and when they'd managed to get her out from underneath they found an artery was cut and the blood—the blood of a singing blackbird . . . was flowing away like precious liquid from a bottle . . . hurry, hurry . . . she was driven to the nearest hospital but at the gate they said they were sorry but they weren't allowed to admit negroes . . . gloo-gloo, said bessie smith's blood, flowing away . . . and they drove her to another and yet another hospital, till finally they found a small, primitive hospital for negroes: but when they got there the bottle was empty: oh what wonderful bottles flow empty in america

msieu colson of the ministry falls silent and all the others are silent as well. Only your wife, with the authentic, shrill, sardonic humor of the american negroes, says: on this rainy day I think I can hear bessie smith's blood saying gloo-gloo . . . but I suppose it's only the gutter of our shed.

## BUTANE GAS

It's 1 of those abysmally dreary sunday afternoons and l.p.boon, the author, sits alone and when he's alone he's alone:

weary of fighting against the ever growing flood of Folly, against the creepers which close behind the pioneer in the jungle, blocking the path which he has hacked out, struggling for his life . . . weary of fighting against those who sell ideas that resemble his ideas and penetrate everywhere like butane gas: very light in weight but stinking and dangerous. Because although l.p.boon proclaims a brand of nihilism, his nihilism isn't hopeless: he knows, he has a vague premonition that out of the collision between the existing world-ideologies, something new, something different will emerge . . . and even if it isn't going to be any better, there will at least be new l.p. boons. Neither is his nihilism sadistic, like that of others, whose nihilism looks deceptively like his. They dance the carmagnole on the ruins and walk with their thing poking out of their fly, raving and swearing and smashing things up: l.p.boon, however, proclaims the nihilism of the future, in which the earth will have come closer to the poet's dream

but this isn't the reason why it's 1 of those abysmally dreary sunday afternoons, on which the author is alone . . . it's an abysmally dreary sunday afternoon because he was unable to word this last piece, this bit in parentheses, clearly and pointedly enough, vividly and brilliantly enough . . . because sitting amongst the books which he himself has written, from which he hasn't even bothered to blow the dust away, he sees 'forgotten street' lying on the table . . . it lies there indeed forgotten. And when he sees the name: louis paul boon, and reads what this louis paul boon has written, he thinks: god almighty, what a fool. And he wonders where this louis paul boon gets it all from, writing down things he doesn't mean! Forgotten street, look at that: everybody chooses a title with something forgotten in it . . . forgotten street, forgotten village, forgotten house, forgotten man . . . and so every writer walks around with the idea of living in oblivion, of not bothering about anybody else, because even though community life is becoming an ever greater necessity, it breaks the individual. And every writer chooses something with street in it . . . forgotten street of the fishing cat without joy without end. And so you see how small a man is as a writer: he thinks it's all coming out of his own head but it isn't, they're ideas hanging in the air like butane gas, penetrating into his little brains. That's why it's a sunday afternoon of abysmal dreariness: because only these things get down on paper . . . but the things about which he broods till he's worn out, are never born.

## RAIN AND OLD LACE

It's mid july and still raining; all day and all night it rains and rains . . . and your wife, whose blood is too thin and whose nerves are playing up again, stands by the window looking at the rain, and says that in other years we were in the ardennes, camping . . . do you remember we were by that spring in the forest, or by that brook rippling over the stones, suppose we were there now, in this rain, it's bad for my nerves, and in other years we used to be in the kempen with our tent . . . do you remember we were behind that grove of fir trees, just suppose we were there now, in the rain, it's bad for my nerves . . . you interrupt her: yes, sure, it's bad for my nerves too. But your wife doesn't bother about your nerves, she goes on praying her rain-litany and says that the pretty lucette is bound to be disappointed too, because whereas she used to come with us to the ardennes, with her music master in a tent next to ours, she can't go to the ardennes now . . . in the 1st place because of the rain which is so bad for my nerves and in the 2nd place because of that tiny piece of shrapnel which is festering in her thigh, because she was in the bombing, way back in the war, in 1940 . . . she's in bed now and the shrapnel has been removed . . . she won't be coming tonight and we'll be all by ourselves again and we'll have to amuse ourselves listening to the july rain, it will be bad for my nerves. Your wife is still standing by the window when someone knocks and you let msieu colson of the ministry in. He sees her standing there—she on this side of the glass and the rain on the other side—and he says that he's suddenly found a title for his story: rain and old lace; first I took arsenic and old lace, like that film in which 2 old ladies, dressed in old lace, murdered several people in their cellar with arsenic . . . but the film will soon be forgotten and so the title would be pointless . . . well, I use the rain as the setting of my story and I'll call it rain and old lace. Are you listening?

there used to be 3 Lammers sisters . . . the 1st one is now a doctor's widow, living in a house which is spotless but worn with scrubbing, together with the 2nd, almost equally old sister, who'd been courted in her youth but had never got married . . . both have grown old and grey, only to peer into the rainy street from behind the curtains . . . but now, in the evening rain, they take their umbrellas and go to visit the widower, who was married to the 3rd sister after he'd courted the unmarried sister for a time. And here the drama begins. When the 2 grey old sisters are leaving this grey old gentleman and he opens the door to see them out, he very briefly kisses the unmarried sister, in the corridor . . . at that moment the oldest sister, the doctor's widow, who has just taken the 2 wet umbrellas from the umbrella stand, looks round and sees what's going on. Here the drama ends. But when they're back behind their curtains and look into the street to see what *might* happen there in the rain, the oldest sister keeps saying: you let him kiss you in the corridor.

## ONDINE HOPES FOR A DELUGE

*That traveler from brussels had said in a mood of tender love that he'd wait, but his more and more, frequent visits showed that he was becoming impatient. He started going there every sunday, he even stayed all day; at first he used to bring a packet of sandwiches so as not to be a bother at lunch time . . . but soon he was there on Saturday evening and stayed till monday morning. He ate and slept there. He sat by the stove, watching the peasants playing shove ha'penny, making a lot of noise and amusing themselves with cousin maria . . . he tried to save his face by sitting in a corner playing cards, as if he didn't care about her and didn't mind that there was a bit of rough-housing going on over there; but he was a poor actor because he couldn't remember a single card and kept losing the game, no matter how hard he tried to keep his mind on it. He yawned and got a headache, he got tired waiting so intently for closing time, when he'd have her alone for a few minutes in the courtyard: there he suddenly became quite different from what he had intended to be all evening: irritable from the long hours of deadening boredom, he kept nagging her that she shouldn't be so free and easy with those peasants. They're not peasants, they're termuren boys, cousin maria replied. He knew this as well as she, but it was a habit; once she was a madam in brussels she'd call everyone a peasant too. And I even noticed someone touching your heart.*

*It wasn't true, he hadn't seen anything, he only said what he'd imagined during those boring card games; cousin maria was still too young to understand that his impatience and his restrained passion were the cause of his bad mood. She was also too simple-minded; her mother had said that this traveler would be a good husband for her one day and that she must be nice to him. And she was nice. She smiled at him now and again and she allowed him things which she might not have allowed others—apart from valeer perhaps, but he didn't show up any more. Ondine was amused when she saw these 2, necking clumsily . . . once she asked with a laugh where the traveler slept, probably in maria's bed; and they answered, also with a laugh, that yes, that was so. But as soon as ondine had gone, she strewed this news around as if it was the honest truth, and as a finger is quickly turned into an arm, she soon heard from the mouth of others the lies which she had spread herself. Yet it bored her, this whispered slander without an open quarrel; such things were after all too trivial to cut any ice: so what, she replied; what's it matter if a girl sleeps with a boy sometimes! Surely you don't think that's going to bring on another deluge? A deluge, yes, maybe that's what she was longing for . . . war and disaster, plague and famine and cholera and vikings . . . because she was going to crack up if there was never anything better to do than spread a few paltry lies.*

## JEANNINE THE CONTEMPORARY ONE TURNS UP AGAIN

She's painting, tippetotje, and at the same time she's explaining to johan janssens, poet and journalist, that of late there's been far too much talk in our book of those things . . . you know . . . as if it was the most important theme and the chief phenomenon of our time . . . whereas these things . . . well . . . are as common and as old as the road. Which road? asks johan janssens . . . the via appia, replies tippetotje. And choosing a clean brush she says: here we've got these stories by boon with his big moustache, which are supposed to show us a picture of the world and we've got the stories of lady emestine which are supposed to show us a picture of the encyclical world . . . but what can I say about jeannine, you know, my jeannine, the temporary one, who lives in the 1st dirty houses behind the labor? Well then, this jeannine is now about 17 and tumbles from one crisis into another, she screams and stamps and kicks . . . it's her nerves, says her mother, . . . they're nerves all right, between her thighs . . . and one day somebody from the police comes knocking at the 1st dirty houses asking what kind of people they are, those parents of hers . . . oh, very nice people, say the neighbors . . . What about this then! says that person from the police, his moustache menacingly thrust upwards . . . what about that? Their daughter, jeannine, was caught by us, offence against public decency, she was walking outside termuren, stark naked . . . and we ought to put her in the mental hospital. Tippetotje stops imitating the menacing voice of the policeman and goes on: she isn't ugly, jeannine, far from it . . . although her teeth are a bit higgledy piggledy . . . but just imagine you're taking a walk outside termuren and suddenly there's jeannine jumping in front of you in her birthday suit . . . heaven protect my prim and ladylike soul from shock.

Johan janssens, poet and journalist, nods his head gravely: it's true, too much attention has been paid to these things . . . just suppose the story was set in a metropolis, what on earth would it be like then? . . . like this morning in town, in the flower shop where a young woman was cleaning the shop window, squatting . . . no, she shouldn't have done it, surely she remembered whether she'd put her knickers on that morning or not? . . . no, she shouldn't have done it, because just in front of me there was another man, he saw it too and he stopped . . . and she stayed as she was and god knows what that man's going to be up to this evening, because even I walked on with a double beat in my blood, or with a slowed-down beat, because I still can't make out whether it beat once too often or once too little.

## A RADIANT SUNDAY AFTERNOON

*It was a radiant sunday afternoon and ondine saw liza standing in the door rocking her 3rd child to sleep: she told ondine that mr brys had been to see her. What did he look like? asked ondine without enthusiasm. Well, he'd had to sell his cottage and had holes in his shoes, he stuffed newspaper in them so as not to let the water get in . . . she, liza, had offered him a cup of coffee which he first refused but later accepted. He'd held her hand and pressed it for a long time . . . he cried a little and confessed he hadn't eaten for 2 days; even so—he still wore his bowler hat and his pince-nez, you couldn't tell straight away what a bad time he was having. He'd told her that at the filature they'd made him a disgraceful proposition, to which he hadn't wanted to reply . . . they hadn't been able to stop his fund from growing, but the swine—yes, for the 1st time in his life this respectable little bourgeois uttered this term of abuse, and he apologized for it—the swine had thought of something else: he'd gone to church as on every morning and the priest had refused him communion; the priest had come forward carrying our lord in his raised hands, had stepped back and walked past him . . . as if christ, who was born in a stable and died on a piece of wood, had no dealings with someone who wanted to give the workers a sick fund. He had at once called his members together, but it was too late, it had spread through the small town of the 2 mills like wild fire: mr brys has been refused communion! And they'd got scared, the members of his sick fund . . . the few who'd come to the meeting at his house were riff raff who'd only come to get a rise out of him . . . he'd spoken to them with tears in his eyes . . . but they'd left, after breaking 2 chairs, and one of them smuggled out something in his pocket, a trinket, something of which mr brys' late wife had been very fond . . . they'd left, stealing and destroying, reproaching him with being a thief and a swindler. Only 2 members had stayed. They'd suggested joining the socialists at once, but he hadn't wanted to: you can go, he'd said, but I'm too old to join such a new movement. He'd also said to liza: if your husband has got any sense, let him be a good boy, don't let him join the socialists, because he'll be persecuted all his life and it won't be worth the trouble . . . He himself was leaving, for england . . . what are you going to do there, liza had asked. Well, find a job and be good, he'd said. This was news to ondine, she'd never seen such a glorious sunday afternoon, full of hope, full of sun, and whistling like a man she walked into the café by the level crossing where the boys of termuren were playing peck-a-bird.*

## LONG LIVE THE KING . . . NO MATTER WHICH ONE

This is the fable of the kiss from reynard the fox . . . in contrast with the fable of the peace of god, which will come much later and which resembles it. But in the fable of the kiss of life the pilgrims are returning, carrying in their limp hands the even limper flag from the shrine . . . neither sapine the goat's rosary nor black sheep's rusty revolver nor carcofas the donkey's spectacles, had been of any avail to king noble's recovery. What kind of illness could it be, sapping king noble's strength? . . . it's the noble disease, said carcofas pompously, making a gesture to indicate how the old kings had to make way for the new kings of steel, oil and uranium . . . it's all the same, replied bekard the billygoat, unaware of what he was saying; he only began to realize it when sapine looked at him angrily. By the side of chapel road sat an old, stupid sparrow, who'd lived all her life on the droppings of those whom she had always looked up to so respectfully—having brought many children into the world, as she had been told to do, and now hoping for something or other, she didn't know what, maybe to be taken into the old sparrows' home—this old sparrow twittered after them: long live the king, no matter which one. But sitting in the midst of her flat-trodden droppings she saw that nobody took any notice of her, and shaking her head sadly she repeated: long live king noble or uranium, no matter which, as long as he gets me into the old sparrows' home. When the last pilgrim approached in the distance she flapped towards him with her aged wings and called again: long live . . . But reynard lifted his paw to silence her: no pilgrimage is of any use to noble's illness, he said . . . and to illustrate his thoughts he quoted the poem of the w.ild b.oar:

the wretched bearded scoundrel, stood gaping at us all, as if we were hired soldiers, I still don't understand, how those nine thousand heads, suffered it all so meekly, they should have taken off his pants, to smack him on his back; but though this was not done, all is not lost that is delayed, we are ready for revenge, but we shall not break his back.

and then reynard evoked a picture of our future society and universal peace . . . swinging his arms he once again proclaimed the republic. The sparrow, however, went on twittering regardless; of her hope to be admitted to the old sparrows' home; she called reynard an anarchist and a nihilist and asked what one had to obey if there was no one left one could obey? This made reynard more depressed than ever: come down from that tree and give me the kiss of the free brethren, and I'll take you straight to the old sparrows' home, he said, closing his bitter eyes so as not to frighten her too much . . . but a clump of moss falling from the tree, which made him snap with his big mouth, roused her suspicion; come on, he said, that was only to show you in what way the pope is infallible with regard to faith and morals, and also to show you that noble in his inviolability is raised above all treason. But while he tried to smile amiably, he saw his old enemy approaching in the distance: baron constant derenancourt with his barking encyclical dogs. Reynard took his tail between his legs and hurried off, while the sparrow twittered: why are you running away if the republic has been proclaimed? It's been proclaimed but not yet signed by the dogs, he called back, before disappearing into the wood behind the castle. johan janssens

## BLINKERS

On this Saturday afternoon in july, when the summer weather has come at last, the people of the 4 villas stand in their front doors in the shade: 4 young little housewives discussing chapel road life in their own little way like you write about it in your way. And talking about writing: tippetotje tells you, shaking her head: msieu colson of the ministry has a touching but rather simplistic desire to stop people in mid course as they hurry downhill . . . like someone standing under niagara falls holding up his hands in protest . . . and it's also a touching but simplistic idea to think that human civilization will end with the atom bomb—because it's quite possible that my own fear, of which I told you the other day, is nothing but a stomach ache after all—just as it used to be thought that the invention of the steam engine would inevitably bring human civilization to an end . . . whereas the history of man has really always been a history of dangerous discoveries . . . for instance the art of printing and gun powder . . . because man has read and read till he fell to pieces but he still goes on reading, he wears glasses of all sorts and shapes and reads newspapers and can pee his name in the snow . . . and man has fireworked himself to pieces so that hands and legs and bits of penis are lying in the ditch by the roadside, but he always goes on and will go on, even after he's exploded into atoms and after he's reconstructed himself artificially. Because man adjusts himself. He adjusts himself and that's why he has become the king of creation . . . he adjusts himself to the cold of antarctica and the heat of the sahara, to the trenches of 14-18 and the air-raid shelters of 39-44, to the convent school and to nazi, marxist and encyclicalist regimes. He adjusts himself and that's why he has the advantage of being the master of creation . . .

At this moment a new car drives along chapel road, hooting by way of greeting, and tippetotje says: look, there's jaspers the commercial traveler, he's the living proof, the three-dimensional image of my argument: he always used to be jaspers the commercial traveler, trudging to the station with his 2 heavy suitcases and talking in commercial traveler's jargon . . . but as soon as he's become a car-owner he speaks motorists' jargon—he talks about his 'beast' and looks contemptuously at the highway patrol which he calls the 'tse tse flies of the road' but being the king of creation he is also the slave of creation: through his faith in himself he can only cover 1 particular field of vision and according to Christ's words he's one of the poor in spirit entering the kingdom of heaven.

## A SUGARPLUM

*So the boys were playing peck-a-bird and the traveler from brussels sat by the window, staring at always the same old level crossing: ondine suggested to him: as maria is busy in the café, shall we go for a walk together? From then on it looked as if it was ondine who was flirting with him . . . summer came and they went for long walks along the railway, through tralfene woods far beyond termuren, as far as the river dendre. She asked him to hire a boat to go rowing, it was so nice on the water, but he'd never been in a boat and was afraid he might drown. She felt like laughing . . . and the question lay on the tip of her tongue whether a little while ago, in the woods, he'd been scared too? But it was useless to waste her powder and shot on him: the more you saw of him, the greater dunce he turned out to be. She didn't even want to take the path back along the dendre past the town of the 2 mills, for fear that mrs monique van wesenborgh or someone else from madame berthe's school would see her and would think that he was her sweetheart: they made a wide circle round termuren and came back to chapel road towards dusk. She showed him the villas which were almost finished, she got a key out of her purse and opened the front door of the 4th villa. They had a look round, downstairs and upstairs and sat for a while in the attic room, looking at the twilight settling on the level crossing and on the chapel and the trees round it. Then finally they spoke of her cousin, because so far they had avoided the subject . . . you ought to have a wife like me, really, said ondine, a woman who's got some idea of building up a business, but of course, as you see, I can't leave here. And she made a grand movement with her hand as if to show him the unpainted windows and doors and skirting boards, as if she had made it all and put it in place. Perhaps he didn't understand her gesture because the falling darkness made it difficult to see anything clearly; perhaps he thought she meant the whole of termuren. She took advantage of the darkness to say that her cousin wouldn't be much good to him, she was too stupid. He defended her . . . or himself . . . by saying that she was hot, though. But hot, what's hot? Anyway, you look around and you'll see that girls who grow up early, who at 15 have got a heart making all the men's eyes pop out of their heads, look like withered old hags at the age when other women start blossoming. Is that true? When she's 19 her breasts will be shriveled, you can be sure of that . . . and she asked him, had he come all the way from brussels and didn't know the first thing about women . . . then the fool wanted to show her that he did know something about women, but ondine rapped him on the knuckles. This was her triumph, that she could rap him on the knuckles: yes, burning your fingers, you know all about that, but not what a woman really wants . . . . They left the empty villa and walked down chapel road in silence. By the chapel she said: a woman is more than just her body, don't forget . . . and then she suddenly left him, and disappeared into her parents' house: ugh, he was a yokel like the others . . . look at him hurrying off, running to make up for lost time, even though a little while ago he tried to get under my skirt . . . he's a bull, a bull travelling in buns and sugarplums. She pushed aside the thought that he might have a sugarplum hanging between his legs, too: I should have had a look.*

## ARTIST IN UNIFORM

Journalist johan janssens is walking down chapel road, he almost picks the wrong house, he's so absorbed in surveying the situation: yes, so they set up a committee to decide what I shall write about and what of it shall be published . . . I was almost pleased, wickedly pleased, because now I would at last see what they thought about art

there's an artist amongst them too, a pianist who has no longer any contact with the world but sees everything through the navel of his piano . . . before giving a recital he lies down naked in a dark room with wet, hot towels all over him . . . he lies absolutely still before giving a recital . . . that's to say, before playing music which someone else has written . . . like a poetry reciter bellowing out a poem written by someone else. And then he goes home and demands the best food . . . but never anything animal, never fish or meat or eggs . . . and then his mother makes pancakes for him, with eggs; he doesn't know, he gobbles them up and says: my mother can make the best pancakes, and Without eggs, too!

I was curious what that idiot would have to say about pancakes . . . no, about art . . .

because you see, walk out I won't; to rebel again I refuse, going on hitting my head against the wall, I'm damned if I will: my wife has a right to a new dress once in a while and my son jo to a new toy . . . I want to see Them happy for once . . . I have no longer any desire to go home and say: I rebelled and I walked out. Having said this to himself, johan janssens, the journalist, discovers that he's standing on the wrong doorstep of the wrong house . . . and when he finally pushes his own door open, his wife meets him in the hall and asks, with a kind of intuitive fear: well? . . . johan janssens answers: oh, they weren't there, they didn't have time, so I just wrote a page of cultural life, all by myself . . . but I had to laugh when I sat there writing down my thoughts in my usual mocking way: yes, what am I going to write which isn't going to be good, or suitable, or politically correct? And then I laughed again when I answered myself, mockingly, I'm an artist in uniform . . . and most peculiarly of all, I don't get any orders because they're not capable of giving me any orders . . . but yet after the battle I shall be told that I'm going to be demoted.

## COUSIN MARIA IS PREGNANT

*Coming home, ondine looked around the house. She didn't feel like sitting down with the others in the lamplight, aimlessly waiting till it was time to go to bed;*

*eating a piece of bread she looked at valeer who was winding bandages round his cut and chafed fingers. She beckoned him to come out into the yard, where he stood in the bright square of light falling through the small window, while she had made sure to stay in the dark; she asked him why he was so clumsy with cousin maria that he allowed a sugarplum to pinch her from him in front of his eyes? With halting words, which hurt him, he explained how it had all happened: they'd never talked about That together, he said. About what, asked ondine . . . Well, you know, That, he replied. And so she had to squeeze the words out of him . . . he daren't accuse his sister but ondine could gather from his words that he saw in her the cause of his unhappy love: hadn't she always told him he should be good, and a Christian? She laughed scornfully in the dark: not when nobody can see you, she said. And as he looked surprised into the darkness where she was standing, she explained further: he should be good, that meant he should be polite to the priest and should go to church every Sunday and should be holier than anyone else . . . outside . . . but that didn't mean that in the dark he couldn't get under a girl's skirt to see how she was made there. She gave him advice, she even talked of things that made him turn away in shame: I'm too tired when we get home in the evening, he said in escape. And anyway, is she still worthy? He told her that their cousin slept with that traveler from brussels. O you fool, laughed ondine, that's a pack of lies I started myself. No, no, it's not a lie . . . and falteringly he managed to get out that he'd been standing by the level crossing for a long time and had seen that man's shadow in cousin maria's room; and don't ask me if I'm sure where maria sleeps, because I've often enough played with her in bed. Ondine understood that he was so madly, so miserably in love, that he even sacrificed his nights to look up at her window . . . longing to see her shadow, and discovering in self-tormenting pleasure that she now shared the bed in which they'd played as children, with someone else, a rich man, a gentleman from brussels. Ondine remembered how she herself had suffered because of . . . well, because of that flatfooted one. And if her nature hadn't played her nasty tricks as usual, she might have reflected further on these nocturnal wanderings of valeer's; she would have asked him if this was what he usually did . . . spying secretly on the doings of others . . . but the unbridled desire to make a rift between cousin maria and the sugarplum and put valeer between them, made all reasoning impossible. He listened to her orders with open mouth . . . and now and again, in the middle of a torrent of words, how he should do this and that, she said: shut your mouth, for heaven's sake . . . as if he'd done something wrong; she snarled at him angrily that he had his mouth wide open but that his ears were full of plaster and cement from the 4 villas. He left her like a lion, bristling with courage, but when he arrived at the crossing he was like a frightened sheep: he was a bucket with a hole in it, on the way all the will-power, just poured in, seeped out again. And besides, he was incapable of quarrelling, he entered the café and looked for a lonely corner . . . and as all the corners were occupied, so that everybody noticed him, he turned his fat head this way and that, bumped into everything in his blind shyness, and went home again. Well? asked ondine. There were too many people, they were looking at me. And the next day, when he'd been sitting in the café for hours on end, he returned with a handkerchief . . . ondine found it later: that's not one of yours, she said looking around questioningly . . . valeer hung his head in shame, it was one of their cousin's handkerchiefs which he'd been carrying about like a relic. You bloody idiot, she called out . . . and she wanted to crush the holy image he carried about in him of cousin maria, to throttle it, and to show it to him like a plucked hen: don't you know that maria, big, hot maria, does not even bleed proper red blood when she has her periods? She asked it maliciously, derisively, with her hands stretched out as if she almost had his sacred image of maria in her clutch. Periods, he stammered, his mouth hanging open . . . a mouth with a faint, happy smile round it, because he longed to hear precisely such things about her. She grabbed him by the sleeve and dragged him to the café, intending to create such hell that the dust would fly all over termuren, sky high . . . but although she came too late, she came in time to witness the most wonderful row she could have dreamt of: it turned out that cousin maria was pregnant. The sugarplum, who'd first sworn, raising 2 fingers, that he'd marry her, had now come back with hanging head: he explained that the formalities couldn't be complied with yet because cousin maria was too young. We could have told you that, you bloody ass, they said in the café. . . you're lucky they didn't put you straight in the nick, up at the town hall.*

*Ondine listened with a blissful smile on her lips . . . she fluttered from house to house like a butterfly.*

## THE GOOD ONES GO AND THE BAD ONES STAY

*One day at the café ondine announced to a room full of people that they'd soon find out how the horse had been harnessed: when the child arrives and it's only got 4 fingers. They didn't understand her at first, although cousin maria turned bright red and started to cry, the sugarplum looked round questioningly, till his eye fell on valeer who was staring sheepishly at his maimed hand. Then christ stood up straight: he had never said a word in the whole affair, and he still didn't speak, but he went to the door, opened it wide, and pointing silently at the doorway he looked at ondine. Ondine got up and left, her head high, and she quoted something from holy scripture, about the dry wood which will be burnt, and the green wood which will blossom . . . and don't forget it's always the same, she said: the good ones go and the bad ones stay . . . come on, valeer.*

*And so time passed: the sugarplum went here and there with his bride, got married, and finally the day came that he was going to leave for brussels with his little wife: she walked heavily, she was nearing her time. People were telling the sugarplum to hurry, as if he had to drive the train himself . . . they would walk down chapel road, and catch the train at the station in the town of the 2 mills, but they were not a little surprised to find valeer by the 4 villas, with a large suitcase between his legs and a funny hat on his bulbous head, and still with a bandage round his fingers . . . he was coming with them to carry their suitcases, he said, but he was encumbered enough with his own. The sugarplum asked him why was he carrying a suitcase of his own then, and valeer explained, haltingly, that he was coming with them to help them, the work here at the four villas way almost finished, there were only some small jobs left which his father would do by himself. The traveler was perplexed; it seemed impossible to him, a nightmare, a bad dream, sent to him by the person he hated, whom he feared like the plague: ondine. Cousin maria, on the contrary, who'd been pushed this way and that with her bump these last weeks and who'd been scared stiff at the thought of having to go and live in that totally strange city where she knew no one and where people spoke a language she didn't understand . . . cousin maria brightened up visibly. She'd been looking sad before, because of her condition, she said, but now she beamed and started chattering at once: she winked at her husband and said: oh, come on, the poor chap, let him come . . . I'll have somebody to talk to then from my own village when I get amongst all those strangers. So the 3 of them went together and cousin maria, looking round once, saw someone staring at them from behind the window of one of the villas: it was ondine. She'd given valeer strict instructions: how to mess up their honeymoon good and proper. But . . . valeer was walking beside his cousin, his dream . . . and he too turned round to ondine and called out, laughing: the good ones go and the bad ones stay. He laughed, but then shrank, because he felt he'd said something wrong.*

## IT'S ALWAYS THE OTHERS WHO TELL STORIES

Instead of going home, johan janssens, the journalist—yes, how about that, is a sacked journalist still a journalist?—johan janssens turns into the road behind the castle, thinking that there hell be alone with his thoughts. But look, he bumps into msieu colson of the ministry and says: I must tell you . . .

But msieu colson, who's full of his own encounters in his own life, says: let *me* tell *you* something that you can put in the paper . . . the history of mr lyon the silent, who spent one part of his life behind the counter at the discount and credit bank and the other in bed with his young wife whom he tortured and put on the rack day after day. When the doctor told him to stop it he answered that he Wouldn't because he was married and had a Right to his wife . . . he hardly ever spoke a word at home, but poured himself a glass of wine, lit a cigar and sank away in a deep armchair . . . and when finally the doctor said his wife had to have an operation urgently, he didn't even reply, didn't even ask why or for what she had to have an operation . . . but he stood in the kitchen early the next morning, chattering to the maid, the devil knows about what . . . and when he had to go to the head office of the discount and credit bank, in brussels, he walked about the streets all day long, in the department stores, in the parks, and saw legs and legs and legs, and worked himself up into a frenzy . . . he went home and took his wife straight to bed . . . crawled on that pale, transparent little wife who'd only just had her operation, and exercised his Right on her, gave rein to his Right, and smiled at the immeasurable drop of blood which came flowing from her pale, transparent body, and then finally he said casually that he had raced a mounted policeman, he on foot and the policeman on horseback . . . and he triumphantly concluded that the policeman hadn't managed to overtake him . . . he finally died . . . in a very ordinary way, not in a madhouse as you might perhaps have expected.

right, says johan janssens, but now about what you suggested, about writing that story for the paper . . . let me tell you . . .

but just at that moment they've arrived at the 1st dirty houses behind the labor, and under the last falling raindrops there are a big crowd and several policemen . . . msieu colson of the ministry asks: what's going on here? Someone turns to him and says: I'll tell you, you know there's a sailor lived here who used to sail on the big hamburg-riga line . . . well, all his life he's been saving up for his old age, but now that the war is over and they've called the money in, the sailor had to hand in his few savings and he's obliged to go sailing again in his old age . . .

and now the police have come to find out if maybe he was a fascist in the war . . . listen to the racket . . . it's the people of the 1st dirty houses crowding round the police asking them were *they* fascists, they used to bully us enough in the war but they always said: it's the germans, they're giving us the orders

msieu colson of the ministry shakes his head and says: you see, johan janssens, I thought: when I see johan janssens I'll tell him the story of mr lyon the silent . . . but I've hardly finished when there's already a new story: everybody's got a story to tell.

## THE DREAM

In the night johan janssens dreams, restlessly tossing about, frightened, fighting for his life . . . his wife wakes him up and asks if he was fighting in his dream? . . . she tells him that he was squeaking and squealing like a mouse. I fight like a mouse, thinks johan janssens.

## WHOSE FAULT IS IT?

*Cousin maria had only just left when new trouble started for ondine . . . but it was precisely what she longed for with all her heart: she languished if there weren't any quarrels or troubles. And now she'd seen the old priest, father voncke, half sobbing in the pulpit: he said that the devils had broken loose—thanks be to god the people of termuren were still living in peace—but in the town of the 2 mills they were walking about with knives between their lips and they ate human flesh: and now they've got a trade union and there'll be universal franchise as well, and I wonder whether now you'll be for me or against me. He sobbed and asked whether he hadn't always been good to them . . . as if he imagined that this was the last time he was allowed in the pulpit and that he'd have to make way for the devil incarnate. People left the church talking about it and shaking their heads and in every house prayers were said: deliver us, o lord, from the godless socialists. Only at ondine's no such prayer was said: vapeur, looking 10 years older since he'd started on the 4 villas, thought everyone had better paddle his own canoe and whether it was the devil or the priest standing in the pulpit—he said—it is still us, the middle class, that have to pay for the candles. At first ondine laughed at her father's metaphor, but then the truth of it struck her . . . she was once again amazed at her father: how did he manage to hit the nail on the head so precisely . . , expressing Everything with that 1 little sentence . . . and yet without being able to benefit from his wisdom, but going through life like a clumsy oaf, allowing himself to be cheated by the smallest child? She came to the discovery that with her the reverse was true: or would have to become true . . . that she wanted to profit from her intelligence as soon as she'd managed to bring some order into the chaos of her thoughts. A t the moment this was impossible, she couldn't bring clarity to her hundred and one thoughts, she couldn't reduce all those stormy ideas to the One idea which would tell her which road to follow. The socialists, for instanced . . she had to agree with the priest and she had to agree with her father, and beside this, she had other cobwebs of her own in her head: first and foremost the 4 villas which were finished now; people were already living there . . . for instance that mr schatt, whom she still hadn't met, let alone got any money out of . . . and at the same time, thinking of the socialists, she wondered whether it wasn't the priest's own fault: take the pope now: how could one person possibly rule the whole church without someone . . . somewhere . . . how, for instance, could he know that in termuren there was a girl to whom a miracle had happened? . . . a girl who would have been able to nip that whole business with the socialists in the bud, if only she'd been allowed to marry a derenancourt. But whose fault was this then? . . .*

*not hers, she didn't rule heaven and earth, she didn't know things in books, but Someone Else did, who didn't bother about the fate of the world because he was safe and well in heaven and had it good . . . a fat pig doesn't know that a lean pig is hungry . . . and so everyone was going to have the vote? That really gave her a wicked pleasure, she hoped they would all, to a man, vote for the socialists . . . ha, that would teach them, the gentlemen, to cover her with shoe polish. She laughed at it, but when she'd finished laughing she repeated it: that will teach them to cover me with shoe polish and refuse to listen to my advice.*

## DEATH DUTY

You're not writing in the daily paper any more, then? msieu colson asks johan janssens . . . and johan janssens says: no, but I still write in the weeklies, in so far as weeklies still appear, and this week I wrote a story called 'death duty':

just as there is all saints' day, so there should be all wars' day and on that day a good-for-nothing little mass might be read in memory of rené vennekens, who died for the fatherland, who was burnt to ashes, but not buried: you probably knew rené vennekens: he belonged to that noisy high school year to which zillens also belonged, who took the wrong bottle one day and drank ammonia, and jespers who always insisted on carrying a portable record player about, with pop-records . . . but rené vennekens was quieter, he was his mother's pride, and therefore felt a kind of duty weighing on him . . . maybe you lost sight of him in the war? . . . yes, so did I . . . we went through such a lot, bombs and famine and so on . . . well anyway, rené vennekens was in ghent prison, the sicherheit had picked him up, and not long after that, little pros was put in the same cell. Little pros was kicked inside and from a corner rené vennekens came to meet him: my name is vennekens, I come from the small town of the 2 mills, why are you here? Naturally, little pros wouldn't say anything, and he only said: I don't know. But rené vennekens pulled his pants down and showed him his buttocks: 1 huge raw blue wound: you'll soon find out, he said. Yes, and then, because I must be brief—rené vennekens, ordinary simple little resistance fellow, was sent from sicherheit to gestapo, was jeered at, spat upon and beaten, and was put on transport to germany to die on the cross of the furnaces. His mother, whose pride he was, sent him food parcels. But of course, you must understand that his mother was a humble lower middle class widow who'd made her son and pride join the old boys' association so as to get school books more cheaply . . . etc . . . and she no longer got any stamps for him now, and had to put smuggled food in the countless parcels and had to mortgage her cottage—but never mind, as long as she'd get him back alive. And then . . . she didn't get him back alive . . . she waited and hoped, partly also because he'd have to help her pay off the mortgage . . . but hoping and waiting and wandering here and there, she came home one day and in the letterbox there was a letter from the belgian red cross: the news that he'd been tortured to death out there. Naturally, everyone tried to console her saying that she was the mother of a hero . . . but then suddenly there's another letter, that she's got to pay death duty to the State for her killed son. She hits her blind head on the blind wall because instead of paying off the mortgage she now has to sell her cottage and maybe go to work as a house maid to a bloated collaborator: that will teach her to have donated a hero to the belgian State.

## A NICE STORY

The music master, having listened to this death duty story, nods and says that it is a very nice story. But johan janssens says with a grimace: it may be a nice story, but the nicest part is still to come: rené vennekens' mother has indeed become a maid in the house of a rich collaborator and as you can imagine they don't read the weeklies in which I write about the mothers of rené vennekens, but the weeklies in which the mothers of rené vennekens are maligned . . . and so, being a maid there, she comes across one of those weeklies and reads in a dirty article that I johan janssens am a leper, writing now in the socialist papers and then in the ultra-marxist papers . . . that I shouldn't talk of fascists because I'm one myself . . . or might easily have been . . . anyway, you know their prose, the filthy bastards. So rené vennekens' mother folds the paper up and puts it in her apron pocket and takes it to the house next to ours: there they're pleased because I get what I deserve

. . . and rubbing her hands together rené vennekens' mother says: my boss says so too, they've given that insufferable johan janssens what for, haha!

## THE GENTLEMEN

*You sit down to write about ondine, that she shook her head at the gentlemen's latest stupidity . . . but just as you're putting pen to paper, tippetotje enters and the first thing you notice about her is a streak of paint on her left cheek; don't look at that paint on my right shoe, she says, I've just come from brussels, I've been working for the rich, I've painted angels' heads on their walls and ceilings and golden borders on their doors . . . and I've come here in a hurry to tell you you should change your view of the gentlemen if you write about them again . . .*

you told us about achilles derenancourt and fat glemmasson, you described the orgies that boone with his big moustache told you about, from the time he was still a coachman, but now I'm going to tell you something: I've been working in tervuren avenue, for the viscount . . . and this viscount is an encyclicalist of the purest water, that's to say, he's not political but a very devout man, like émile zola described him in nana . . . a tall, lean man who has known blow upon blow in life and who says in resignation that everyone has to carry his cross, that Christians are put to the test and non-christians punished; one day he's ill and lies in a lonely big bed in a lonely big cold bedroom and the next day his wife is ill and lies in the lonely big bed in the cold big bedroom; his son was killed in an accident and his other 2 children are ill whenever their parents are well for a change—oh, and the candles that bum there, and the holy water that's sprinkled and the consecrated palm that's carried about and the rosaries that are solemnly said—oh, you should see them sitting in that dreadful big, somber, empty dining hall, the viscount folding his hands in prayer and the others following his example and praying and crossing themselves, and then everyone starting to eat in mournful silence . . . but when he talks about politics to me he talks the greatest twaddle, the biggest hotch-potch of contradictions you can imagine: first that the workers are never satisfied anyway, and then that everything would be a lot better if only the worker was paid a proper wage. But it isn't the viscount and his family who go in for orgies, it's the maid; she was getting her bath ready one day, naked, leaving the door open so that I could see her plainly and she told me from her bath that I could come and see her that night, using the servants' staircase . . . and that night she told me about the sad, somber life in that sad, somber viscount's house.

Another day I went to paint the house of a big industrialist . . . the viscount had recommended me there . . . I rang and I saw someone I thought must be the chimney sweep, but no, it was the industrialist himself . . . a fellow with hands like this, he waved to me and said bonjour, high above my head—the plumber told me he'd told him that he used to be a racing motorist when he was young. When he heard I was a painter he took me round his collection, a good million francs he's got hanging there . . . breughel and bosch and rembrandt, van eyck and van dyck, metsys and van der weyden and van der lubbe . . . no, I beg your pardon, that wasn't a painter . . . a million francs; what am I saying? billions of francs . . . there are things there that are coveted by all the foreign museums and he told me what they'd offered him . . . and he stopped in front of one painting and showed me a drop of blood, jesus's blood and he said: look; look with what realism that's been painted, it's just like real, they can't do that any more these days. Yes, that is his art-appreciation: the art-appreciation of a chimney sweep who was a racing motorist once upon a time; the art-appreciation of an industrialist who got a 120 million franc fine for collaboration with the enemy, which he paid promptly, in cash. And coming to the end of the gallery he looked back at his collection of paintings, at the glass cases full of gems and rarities and art treasures, and he said: yes, a man must have something to fill his old age. And then, his wife; a thin, spindly creature, off to buy half a pound of margarine, because real butter is too expensive . . . wearing a shabby black dress: I bet if you saw her in tervuren avenue you'd swear she was some poor office clerk's wife.

## THE MUTINEERS OF THE FILATURE

*Standing in the front door ondine saw that the gentlemen had been stupid once again: some 3 men were returning from the filature, in their blue overalls and with their bread wrapped in a piece of paper . . . it was getting towards noon, and the children from the convent school ran shouting ahead of these three unusual homeward bound men; a pregnant woman went out to meet them, an out-worker came to his front door and asked them: what's happened? Yes, there they stood, hardly knowing what to say, looking at their packed sandwiches: at the filature the chief members of mr brys' sick fund had been dismissed; some had been suspended for 6 months, and these three here for 2 weeks . . . mr brys himself had fled to england, it's easy to escape to a different country when you're educated and know languages, but they? They wondered whether the socialists would do something for them now. Ondine listened but didn't join in the conversation . . . she shook her head at the gentlemen's stupidity: now that mr brys had gone it would have been far better to treat the ignorant people to beer, instead of chucking them out and making them rebellious. She knocked at liza's door, to see what had happened to her husband; he hadn't had any better luck, he'd been taken off his work at the mill and put back on his former job in rain and wind in the yard, at his previous wage . . . liza and her husband had discussed things till deep in the night: they'd wondered whether it wouldn't be better to look for work at the labor, where they didn't bother about religion . . . and they'd totted up all the advantages of working at this godless mill: firstly, it needn't worry him any more that he didn't care for priests and therefore he needn't go to mass against his will any more . . . and secondly that he'd be home sooner if he worked at the labor, he'd be there in 2 minutes and so he could work a bit in the garden afterwards . . . maybe grow some vegetables and sell them early on sunday mornings at the sunday market in town . . . and the more they looked at it the better it seemed. But when he started at the labor, he had to work in the yard there as well, in rain and wind and snow, and for an even lower wage than at the filature . . . and the foreman looked at him suspiciously: aren't you a fellow from the filature? He had to work overtime, too, for which he way supposed to get paid, but for reasons they didn't understand he didn't get paid. But it's going to get better, said liza hopefully . . . oh, the more liza was up against it, the more hopeful she became . . . she said there was a foreman who liked her husband and who might get him a place in the machine room . . . where it was warm and where you could earn an uncommonly high wage for termuren. But ondine dashed this hope to smithereens at once: if you earned a higher wage then there was probably a snag in it: 'maybe you risked your life every second. And then—get better? It can't get better if you live without god, she said. Liza shook her head and said that ondine didn't understand: we don't live without god, we just don't care for the priest . . . the children kneel down every night to pray, you should hear our oldest rattling off her our-fathers and her hail-marys, and saying: deliver us, o lord, from the godless socialists . . . but liza's husband only went to work at the labor because he couldn't bear to see the injustice that was done to mr brys. Ondine had an answer to this too, but it was nothing new, nothing we hadn't heard from her before: for instance, that god didn't worry whether you read stupid pater-nosters but that he wanted a great deal more: that you behaved yourself and were always humble and obedient.*

## VAPEUR TALKS ABOUT MONEY

*The next day, however, there was a registered letter, that carolus bosmans had to pay for the timber, or else. Vapeur started running around, flourishing his arms: there you are, I told you so, tomorrow the police will be here and confiscate the whole caboodle; I saw it happen once when I was young, but nobody listens to somebody with experience. Ondine looked at him in contempt and said that surely he knew that if he bought wood he'd have to pay for it, or are you such a dunce that you think they'll give it to you for nothing? All right, pay then, shouted vapeur. What with, ondine shouted back. They looked at each other and in the silence they heard zulma laughing. Vapeur went to look, out of old habit, in the canvas purse on the cupboard, and ondine gratefully took the opportunity to sneer at his ignorance: you don't even know there's an iron casket, she said. But in the iron casket there wasn't anything worth mentioning either: ondine herself was startled that it was so little . . . she looked her father deep in the eyes, so that he became nervous and turned his head away . . . yes, finally he admitted having taken some of it, a trifling sum, surely he didn't plod and toil for nothing? . . . he'd heard of electric lamps which were being sold in town for his perpetuum mobile machine; he raised his finger and said: if vacuum bulbs turn round on a wheel and come down in a tub of water, they will rise to the surface again. Ondine laughed scoffingly and asked how much he'd taken . . . valeur stammered in shame and mentioned a sum, a ludicrously small sum, but she knew he was telling the truth. Where was the money then? She started calculating feverishly what she herself had spent, apart from what she had put aside as a reserve and put in a tin in the attic . . . but the calculations didn't tally, there should be more . . . her mother was giggling stupidly, looking at the iron casket . . . a suspicion rose in ondine and she started questioning her mother, who told her, in a shrill, piercing voice, that she'd listened very carefully to the priest—that in town there were savages eating their own children, and that therefore she'd given a donation for the repair of the chapel . . . ondine started swearing and asked how she figured a repaired chapel would stop the socialists? But seeing that stupid face she fell silent . . . it was useless to waste words. But she had to do something to cool her fury: she lifted her hand and slapped the stupid face. Carolus looked in defeat at the white cheeks on which 5 red fingers began to show. And now I've had enough of it, she said to her father . . . in future you can go and get the money yourself, you can go and see that man schatt and ask when it will please him to pay. Vapeur went. He washed and shaved and put on his mouse-eaten overcoat . . . he only had 1 coat and daren't wear it for fear it would get worn, and so he left it hanging in the cupboard till a family of mice came to live in it and started eating the lining. He left, rehearsing the words he was going to say; and that he was ondine's father he proved by even imagining what they'd answer . . . and by seeking new arguments in reply to those answers. He stayed away for 3 hours and when ondine asked him: well? . . . he only muttered something . . . yes, he'd been talking about his perpetuum mobile machine for 3 hours and hadn't dared open his mouth about money; he'd talked about the bourgeoisie and the men with knives, about mr brys and the socialists and that it was foolish to try to change the world by means of a trade union if people themselves remained ignorant: science and intelligence, understanding what remained dark to people, this was the starting point for a happier mankind. And he, with his invention, would bring about more happiness and prosperity than all the trade unions put together: the others quarreled today and rebelled tomorrow and made a revolution the day after . . . but whatever one did, the petty bourgeoisie would pay for the broken pots . . . the petty bourgeoisie is the milch cow: take me, for example, I've got to pay for all that wood . . . And he halted, with a start, because there he was talking about money after all, unwittingly: soon these people would think that that's what he'd come for.*

## IT ISN'T NICE OF JOHAN JANSSENS

Today is thursday . . . which is the day when the young folk of termuren go and see their sweethearts in the evening and take a walk in the wood behind the castle, to tell each other that they will do everything differently from the way their parents did it. But today is also the day when the papers carry their page of cultural life . . . and so love-life and cultural life cross paths on this day: this is what johan janssens thinks as he walks down chapel road, with the paper opened at page 3: art and literature. He reflects that it's odd, you've always filled that page all by yourself . . . when you're used to see your own prose in the paper, in the morning, like you find your own face when you look in the mirror . . . to find now, looking in the mirror of the paper, a stranger's face.

a column with the title: book of the week. This was actually still johan janssens' idea, but it's been mutilated and made respectable: he'd explained the idea to a young poet, that each week a book from world literature would be discussed, along socialist guide lines, in order to build up, bit by bit, a kind of literary history on a socialist basis: starting with flanders: nivardus' isengrinus; willem's reynard the fox; van maerlant, the father of all dutch poets; j.f. van kerckhove, and eugene zettermom . . . but now it has been reduced, as we said, to a respectable book review. And then there are articles lashing out, reviling and abusing everything and everybody and therefore nothing and nobody . . . but with big, hollow words and threadbare slogans worn to the last shred, about the proletariat and the new society. And in clumsily camouflaged terms it is said that johan janssens' work didn't enough . . . was too much . . . well, er . . . didn't sufficiently deal with the worker, collapsing at the factory gate gasping his last breath . . , and also, that there was never anything worthwhile amongst all those subjects johan janssens used to discuss: bosch and breughel and goya and magritte, louis paul boon and the sculptural element in literature: none of these things depict the proletariat, clothed in rags, showing a living skeleton beneath.

Johan janssens folds the paper, with wistful regret, because all these younger people who now fill the cultural page are the same people who vied for his friendship, in the time when he still used to fill that page, who wrote enthusiastic letters to him and sent him poems and short stories and asked his advice . . . but now, having climbed on the horse, they try to trample on him . . . no, they make that horse kick mud at johan janssens with all 4 hooves at once. And meanwhile, in every small town with 2 or 3 factories, or if need be even 5 or 6 factories, the workers open their paper and look for a piece by johan janssens, and if they don't find one, they say: dammit, we used to be able to swear or laugh at those articles about our misery, but now . . . it's not nice of johan janssens that he doesn't WANT to write in our paper any more.

## AT ELMAEREN*

I created a monk at elmaeren . . . so it says in the old books of reynard the fox, but before the foolish wolf is going to ring the bell that turns the friars loose on us, let me tell you about how he read mass; whenever reynard set his traps to catch a hare, in the wood behind the castle, in the fields, along chapel road, or anywhere else, he'd invariably meet a friar with a briefcase under his arm. Although he remembered from long ago that all roads lead to rome, he now began to realize that the road on which most hares were caught—though not by him—led to the monastery of saint one-eye, some way beyond termuren. Birds of a feather flock together, he thought, and at the umpteenth bend in the road he found a tin of rolled wafers, and started to nibble at them . . . but who was coming along there, with hollow eyes above a plaster on his cheek? . . . wasn't that his uncle isengrinus? Aha, so you too have found the road the hares take, never to return, said reynard . . . but isengrinus looked at him glumly, admitted to be on the way to the monastery, and humming and hawing, gave his views on the state of the world, which was going to the dogs, according to him; he gave his views on noble's illness, and then he told reynard about the goats who'd promised him something that wasn't even edible: the souls of children, how do you cook them, how do you dish them up? The louder reynard laughed, the gloomier the wolf became, counting all the times when someone had 'painted him a friar',

* I, johan janssens, write out of pure, stupid habit my pieces about reynard the fox, and afterwards I realize that I needn't have bothered . . . never mind, it's been written now, but what am I going to do with it?

and now that I've become a friar myself, who'll be able to paint me one now? Then reynard took out the last few wafers, gave 1 to isengrinus, and stuffing the rest in his mouth, he pointed significantly at the monastery: isengrinus got the point, he at once started to run, and reached the back gate of the monastery garden 2 paces ahead of reynard; there he stopped, pointing at the friars, as if trying to put his foolish dream into words: by our lord's beard, you renounced the world, except of course during an election campaign, after they'd pulled the pope's sock over your head and tried to make you believe that everything you saw would be yours—and you entered between these walls where you may not even have a stone to rest your head on . . . because, and this is true, too, it's much more comfortable to rest your head in the lap of some youngster or other. He wanted to go on singing his vespers, but reynard pulled him away, into the coolness of the vestry where they found meat and bread and wine. But inside the wolfs stomach the wine changed into devil's blood: he insisted on singing mass and stood there swaying his arms and jabbering double latin—vobiscum he pronounced as vobis-come, meaning: come on, give me so much for a requiem mass with 3 Hosts and twice as much for a wedding mass after ten o'clock—opening his arms he turned to the empty chairs calling: suckers suckerorum . . . and reynard, almost peeing himself, replied: amen. johan janssens.

## FOR THE 1ST TIME: OSCARKE

*I'll go and see those schatts myself, said ondine, and she went with the golden bracelet round her wrist and the sunshade over her head, although it looked as if it might rain any minute . . . but they must have seen her coming, because when she rang, it remained dead silent in the house . . . much too silent . . . they must be scared stiff of her. She heard from the hollow sound of the bell that it was an empty house, that they hadn't got 5 cents' worth of furniture; they probably didn't even have a table and ate on the floor round a wooden trough! She started sneering at herself for having let herself be caught like this: if she was ever going to build any more houses this would serve as a lesson. She gave another savage pull at the bell, with no other intention than to go home at once, to spite those who were inside. She was about to walk back to termuren . . . but she must have misjudged the situation, because the door opened and a nervous boy with disheveled hair looked at her. He was foolish enough to leave the door wide open, so ondine took her chance: she stepped past him into the corridor and closed the door herself. She stuck her sunshade out at him like a dagger and told him to go and fetch his ma: he was embarrassed and stroked the fluff on his chin . . . he was too shy to tell her that there honestly wasn't anyone at home. Ondine smiled at him, said that he was a good boy, and resolutely walked into the kitchen, but indeed, there was no one there: it was cold and empty; she was all alone with this young chap who'd have to start scraping the down from his chin for the 1st time some day soon. I'll wait, she said, and one by one she wheedled the worms out of his nose: she soon saw that apart from his mother he had never been alone with a woman and that now, while talking, he couldn't take his eyes off her skirt. He was as malleable as wax: ondine could easily imagine what a lonely life he must be leading in this new villa: and at first in order to put him at his ease, but later with wicked pleasure . . . and finally because she began to like it . . . she told him all the things which probably touched his heart to the quick, but in a way as if they'd really happened to her: that she felt lonely, that she had dreamt she would achieve something in life but that there was only restlessness and doubt. He forgot the hem of her skirt, because he was deeply moved to find someone who had the same feelings as he: his frank eyes sought hers . . . which were grey . . . and he told her of his own restlessness, told her that he wanted to become a sculptor, that he could look at a chunk of stone for hours, unable to put his hand to it . . . and that he sometimes cried without knowing why. He was called oscar. He asked her to come up to his studio . . . she realized that there wasn't a trace of guile in him, nothing but childlike innocence . . . so she went upstairs with him, wondering what his mother would think if she were to come back unexpectedly. She looked round the bare attic room and saw that it was the room where she had stood by the window with the sugarplum: they might as well have stayed in the kitchen, because it was just as cold and dead here: there was only a bucket of clay and on the back of a rickety chair hung some wet pieces of cloth. She looked out of the window at the long, long wall of the labor where a scraggy dog was limping past . . . she realized that the boy had nothing more to say . . . maybe he thought that she could see, in that shapeless lump of clay, the statue he wanted to make . . . melancholy, he was going to call it . . . oh, wasn't it exactly the same as in her youth? When she'd wanted to show her dream to someone, what had come out? the rusty chapel key or the chipped plaster saint she had kept in the attic. She felt pity for herself and for this boy, because all childish dreams are so infinitely small and infinitely sad . . . she smiled, with melancholy, like the statue he was going to make . . . she kissed him briefly and went away, leaving him in utter confusion.*

## AM I BECOMING AN ORDINARY MIDDLE CLASS WOMAN?

*When ondine came outside, she thought with self-mockery that she, too, hadn't mentioned money . . . but what use would it have been? There was no money there, they were as poor as church mice. And as if it had happened to someone else, she concluded that she'd been taken in. With self-mockery, yes, but at home she wrote a peppery letter addressed to mr schatt, which she was going to send by registered post. But she forgot the letter, she found it in her pocket, days later, in chapel road on her way to town . . . she remembered the days when she still imagined that the world was waiting for ondineke and wouldn't dare revolve without her . . . now she wasn't quite sure why it should ever have waited for her; it was clear from everything that she was too good to wither and waste here in termuren . . . but was this a reason for such wild dreams? She noticed that she'd become more modest—how had this come about, without her seeing it coming, seeing it happening?—that she was no longer such a world beater, but only cherished a very modest middle class wish, of marrying a middle class husband and being comfortably off. She asked herself in vain what her dreams had consisted of . . . and also she tried to sum up her childhood: a miracle happened to me. She laughed bitterly, she wondered why: so that she should become an ordinary middle class woman? . . . surely, in termuren an ordinary middle class woman was no less than a miracle, but then, what was termuren? . . . take cousin maria, for instance; in brussels, there must be swarms of ordinary middle class women there. And arriving at the 4 villas she thought of oscar and concluded: yes, I told him I way restless . . . but it wasn't all a lie. Just then the Schatts' front door opened and a woman came out . . . if ondine had been a child still, she would have called this a miracle too . . . she saw that this woman was someone who'd become grey from her little day to day worries, from the little hour to hour troubles . . . she was the archetype of the lower middle class, ondine thought. Suddenly she remembered the registered letter. And also, she didn't know why, she felt such violent aversion, such hatred, that with the best will in the world she couldn't look at the woman. But mrs schatt beckoned her . . . ondine went . . . she saw that this was a woman who hadn't lived, who had shriveled up beside a man who probably spent his time in brothels . . . yes, that's how it must have been, that's why this woman had no cash: her body had withered amongst the bare walls of empty houses, and her petty bourgeois soul had shriveled in the vain struggle to get some of her husband's salary. He probably took that salary straight from the office to the whores . . . or maybe a filthy tart in a room furnished by him, with no slip on her buttocks. The woman talked to ondine . . . but it didn't penetrate, she was still following her own train of thought, a train of thought full of odd jumps: from the tart in the furnished room to her own nights at the castle, to the crazy hours in the room by the station . . . and yes, a wry thought: to the bushes which used to grow here, at the place where the 4 villas stood . . . and she wanted to know whether any will o' the wisps had been noticed yet . . . but she didn't ask, she took the forgotten letter from her pocket and said that mrs schatt should think of paying at last. Not that they were short, but this week a bill of exchange was going to be due. A bill of exchange—ondine had heard this phrase once, at the iron-monger's. Mrs. schatt said she would think about it . . . she was going to talk to her husband about it, they might pay everything at once, then it would all be settled. Ondine felt herself turning grey with nausea; she had to turn round and leave, or she might have vomited in mrs schatt's face.*

## GREY DAY

To your eternal vexation you see yourself sitting there again like a stranger . . . with your head between your legs and with limp hands in your lap and with the unbearable feeling that inside your head something is swinging between 2 poles like low tide and high tide, day and night, winter and summer: one day you're being pushed away from the world which is in evolution, so they say, but you see as little of this evolution as of the angels in heaven: and if you dare think, at times, that you're beginning to know the world, it's nothing but arrogance, because in this grey day the world is an unknown planet, a closed house, a cracked mirror . . . and you're being driven away from people, because wherever you go you see ignorance and bad faith and self-interest, and most of all, stupid misunderstandings, enough to kill you . . . so that you almost begin to think: anyone who mingles with people carries a heavy burden . . . and you're also driven away, how is it possible, from your work, in which there isn't a trace of ambition . . . all your writing seems useless to you, because your wife and child have left you alone with your papers and have gone to sleep, and asleep they're still as much participating in this . . . well, this evolution . . . as you, writing about your dejectedness, or thinking, with your head near the floor. And the next day you're swung back to everything and everybody, because when it comes to the point you need more than just yourself and your possibly wise but rather unworldly thoughts . . . and you long for that work of yours, that work without ambition, while the lamp hums softly above your stumbling pen. So tonight is the evening after a depressing day, no, a grey day . . . you have done nothing but sit around, although you keep saying that sitting isn't good for a person, because from the stars down to the atoms the universe moves, and you must move too if you want to understand the meaning of Things. You hear the rain beating down in your little garden, so that you're glad when someone knocks at the closed front door, for shelter. It's tippetotje the painter, who's on the way to eenighem, half an hour's walk from termuren . . . you turn the lamp a little lower and say: I'll come with you . . . and while the pouring rain streams down your nose in rivulets which you blow away with your mouth, you shout out your dejection into the wind: I don't know what's the matter with me, but I don't feel like anything, I'm becoming a damn buddhist I'm so apathetic about everything. Tippetotje shouts into the wind too—on that slippery, lonely road to eenighem, beyond termuren—this is quite normal at your age: you're now let's say about 30 years old and maybe you've more or less achieved what you hoped you would, in your youth, and on top of this you're bound to feel a certain unrest because your blood is getting a bit less wild: it's the time when your reason has to whip up your blood to its former savage pitch.

But you wonder whether she's right, whether now you shouldn't rather have time—time and money—to study a bit: because what do you know of all the things there are to be known, apart from a few commonplaces? . . . And as goethe said . . . haha, goethe and boon . . . as goethe said: it's not enough to have talent, there must also be money to let it run its course. So that the conclusion to this grey day is: you swing back to the world and its people and your work . . . and you swing away from the world and people and your work, because you lack time and money to understand things better.

## A SCHATT WITHOUT A TREASURE

*Returning home, it occurred to ondine that she hadn't for a moment worried about the money and moreover, that the only reason why she wanted to go to town was to walk down chapel road and . . . yes, it was the unvarnished truth, in order to meet that snotty-nosed schatt boy. It hadn't been just a pack of lies, what she'd blurted out in that attic room, by god, no, it had been the truth, and after all, he'd been the first man with whom she could talk about the soul of things; he'd been the first who had listened, who'd been aglow at her words and who hadn't crawled under her skirt. She was sorry she'd rushed away from that attic room so soon, that she hadn't raked up all her foolish dreams and uttered all the thoughts to which no man had ever listened . . . she'd always felt bitter because a man doesn't understand that a woman has got brains too. And in bed she thought of that small, insignificant boy with his bristly hair: he's a schat, a treasure, she thought and she had to smile at the pun: a schatt without a schat, a treasure without a treasure . . . She searched for a pretext to meet him again. The next morning, however, she woke up with a feeling of nausea, of disgust with this whole life . . . termuren and the nearby town: it was a noose in which higher powers kept her head ensnared . . . where were the dreams of her youth, where was her will to fight, if now she was almost willing to marry a boy who had never yet shaved? She took her sunshade and her golden bracelet and said to vapeur that he needn't cook so much mash at noon, because she was going to brussels . . . and with the address of her cousin maria in her pocket she got on the train. She'd never seen brussels and was overwhelmed . . . as she walked around, asking in the big stores, they looked at her with pity: her cousin lived at forest and the tram took her further and further through ever more streets; soon ondine saw that brussels was too big for her, she'd have to wage a giant's war to get to the top here . . . she would grow old and grey in that superhuman struggle . . . and an old, grey ondine, what was that? No, she must be young, with golden bracelets round her wrists and ribbons in her hair.*

## THE PROFESSION

Little pros bursts into the room, his mouth looks sharp and fierce like a notch in a block of wood: you, writer, have chosen a profession which has never become a proper profession . . . or a science . . . but politics has already become a profession and a science, taught at the university . . . political science . . . and what does that mean? that means that the sons of the rich can go to the university and choose to be a doctor, a lawyer, or a socialist minister . . . professions in which you get rich. And having said this, little pros is gone and away, because he's said what he knows, but doesn't want to know what you say.

## I LACK SOMETHING

*Ondine asked about 3 times whether they hadn't got to forest yet . . . and finally the tram stopped, it was at the terminus and with outstretched arm the driver showed her a muddy suburb: a chapel road and an unguarded level crossing, the long, long wall of the labor . . . no, it wasn't the labor, how odd, it was the f.f.f.: filature et filterie forestoise. She plodded along in the mud and twice passed a little cake shop, in search of the large business . . . and then an intense joy rose in the goitre under her chin: it's only a little cake shop, she jubilated . . . she's only a little lower-middle class woman who's got to serve in the shop and be polite to the children who come with 10 centimes asking for a half-franc cake. She went in with feverishly glowing eyes. They were surprised, they hadn't expected her, and had no food worth speaking of; there wasn't a bed for her either, unless she slept with valeer, in a bed by the trapdoor, where it was cold and draughty. Ondine was content with everything . . . she jubilated . . . the only thing which hurt her that day was to see that they were happy, that the child thrived, and tattled, and had 5 proper fingers. Valeer hardly answered when ondine asked him a thousand*

*and 1 questions, in the narrow bed . . . he was tired, he'd been unloading sugar all day and fell asleep at once . . . it was good to see that here too he was a seedy beggar, his worn jacket and frayed trousers hung on a nail beside him . . . and on his finger—how could it have been otherwise—was a bandage again. There was something about him which ondine couldn't bear: in his tiredness and shabbiness he looked happy. And the next morning, when ondine asked what was this, about sugar, cousin maria replied that they'd been able to expand the business thanks to 1,000 francs that had come their way; they'd bought sugar with it which was going cheap. Ondine said that at home they'd got many thousands of francs, that they'd accepted a contract for a whole row of workmen's dwellings and that she was about to get married to someone called schatt . . . his name isn't far wrong either, and if their cousin needed 10,000 francs she only had to say so, but ondine could see that no help was needed here. And as she was flattering them, she became malicious: on the train there had been a man who wanted to make a pass at her, but she'd make sure that wasn't going to happen to her, to go to the altar violated: when she, ondine, married, she would still be a virgin . . . and also, she roared with laughter remembering that she'd asked for her cousin in the big store: I thought you lived in new street. Cousin maria listened, her hands in her lap, and laughed too, so stupid was she. Ondine became furious, all her marvelous fabrications fell flat, and also the things she'd wanted to fling at the sugarplum's face didn't materialize: he didn't look at her, but sat by his sugar calculating and counting. She took her sunshade and left; it was pouring with rain; she was covered with mud before she even got to brussels . . . and then she had to get on the train . . . she could have cried . . . I lack something, she said. Everybody has got something to hold on to, except me. Look at that priest there, running to catch the train clutching his skirt . . . what do I care if the train has gone, I'll take the next one. And she thought all people were small and silly: the ticket collector and the station master; she could have thrown herself under the train.*

## BITTER, TOO BITTER

*As soon as ondine got home, she went to look for oscar. She walked up and down in front of the villa, but as she didn't see anyone, she rang and asked for the money . . . oscar saw her out, in the hall she asked him to come to termuren that evening, behind the level crossing. She sat by the window, looking out, waiting . . . at last he went by, sheepishly, with a somewhat stooping gait . . . he didn't look at their house, he looked neither left nor right, but lurched like a diver . . . and as she watched him pass she saw that his shoes had just been resoled. It was ridiculous. She was suddenly afraid, it was abnormal that she could never see anyone without finding him ridiculous, small and pathetic. She went after him and together they followed the railway till they came to the broom . . . the broom wasn't in flower; it was october, they were black bushes without a soul . . . and she heard herself saying things to which she listened without believing a word: that she'd been on a train, alone, and that a priest wanted to molest her . . . but that she'd thought of him, oscar . . . of his wonderful soul, of her life which would become altogether different with him. She longed for something spiritual. Oscar looked at her helplessly . . . he sweated, although it was chilly . . . because what he was hearing now was so unreal, he had never known anything but that bare attic room where he sat dreaming by a piece of stone; he knew nothing of life. Soon after they'd moved into the villa his mother had sent him out to fetch a bottle of paraffin; he'd almost cried, clutching the empty bottle under his arm, in search of a shop. In search? That was precisely what he didn't understand, that there are things in life for which one has to search. Ondine laughed when she heard that he was already 20, instead of 16 as she had thought. And you've never been out by yourself? she asked. The devil raised his horns inside her, began to itch inside her to make a fool of him so that he'd run away crying. But for some reason he began to talk about his stone again, hesitantly, as if he expected her to laugh at this too: now I know what I should cut, he said, I'll cut your head in stone. It touched her. He made a drawing of her, as they were sitting by the dead broom . . . it was a sweet girl's face he drew, without the lines by her mouth, without the bird's nose or the over-round, over-smooth neck. Maybe he didn't notice all this, or maybe he had drawn it first, but it had looked too much like an old woman. Ondine couldn't part with the drawing, she put it in her pocket and said he could always make another one for his stone; she was afraid of crumpling the paper. He had never known anyone to be so grateful for anything he'd made, and he bent his face towards hers so that she might kiss him again. She laughed, kissed him very briefly, and lay still, in the not very dry grass, her face towards the grey sky. She cried. She thought of all sorts of impossible things, of her struggle against the socialists, of mr brys who was now in england suffering god knows what poverty . . . she thought of the first doubting socialists who'd left the sick fund out of fear, because mr brys had been refused communion, how they gradually went back to the meeting room by the station, one by one, frightened, and weighing up their fear of hell against their hope for a better life . . . she thought of the timber yard which they'd never been able to pay, and whether they'd now be put in jail. But these were all side-thoughts, trying to distract her mind . . . because she really thought of the child which she had dropped in the lavatory, which would have been about 3 years old and would have been able to chatter by now. She felt so miserable, and kept looking at the sheet of paper with the drawing of a girl that didn't look like her . . . and suddenly she flung her arms round oscar's neck and asked him to marry her.*

## THE END?

This is the end of the 2nd chapter: today some sunshine and tomorrow some rain and wind . . . or what was it again? . . . we don't feel like looking back, because god knows there might never be a sequel. We, you say . . . msieu colson of the ministry has long since ceased writing in his notebook, he's got to study hard, to become chief clerk, and he has a weariness on his eyes, so that he can't read anything except the bare necessities. And tippetotje the painter is still with those rich people in tervuren avenue . . . far from creating new roads in the art of painting . . . cold and unmoved. And johan janssens . . . oh, don't talk about johan janssens! . . . he's got no profession, no job, no bread; he went to see the old house painter by the 1st dirty houses on the corner of thrift street and prospect street and asked whether there was any work for him. Now he walks along chapel road in white overalls, with ladders and pots and brushes, painting walls . . . he, who used to describe our cultural life, now paints wall-life. And you?

You, boon?

Your wife enters and surprises you, lying with your head in your arm on the writing desk . . . she asks: are you asleep? . . . and you answer: no, dammit, I'm not asleep, I'm crying.

# AND NOW THE THIRD AND LAST CHAPTER: YESTERDAY SOME SUNSHINE AND TODAY SOME MORE WIND AND RAIN AND MUD

## MRS PROUST

Why should this be the end of our book on chapel road? asks johan janssens, poet and House painter . . . who has wound a bandage round his work-worn finger . . . he makes a grimace when the pretty lucette asks him: did you get paint on your finger, johan janssens? . . . he takes his notebook out of his pocket in which he writes down his hours of work, and reads from it:

today: painted front of widow proust's house, wrote down everything I heard and saw . . . but simply and soberly, without any literary comment; why should I? it isn't going to be put in the paper, is it . . . so today I painted the front of a house and wrote down what I heard and saw: the blind man opposite crosses the road to ask me whether it's oak that I'm painting on and whether I'm using pre-war brushes and whether . . . well, it would be quicker to write down what he wasn't interested in . . . and when I didn't answer any more he calls out, with his face close to mine: are the painters still here? Then another blind man comes along, blind jean, and I say: be careful mate, there's a ladder there . . . thanks, he says, stepping aside . . . and the first blind man hears that it's his fellow-sufferer and calls: hello jean, how's life? And the other blind man, walking past, calls back: well, as you . . . as you . . . and suddenly he realizes who's talking to him, so he goes on: as you hear mate. The next moment widow proust herself appears round the corner, looking at her house. She starts talking about her life: that she goes out cleaning and scrubbing for the rich, to earn a bit of money so that she can have her house painted—so she's never at home in order to pay for her house to be made beautiful—and she tells me how vicious people are: today she saw a lady leaving the house of a well-known collaborator and she, mrs proust, called: good morning, madame, just to show her that she'd seen her going to see that collaborator. And she tells me that her mother had never been inside a car, and on her deathbed she asked to be buried by car: then I shall have been in one after all. Then she tells me that she's already made her will, and has stated in it that she wishes to be burnt in the crematorium . . . all the formalities have been completed, + a signed telegram which has to be sent off as soon as she's dead. And when all the formalities were completed I was so happy, she says, that I thought: I wish I'd die soon now. Because she says she doesn't like the idea of being buried by a priest sprinkling holy water on a corpse that's beginning to smell, and with people standing around crying with 1 eye and laughing with the other, saying: so there you are, she's dead and gone . . . They're not going to know when I'm gone, she says, I'll be dead and the car from the crematorium comes to fetch me; people will turn pale when they don't see me around in the street any more . . . they'll wonder: where has she gone? . . . haha!

Haha . . . johan janssens bangs his notebook shut and stares at the bandage round his worn finger.

## A HOUSE PAINTER'S TIMETABLE

Actually, I told you a lie, says johan janssens, poet and House painter . . . when I said I hadn't added any literary comment . . . penmanship still runs in the ex-journalist's blood . . . and I'm ashamed of it . . . so let me repeat it all the way I actually wrote it down in my notebook:

monday, 28th or 29th, painted the outside of the blind man's house . . . the father looks like a 7-hour-slobber and has been operated on his eyes 3 times already . . . veils come over them . . . his son is 30 and blind; I remember him from school: I believe I used to see you at school? I say. Yes, he says, that's possible, I used to go, for a time, but that was only so I wouldn't be on the street. He's interested in everything, in paint and varnish and putty and how many brushes I have worn out and what kind of hair is best for paint brushes, all sorts of things I don't know myself. While we're talking another blind man comes along, he stands still about 1 meter from our ladder, as if he could smell that there was something in his way, and I call out: careful, mate, there's a ladder there. The first blind man asks: is that jean, going there? . . . hey, jean! And jean calls back: hey, frans! . . . how's life? And frans calls noisily: well, as you s . . . as you hear, he says, more quietly. In the morning I worked four hours and used 2½ gals, of paint—actually, it wasn't even 2 gals., but never mind, there's no need to be fussy—and two sheets of sandpaper, 1½ lbs. of putty and one pint of naphtha—that lamp should be looked at, it hums—in the afternoon I worked 2 hours painting widow proust's house, opposite, had a chat with a passing policeman; he's married and has a child and earns scarcely 2 thousand francs per month . . . he won't get fat on that . . . and then people are surprised when there's corruption in the police. Then I worked at the music master's, with the boss's son, who split his sides with laughter, I forget why—I½ hours, the varnish has already been included. Then I had a look at liske's front door and I saw I'd got the color wrong—and liske, who's always so particular!—I'll have to see what I can do about that: ½ hour. Tuesday: I½ hour second coat at the blind man's house—yes-yes, yes-yes, he always says—and I saw frans' sweetheart, from behind because she'd already gone past, and I said: I don't care for her legs much . . . and frans said: neither do I. Then we worked in the bedrooms of an ailing old woman who's got a sickly husband. She only worries about one thing: whether her floor stays clean. Pink paint—let's say two gals., because I forgot to measure it, and 4 sheets of sandpaper and a ball of putty. Finished at 5, because frans got bored. So did I, but well . . . what isn't boring? Didn't look at liske's door.

## A GOD OF SCIENCE?

*Ondine saw her father going greyer every day . . . he kept telling himself over and over again how this whole business of the villas had started . . . she sometimes surprised him, walking up and down in his workshed, talking, as if somebody was walking beside him, listening. The tragic peak in his thoughts seemed to be the moment when he'd discovered that false signature: he'd stop walking and shrug his shoulders as if to show that he couldn't have done anything about it, that the world was too big and he too small. Making excuses for himself, he'd look up, as if a god, a supreme judge, was hiding in the rafters. Yet, he couldn't easily believe in god . . . to him god was science, or would become science . . . he wasn't much good at putting it into words but it came down to this: that science in its searchings would arrive at something, at a positive image, embracing everything . . . and that this something, which would be discovered, would turn out to be god. He explained to this idea of the future, to this god-science, that building these villas had been beyond his strength . . . it was pathetic to see him pushing his sleeve up, in the silence of his workshed, and showing his bruised, wasted arms, to this something which wasn't there yet. But he was also able to see things from a different point of view, from a practical point of view . . . for instance, he saw very clearly that one day ondine would skedaddle off, would marry and leave him to face the music. But strangely, although he realized this, this knowledge seemed to hang in a mist . . . or rather, it seemed to be something that would happen to someone else, to another ondine and another carolus—nick-named vapeur—somewhere far away in a different termuren; that other vapeur would be put in jail and he himself, the real vapeur . . . the inner one, carolus . . . he would be prevented by this whole business from working on his invention. He would have to forsake his god, and his perpetuum mobile, for which the world was waiting because it was going to be transformed by it, would not get invented. For all these reasons he hardly ever spoke to ondine; to him she was the devil incarnate, the devil in Christians' clothing, standing behind the priest in the pulpit, to prevent the rise of truth and science. He left by the back door, through the humble garden, when it was getting towards noon and ondine had cooked something for dinner . . . he waited till she'd gone and would then, all by himself, as before, make some kind of mash that didn't have a name. He hurried to get away from the house, muttering to zulma that he had a headache and was going for a walk in the fields—if anyone calls, tell them to come back this evening—yet, there was no reason to make excuses to zulma, she didn't understand anyway . . . actually, he was making excuses to himself, because there was work, he had to repair a gutter at the castle, but he daren't start on that gutter, it was too high up and too heavy for him alone, and he needed wood for it but daren't go to the timberyard. He walked for hours and hours, he sat in tralfene woods chewing a sprig of grass or cutting himself a whistle, or snipping an elderstick and engraving inscriptions and alchemists' symbols in it . . . all the while expanding his idea of god, which was still very vague. He argued with himself and was all the time utterly and completely in the right. It was wonderful how clear it all seemed to him, in contrast with those evenings when he used to talk about it with ondine . . . ondine had beaten him . . . she had come up with arguments which had made a mockery of all his beliefs . . . and he didn't know that she herself doubted and doubted these arguments, wondering whether maybe he wasn't right. But she had dismissed this with the thought: if he's right, then it's no more than a small, unimportant truth . . . for how could such a fool ever discover the great, universal truth? What little he knows today he will have forgotten tomorrow. But the next day, or even that same night, she had to convince herself that there had to be something else, something More, than only science and self-sufficient laws . . . because, what else to do with the devil of her instincts and fears? It wasn't for nothing that norbert had made her pray: o thou lucifer, son of the morning, thou shalt become an angel of light once more.*

## THE ORDER OF THE DAY

You tear open a letter from tippetotje the painter and read: I, tippetotje the painter, have heard that all the chairs in your livingroom are empty . . . and I know that my empty chair is amongst them . . . and that there's only johan janssens talking about house painting; I'm sorry, but I've got to write to you about painting too, with this difference that johan janssens is working for the common folk and I for the rich . . . I'm still working for the big industrialist, you know, where the maid prepares the bath naked, did I tell you she's Spanish? . . . well, she came to belgium because here she can earn 2000 francs per month, an incredibly high wage which she can't get anywhere else in the world . . . and she tells me, when I've saved up enough I'll go back to spain and open a shop . . . and I ask her, how are things in spain under franco? And she tells me, with an inscrutable smile: oh, franco is good for us, he gives us food and clothes and jobs, it's only a pity he doesn't belong to the people. But yesterday she quarreled with the other maid and went for her with a bread knife, and now they're both in hospital. Now there's only a very old woman who's got to do all the work by herself: she's 72 and she's got to cook and serve the meals and wash up and put everything away . . . meanwhile the chimney sweep, I beg your pardon, the industrialist, sits with his wife in the immense dining hall, where the huge table is laden with crockery and silverware, as if the whole naval college was coming to dinner . . . and I, tippetotje, surprised the old woman on the stairs, she was sitting there panting and out of breath, with a dish in her hands, while the industrialist was waiting for his dessert. And then there's something else, I'd almost forgotten: talking of spain, he'll do whatever's necessary to let me travel all over spain unhindered, because he's a friend of franco's, and another thing, that's two things I'd almost forgotten, I can't get a telephone ... What! no telephone? roars the industrialist ... and 3 days later they were busy putting a telephone in.

My regards to your wife, to the pretty lucette, to the girl with the fat behind and to my jeannine, the temporary one ... oh yes, and to the daughter of the machine man too ... yours tippetotje.

p.s.: don't write those things about the big industrialist any more, he might get nasty.

You read the letter to those who occasionally come to visit their empty chairs ... but the music master says, with something of a hesitant contempt: I think our little tippetotje is becoming a bit of a boaster ... telephone, paintings sold to the industrialist, paintings sold to the baron, journey through spain ... kind regards to all the women of termuren ... wasn't this tippetotje nicknamed the 'ship of lies'? Long ago, when she was younger but just as naive?

## ONLY APPEARANCES MATTER

So the music master is a bit contemptuous of tippetotje, is he? says johan janssens ... I, johan janssens, I'm not just a bit contemptuous of her, I'm downright angry ... especially about that last bit: don't for heaven's sake write anything about the industrialist, because he might get annoyed. Poor tippetotje, having dinner with the rich, having a telephone installed and selling paintings ... poor tippetotje, for whom only appearances still count. And I'm also angry because she says that I, johan janssens, write only about house painting ... that's a lie ... when I wrote about house painting and the common people for whom I work, I wrote about something quite different, far more important ... writing about house painting and about the common people amongst whom I work, I might for instance say this:

that everyone likes to be what he's not: all the workers you see walking around these days, painters and glaziers and plumbers and electricians, and all the truck drivers and all the people pushing hand-carts: they all wear khaki caps like american soldiers, and they all push the peak up, like the american soldiers used to do. Naturally, the son of my boss wears one of those caps . . . like he used to wear a student's cap. And talking about that student's cap, I asked him once, was he going back to school then? . . . and he answered, no, but all my friends wear a cap like this; willy works in a shoe-factory but he still wears a student's cap. This morning he turned up with a badge on the lapel of his jacket: royal painters' school, brussels. And when he saw me looking at that badge with a smile, he said with a mixture of defense, apology, and indignation: in the school of graphic art here in the town of the 2 mills they don't have a badge. That's why we all wear the badge of the painters' school in brussels.

you see, when I write about this you can say: johan janssens is on about his house painting again . . . but that isn't true; I'm writing about appearances, the only thing that still counts today . . . and I smile because the son of my boss believes in and lives by these appearances and is blessed . . . but I get angry when tippetotje renounces our flag and runs after the appearances of the rich in tervuren avenue.

## AT THE LEVEL CROSSING

*And then, in the woods, vapeur decided he never wanted to have anything more to do with ondine . . . he couldn't be her real father; he might have begotten her, he might have had a part in the origin of her sinful body, but her spirit was nothing but a continuation of zulma . . . a continuation of the spirit of the castle, so to speak. He returned by a short cut which he'd got to know by heart, this autumn . . . and one day he decided to go much further still, and go home late at dusk . . . however, he didn't know the way very well, in the fields, and he was as pleased as a child when he finally found the railway; he decided to follow it, and crossing the track he began to think—after all, he was human—of all those unguarded crossings everywhere . . . couldn't there be an invention so that the train itself, approaching in the distance, would open the gates, or rather, close them? Where were his thoughts? . . . and then, vanishing, would open them again? He puzzled and calculated and suddenly . . . because he'd reached the broombushes . . .*

*he saw her whom he was shunning like the plague. She sat there with that boy schatt, wasting her wretched life. He was so startled that in his perplexity he said good-evening, and then remembered that he'd sworn never to speak to her again . . . he looked at them blindly, turned away and walked on, almost in tears. He stumbled over everything that could be stumbled over, he stood by the level crossing and heard the train approaching, in the distance. And right through his confused thoughts, right through his shame about her, lying there with that child, he thought again that something ought to be done to make level crossings safer . . . automatically he took a piece of chalk out of his pocket and started drawing, but he wiped it out again because it had become too dark . . . he hurried to his workshed where he could give free rein to his ideas in the light of a stable lantern . . . he started drawing lines on the floor . . . because he had an odd way of inventing things, he figured and calculated, he made a hundred and one drawings, without knowing what it would lead to . . . suddenly something would flash through his mind, he'd wipe everything out and start anew, wildly drawing lines in order to seize this flash of lightning, to lay it down in figures. But this time he found it impossible: each time he thought he'd got it, there was something else, a side-thought hampering his brilliant impulse, chasing it away: he gazed around, brushed his forehead, wondering what it could be that was troubling him; it was the slumbering worry about the debt which he couldn't pay, it was also the memory of ondine who was lying in the broom bushes with a child surely no older than 14, whom she was probably spoiling so that he would never come to any good: he knew her. Such thoughts confused him, made it impossible for him to draw anything that made sense . . . he should have been able to talk to somebody, to get rid of all these cobwebs . . . but even suppose anybody would have heard him out, where should he have started? Which thread from the tangled skein should he have picked up first? Ondine, who had come home by now, saw his inner struggle, saw that he wanted to put into words something that was beyond his comprehension, and saw, most of all, his inability to begin: he feared a quarrel, he worried that she would reproach him for being powerless, he feared the days and days when there would be no conversation in the house: they would be like ghosts, almost touching one another amongst the close walls and yet not opening their mouths . . . ondine, on the contrary, imagined him falling ill . . . she saw that he wished to be dead and that he was trying to hide this, but it was so obvious to her; she understood him. She had suffered from such whims too, lying in bed with the secret wish not to wake up again . . . and she also saw that he was too cowardly, that he would rather be taken for a thief, for someone who hadn't paid his debts and who'd been in jail.*

## ALL SAINTS

Again it's all saints and the white chrysanthemums bloom in your little garden . . . again the stove burns and your wife is knitting, although knitting isn't good for her nerves . . . but what else can she do? She's knitting something without name or shape, which she calls perhaps, deep down in her mind, her illegal knitting, like you write and write away at something without name or shape which you call your illegal book. As you're writing you look out of the window now and again, at no-man's wood with its trees in their late autumn attire, where the bells of all saints chase away the last leaves with their bim-bom. Because it's all saints' day again, the white chrysanthemums are in flower and the girl with the fat behind has come back in her rolling camper, and stands by the roadside beside the autumn leaves, beside the castle brook, beside the place where the people from the 1st dirty houses throw their empty vegetable tins. She stands there with her camper to let the winter of termuren descend on her, like the bats hanging from a beam in the darkest corner of the bam . . . termuren is the darkest corner of the barn, to the girl with the fat behind . . . with your pen raised in your hand you look at the steps of her camper, longing to see her come out; the door opens but it isn't her . . . it's a wild boar, a tall, lean man . . . his name is woelus . . . woelus wildboar . . . he's the husband of the girl with the fat behind who made the blood of jaspers, the commercial traveler, race through his veins, who made tippetotje reach for her sketch book, made boon write columns full of poignant nostalgia . . . you got married somewhere in the land of the sun and the fairs and the shooting tents . . . now that it has become winter and the weather is getting bad, now that it's all saints' day and the death bells toll, you come to the darkest beam in the bam: termuren . . . to hibernate beside woelus wildboar . . . you will rest your fat buttocks in his bony lap, while it's raining and snowing and freezing and it is dark outside ... and you'll say: listen to that, outside, woelus wildboar, and here I'm lying so snugly against your hard belly. But just as you're writing this down the doorbell rings, your wife puts down her illegal knitting and goes to see who's there; it's woelus wildboar himself ... but he's not wild, he's subdued and turns his cap nervously in his hard fingers, and says that the girl with the fat behind is ill, she's got something in her tummy, she's sweating and has a fever ... your wife says it's probably flu, flu in her intestines, she gives woelus wildboar some aspirin and the advice to tuck his wife in warmly. Woelus returns to the camper reassured, but you, picking up your pen once more, know better: it's all saints' day and the death bells toll and even the girl with the fat behind marries and grows old and gets something wrong with her belly and dies. Bim bom.

## THE PROLETARIAT OF OFFICE CLERKS

You see, says msieu colson of the ministry ... I didn't come to see you on all saints' day; first I thought: they're probably baking all saints' cakes ... and then I thought: he's probably busy writing about all saints ... and you see, I was right! You reply: you were right, msieu colson, I was writing about all saints, but you were wrong in not coming to see me. He sits down smiling in the light of the reading lamp, which you made last week out of an old kerosene lamp ... as he sits down in the light of this lamp, you see a nervous twitch flashing across his tired face. He says: I'm glad this exam for chief clerk is over at last, because I didn't read a thing any more, I didn't write any more, I didn't live any more. I studied to be a head clerk ... now the exam is over and I've passed ... but I haven't got my promotion yet and I won't get the extra salary either ... although I've been doing the extra work for months and months ... and now that I've passed the exam all the employees at the ministry come and see me, all the deputy head clerks and the drafters and the clerks and the ushers and the lift girls who are taking exams or want to take exams. They come to ask me what they should do in order to pass ... there's this boy from tralfene who writes stories about the train on which he travels back to his remote village every evening and about the bridge in his mouth which doesn't fit properly so that he daren't laugh when he's at the office . . . and there's that other boy who's interested in the theatre . . . the catholic-sponsored theatre; he and his wife have three children and she's expecting the fourth; he earns less than 3000 francs but has to pay 1500 francs rent for his apartment . . . apartment, don't laugh, it's only one room . . . for their one-room apartment in which they keep their coal and their firewood, where they cook and eat and sleep and expect a child, the fourth, as I told you . . . and they all come and ask me whether they ask a lot of math at the exam or a lot of economics or a lot of . . . a lot of . . .

Msieu colson says: 2 weeks ago, when I was in the middle of the exam and didn't read or live, I still found time to write down this here: people don't go to school to acquire knowledge for themselves, but to lay the foundations for earning money. I wrote this down with a certain irony, even with disdain . . . but today I wonder what anyone could do, in a one-room flat, with knowledge with which one can't earn money? 2 weeks ago I also wrote in my notebook that all those who've been to school and have learnt some math, some economics, some business science, are ashamed to be farmers or laborers . . . they want to be office clerks . . . but today I can see their need, and I see with dismay that their problem has no solution: the problem of the proletariat of office clerks.

## HE TOLLED MUCH TOO LOUDLY

I do paint houses, says johan janssens, but I also write my reynard the fox . . . actually, I don't want to tell anyone before I'm sure, but there's going to be a change in my circumstances; I shall soon be needing these reynard stories . . . well then, I told you how the wolf sang mass:

when the wolf in monk's habit preaches the gospel: the poor had better watch out . . . this was the last thing isengrinus sang at the altar, then he turned to the empty chairs and preached the famous sermon which is known in church annals as the Dubonnets sermon:

dearly beloved doubters, beside the image of king noble you have seen in every window a church advertisement, every day; first a man going to catch a train with a suitcase in his hand, and then a man going to church with a missal in his hand, and then the legend sun sunday sunday mass, after the wonderful example of dubo dubon dubonnet, and then again another advertisement . . . but now the advertisements are finished, beloved unbelievers, because there's no longer any need for you to wear your shoes down in order to go and drink a dubonnet mass: the elections are over and mr derenancourt of the castle is in the government. Bravo, reynard wanted to call out, but he remembered in time that one shouldn't make a noise in church but ring the bells instead. So he rushed to the bell-rope, to announce to the world that the dubonnet sermon had come among us. This bell-ringing disturbed isengrinus who hastened away from the altar and came rushing along: what's the matter? Are you sounding the alert to start the war all over again? But reynard asked him what kind of a monk he was: here you come preaching the truest sermon that ever was, and then you go all shy and bashful, like girls and geniuses when they notice that the bells are ringing to make people look at them! Yes, but . . . said isengrinus, turning and wriggling his long body . . . but surely you know that the small man is free to think what he likes but not free to speak his thoughts as freely as he likes . . . and anyway, why don't you preach, you know what I said, you only need repeat it and I'll ring the bells if you like. All right then, said reynard, remarking once again what a coward his uncle was, and he showed the wolf how to hold on to the rope, as high up as he could, and then to pull as if it was for a death vigil for which somebody was paying through the nose. And when the wolf stretched his long arms reynard grabbed the end of the rope and tied it round his uncle's feet: you must ring much louder, he said. Isengrinus discovered the trick too late and struggled to escape; he tugged and pulled, and cursed the bells which went on ringing; he implored reynard who called to him from a distance: that's right, uncle, lots of people will come to your mass, I'm sure; I can already see the friars hurrying round the corner.

. . . he would like the din,  
he thought, of tolling the tocsin,  
that he would learn it at any cost.  
But the result was honor lost.

For he tolled much too loud,
so that down in the street the crowd
and all who were inside the Elmare
thought it was Satan and ran in a scare
to where they heard the bell being tolled.

And before isengrinus had time to say that he wasn't a fascist but that surely he too had the right to leave the world and go into retreat in a monastery . . . I shan't eat more than 1 goose a day . . .

The mob had nearly beaten him cold
before he had time to speak and say,
"I want to become a monk and pray."

because the louder he talked the more savagely they broke the sticks across his back. johan janssens.

## THE WEEKLY PAPER

All saints' day is over . . . and whereas in the summer it rained and rained, it's now all the time mild and fine . . . msieu colson looks down chapel road with johan janssens, at a man engaged on burying the footprints of hundreds of generations with new cinders . . . the man leans on his spade and says to every passer-by that it's very nice weather for the time of the year, a bit damp, but very mild . . . and msieu colson of the ministry says that at least he'll get home with dry feet now, *but that all the same he'll miss the holes and puddles and cart tracks and ondincke's footprints* . . . things that were familiar ever since his childhood . . . he remembers that his mother used to say: look out little colson, don't step in that puddle . . . and that later she changed this to: you rascal, you've been walking in the puddles again, your shoes are wet and your socks are soaking, you'll catch a cold and do you think shoes don't cost money?

Johan janssens nods, very profoundly, like all people nod profoundly who haven't taken in what was said to them . . . shoes do cost a lot of money, he says . . . I've just bought a pair of shoes for my son jo, he's 9, and he keeps running up and down those heaps of cinder, up and down, wearing down his shoes . . . shoes cost a lot of money . . . the other day I mentioned something to you and I said I wasn't sure yet, an improvement in my income, for which I would be able to carry on with my stories of reynard the fox . . . well, it was for the weekly . . . they're asking me to fill a column in the weekly like I always used to do in the daily paper . . . they're not paying much, but still, it's something . . . and I worked out how much of an improvement this is going to be in my income, if I add to this what I can earn if I go on writing for the literary monthly The New Times, and for the belgian radio . . . Stop, stop, calls msieu colson of the ministry—and the man who's supposed to be tipping cinders all over chapel road thinks it was meant for him and replies: what d'you mean, stop? I haven't lifted a spade for 2 hours—but it was to johan janssens, poet and weekly journalist, that msieu colson called out: stop; soon you'll have too many sources of income! But johan janssens smiles grimly and says: don't worry, msieu colson of the ministry, because weeks and weeks have passed since then . . . and all I've received, apart from my returned manuscripts, is a tiny fee from the weekly: look, it's in this box here. Do you get it in a box, asks msieu colson of the ministry. No, but the shoes for my son jo, who's 9, I bought them with that money.

## ONDINE LAUGHED AT IT

*Ondine had to laugh at her father's death wish, which became watered down to a wish to sleep and to go on sleeping . . . she forced his mouth open by asking when he was going to start on this gutter . . . when he replied his voice leapt at the first word, so that even zulma laughed and started imitating him. Whatever he managed to wring out of his mouth, she still went on crazily repeating that first word . . . he looked at her sadly and forgot what he was saying: ondine laughed at him: it was a terrifying, artificial laugh. But she was terrified herself, she knew that something would have to be done about all those unpaid bills . . . but what? . . . and she shouted that it was all up to him now . . . she named all the things she'd done: saving, trudging all over the town to collect money, walking herself into a sweat, suffering all sorts of humiliations . . . but you're the smart one here, buying valves for an invention that will never come to anything, and you spend money to repair burnt down churches and chapels as if you were related to the bishop. Amidst this flood of words vapeur no longer saw his own skein of thought, he searched and searched for a thread, to say at least something. Earlier on, when he was alone, it had seemed to be anyone's fault but his, and now . . . now . . . soon he would turn out to be the only one to be blamed. He clung to what she had said last, although he realized that he ought to say something quite different—that he hadn't spent the money on the chapel. But ondine cut him off saying that someone who wanted to play the contractor would have to make sure that his crazy wife couldn't get at the money. This made zulma shriek with laughter and again she began to repeat what vapeur had just said. He started to retreat and make excuses . . . there were tears in his eyes . . . he wanted to say . . . no, he wanted to ask, hadn't they better put their heads together instead of quarrelling. This made ondine laugh even harder, even more artificially: I earn it, you squander it, and then we've all got to put our heads together and we'll get jailed together . . . you can go to court by yourself and make excuses about your crazy wife there, but not to me. Vapeur didn't contradict her, on the contrary, he sat quietly in his chair staring at his weary hands, thinking that everything she said was the truth: it was the truth that he shouldn't have married a loony, and it was also the truth that he shouldn't have let ondine be the boss over things which he should have kept under his own control . . . not she should have signed that order book, but he. And in order to get away from it all he went out by the back door and sat down on the lavatory . . . and there, in the silence of the falling night, everything ondine had shouted, faded, and he saw again the pattern of his own tangled thoughts and he was in the right again: he wasn't the only one to blame, surely others had done wrong too! Like that girl talking about her mother now, saying he had a crazy wife, wasn't that a crying shame? If god was what they all imagined him to be, someone who was watching them and who punished or rewarded them, why didn't he punish her right away, why didn't he come down to slap her face? And the way she'd been lying in the bushes by the railway . . . Yes, of course, he'd forgotten to say what he'd seen there . . . and he wanted to jump up to go and reproach her, but, what would be the use? She would have twisted it till he'd been lying there doing dirty things. And he sat down again; he reflected that it had always been like this in his life . . . all he desired was to sit quietly in a corner, messing about, making unbreakable glass, melting something which it had never been possible to melt. And all the others, the whole world, wanted to do things which overstepped the mark, which were punishable. And the most incredible thing was that they always held him responsible for it. Oh, he needn't ask why, it was because they took him for a fool, to be taken advantage of. He also reflected, bitterly, that it was very well possible that god was really sitting up there, just as they all imagined, and that he was precisely as unjust as all the others . . . that his son christ, plus vapeur, would be punished for the wrong done by others, that god would say to him: get out of my sight, into the everlasting fire . . . and that ondine, who'd never done anything except teaching children dirty things, would be allowed into heaven.*

## I HAVE NOT LIVED IN VAIN

Among your mail there's another letter from tippetotje, in which she talks of a plan for a painting . . . I've seen the surrealists, she writes, and I think I could paint such things too: I imagine the corner of an immensely tall room and in this cold, empty corner of this immensely tall room there is kramiek, standing by the telephone . . . that's to say, he's on the telephone but there is no telephone . . . there's only a cold, empty corner with kramiek in it thinking he's telephoning . . . he brings the receiver to his ear but his hand is empty and by his ear there's nothing . . . he's wearing very large glasses and through one of the glasses you can see his eye, smiling at the message he's not hearing, through the telephone . . . and through the other glass you don't see an eye, but on the glass a text has been stuck, a cliche, a winged word, a dogma. You see, that's what I would paint if I were a surrealist . . . writes tippetotje . . . but I'm not a surrealist, I'm tippetotje, and I must take a subject that suits me better:

a dream:

a row of workmen's cottages, painted very realistically, although they stand in a kind of dream-landscape, under a dark, closed sky, with a reddish glow, but lit by a brightness which seems to come from the painting itself, coming out of this otherwise very realistic row of workmen's cottages: and in the front door of the first cottage stands the most wonderful dream of a naked girl . . . she's naked up to her waist so that you can see the dream of her legs and thighs and the devil's hair on her sex, but above this she wears a red, hand-knitted pullover. This is tippetotje's letter.

Yes, that's tippetotje's letter, says the music master, matter-of-factly . . . he looks over your shoulder and sees a p.s. which you didn't read out, in which tippetotje apologizes about this business of the industrialist: I only meant, she writes in the p.s., that you ought to camouflage the names a bit better, because there's someone mooching about here who might give me a kick in the arse.

So that's tippetotje's letter, says msieu colson of the ministry gently . . . I think tippetotje is a nice girl but she's rather fond of chattering about you and she's been boasting about your work to the industrialist himself and to the baron himself . . . and now she finds herself in a tight corner, she's introduced them to your work in which you're making it hot for them.

So that's tippetotje's letter, say johan janssens, poet and weekly journalist; and what she says about her paintings is right . . . it reminds me of a film scenario I'd like to write . . . in which I'd make fools out of all those people talking about painting without being painters: a parody on the film about rembrandt, in which they said the nightwatch was his greatest painting because it was the biggest . . . and in this rembrandt film, the one I'd want to make a parody of, an old, half-senile man stumbles about in an attic; he wipes a bit of dust from the night-watch and says: I haven't lived in vain . . . and then he very symbolically blows out his candle . . . and then afterwards in this film I'd have this nightwatch cleaned and a quite different nightwatch appears from underneath and I'd make all the experts say that now it's even greater . . . so that the old man has got to light his candle again and look at the cleaned nightwatch, stammering; I have twice not lived in vain.

## VAPEUR IS GOING TO EXPLAIN

*Vapeur was tossing about in the night and in his mind he went 100 times to the timber yard to explain, although there was nothing to explain, only to pay. And yet . . . He was waiting for the morning, he wanted to go before he'd have second thoughts stopping him, making him incapable of explaining and settling things . . . he'd have to go now, at once, or he'd become like zulma. He got up, to make himself some coffee and eat a piece of bread and he walked through ondine's bedroom . . . which wasn't really a bedroom but a kind of landing by the stairs . . .*

*she'd been tossing and turning, her blankets were tangled like a rope, a sign that she didn't have a quiet conscience either—but this didn't occur to vapeur. He woke her up and said he was going to the timber yard to see who'd get the better end of the stick. She stared at him, drunk with sleep. Wouldn't you have thought she'd at least cover herself up, he said to himself . . . no, she lay there with her dirty behind bare, her flesh covered with devil's hair—devil, Devil, he thought—she stayed as she was, shamelessly, and laughed at him into the bargain: with a scornful snigger she pulled the bandage from his eyes which he'd been busy blindfolding himself with all night. She asked him, hadn't he better go a few blocks further and report at the police station, in order to save time. And then there was something else she wanted to tell him . . . something, a side-thought that had just occurred to her when he talked of going into town . . . But, what was it? . . . I'm still half asleep, she thought. She brushed her hand across her forehead: how odd, it was the same gesture that vapeur always made when he couldn't remember something . . . but he didn't understand that she wanted to tell him something, he thought she was only rubbing the sleep out of her eyes and he also thought, it's easy enough to lie there showing your private parts, laughing and rubbing the sleep in and out of your eyes; I sacrifice my night's rest and lie awake for hours, brooding how I get out of the trap you were fool enough to set for me . . . and so you really ought to be in it . . . it's all very well for you, filthy slut, lying naked in front of your father and behaving indecently by the railway, depraving children. And what about you, ondine shouted suddenly: what did you do in brussels if you had to come and live in this dump . . . I think you must have come here to hide . . . and if you saw me over by the broom, so what? . . . my love for that boy is one of the purest things in the world; he hasn't touched me that much, do you hear, not that much—she flicked her fingernails to show him how little he'd touched her . . . and anyway, why shouldn't I have a right to be in love and get married, like anyone else? Marrying, you see! said vapeur . . . you see! . . . it made such an impression on him that not another word, not another thought, would come to him . . . Marry! and leave him to cope by himself. He went down the stairs, speechless; ondine saw him, walking with his head between his legs, so to speak, and she suddenly remembered what she'd wanted to tell him: the socialist band was going to play in the streets for the first time, and would pass through termuren, through chapel road.*

## THE TOBACCO FACTORY

Kramiek rang the doorbell, irredeemably ruining, spoiling, poisoning your evening. He talked about the little tobacco factory which was built some time ago behind the hatter's shop, behind the waste land with the empty tins and cans, just before the 1st dirty houses. He's an office clerk there; he has enriched the proletariat of office clerks . . . and being a socialist, or an ultra-marxist, fighting for equality, freedom and brotherhood, he speaks slighteningly of the other, common workers, who have to handle alum and get themselves black and dirty: I, kramiek, office clerk. And he, kramiek, office clerk, talks: mr alfons, the son, has finished his university studies, he's a lawyer but doesn't want to practice, he stays in the tobacco factory and is the torpedo boring all other tobacco factories into the ground, quite legally. In the summer he lives at the seaside, does mr alfons, in a villa in the dunes, and in november, when the weather is damp, like now, he lives in brussels where there are parties and bars and defenseless naked women. Kramiek tells with verve of mr alfons driving to brussels with his factory girls . . . he picked them dirty and black from by their machines, put them in a closed, dark van and drove off to brussels with them to put his house in order; he took them into a posh hotel with their dirty aprons still on and let them eat and drink. Then, when they were tipsy, they had to go back home to the town of the 2 large mills and the 100 and 1 little shoe-, tobacco- and knitwear factories. He tells it without comment, kramiek, only with a tinge of audible respect for his mr alfons of the tobacco factory, and with audible regret that he wasn't among those tipsy factory girls. And then he talks of the people from the prefabs on the other side of the town of the 2 mills . . . snotty-nosed girls of 14, 15, straight from school, creeping into the lavatories with the men, with their skirts up and their pants off, and they join the Christian workers' youth, but all they're good for is making a mess of their work, walking around with little dancing steps, and filling up their bags with stolen goods every noon and evening . . . so mr alfons ordered the gates to be locked at noon one day and had them all searched: they were standing in a row and they all furtively emptied their bags and dropped the stolen stuff on the floor. Kramiek laughs. But then he frowns and says:

there's one thing I don't understand: when all the war money was called in but we hadn't been issued with the New money yet, a cart-load of tobacco arrived and mr alfons paid with the new money which nobody had seen yet . . . how was that possible?

Yes, and how is it possible that you're fed up to here with kramiek.

## WHERE'S YOUR DIPLOMA?

Johan janssens, poet and journalist and house painter, says msieu colson of the ministry . . . he goes now here then there, trying to find some government job somewhere, for instance as a librarian or inspector of libraries, or assistant in a museum, anything . . . not that he's so keen on being somebody's assistant but he's keen on a regular monthly wage so as to give his wife and his son jo a more or less decent standard of living. But the socialist-minded poet and journalist johan janssens, . . . says msieu colson of the ministry, can't get such a job in a state with a socialist-minded government, because he hasn't got a diploma . . . and the socialists proclaimed this from the earliest days from the roof tops, that in a socialist state no encyclicalist friends and sons of encyclicalist friends would be let in through the back door without proper qualifications—liske used to say this too, she's dead now; she was a very socialist-minded girl when she was alive, rather of the far left, and with ultra-scarlet tendencies too . . . so liske would have said that it was fair if even her friend johan janssens would be unable to get a government job without a diploma. But let's look at things realistically . . . says msieu colson of the ministry . . . suppose that someone like kramiek, who's been to the university but knows nothing about anything, gets a government job connected with books on art! But liske, who was a friend of johan janssens' . . . says msieu colson of the ministry . . . liske didn't understand this: the socialist government demands a diploma and professional knowledge in the case of humble ushers and clerks and drafters and deputy head clerks . . . but it doesn't demand diplomas in the case of socialist friends and sons of socialist friends—like that son of a distinguished person in the socialist party, who's a student at the university but is never there . . . a government post was created for him: he got a smart office with pictures on the walls and carpets on the floor . . . a government office, but he's there no more often than he was at the university. So the point is not . . . says msieu colson of the ministry . . . the point is not that our friend the poet and journalist and house painter johan janssens hasn't got a diploma, but the point is that while we have a socialist government he's a poet who goes on writing unpalatably hard socialist truths.

## THE SOCIALIST BAND GOES BY

*So the socialist band went out for the first time, and would pass through termuren along chapel road . . . the simple folk had discussed it yesterday and the day before . . . they were frightened, they didn't know what evil that band would commit, nor did they understand that liza's husband was pulling their legs when he said: you'd better bolt your doors. They did: they locked doors and shutters and decided to go out into the road as little as possible. Ondine stayed in bed, with a strange, empty feeling: she had heard people talking about it and like a storm, like a hurricane the realization swept through her that she had drifted infinitely far away from her childhood dreams. Instead of conquering heaven, of halting the earth in its course, she was frittering away her days quarrelling about trivialities, about paying a timber yard. And her grief, her pain at this awareness was so intense that she daren't think of it any more, but shut her eyes tightly, and said to herself: I must forget it. Also the thought troubled her whether she wasn't applying her energy in the wrong direction . . . because look, she said to herself: I must try to forget . . . and really, she did forget it. Wasn't it in fact the reverse, though, shouldn't she use her energy to find mr ludovic and persuade him to put a stop to . . . this music . . . this timber yard . . .*

*In her mind she followed her father on his way, his stations of the cross . . . and so she arrived at the amazing thought that maybe he was a new christ: what would he do if he met the music on the way? She imagined that she was vapeur, her father . . . and being vapeur she saw all these socialist faces coming towards her—and meanwhile That which she'd been trying to forget, rose in her more strongly than ever—and she tried to remember all those sinister faces that were passing before her mind's eye, so that later, some dark evening, she might attack them one by one . . . pounce on them, on all of them, and . . . well . . . amuse herself with them. She was still lying in her narrow bed, on the landing by the stairs, and her hands moved down her loins to the hair on her sex . . . she burrowed her fingers in it, restlessly . . . her eyes were wide open, the pupils abnormally large.*

## PROFESSOR SPOTHUYZEN ABOUT THE SOCIALISTS

As you had to be in the town of the 2 mills anyway, you went to see professor spothuyzen . . . his doorbell didn't work; the front door was ajar, so literally and figuratively you plunged right in. He welcomed you with his hands, his eyes, and his lips, all moving as if electric sparks were jumping out of them and he took you to his livingroom which is a study and into his kitchen which is also a study and into his bedroom which is also a study . . . and finally he took you into his study, which isn't a study but a place where his children play, where his sunday suit lies on a chair and his wife's bicycle stands. Sit down, he says . . .

pointing to a chair on which there is a pile of books, on which are a full ashtray and a dirty coffee cup. Professor Spothuyzen teaches literature in the factory of universal intelligence, but although he knows each name, date of birth and collar size of any one writer, he has missed his vocation and should really have been teaching political science, because he daren't have an opinion on writers and books without first reading 100 fat books about them and writing another 10 . . . and then he still says that it doesn't reflect his opinion exactly, because his views have slightly changed in the meanwhile. But you should hear professor spothuyzen about politics! about the local politics of the village where he was born, in which he still takes a passionate interest, and of the town of the 2 mills where he lives . . . and about the national politics of this country, which isn't politics but a question of individual interests . . . and about world politics which isn't politics either, but a collision of capital and power. Professor spothuyzen's political persuasion is the libertine one . . . *the one of mr ludovic gour-monprez of the labor, whom we know from the days when ondine was a young, fast girl.* But although professor spothhuyzen's libertine ideas are the same as those of ludovic gourmonprez, they are yet quite different . . . like the pope's Christianity and the Christianity of the squinting old charwoman are the same and yet quite different . . . like the ultra-marxism of dr pascalius prostituaan and that of hoedje are the same and yet quite different. Professor spothuyzen, who usually wears a fine little smirk round his lips . . . thinking he can hide his inferiority complex that way, which isn't true, on the contrary: it gives him away . . . professor spothuyzen puts his mocking smile down on the chair with the books and the overflowing ashtray and stretches out his arm like a machine gun: look at those houses on the other side: respectable bourgeois houses all of them, wealthy houses even; well, officials of the ultra-socialist party live there, and civil servants in the ministries of the socialist government: they whore and they fornicate and gamble for high stakes and don't know what a book is . . . I bend over fat books in order to read them and you bend over fat books in order to write them, and they don't know what a book is . . . and I, professor spothuyzen, see that the socialist party has collected the savings of the socialist laborers and now they don't know what to do with the capital; they are afraid of a real socialist state and they always take care not to be in the government on their own, but always to have the old encyclicalists and the old libertines around them: they have evoked the socialist ghost and now they're trying to push it back into its little box, and they only want to take it out when it suits them. They've taught the people that decency and virtue were only the reins with which to keep control . . . but now the people have thrown these reins aside and steal and lie and swindle and whore and fornicate, like in the old days only the great did . . . and so now the world is going to the dogs, at both ends . . . and now the socialists sit in their ministerial saddles and they are too stupid to see where they've failed.

## BLANDINUS HILL

Maybe you shake your head at that story in which the wolf rang the bells in the monastery at elmaren, was beaten half-dead by the friars, escaped and found himself . . . on blandinus hill—because elmaren monastery, in those days, was over at dingen, far away . . . and the monastery of blandinus hill is somewhere near ghent—yes, but the learned professor fossejaegher will do more than shake his head, he'll say that it's an erroneous combination of william and nivardus. But that isn't so: in an odd way it's supposed to prove that one monastery might just as well be another monastery: you enter appelghem monastery by the front gate and you leave it by the back gate of st. arjaen monastery, where 2 pairs of slippers stand under the bed, as the song has it. There's also a surrealist notion that the door of the most ordinary livingroom can open out into the land of darkness and death . . . into the fantastic world which william of madoc created. No one has read madoc and yet it must be the description of that dreadful land where people go never to return. Now you can understand that it's possible to enter the gate into elmaren monastery to pull the bellrope so hard that the friars feel obliged to give you a black eye with the relic of saint aberdan . . . but that you, escaping with a beating, find yourself on blandinus hill. There reynard lay in a ditch, waiting for isengrinus, and before the wolf had uttered a word, he said: what do you mean, my fault! Could I help it that you pulled the rope so clumsily that it got twisted round your legs or that you preached the wrong kind of sermon that clashed with the number of your ribs? It didn't occur to the wolf to contradict this, he was depressed, his limbs ached all over and he said: I think they were only angry because I wanted to hide in their monastery, in exchange for all the friars who go to america to sing mass and never come back. Then reynard and isengrinus, laughing and grinning, went down the hill together, through the leek field which also belonged to the monastery and there they fell head over heels into a trap . . . no one knew why this trap was there, unless maybe it was in the nature of the friars, who were made in god's image, to dig wells for other people to fall into: now how could reynard and isengrinus get out, with honor and dignity? You wanted to retreat from the world, said reynard to the wolf, so you'd better say your prayers, because the way you swear you can't expect a miracle. Isengrinus, who wanted to become a monk, went down on his knees and began to pray devoutly: lord, grant a miracle to thy servant isengrinus that he may get out of this well and out of his misery. At that same moment he noticed that reynard was climbing on his back and was hoisting himself out of the well . . . but lord god, called isengrinus, it's not reynard but me you've got to help out. But reynard was already a long way up the road and called from afar:

go on praying; it's because you were in a lesser state of grace than I. johan janssens in the Weekly journal.

## HAS THE PLAGUE PASSED ME BY?

*Vapeur knew nothing about the socialist band which was going out for the 1st time . . . he'd put his mouse-eaten overcoat on and had left without as much as a cup of coffee or a piece of bread . . . he'd only drunk from the spout of the coffee pot, but all he got in his mouth was cold grits . . . in the timber yard he almost wept and called everybody sir, even a girl with glasses who happened to be there but had nothing to do with it, so blind was he, staring at the words that came falling out of his mouth. He said they ought to see his wife, and that his son had gone away, to brussels, and that his daughter this and that . . . that he would save all his life, to pay, if need be . . . but that now he had an invention in mind, the plans were ready . . . which was a lie and yet not a lie, the plans were only ready in his head . . . but that was the same thing . . . and anyway, they wouldn't have understood; and once the invention was ready he'd be able to . . . to . . . But why was he taking all this trouble? He looked around to see if the police had arrived yet, and was surprised that for the first time in his life nobody interrupted him. He heard himself speaking and the others listening . . . they even gave him a glass of beer . . . oh, they didn't take it too tragically, they also gave him a cigar and he decided he'd work on his invention with heart and soul in order to pay these people; he had to sign a paper that he should pay interest every six months, for as long as the money hadn't been repaid; he signed anything they liked, blindly; he was grateful that they were treating him like a human being, not like a thief. He went home happily and told himself he'd been a fool to worry all these days and nights, all for nothing . . . and he decided he'd always do this in future whenever there was any trouble: go straight to the people and explain: you drink a glass of beer and you sign a paper and that's the end of it. On the way home he met a music band in chapel road, they were playing a battle song and however much he tried not to join them, it was useless: it was as if termuren itself was welcoming him festively. He shouted to the musicians and started to sing, in french . . . he danced and walked at the head, in front of the drums, swinging his arms . . . he sang with the others: this is the goal for which we die, this is our ho-ho-holy ideal. And behind the few musicians there were about 7 people: the sailor, the one with his 1 hand, the student and boone . . . The student spoke to him and in his crazy, happy drunkenness vapeur didn't understand him too well; he went home, content with the whole world. Yet, as he walked along, it surprised him he didn't meet anybody. Isn't termuren empty, he thought. He looked at the closed shutters, the barred doors, as if the plague was on its round again. Come on, the plague . . . what was he thinking of, it was years and years since the plague had last been heard of. He hurried home and found zulma, all alone, huddled in a corner with her apron over her head. What was the matter? He went outside and was startled to hear that the 1st socialists had passed by. And now he remembered that they'd all been on clogs, the whole band, and all the followers as well . . . the clog band, the socialist band. And vapeur muttered very quietly, very softly and shamefacedly what he had sung together with them: this is the goal for which we die, this is our ho-ho-holy ideal.*

## THE FURTHER HISTORY OF MR POTS

I met tippetotje in brussels . . . says msieu colson of the ministry . . . she had a wrinkle round her mouth which was waiting to become a smile: she talked about the chapel road book, from which she's been removed, she says, because she earns her bread licking a baron's arse . . . while in her opinion there are sadder ways of earning a living . . . this baron wants to put her in a shop of objets d'art, in the avenue des arts . . . and talking about the chapel road book she offered a piece of criticism, justified, I think, that we're neglecting too many of our heroes . . . for instance the poet johan brams, johan janssens' colleague . . . and our national mr pots, who said that bitterness is an illness.

True, you do occasionally quote these winged words, but where is mr pots himself? Which illiterates receive advice from his fat law books today, which air receives his used carbonic acid, which new mistress his sperm? You're a useless writer if ever there was one, said tippetotje the painter, a romantic of the worst kind, a prize fool, an idealist like mr pots was when he still wore the romantic honorary title of Advocate of the Poor . . . he was the advocate of the poor all right, they all came to him for advice, with the paper clearly visible in their pockets in order to get free service . . . and the advocate of the poor put a complete smoker's set in his waiting room—a big box of cigarettes with matches, and an ashtray—and they grabbed the cigarettes with both hands and stuffed them in their pockets, they took the matches, box and all, and put them in their pockets and one day the ashtray had disappeared too . . . they sat in the waiting room and sat in the hall, they walked in the courtyard and besmirched his shit house, they sat in the kitchen, cooking steak and chips—this sounds like kafka's novels but there's nothing imaginary about it; they actually did buy steak and butter with mr pots' money and fried it in the frying pan on his cooker—and mr pots, the advocate of the poor, became the poorest of the advocates and his colleagues in the town of the 2 mills shunned him like the plague because he'd been an election candidate, and also, he was a man of free morals, with a new mistress in his bed every week—when they came downstairs in the morning, both in pyjamas, while the people were already sitting in the waiting room and in the hall, on the stairs and by his bedroom door, one man said, as he was coming down the stairs with his mistress: you picked up a nice one there, comrade pots! So his colleagues in the small town of the 2 mills shunned mr pots like the plague . . . the town council, being encyclicalist and socialist and libertine, kicked mr pots out of town: maybe the ultra-marxists would have kicked him out too, if they'd been on the council—and now I, tippetotje, met mr pots in brussels; he's left the small town of the 2 mills and he's lost his title of advocate of the poor and has gone to live in brussels, in tervuren avenue, amongst the rich: he receives the industrialist and the baron and gives them advice; I, tippetotje, lick their arses and he gives them advice.

And msieu colson of the ministry, who met tippetotje the painter in brussels . . . who in her turn met mr pots in brussels . . . msieu colson of the ministry falls silent and the wrinkle round his mouth changes into a smile.

## THE 7-HEADED DRAGON

*No sooner had the socialist band gone past, than people hesitantly peered out of their doors . . . vapeur swore by heaven and hell that he'd seen them, that he'd talked to them, but no one would believe him. They wondered whether that band had gone past the chapel without making the sign of the cross . . . zulma came outside and shouted that they hadn't gone past, but that they'd flown overhead with a terrible scream . . . The people crossed themselves and wondered what was in store for them: a young mother with a child on her arm burst out sobbing with-out knowing what she was doing; a peasant joined them; he'd come all the way from his fields and looked, back at his fallow land as if he was wondering whether it was worth tilling the soil any more, now that the world was going to perish anyway. Vapeur looked at them and daren't utter his unbelief: so it was the same as usual again, that he and only he had seen them and had talked to them . . . he had to conclude that they were people like any others and that therefore all the things these stupid blockheads imagined were fantasy. And god? . . . god was science and progress and struggle and love, and something he couldn't explain to these stupid yokels here. While he was thinking all this, feeling ashamed and guilty, he felt someone looking at him, looking right through him: he looked up, and it was ondine . . . her again, the devil. She smiled as if she understood him, as if she could peer into his deepest soul. That evening, after they'd been sitting in the dark for hours and ondine asked was the lamp ever going to be lit, vapeur suddenly said, as if to see what she'd answer: the time will come when we'll have to pray to god by making inventions. Ondine didn't understand: she started to think frantically in order to grasp what he meant . . . she thought it was connect-ed with the wooden clog band which had put even him in a rebellious mood . . . she looked at him in the dusk, wondering what in god's name she should answer. And because she was silent, vapeur saw this as an admission, as an agreement to something which in his eyes was undeniable. He laughed. But he halted in the middle of his laugh, because as suddenly as he had felt joy at having discovered the truth, came fear, because ondine was after all one and the same person as the devil . . . and to him it didn't seem to add up that he no longer believed in an omniscient, almighty, supreme god, but that he couldn't get rid of this childlike belief in devils. Well, he admitted to himself, if I see the devil in her, that means that I see her as a child of darkness. And when he said 'darkness,' he meant That which was connected with zulma.*

*However, the reason why ondine didn't answer and didn't even ask again for the lamp to be lit but remained sitting in the dark . . . was that there were too many worries hovering around in her mind; she'd known that the band was coming and what had she done to prevent it? She'd got dressed and had stayed in the garden, sitting in the sun . . . and what else? . . . she'd wandered about the house, waiting for oscar, and had gone to the broom bushes with him . . . and what else? Nothing else. Nothing of all the things she'd once imagined she'd do with those socialists. God had deserted her, god had made her heart empty, had made her senses sad and had robbed her will of its strength . . . why, why? . . . that's what she wanted to know, and as they were sitting by the broom and she was looking at oscarke, at his tousled boyish hair which stood on end in a tuft, and at his wet nose which he wiped on the sleeve of his jacket, she heard the wooden clog band approaching in the distance . . . the drum beat on her heart and the trumpet stabbed her brain, it hurt her hurt her hurt her . . . oscar, on the other hand, got excited hearing the music, he laughed, he fumbled in his pocket and wanted to show her a drawing of an ornament he was going to sculpt in freestone, to put in the façade of their house, later: two intertwining o's,*

*Oscar and ondine, and he beamed with pleasure at his wonderful find. But she pushed him back roughly, she hated him because he too was stirred by that stupid poorman's band . . . they'd talked of marriage, but no, it was impossible, she saw it herself. . . . her place was where the fight was on, where the 7-headed dragon of the socialists was going to be crushed. She lay on her back, dreaming and thinking of those who used to be her friends and who had now deserted her . . . and she started because oscarke had quietly come nearer by, and pressing himself on top of her, kissed her as she had taught him. Oh, it didn't mean that he felt any kind of desire . . . but he saw her lying there, so withdrawn, so dejected, and he was like a faithful dog, anxious to show her that he was there . . . but she, she couldn't have felt more revolted if a worm had crawled across her lips. She shuddered and began to vomit, she pushed him aside so gruffly that he rolled down the bank . . . she walked away, home, and he followed her sadly, calling her, and showing her the drawing with the two o's, like a child.*

## MISUNDERSTANDING I

*When you've finished elaborating on how oscarke sadly followed ondine, msieu colson of the ministry is full of pity for poor oscarke . . . to be running after that vixen ondine, who'll never understand him, while he will never understand her! he says regretfully. And he adds that quarrels and vexation are usually caused because in spite of all that's said and written, people are still inadequate in the use of words and have to express the most complicated things in their poverty-stricken language. Johan janssens agrees with him and adds that on the anniversary of multatuli's death he put a piece from max havelaar in the weekly journal—the address to the lebak chiefs—and that a reader wrote to him: I read your article on multatuli but in my opinion you didn't say enough about max havelaar. The music master raises his hand and says: not only are we poor in words, but the result is this: one word has to cover a number of completely different meanings . . . for instance, we say: Man . . . but what does the word man mean as long as we can't comprehend the concept of man? . . . sometimes I almost think, in my capacity as a music master, that there is just as big a difference between one man and another as there is between my streptococci, my sperm, and the stars of the milky way: completely different beings with completely different relationships which can have no contact with each other—could you imagine my sperm having a love relationship with my streptococci and can you imagine my streptococci discussing the mystery of the holy 3 with the stars of the milky way? Maybe one of my streptococci went to confession and communion this morning somewhere in a deserted corner of my larynx, which they converted into a temple . . . but his sense of justice, his fear of punishment and his hope of a reward are so infinitely far removed from me, who am his god, that I simply spit him out together with hundreds and. thousands of others of his kind. And you, who have been listening to msieu colson and johan janssens and the music master, you know that they've simply been describing what you depicted in ondine and oscarke . . . but—what's the point of upsetting them unnecessarily?*

## . . . AND MISUNDERSTANDING II

As you dip your pen in the ink . . . *in order to explain how far removed ondine and oscarke really are from each other . . .* the doorbell rings and msieu colson of the ministry enters, to tell you something, as an afterthought, something he forgot yesterday, that he's been to the picasso exhibition and that there was a little petty bourgeois with a pince-nez walking beside him—it could have been mr brys, but I suppose he's been dead a long time now, hasn't he?—When they handed him his entrance ticket he made a very friendly, courteous bow and trip-tripped into the exhibition rooms . . . looking at pictures, lovely . . . but suddenly he stopped with a start and in the glasses of his pince-nez I could read anxiety: what kind of a wild animal is this, this picasso? is it going to grab and devour me? The music master who entered together with msieu colson of the ministry, begins to expound how his 2 cats tried to grab a piece of meat which was out of their reach and how after a while they gave up their fruitless efforts and started looking elsewhere, in animal resignation, scratching behind their ears in an almost human way . . . and because this gesture was almost human, it looked extremely funny, so that the pretty lucette started laughing uncontrollably . . . then one cat stopped scratching for a moment and looked in amazement at this creature that was uttering such a strange sound . . . so that the pretty lucette began to laugh even more uncontrollably. I, the music master, looked at her in amazement too . . . don't you think that's funny, she asked, still laughing . . . and I looked from the surprised çat to the laughing woman and back, and had to admit: no, actually I think it's sad that animals copy our gestures with which we express regret, but find our laughter a strange, disturbing noise. Johan janssens, the poet and weekly journalist, who arrived together with the music master and msieu colson of the ministry, now begins to tell the story of when a door-to-door book salesman came to his house once . . . it soon turned out that he wasn't only a salesman but also a Poet . . . and that this salesman offered him a copy of his collections of verse to read, and maybe to review in some journal or other . . . of course he was a respectable man like any other respectable man, a man of the resistance, a Democrat, who'd been in several concentration camps and could tell very moving stories about them . . . but he had an idiosyncrasy: out of professional mis-training he had started to talk in book-titles . . . he couldn't tell a story without illustrating it with the title of a book . . . and I, johan janssens, though this was so peculiar that I devoted a column in the weekly journal to it . . . unfortunately, however, he read this column too and promptly sent me a furious letter: that he didn't talk in titles and that anyway I still hadn't reviewed his collection of poetry yet: you see, he was as remote from me as the cat from the pretty lucette and as the music master from the pretty cat . . . I mean the pretty lucette.

## A DREAM—OSCARKE

*Ondine stole away from the kitchen and lay down on her bed to think about how utterly far away oscarke was from her . . . she pulled the covers over her ears, which first gave her an anxious dream in which norbert pushed her into an empty room to repeat her prayer to the devil . . . and once in this room she saw it had no door or window, but she felt that Something was standing behind her and was looking at her back . . . she wiped the sweat from her upper lip and knew that she would die if she looked at what was behind her, because it was too big and dark simply for her to look at it and then to go on living as if nothing had happened . . . but dying with fear she would KNOW: however, it was too sly, or rather, it was more endless, more unreal than she was herself. When she turned round with a jerk it was AGAIN behind her back; she screamed and woke up with a jolt. Sweat was pouring off her. I'd got too much cover on me, she thought. Yet she thought about the dream for a long time, it seemed to mean something which was of importance for her future life . . . it was as if something deep down inside her FORCED her to think about it: I was afraid; something was looking at me, I had just said the prayer to the devil: thou angel of darkness shalt become an angel of light again . . . so it was the devil . . . but how was it possible, aren't we ourselves the devil, the angel of darkness who will become an angel of light . . . who will become god, through science, as my father says . . . was I afraid then TO SEE MYSELF in that empty room?*

*She couldn't solve the riddle, she kicked all the blankets off and lay naked . . . only the night and the darkness were her cover . . . while the sweat dried cold and chilly she began to shiver violently in the december night: she thought of valeer and of this person and that person and of everything that had happened in her life so far: it all came creeping before her eyes, some things slowly and others fast: I'll get up and go for a walk round the garden, she thought, and fell asleep at the same moment; she dreamt of oscar, a love dream of which she was ashamed even in the dream itself . . . strangely enough, while knowing all the time that it was a dream, because she said to oscar: it's a good thing that I'm dreaming and that I feel dreadfully cold in this dream, otherwise you wouldn't be allowed to do all these things you're doing to me now . . . she laughed and encouraged him with scorching, whispering words: hurry up, make me passionate, make me hot, I feel much too cold. And oscar laughed too, he was big and strong, he was beautiful . . . no, that wasn't how it was . . . he was the same oscar as always, but now everything about him was good and strong, as if she was looking at him through colored glasses . . . even his spiky hair was beautiful: he was the same and yet different. She pressed him against her body and woke up like this: clutching her pillow against her breasts; all that day she longed for the evening, to see him, to tell him that she'd dreamt of things which he shouldn't do again, naughty boy. She stood on guard by the door although she knew he never passed this way . . . it was Saturday, cleaning day, she frittered away the time by the front door and the house remained dirty . . . she kept carrying more buckets out and as there weren't any paving stones in front of the house, it soon became a pool of mud in which she sloshed around on her bare feet . . . she took a bucket and washed her feet and legs by the front door . . . she couldn't care less that people shook their heads at her, she also washed her left thigh which had got a spot of mud on it; she defied these people, she had nothing to do with them, she had nothing to do with anyone; tonight she wanted to be beautiful, everyone was allowed to see that she way a mare, longing to get to her stud. As soon as she saw oscar she started talking about marriage . . . she spoke of it as if it was something that had to happen the next morning . . . she painted a picture of what their life was going to be like: he making sculptures all the time, of her, and holding exhibitions and selling. He listened in rapture, his mouth hanging open: no, he wasn't the one from her dream, he looked like him, he was oscar, but without the piece of colored glass which had made him so beautiful. She daren't tell him of her dream; it wouldn't have been the same any more. She couldn't recapture this dream-person, this better, more beautiful dream-oscarke . . . but she imagined that this would come in time . . . she ignored the poor fellow beside her, and when she spoke, she spoke to the being that was hidden inside him, the being she had dreamt of and who wasn't really him.*

## THE CHRISTMAS TREE

It's almost Christmas, did you get a Christmas card from tippetotje the painter? asks the music master . . . and while they look at each other in surprise, msieu colson of the ministry replies: I only get children at my door singing carols because christ is going to be born and they don't care a damn that christ is going to be born because when I told them it wasn't nearly Christmas yet and that you only sing carols on holy innocents' day, they said: we don't care, we are born and so couldn't you give us something anyway because it's winter and times are bad.

It's winter and times are bad for them and it's going to be Christmas soon and I had a Christmas card from tippetotje the painter . . . the music master repeats . . . I'm surprised at it: why should she send me a Christmas card, of all people, with a rather hackneyed subject, in my opinion: poor children looking through a window into a room with a Christmas tree? look:

everybody looks and johan janssens hits himself on the forehead and says: I've got it. One day I gave tippetotje a Christmas story to read which they'd rejected at the paper because in their opinion it mocked the small worker . . . but that wasn't true at all, it wasn't trying to make the readers split their sides with laughter at the stupidity of the small worker, it was intended to teach the stupid worker to live the way he ought to live . . . because on Christmas day he's got a Christmas tree in his front room, a very big one with a double row of lights, red, yellow, green and blue, and with imitation snow; and he's left the shutters of his little terrace house open—his little house: so much a month and it will be his in due course—in order to impress the passers-by on Christmas eve . . . but at the very moment that a passer-by really does get overwhelmed, and the man's children have gone into the front room and stand gaping at the Christmas tree, then the mother comes rushing out of the kitchen, cursing what the hell do they think they're doing in the front room by the Christmas tree, go and play somewhere else or you'll get a thrashing you won't forget in a hurry. And at the end of this story, which was rejected by the paper, there was a postscript: beside that Christmas tree in the front room there was a club armchair . . . in which the husband isn't allowed to sit when he comes home from the filature or the labor, what the hell does he think, that a club armchair is to sit down in, perhaps? . . . no, it's only there to give the impression that we, working class people, aren't really working class people, but people with Christmas trees and club armchairs and the story ended with the moral, that the worker likes his boss to think that he's earning more than enough; because you can see for yourself; he can afford a big Christmas tree.

The music master gazes again at the Christmas card which tippetotje sent him . . . although he still doesn't understand why she sent it to *him* . . . and he says: I see, it isn't really the hackneyed theme of children standing outside a strange house gazing at a Christmas tree, but they're standing outside their own house, looking longingly at their own Christmas tree—look at that girl, rubbing her hand on the window pane, the way kids do! Msieu colson of the ministry takes the card in his hand and looks at it, but when he unthinkingly turns it over, he reads the address: poet and weekly journalist johan janssens! Everybody laughs, because the postman must have made a mistake, delivering the card at the music master's instead of johan janssens'.

## HONESTY

It's new year's day and your friends-heroes come to wish you everything you'll need in your life and work . . . you wish them the same . . . it doesn't cost you anything . . . but suddenly the poet and weekly journalist johan janssens says: most of all I wish you honesty in your work. It's as if the earth splits in half: a chasm appears and johan janssens and all your other heroes stand on one side of it and you on the other side:

and standing on the other side of the chasm you stammer that you're always talking about honesty but that now, because of this wish of johan janssens', you have to ask them a question, man to man . . . some time ago you went to the letterbox to post your usual article for the world-of-today, by the 1st dirty houses behind the labor, and out of a house under construction came a workman, a white cigarette in his black hand, looking left and right for a passer-by who could give him a light. Be quiet now, you've worked on building sites too, you used to stand on scaffoldings and had to walk on the cross beams carrying sheets of glass, to be placed in the gaping window holes. And at the moment when you were about to put the biggest window pane in . . . thinking how difficult it is to span it, that the hole is so high up and so damned hard to get at, and what the hell some architects think they're doing, making drawings without ever giving a thought to the poor workmen who've got to carry out their plans . . . and just at that very tricky moment you feel like lighting a cigarette first, but you can't find your matches. Where could I have left them? You jump down quickly, looking around for a passer-by and you ask: could you give me a light, mate? Alas. Now reverse the roles . . . suddenly, walking outside, asking for a light, you're no longer boon the glazier, but you're boon the writer going to post his article. You barely touch your pocket and say: I'm sorry, mate, I haven't got a match. But you know you have. And now you ask: why did I say to boon the glazier that I hadn't got any matches, and do I still keep talking about honesty and humanity?

Over at the other side of the gaping chasm stand your friends-heroes, and amongst them the music-master takes your side: he says that maybe you had no time . . . and by time he doesn't mean that for instance you had to catch a train and would miss it if you gave a light to everybody on the way . . . no, by time he means that you might have been thinking about a difficult problem, about an article, about a novel, about your philosophy.

But you, on the other side of the chasm, know that this isn't true: you had plenty of time, there was no question of a train or of a problem: it was really because you find it hard to bear with people who always forget something—now their matches, now their cigarettes, and then their money or their philosophy or their trousers,—and then maybe what's inside them—and also because you're beginning to hate people who think they're the relatives of machines; they're born to let themselves be bullied by everybody, even the dumb machines themselves; they accept things and forget things, they live a bit and then they die a bit.

But on the other side of the chasm there is also tolfpoets who with his deviate mind has become a relative of the machines; and he says: I can't agree with this . . . because if you regretfully decide that most people have become relatives of machines, it would have been better if you'd promptly taken a match out of your pocket and given boon the glazier a light . . . then he might have realized that a different kind of person does exist, while now he probably only watched you going with scorn in his eyes and maybe he thought what I think and what johan janssens thinks: that it wouldn't do boon the writer any harm to go back to putting in windows now and again.

## CRIMINALS AT LARGE

So here we are in the new year, says msieu colson of the ministry . . . and when I pick up my file of newspaper cuttings to see what happened last year, I have the same feeling as magister nivardus had in the year 1100 and something, when in his bitterness he wrote isengrinus and thought the end of the world was near: gandhi murdered at new delhi, attack on the italian ultra-marxist togliatti at rome, bemadotte, the u.n. mediator, murdered in jerusalem. And then there are also the Black days . . . for instance the day on which france announced the number of her war victims . . . 267,469 soldiers and 378,457 civilians killed. And what about germany russia poland england and all the others, from the remotest corners of our village, the world? I go on leafing through my file of newspaper cuttings and I only find disasters, murders, rapes, assaults, wars, ominous army maneuvers, financial and political scandals. And just like magister nivardus wrote his grim isengrinus, we write our book and think in our bitterness that the end of the world is near, because I, msieu colson of the ministry, can only measure the world with my own small yardstick: all of those disasters and wars and assaults and scandals take place high above my small person. But listen to this: I was at north station the other day waiting for the 18.25 and 2 gentlemen were walking up and down the platform, they daren't use their car in this frost so they take the train . . . walking behind them I heard one of them say he's doing well, because he makes gunbarrel covers . . . and these covers have to be sent to spain through Switzerland, he says. The other gentleman who's walking beside him, replied that the new war which is coming, of which there's talk, is really necessary . . . trade will boom again. The first gentleman, the one who makes barrel covers, agrees . . . but suddenly he stops and says: but the atom bomb, couldn't that come this way and hit us? And I, msieu colson of the ministry, was perplexed because there was the 18.25 coming in, just as usual, stamping and shrieking and vomiting smoke, so innocently, full of its own importance: a train . . . and yet unaware that soon it won't be needed any more, if the world remains the way it is: full of criminals who can't be arrested but who walk up and down a station platform when the roads are too slippery for their cars and who are called gentlemen.

## ONDINE SPEAKS OF MARRIAGE

*Ondine talked to oscarke about their marriage as of something which had to happen tomorrow morning . . . but she hadn't counted on 1 thing: on oscarke's fear: he didn't like the idea of getting married at all and tried to shake it off. True, he did like to hear her talk about it, as of something very far, very vague . . . a dream in which he made her statue and won the prix de rome and had a studio as big as a theater . . . but when this marriage became something real, which was going to happen tomorrow, he felt incapable of making anything that could win even the measliest little prize. And anyway, he'd never dare show himself with her in public . . . he suddenly remembered painfully that once he'd walked home after school with his girl cousin . . . and that the others had laughed at him . . . that he'd been cowardly and had hidden in a corner till long after his cousin had gone home with another boy. And now he still felt the same shame at being seen with a girl . . . but he daren't say this to ondine: he thought up another reason to put off the marriage: a reason which wasn't a reason, something so childish and naive that in any other circumstances it would have made her angry . . . so angry that she would have broken it off . . . but now this dream, this dream which put a gloss on everything, was still in her head: she laughed and kissed him and called him her sweet boy; he mustn't worry, she would see to everything.*

*She started seeing to things by turning the house upside down, raging, cursing, raising hell . . . her father had cleared the kitchen table and had sat there with a home-made wooden train in front of him . . . he'd also made rails and was busy trying to get the train to run smoothly on the track . . . but in the curve it made too sharp a turn so that the carriages derailed and fell on their sides. When he'd adjusted the rails and his miniature train came rushing along like a real one, he forgot his invention for a moment, forgot what purpose this experiment was supposed to serve, and imitated a train whistle when the engine entered the curve; he laughed at his own silliness. This was ondine's moment. She asked how much this toy was going to cost and whether she hadn't better buy her mother a doll so that they could amuse themselves together? He started to make excuses, he began to explain that he'd got so far now that his invention might take a clear and exact shape in his mind any day now, that we're entering on a different age and so on . . . he even became moved by his own thoughts and was about to call her 'my ondineke' . . . she saw it coming, she didn't care two pence about his invention; his joy infuriated her . . . with mock tears she began to explain that now she had finally fallen in love and wanted to marry . . . but as for money to get married, she didn't suppose there was any in this house. She looked around sadly as if she was ashamed of having such parents . . . she repeated again that it was thanks to her that there ever had been money in the house . . . but now it was gone, now, just when she needed it. And as vapeur sat there in silence, waiting for the storm to blow over, she emptied the table with one sweep of her arm and kicked his toy train in a corner: I want to get married . . . and I want to get out of here. But in an amazing moment of lucidity zulma replied that if she wanted to get married and needed money, why didn't she go to the schatts then, they haven't paid yet. She laughed shrilly. Vapeur looked at his daughter and ondine looked at him, and it was strange: again they both had the same odd thought at the same time.*

## OF DISEASE AND MAGIC

How long have I been staring at this title and how long has this sheet of paper been lying empty and cold and silent under my hand while I don't know how to start? . . . under my hand, I say . . . because for Once I can't think of a mask and my own tormented and pained heart has to write all by itself . . . my pained, tormented bleeding heart writes about disease and death and grief, about the transience and fragility and uselessness of this life: once my little sister jeanneke sat on her potty-chair and listened to the tinkling of a small brass chain round her plump wrist . . . she sat there and was the darling of the neighborhood: look at jeanneke, hello jeanneke! my sister jeanneke grew up and wanted to be friends with nobody, go out courting with nobody, dance with nobody . . . she became dry, cross and surly, swallowing powders from the out-patients' clinic, like this, with a sour face . . . my sister jeanneke was a difficult girl, and dammit, I've often said she was going to go to seed, like an onion that's been left standing in the field, forgotten . . . later, she went from one doctor to the next, fussing and whining, doctors who gave her tranquilizers and pain-killing drugs, doctors who gave her injections for her gall bladder and her liver and her thin blood, doctors who prescribed pills and powders and complete rest, or a fattening diet or some strict, ascetic regime. And then one day she collapsed and had to be dragged to hospital, to the operating table . . . yes, dragged, because she didn't want to go in an ambulance, because then people might think I'm ill, she said . . . and it was only a growth, a growth in the stomach which had to be cut out, nothing important, that's to say, fairly serious, but well, lots of people have stomach operations . . . stomach . . . stomach . . . I see my father standing by the window behind which I'm writing, I see his eyes and I have to listen and all the time I only see his eyes . . . his shriveled, dry eyes which daren't cry . . . cancer, he says . . . damn damn, and he bursts out in sobs . . . cancer, he says . . . oh please don't tell anyone, louis, my boy, don't tell anyone . . . cancer, he says . . . the operation was successful, but it's cancer, eating away . . . the dreaded word the murderous word the word that gnaws to death . . . she'll come home and everybody will ask, how are you now, jeanneke? . . . and my sister jeanneke, who was once the joy of our neighborhood, who made the brass bracelet tinkle on her plump little wrist, my sister jeanneke will say: oh, I'm very well, thank you. It's cancer; oh, the eyes of my father who will stand behind her trying not to cry . . . and my mother suddenly calls out: dammit, god, I don't believe in anything any more; I no longer believe in priests, I promised everything and now you see . . . I see . . . it's cancer . . . oh the eyes of my father . . . oh this swearing of my mother who used to believe everything and who now no longer believes in anything . . . who promised everything to god and his saints and who now . . . you see . . . My sister jeanneke is afraid, afraid of what an old soothsayer predicted . . . he's bewitched me, says my sister jeanneke, he's bewitched me, I feel it, I feel it, I feel it, my sister jeanneke shrieks.

But bewitched? . . . I no longer believe in anything, said my mother. Neither do I, not in god and his sorcerers, the priests, nor in science and its sorcerers, the doctors.

## ABOUT ILLNESS AND DEATH

With the mud of chapel road still on his shoes, your father stands in your house and msieu colson of the ministry says that he's having trouble with his blood, which is too thin, and with a nervous tic by his eye which is getting worse, so that one day he went to the clinic and waited for hours in the mental patients' waiting room. Your father is still standing there, with the mud of chapel road on his shoes, listening to msieu colson with withered eyes . . . msieu colson talks about the mental patients who were waiting there: first a tall, thin man, whose trousers were too short, the legs didn't even cover his ankles, and he was shaking and nodding his head all the time, like this, like this, nothing but a bunch of nerves . . . all the same he was trying to jump the queue, to be seen first, because he'd come on The train, he said . . . the way he said it, it was just as if there was only 1 train in the whole of belgium and that it only ran Today. Next to him there was a thin lady with an enormous hat and she told everyone that it was because of her nerves that she'd already squandered enough money to buy a house and that her maid had robbed her . . . robbed her of a sum large enough to buy another house . . . so that was 2 houses . . . and so you knew right away that this was that lady's dream: to own a house of her own. And if anyone turned away from her endless lamentations she at once fixed on a new victim. Next to her was a very old, very small creature which you might have taken for an animal, with spectacles and with a pasty, indoor complexion . . . who said: if the doctor doesn't come soon I'm going to hang myself. The doctor should have started at 2 but it was already 3 and all those patients sat there waiting in vain; maybe the doctor has crashed into a tree, they said . . . maybe he this or maybe he that . . . anyone can have an accident. If these were mental patients, I'm a mental patient 3 times over, msieu colson of the ministry concluded.

And because your father is still standing there, listening politely to msieu colson of the ministry, you say, in order to fill the silence: when you go to a clinic you never see anyone but peasants and yet more peasants . . . so you begin to wonder which clinic or hospital the townspeople attend, and then you begin to believe that townspeople keep going till they die of their illness because science is always making such great strides and people don't believe in doctors any more. Hereupon msieu colson of the ministry says good-bye, leaving you alone with your father and your father says: in the clinic your mother almost knocked her head on the wall and she shouted in all the corridors and rooms and in the operating theatre, at the nurses and the sisters and the chrome instruments: murderers, murderers, she shouted and then she fell and I had to pick her up.

## AGAIN AND AGAIN ABOUT SICKNESS AND DEATH

The next day you sit at your desk again like a patriarch raised high above time and sickness and death and all other transitory things . . . but your blood flows more slowly and more quietly like a brook in the ardennes which first falls from rock to rock and then finally, numbed, perplexed, flows quietly away . . . Your hand goes on writing but there's a shadow hanging over your mind and your eyes gaze at the white paper with a kind of disdain:

I write but I know they're only words that don't touch the core of things. I write but I know it's got no use, no purpose, no meaning. Msieu colson of the ministry sits down beside you and says excitedly, with a glimmer in his eyes: do you know . . . that doctor who was supposed to start his clinic at 2 o'clock and hadn't turned up at 3 yet, well he'd really had an accident, he'd driven into the canal with his car and 2 women hitch-hikers, who were in the car with him, went down as well . . . they're dead and drowned, the car, the doctor, and the 2 hitch-hikers. And talking of doctors and clinics, johan janssens says he's heard of a charge made against a doctor who'd given a blood transfusion as a result of which the patient had got syphilis . . . and the doctor's lawyer said in court that one had to consider it as a transaction in which the merchandise had certain faults which neither the purchaser nor the vendor had noticed. And talking of blood transfusions and operations, your wife butts in and says that somebody told her about a doctor's wife . . . this doctor's wife said to another lady: why did you bother to have that operation, don't you know that in hospitals they simply follow fashions . . . now this disease and then another? Tolfpoets, who's been listening, adds something of his own, a product of his deviate mind: the story of a man who fell from his cart, with his head on the paving stones, and while he was lying in the road he was kicked on the head by the horse's hind leg . . . and now he's in hospital, raving and shouting that they should give him a new head because his old head is busted. After listening in silence, out of politeness, you add your story—life moves on, after all, about a little girl whom they were trying to scare with johnny death . . . but the little girl wants to know what exactly he looks like, so they drew her a johnny death . . . and when she'd given johnny death a long, close look, she said: now draw jenny death.

## THE POEM OF THE ATOM BOMB

Cibazol, thermopirin, and aspirin, plus 7 wet handkerchieves: there's the portrait of johan janssens, Poet and weekly journalist, as he enters the room. He's got flu and says: at least you can get rid of flu . . . but who can rid me of the chief editors of the weekly papers, they get troublesome and cross all the time but they're so naive they don't know who to be cross with, yet they're crafty enough always to take it out on somebody else. Start making room for your eye-witness report on Life, they say, where shall we put it? . . . on the front page, no, then it would be a bit too obvious that we are what we are . . . on the second page, no, we've never had reports there . . . on the back page, no, that's the rubbish page. The next day they no longer talk about your report on life, they're cross and gruff as usual. And finally, they accept a report by a Walloon, in french, which has got to be translated first . . . I make a lay-out with the report on the middle page, but they chuck it out and throw it on page 7 where there's never anything worth speaking of . . . I make up a new lay-out and they move the report from page 7 to page 3, so I do yet another lay-out . . . but now they don't want to discuss the position of that report any more, now they start fussing over a detail: the title: Life. And life has to be written with an 1, they say. So they start messing about with the L, with a red pencil, as if it was a knife: about life, they say. And still holding the red pencil like a knife, they start working on the other pages, they work on cultural life till their eyes fall on a poem: hiroshima. They ask what kind of a poem is this, they shout furiously, hacking at the title with their red, pointed knife. I explain to them that my friend the music master has read a book in which an american reporter reconstructed the tragedy of hiroshima, and that my friend the music master was so disgusted with this civilization of ours that he wrote a poem in which he says he spits out his spittle . . .

I spit out my spittle
but on whom should I spit?

they get to work on these last lines, I spit out my spittle but on whom should I spit . . . they spit on these lines with the red pencil, they push the lay-out aside, out of their sight, and say: anyway, you have no right to accept poems without our knowledge . . . you can put it in now, on your own responsibility and add a note from the editor that we think this is a remarkable poem but that we do not agree with its political . . . no, not political, with its ideological premise. And by the way, don't bother to do any more lay-outs, that's no use; we'll see in the printing room where to put things. They almost said: we'll see after the paper is printed where we should have put everything.

## PANDORA'S BOX

*Actually, ondine wasn't really so much concerned with getting the money . . . her cursing and raging were only a kind of introduction, making a noise on purpose, in order to put herself in the right against all better reason: she knew as well as the others that there was no money; she thought with secret pleasure of the 1000 francs in the attic, which she had hidden long ago in an old tin. This stolen money was her support, on which she could fall back during the battle. She looked for quarrels, but it wasn't only in order to shout down her own mistakes; it was first and foremost something in her blood, inseparably bound up with her personality. It was her life. She was a plant thriving in the jungle, obliged to kill, obliged to kill the surrounding plants in order to stay alive . . . she fought . . . it was as if she throttled those around her, in order to have light and air, to reach the goal which she had set herself in her youth and which she didn't really remember very well. She found it hard to go to sleep if a day had passed without struggle . . . she snuggled down in bed to dream all sorts of things but unconsciously her mind wandered back to those evenings when she'd baked cakes at the castle . . . finally she fell asleep and dreamt of him, of mr achilles, of whom she daren't think during the day . . . he had strong white teeth and bit her . . . she was a child again, letting him touch her young little breasts . . . it was blasphemy, really, because she way a very young mother-of-god and he was a lascivious devil, yet night after night she asked him to come to her in her mother-of-god's bed and forgave herself time and again their sinful copulation . . . it way such an impossible moment of deep sinful happiness that she hardly dared move when she woke up . . . her dream way still alive in her but so delicate and fragile that she feared the slightest movement would make it wither and vanish. Oh achilles, she said. She kept her eyes closed in order to keep reality at bay which came storming towards her: she didn't want to know that her father was going downstairs, that outside in chapel road a cart was rumbling past . . . she didn't even want to know that she was planning to marry oscarke: . . . however, she couldn't defend her dream and go on defending it against the forces of onrushing reality, she searched desperately for that which had been her strong support in the last days, so that she might take refuge in it . . . what was it? . . . what way it? . . . it was that she'd got a thousand francs in an old tin. But was it enough, what was a 1000 francs compared with her dream? Oh achilles, was all she could say. She didn't want to remember oscar's face, she daren't; she couldn't possibly compare the things from daily life with the things she'd seen in her imagination. Even so, she tried to cheat herself, as if it concerned another woman: if I've had a dream about something which is irrevocably gone, is that a reason to give up in despair forever? She said, almost involuntarily: life must go on. She looked around as if looking for something to distract her attention, she went downstairs, opened the cupboard and drummed absent-mindedly on the door as if there was something there which she needed . . . but she didn't know what she was looking for . . . she shut the cupboard and yes, then she remembered: she was looking for a cup to pour herself some coffee for her breakfast. In a kind of mental stupor she climbed the steps to the attic and picked up the old tin from under a layer of dust . . . she looked for something to wipe the dust off, she cleaned it and cleaned it as if it was a holy shrine, but it wasn't out of respect for the money, it was out of listlessness, because she had already forgotten again why she was standing there and what she was supposed to do with this tin. She opened it and stared into it . . . and very slowly, very hazily, it penetrated to her that there was something wrong with the tin. It was . . . empty.*

## GOD HELPS THOSE WHO HELP THEMSELVES

Today is a day without a name without a meaning without a purpose . . . in which the rain is like melted snow outside in chapel road and in the garden at the back of your house . . . your wife sits by the stove with her illegal knitting in her lap, but the needles are at rest . . . and noticing that you're staring in front of you she says: I'll tell you something with the title: god helps those who help themselves . . . have you got that down? . . . well, some time ago a woman was walking past the 4 villas here and she asked me and the other women if anyone wanted to buy her dog: would you like to buy my dog? because just imagine, I went to buy a dog and nobody at home likes him. Heavens, what should I do with a dog? asks johan janssens' wife . . . a dog is a dog, says the pretty lucette philosophically . . a dog shits and pees all over your clean house, says maria, child of nature, with her ribbons and her frills . . . and then some brat comes round the corner, from the level crossing, calling: whose is that dog that's just been run over? The woman who wanted to sell her dog looks and calls out: jesus christ, that's My dog that's been run over.

Have you written it down, your wife asks . . . right, then I'll tell you something else, you can use the same title: god helps those who help themselves: and it's about somebody else being run over. Well, there was a woman and she had a husband who worked for the state, a stoker on the railways he was, and this stoker was run over by his own train . . . and years later this woman, in a moment of violent anger, says to her son who also works for the state, an engine driver: they ought to run you over as well. And they did.

Your wife is about to pick up her knitting again and suddenly laughs: haha, talking about the state: I remember something else, you might write that down as well, under the title god helps those who help themselves . . . but it's a parody of it, a farce . . . it happened in the war when a long queue of people were waiting outside the food office, and the policeman at the front called out that all women in that state could come to the front . . . and a locomotive fireman's wife at the back of the queue came forward at once, and the policeman asked her: are you in that state? . . . the woman looked at him in surprise and said: oh, I thought you meant anyone who works for the state.

And as you hear the click-click of the knitting needles again, you ask: right, but what do you mean by the title, god helps those who help themselves? Without looking at you she replies: can't you see? The wish is the mother of the . . . or is it the father of the . . . what's its name . . . I say, I sit here telling you stories, but do you think I'm a preacher?

## LEFT IS LEFT

God-almighty-holy-writer, thought isengrinus . . . who'd stayed behind in the well and in his misery . . . I wonder whether that's true that I'm in a lesser state of grace? Other people only need to lift a finger and the roast turkeys start fighting to be picked up first . . . but whatever I try to lay my paws on, it's no damn use . . . what's it called again in latin? So he sat there, singing his strange credo in the well on blandinus hill and the friars, who'd been chasing after the 2 rascals, stopped to listen with unusual interest to the husky tone of the wolf's somewhat vulgar voice. This would add a terrestrial touch to the seraphs' song in the Christmas choir, the superior suggested . . . and friar pascalius prostituaan, who'd painted the stations of the cross, said it was always the shadow that made the light seem even more brilliant . . . and friar editor-in-chief, who was a poet, added that this voice sounded somewhat cynical, like that of the good murderer of mary magdalen. They hauled the wolf out of the well on condition that he'd sing in the midnight mass: do you think that's all right, asked the wolf, in spite of my shuttered eye which stares at you from this god-forsaken monk's habit. We'll put you at the back and blacken your face, the friars persuaded him . . . do you think that's all right, asked the wolf, I used to have the reputation of being a bit of a dirtyist, not altogether orthodox? We'll put you at the back, and make your face red, the friars persuaded him. And so it happened that at the midnight mass the faithful heard in the male choir for several bars the voice of an unorthodox lover of mary magdalen on the far left, presenting with his raw voice the dissonants of life on earth. Later he suggested to the abbot to eat the sheep raw, which wasn't at all taken in good part; as a result he had to preach more sermons than anyone else and was least often sent to check the wine cellar. Even the new bishop of houblon, waldricus one-eye—because in those days the bishops followed one another in rapid succession—waldricus one-eye, who came to inspect the wine cellars at blandinus hill, asked him whether he had enough to do and whether he wouldn't in addition to his sermons also like to sing matins, benediction and vespers, and for the rest of the time, wouldn't he like to be at the service of the other monks. Isengrinus wanted to say that he was even prepared to write the bishop's monthly pastoral letter—if you drink the wine, I shall taste the lees—but at the very first words he made a slip of the tongue; instead of most learned or more honored sir, he said: most dreaded bear . . . and this gave the bishop such a start that he fell into the wine vat. What else could isengrinus do but quickly pull the plug out so that his lord and master wouldn't drown? . . . and again, what better could he do but hold his mouth under the spout so that the precious wine wouldn't rim to waste? So it's understandable that the blandinus hill friars, when they finally came hurrying to the rescue, found isengrinus preaching a sermon: left is left—hiccup—I stand at the back in black—hiccup—and I stand at the back in red . . . and that they found the bishop with his hat cocked at a slant, looking at them with blurred eyes, and nodding amen to isengrinus' sermon. They took isengrinus away from the cellar and said: we might as well make you a bishop. So, ceremoniously putting an iron pot on his head, they rammed it down over his ears till he didn't know whether he was coming or going, and gave him a kick up his behind till he didn't know which way he was rolling. Johan janssens in the weekly journal.

## WE NEED AN AVENGER

*So the tin was . . . empty? Ondine rubbed her forehead and pulled herself together. She looked at the unplastered walls and the tiled roof as if she expected somebody, maybe with 1000 francs in his hands, to be watching her and mocking her. But there was nobody there. She tried to think what could have happened; hadn't she first wiped a layer of dust from the tin? So mustn't it have been a very long time since someone had last touched this tin and . . . had taken the money out? Bloody hell, she said. And with this the mist in her head cleared, slowly she began to remember the day when valeer had come into the attic to pinch a tobacco leaf, and had stared at her . . . he must have been standing in the trapdoor a long time, otherwise he couldn't possibly have seen her hiding the treasure . . . he must have come back afterwards and taken the money out . . . the crafty bastard . . . and yes, now she remembered that her cousin had said: we were given 1000 francs and so we could buy sugar. With her money they'd been able to do good business . . . they'd robbed and cheated her, to enrich themselves at her expense. She nodded her head, her anger and grief were so overwhelming that she couldn't do anything except stand there passively, blindly looking around and nodding her head. But her fingertips started to tingle, a shiver began to rise from her feet, to her heart, to her brain . . . she had to do something or she'd go mad on the spot . . . never mind what . . . she grabbed the empty tin and threw it towards the attic window . . . to break the glass, to hear noise, to hear the world crash and tear asunder. But she missed, the tin fell down beside the window and nothing was broken . . . only her finger bled a little where the sharp edge of the tin had cut her. Oh how wicked is the world, she cried. She fell down on the floor and put her head on her arms, and kicked the floorboards. Oh how wicked is the world, she kept repeating. And when her immense fury had spent itself . . . but hadn't vanished . . . she blamed herself for having been so foolish, for having trusted someone, having wanted to spare someone in life: I should have stolen and swindled and murdered and burnt without mercy; but it's been a lesson: I'll smash the world to pieces to pieces to pieces. She went about termuren hating everything and everyone . . . they were all her blood enemies . . . she went to the chapel to pray, she had no one except him, god . . . thou art my strength and my rock, I have built my hope on thee. She didn't see the christ, nailed to the cross with his arms spread . . . she didn't see the god of her childhood, le bon dieu who spoke french and doled out alms on condition that the poor doffed their caps politely; no, she went back to the god of moses and abraham, the avenger, the thundergod who broke the clay tablets, who sowed death and destruction, who sent diseases to the earth and a deluge and an all-consuming fire. Only in this could she find any consolation . . . she relished the idea of such world destruction, how zulma would shriek and rave, how her father's godless toy trains might cause a confusion of tongues, and how valeer would be thrown to the ground, with the sinful cousin tied to him . . . the thieves, the blackguards . . . and she laughed a baffling laugh in the empty chapel.*

## IN PARTICULAR I BELIEVE . . .

The people who have come to live in chapel road in the course of time, know that you are some kind of writer, and they all come to tell you their life history in the hope that one day you will write it down in a book. Their lives: that's to say, Those things from their lives in which they were the heroes, the shrewdest the best the first . . . but never the things in which they cut a wretched human figure, in which they were the cowards, the stupidest the worst the last. Don't you dare write about that in your stories or else they threaten to sue you. To the priest they say they love lord jesus . . . and to smut, who lives at the 1st dirty houses, in rooms, they say that only last night they caught a girl from behind . . . and to andré the theosophist they say they've heard the dead speak. So the priest thinks that they all love lord jesus and smut thinks that they all chase the girls and andré the theosophist thinks that they all take an interest in theosophy. Talking of andré the theosophist, they told him the story of the man who loved life but who was dying all the same, who rebelled with all his might against his death and said: I'll be back. Well, at about 10 o'clock he died and at the same moment the clock downstairs stopped . . . and the next day, again at about ten, a thud was heard in his room and when they went upstairs it turned out that the mirror had fallen on the floor . . . they came downstairs again and found the clock ticking once more. While they're telling this story, andré watches you with his theosophist's eyes and smiles, nodding his head.

And as soon as andré the theosophist has left—because he has to get up, eat and sleep at very particular theosophist times—they tell you another story: one of those impossible things: about a house where somebody lies dead, a freemason, and a gentleman dressed in black comes knocking at the door to ask is this the house where what's his name lies dead? They let him in and he leans against the wall in silence . . . and when he finally leaves there's a big black stain on the wall and they can't get it off no matter how they scrub or paint. And you, l.p. boon, who've been out painting walls with johan janssens . . . you ask them, out of interest, whether they tried covering it with varnish first. This annoys them and they go on and on telling stories . . . in a moment they'll be telling you that mannikin pis's little thing has flown away and that it gave a loud yell when it flew under the pope's skirts. You leave, wondering when someone will tell you things that don't belong to the darkness of backward flanders but to the darkness of their own frightened hearts.

## A GROSS ERROR, BUT ALL FOR THE BEST

You, boon, you ought to be the writer of this book, but you allow yourself to be pushed in a corner by your heroes . . . you're seized by anger because msieu colson of the ministry keeps talking of a pharmacist . . . there's no pharmacist here in chapel road, what rubbish . . . as far as I know there's only a neurologist and the same thing happened to him once. A fine chap, this neurologist, brilliant etc . . . but when you hear this kind of thing you'd think twice. That's the only reason why it's mentioned in this book, because when he'd told me this, I think he would have given me 1000 francs to get his words out of my ears and back into his mouth.

## CAN CHAOS BE CONQUERED?

You were using a new pen, as if you were going to make a clean sweep, because you wanted to find the answer to an ever more urgent question: can chaos be conquered? But at the same moment the music master knocked, and said that the railway strike was over; the men had been granted a rise of a few centimes . . . but the strike had also been solved on the other side: fares had been raised by 25%. Johan janssens, the weekly journalist, who'd arrived together with the music master, replied at once that the music master was displaying a disturbing lack of understanding of social problems, because soon he'd be saying that the railway company had wanted the strike. With all this, your paper had remained empty and your question unanswered, so that you had to ask it again: can chaos . . . but at that moment msieu colson came in to tell you that a senator had asked a question about certain american army trucks, 10 tonners, which had been bought by the government . . . and the ministry concerned had replied that they had indeed been purchased but that they didn't really have much use for them and they would therefore have to be resold . . . at a loss. And although msieu colson was of the opinion that such errors can occur in the best of families . . . tolfpoets' wife maria also buys things occasionally which they can't use . . . he added something which seemed to bother him more: the ministry concerned had come to the conclusion that the information given had been too good . . . too correct. And the person who had supplied this superior information was now being sought, in the ministry, although the minister himself had signed the written reply.

Your paper was still empty and your question unanswered. And now, on this day, at this hour, you definitely settle down to your writing: can chaos be . . . But it is as if fate is haunting you, because now your wife begins to explain how she's always making calculations: if my husband sells one part of his book to this journal and another part to that paper . . . and if he . . . and that it's always wind in a bottle and that there is always new hope, and that this hope is always shattered again. And now, she says, I sit by the electric sewing machine at the very moment when a man came to read the meter . . . he saw the sewing machine and asked whether I work for myself or for an employer . . . I didn't understand, I looked at him, not committing myself, because you never know whether it might be a dirty trick . . . and this man said that electricity costs more if I sew for myself and less if I work for a factory. She adds with a laugh: so you've been warned, electricity is cheaper if you cut up your work into strips and sell them, but dearer if you want to work on a novel.

And your question: can chaos be conquered, yes or no? . . . remains unanswered, because everything they tell you is rumor and hypothesis, building up, in the middle of chaos, a new chaos of things only half-known, which can never be reduced to definitive facts.

## MY TIME HAS NOT YET COME

*Could ondine remain alone with god . . . no, oscarke was in her life too. She thought of him the way somebody might after a thunderstorm think of his potted plants standing outside the window . . . she decided to be strong for his sake and to resume the struggle . . . yet, she might have done this without him, too, but she was always like this: she always had to think up imaginary arguments and wrap them round even the simplest matters. She started off with something she loved best of all: writing a spiteful letter. When she wrote a letter no one could interrupt her or defend himself, but she was free to invent the most outrageous insinuations, with a cruel smile on her lips. And what she wrote in this letter to her cousin: it was dreadful. She damned them all, she didn't hesitate to talk of her mother, who looked so wretched, of her old father, who could no longer pay his debts and would probably have to spend the rest of his days in prison; but it was no good returning the stolen money, it was too late for that; it was blood money: they would soon find out that they'd have no more luck in life, and even their children would die in terrible pain. Having sent the letter off, she walked around with tight lips, thinking whom she was going to devour next. A master plan took shape in her head . . . a cunning trick to force the schatts to pay, and to put all the money in her own pocket . . . and then, when they'd been stripped to the bone, she'd shake up oscar to marry her and demand his share. God, maybe the old grey cat would drop dead with the shock. She became exuberant, she pulled oscarke close to her and laughed and chattered, unfolding her plans. Oscarke promised her anything she wanted and indeed, he felt excited by her boldness, by her complete lack of scruple. But when he came home it was all different, he began to see everything from a different point of view. Ondine should have foreseen this, but in her blind enthusiasm about the plan, she had imagined that oscar was like her: sly and crafty. Again, it was a mistake, it proved that she still hadn't learnt enough . . . that she still hadn't reached the point when she would no longer trust anyone but would push her way through life all by herself.*

## MY SISTER JEANNEKE'S DEATH

I put my hand on her stomach when the ambulance drove her home from the hospital, says my father, because the tires were much too hard and it trembled so in her tummy . . . not in an ambulance, shouted my sister jeanneke, otherwise people will know I'm ill. I dropped everything and sat by her bed, beside the bed which had been my bed for a long time . . . when I was young and still like my sister jeanneke . . . when I was still young and believed in my immortality . . . when I was young and strong and discovered my awakening sex and thought that I and the world were immortal . . . Now

I dropped this immortality of the world like a stone, and sat beside the bed, day and night, where a little lamp burnt in the dark hours of the night and where the sounds of the fallen world penetrated during the day. I sat beside the bed and from the bed my sister jeanneke shouted that I should leave her in peace . . . that I should go away . . . because otherwise I would know that she was ill and I might tell others. One moment she wanted to sit on the couch, then on a chair, then back in the bed, and her wild eyes tried to escape . . . tried to escape. Oh my mother, crying, turning her smiling face to my sister jeanneke: how are you feeling, darling, is the pain going away a bit now? Oh my father, crying, his hands stricken with lameness and his smiling face turned to my sister jeanneke: can I do anything for you, my little girl? Oh, my own choking tears behind the mask of my own smiling face: do lie still for a bit, jeanneke! Thirsty! shouted my sister jeanneke. But that was only in the beginning, later she stammered it, still later she only murmured it, and then it was a whisper, a soft, quiet whisper, so that my father bent the mask of his smiling face over her and listened: she says she's thirsty.

Look, and then later: the days passed me with dumb mouth and blind eyes, the newspapers piled up with unread news of the world which I had dropped beside me. I smashed and broke everything in my house. I filled up holes where there had been doors and hacked new holes where there were blind walls, I tore up floors and laid new ones; only in order to have noise and movement around me, only in order to see life, but meanwhile my sister jeanneke's dying gnawed at my own dying guts. When the crow bar pierced the walls and the bricks crashed down in clouds of dust and chalk: the dying, breaking eyes of my sister jeanneke . . . those breaking eyes, and what are called 'the last words': I can't keep it up. Her last, betraying words, which suddenly tore all our masks away because she herself was tearing off her mask too . . . she knew that death was near and that it was useless to go on pretending that she wasn't ill: I can't keep it up. My father tore off his smiling mask and I tore off my smiling mask and we wept, deeply and heavily and passionately . . . but my mother kept hers, till the very last moment, and on her smiling mask dripped the tears of her trampled motherly heart. So we sat there, and between us lay the overturned bottle which was my sister jeanneke, a bottle fallen on its side, running empty . . .

Now I sit here writing . . . writing how I broke down the walls of my house . . . but amongst the clouds of dust and chalk and amongst the words I write, I only see your words: I can't keep it up. And I, my dead sister jeanneke, how long shall I, shall this moribund world, be able to keep it up?

## FIGS AFTER EASTER

You're sitting at your desk by the window, for once . . . february and march have gone, it's april and the sun is shining, but in the meanwhile you've been hacking and destroying and turning the house upside down . . . now you sit there, writing at something which should have become your masterwork, *something which should have turned the world inside out, like vapeur's invention . . . but the world is doomed and vapeur's invention will come too late* and your book will come too late . . . oh hell, who said that all these inventions and books push the world over the cliff?—So there you sit at your desk, filling the book with words, instead of doing something useful. Instead of doing what the pepperpot does, for instance, wandering about on the other side of no-man's wood, beyond the brook by the castle, with his fly unbuttoned, ready to get his thing out as soon as a young girl appears. It kills the pepperpot, this urge to show his thing to young girls, as your urge to stop the world in its fall kills you. You sit there writing . . . and there comes poet and weekly journalist johan janssens, with his briefcase full of dailies and weeklies which he's still got to read, and he sees you sitting by the window: so you're writing again, I'm pleased to see it, not because I think the world is so anxious to read your book but because I see that you, little boon, little creature, have found your equilibrium: you sit there writing while I travel up and down to brussels breaking my head on every single wall of every single left-wing paper: we've both of us got something in our head which we might call figs after easter. You with your book and I with my lamentations about the left-wing papers . . . left wing and very left wing and ultra-marxist . . . brys the dreamer was at home in the world of high finance . . . not owning a red cent at the end of the month, wearing socks with holes, eating nothing but stale egg powder and rubbish out of tins, he was nevertheless very well informed about high finance and wrote remarkable articles about it. He was dismissed. But when he'd gone, the empty place was noticed, so he was called back: he can fill that gap again and we'll dismiss him later when we don't need him so much. But . . . as I said, it's all figs after easter . . . I go on supplying the left-wing weeklies with columns, as long as it lasts, because even though I'm in everybody's way, it gives me a better vantage point from which to look at the world. I know the world is doomed; you can write that in your book.

## IS HUMOR SAD, TOO?

You wanted to write about april just now, that the cherry tree in your garden is getting april whims in its blood, that it's sprouting everywhere, but that the ants are coming out of their winter holes as well, they're already crawling all over the smooth trunk: no doubt they'll soon ruin the whole lot again—you just wanted to write this about april, when the poet and weekly journalist turns up and says: I see to my surprise that now that it's spring there is only infinite sadness or infinite sad pity in you. Infinite, sad pity for your cherry tree which is doing its best and yet it will soon be half-eaten by ants . . . and then the rest will be pecked away by sparrows. But do you know, in me too there is this infinite, sad pity; my wife tells me my jaws are too short, I can't open them for a laugh. And she's not altogether wrong . . . I write for all kinds of dailies and weeklies and monthlies, and take my articles to the letterbox by the 1st dirty houses and hardly dare go home to my wife whose blood is too thin, who gets dizzy spells in her head, who's got trouble with her nerves and who's also got something or other in her tummy, like every woman is ill in her tummy: all these things have their origin in the war . . . in the two wars we've had to live through . . . and then, once I'm home, I sit and sit, thinking of everything I've written, I chew over that prose, sentence by sentence, in my mind . . . and I shake my head because again there was nothing in it that expressed my infinite pity: even the jaws of my articles are just that bit too short. Then

I go through the articles written by others in the dailies, weeklies and monthlies, and there too I find nothing . . . nothing. The others aren't ashamed to write about existentialism and personalism. And I think of all those young men and women who've come back from the war, who've known deprivations and who now live like the young shoots on your cherry tree: ready to be half eaten by the ants and half pecked away by the sparrows. I see them and I feel infinitely sad, because I know that they all fought for a better world, that they bore all that suffering in the hope that afterwards there'd be a better world . . . and that they're now deprived of a living, locked out of the trade unions if they want to go on strike. And because they're now living like the young shoots on your cherry tree. Meanwhile, people go on writing about existentialism and personalism . . . but can I write about personalism in the weeklies? . . . I sit here reading what the socialists write about personalism in their party organs . . . they write about it without writing about it . . . as if it's an irrevocable fact that they've failed and seen no point in saving appearances. It makes me so depressed, I see the crowds, all those small socialists whose fathers fought and went on strike, who were exploited and who have ended up as established and acknowledged socialists, led by men who no longer believe in a socialist society. Oh how incredibly tragic it all is, this dead thing built up out of thousands of small ignorant socialists, proudly reading their daily paper in which someone writes about personalism without writing about it.

The music master, who like you has listened to johan janssens with infinite sadness, suddenly interrupts: and do you know, even those whose jaws aren't too short, those who *can* still laugh even *they* make me feel so depressed. Turning to you, the music master adds: take for instance tolfpoets, about whom you write occasionally, well, he too makes me feel infinitely depressed, with his strange, surrealist jokes, with his quibbles and his mental deviations . . . because I think it's precisely those humoristic mental deviations—which seem to support our depression—that push us deeper and deeper into the abyss. Just like the tablets from the dispensary apparently cure our headache, while in fact they give us an even sicker head and a sicker stomach besides. There are today two sorts of people: those who write about personalism and those who're being funny ... but they've all got a headache and swallow pills from the dispensary.

## WHO ARE THE CLIQUE?

*You* write with ease, people say, stressing you ... but they don't know how difficult it is when you, writing with ease, try to say too much. Look at this story now, which is supposed to show how johan janssens, poet and weekly journalist, met the so-called clique at luxembourg station in brussels ... that's to say, all those who got the sack from the daily paper because they were suspected of forming a clique: johan janssens himself and brys the dreamer and tippetotje the painter who used to do the layout in those days. You imagine the scene like this: the unemployed clique, at luxembourg station, in the faint april sunshine. And as you try to describe it, you stumble straight away over this april sunshine ... because people have reproached you that it's always raining in your books and that the sun never shines ... and now, in this scene, the sun does shine ... that's to say it shines on luxembourg station and on the square where the yellow trams go ... but does it shine in the hearts of those who belong to this clique that's been turned out into the street? ... No, it doesn't. Then there's another thought: tippetotje the painter told you once that you should see brussels in the rain, because that is the real brussels ... but you see brussels in the sunshine, when the girls are flowers with bare legs and young breasts ... maybe it would be even better if they had bare breasts and young legs. And then there's a third thought: all of your book is set in chapel road, in the small town of the 2 mills, and suddenly we move the action to brussels ... don't we lose something here, a quality which up to now we've managed to maintain?

But look, the april sun is shining, the trams are yellow, the girls have young, bare legs and dancing breasts ... and johan janssens, poet and weekly journalist, has lunched in the staff restaurant at the ministry together with msieu colson who paid for the tickets—it was vegetable soup and then mashed potatoes with something or other—johan janssens shakes hands with msieu colson and says: see you tonight, in chapel road ... he turns round the corner on his way to the editor's office and bumps into the

Clique: brys the dreamer, who ought to have lead poured into his shoes or he'll soar in idealistic fantasy high above luxembourg station, like marc chagall's figures . . . and beside him is tippetotje the painter, who did the layout for a time, and who was always a plodder . . . this is a long time ago now, but the scene we're describing here is long ago too, and meanwhile tippetotje has become painter to the baron—tippetotje, with her worn sock, her worn shoes, her worn raincoat . . . and her worn smile.

At this moment the sky falls down and all the sparrows are dead, because an old, grey ultra-marxist comes along; he's got a hunchback from hard work and a grooved face from walking in rain and wind, for the party, and something in his eyes, from having been in jail many times, for the party . . . he sees the clique and thinks they're all still editors at the paper, so he says scornfully: you're all young and you dance to the tune, but you know nothing about the background of the party . . . but I've grown old and grey in the party, I wouldn't mind going on dancing to every single tune, but I've been thrown out because I do know something of that history: the old guard must go, you see. The whole clique watches the old, grey ultra-marxist go, as he hurries away so as not to show his grief and his bitterness—because if it hadn't been his party, he would have jeered and spat and maligned—but that was just it: it was The party. Brys the dreamer stammers: the old guard must go and the young guard is turned out into the street. I wonder who'll be left, apart from the *clique* which suspects everyone else of being a clique.

## THE WORLD FALLS INTO 3 FRAGMENTS

*Oscarke looked at the woman whom ondine had called an old grey cat . . . and yes, she did look like one . . . yet, if she hadn't been his mother, he'd sooner have called her an old grey mouse. but that was just the point: whatever she might be, she was his mother . . . she'd been the 1st woman in his life. Evening after evening they'd sat together, hungry, scraping and scrounging, trying to hide their poverty from the world. Evening after evening she had told him ugly things about his father, which might have killed his spirit, showing him the world and its people at their saddest, most repulsive. While he and his mother were sitting by the stove without a fire, his father was acting the rich gentleman, giving supper parties with chicken and bottles of wine, with girls at his table, and things happened which she couldn't tell him about yet. It had influenced his mind, it had given him an intense distaste of those Things, and he'd begun to think that he was born to give his mother everything his father denied her: in the nights when his feet were clumps of ice, he dreamt that he was rich and famous . . . no, not famous . . . that he was rich, and something far more important, and that he made his mother happy. All through his childhood he'd thought of his mother's happiness . . . although his mother had never thought of his happiness and couldn't bear it if he messed about with clay and, well, if he thought of himself at times. She had a husband who thought of himself and she didn't want her son doing the same . . . she fought bravely, cruelly, so that there might be at least someone in her life who'd think of her, of her alone, like a slave, like a lover. And whenever he wanted to go up to the attic to be himself—and this, although she didn't realize it, was only for her benefit—she stopped him, with her tales of what his father did, of their poverty, of what she lacked in life. And now suddenly the world was turned upside down, suddenly another woman had come on the scene, who, just like his mother, wanted him to live for her alone . . . who insisted and who wanted to make him believe that instead of looking after that old, grey mouse, he had to look after her. He asked himself, doubtfully, whether what he needed to do in life wasn't to look after himself. The world fell into 3 parts: his mother, his girlfriend, and he himself in between. He didn't know what to do . . . he couldn't make up his mind, alone. If he was going to look after his mother, he'd be doing it for life . . . he made a quick calculation how long she might live, she was 40 now, suppose she lived till 70 . . . or suppose she only lived till 60 . . . then that would still be 20 years. He didn't think ondine would be patient enough to wait that long. And besides, he'd have to wait all that time before he could start hacking out his dreams in stone . . . whereas, if he got married now, he'd be able to start right away, modelling ondine's head in clay. He sat still, not daring to take life by the horns and demand his own happiness . . . most of all because he didn't know who was right, his mother, who was unhappy, but who begrudged him any kind of enjoyment, or ondine, who had perhaps no other aim than to ruin his mother. Tormented, swinging between two extremes, he became as thin as a rake. And as he looked like a boy of 16, in spite of his 21 years, and with his face looking so withdrawn and wrinkled with worry, he resembled a child with an old-man's head. If he didn't understand others, they seemed to understand him all the better: he couldn't show himself in the living room without his mother starting to talk about that carpenter's daughter, what a suspect life she already had behind her . . . it was said that she had lived at the castle for a year with mr ludovic, and that she used to take all the children to the bushes by the railway, to set them against their mothers, their good, loving mothers. And she talked about marriage, that the time would come for him one day too, and that she'd find a very nice girl for him, with whom he'd be happy all his life.*

## APPEARANCE AND ESSENCE

Who the devil almighty . . . *as ondine had been made to swear, in her youth, when she had for a time been the sweetheart of norbert derenancourt, the spiritualist* . . . who the devil almighty can make sense of this book? Nobody, except me, boon, and maybe I'm only pretending to myself that I can. *There's this whole story of ondine . . . a story in which all the themes are brought together which were mentioned in the very first pages . . . but to which quite a number of new themes have been added as we went along.* Then there's the novel of johan janssens, which underlines the social element in the novel about ondine . . . *but the things for which people were beginning to fight in ondine's time some 50 odd years ago,* have already been conquered in the days of johan janssens: yet what has been the use of this victory? There's msieu colson of the ministry who substantiates everything with facts and proofs, and who in spite of all these dry facts still manages to remain a poet . . . Then there's the music master who . . . yes, what role does he play, isn't it a rather solemn, ridiculous role? And then there's tolfpoets, image of our time, who has invented humor, as if it was a medicine against rheumatism. And finally there's tippetotje the painter . . . poor tippetotje, we're forgetting her more and more, because she's drifting away from us, with that old money-drunk baron under her skirts . . . she was a symbol of art in our book—art with a very small a, because we, artists, scorned by the masses and believing in nothing, find ourselves chased away from our own hunting fields by all the doctors k.k. kakkemans, who Know All About Art—all with capitals like cows—so that we can only use a small a, and become profoundly disillusioned and filled with nostalgia. So they are all symbols . . . and look, now I've made a slip of the tongue; they're a symbol, a reflection of my own self, a counterfeit of my own tom and frayed essence. They are symbols, shadows without a life of their own, only serving to underline something or other. And yet, they have a life of their own, because it would be too simple to reflect myself in johan janssens and the rest; they must exist and yet not exist, they must fulfill some vague role in this book and yet remain People. And if they are people, then outside the role they play here they must have yet another role, a life of their own. The pretty Lucette bursts out sobbing when she's alone with your wife one day; and says that we don't know the music master: you should see him when he gets up in the morning, angry and swearing . . . you should see him with his hair all disheveled, straggling strands of hair in his eyes, like a wild beast, and you should hear him nagging and baiting me—the judas—he keeps nagging me—I don't know why—because he spits on life which isn't worth a rotten cent, as he says, because he wants to be powerful, maybe become a school governor, maybe a minister, be lord and master and have it all his own way . . . and what can I, poor pretty lucette do about it that the world is the way it is? Then he beats me; he hits me in the face with his angry hands and if I ask him what's the matter with you? he answers: you're pretty, that's what's the matter . . . I hate you because you're pretty and you're my wife . . . I spit out my spittle but who shall I spit on?

You see, that's part of the life of the shadow we call the music master . . . but, is there anything in it we didn't know already?

## SICKMIND'S DEFENCE

Sickmind, the student, gets up and says: for some weeks now you've been writing about me, poor sickmind, and you haven't spared me one bit: you describe me as if I were an insect under a magnifying glass. But may I now at last be permitted to show you things from the poor insect's own point of view? When I was still young and naive and not nearly so cynical, I felt like a poet . . . and feeling like a poet I committed my first folly: I went to a university which is supposed to be a state university but where the encyclicalists have remained the bosses, as they've also remained the bosses in the radio and in all other semi-official institutions. Actually, I committed a double act of folly, I went to the university to study literature. I soon found out that literature isn't an art but a trade . . . and that not the poets but the professors are experts in that trade. The evil was so deeply rooted that all the professors looked up in scorn when one day a poet came to give a lecture . . . they thought: what does he know about poetry, he's not a professor!

So I realized I wasn't going to learn anything worth while but I had to carry on with what I'd chosen, because as you yourself described it, my mum made me feel that the stove was burning in the study for my sake alone . . . and the state made me feel that every student costs it a hundred and fifty thousand francs yearly . . . and so my mum and the state gave me an inferiority complex, a feeling of guilt, and also the feeling of being an insect causing harm wherever it goes.

So the years passed and I was crammed full of literature and morally murdered: in ray thesis I dealt with a poet who spat on all that scientific nonsense and I agreed with him in my thesis, and disagreed with my professors. Ass that I was, I should have made a quick job of it, arguing the opposite . . . instead of working at it for months and months, so that I fell ill and had to ask permission to take my exams later. You can imagine that then the bomb burst: I became the symbol of cynical modern youth, believing in nothing, ungrateful, spiritually diseased.

In order to defend my thesis I had to come before a jury and I heard their verdict: they didn't talk about the spirit of my work, only about minor details: that I'd used too many foreign words. Professor X leafed through it and said: there are too many german words in it . . . and professor Y, whose own works are horribly interlarded with german words and whose fault it is that we're all using these words, said: Yes, that is so. For instance, this here, said professor X, quoting a german word. And then the third professor, professor Z, said: yes, but how would you put it in dutch then? Professor Y thought desperately and found . . . a french word. And professor Z asked: yes, but is that dutch then? So they never talked about the contents . . . but later, when I met professor Y in the street, he shook his head: why are you so cynical, you're not a fleming, you're a sick world-citizen. And then, I should really have set that exam at a later date, but it was black on white in the papers that I'd been referred, which meant they'd failed me and I had to do another year, the stove had to bum again in the study and I'd cost the state another 150,000 francs. I went to see professor Z, who after all had been a bit on my side, and I asked him whether professor Y was behind this dirty trick, but professor Z maintained professional solidarity and said indignantly: how could you possibly entertain such a thought . . . it was purely and simply an administrative error!

It was an administrative error, but as with income tax, you've got to pay for the error, and later they'll pay you your money back . . . but how can they give me, my mum, and the state, this whole lost year back? I had enough of it and went to see professor Y, whom I still suspect of having engineered this, and I explained my case humbly and meekly: I asked him if he couldn't get me a job in their encyclicalist educational system, so that I could prepare for my exams in the meanwhile. But professor Y fell on his backside, figuratively speaking: you, with your sick mind, with your ideology, in our schools! . . . I might get you a job as a clerk or as a simple office boy in a factory . . . but I'll tell you what, why not come to my lectures for another year and write me a decent thesis.

And sickmind, having said all this, sits down, like a caught insect which has to go under the magnifying glass.

## HUMOR LEADS US INTO EVIL

The music master dreams at night that the world is massacring itself, and poet johan janssens goes to pieces because of his spleen . . . and yet, you should hear those 2 together: they possess a kind of humor which would make you kill yourself with laughter: they sit there and must have been going on about something terribly funny again, because the music master's face is no longer a face, it's a cruel, laughing mask . . . he laughs and laughs, and you hear nothing . . . tears stream down johan janssens' cheeks, he laughs and weeps, holding his belly muscles with both hands, and you don't hear him either. It's dry humor. It's perplexingly hysterical—crazy humor. But you can't hear any laughter. Johan janssens wipes the tears from his cheeks with the back of his hand and says: christ, look at this wretched business, writing columns in which you're not allowed to say anything; you can't explain to a soul what that's like . . . all right, I've got a wife and a child, but you'd need 2 wives and 2 children to be able to bear it; it's all without guts, without Life . . . the doctors k.k. kakkemans and the doctors pascalius prostituaans fill the cultural pages with their dead brains and their dead sex . . . they go and look at picasso with a heart like an emperor, because they've collected all that's ever been said about picasso in a file . . . but as he's always doing something new, they're always losing their bearings and they never understand the first thing about anything . . . so they go and write in the pink left-wing papers that it wasn't really quite *that* . . . nothing but a pathological case . . . and they write in the ultra-marxist papers: oh, now I've lost my head . . . where is it, maybe between my legs, I don't care for this kind of thing, but never mind, if he hadn't been an ultra-marxist I would have said quite bluntly that it's hideous. And then they put some cliche in the paper: the little lord jesus in his manger, by rogier van der metsysen. And for the rest . . . I don't know who lives at present with elza who's married to van der krieken but who left her husband and lives with van der appelen who left his wife who lives with van der peren whose wife lives with brother hooizolder who in turn comes to visit elza now and again when he's fed up with brother rixensardus' first wife . . . a hotch potch, a hotch potch, a whores' hotch potch . . . now I wouldn't mind this in the least, I'd look at it with a smile . . . although I'm quite happy with my own wife, who's my friend, my playmate, my grief and my joy, my whore, my sweetheart and my consolation—but I would be able to watch this game with a smile if they said: we're ultra-marxists and the only love which counts is free love. But the stinking bourgeois motto under which they live is this: we must live like respectable citizens and pretend we're a party with encyclicalist morals.

Then the music master pipes up again with something terribly funny, so that both of them start roaring with laughter again, laughing, laughing without a sound. So much that once again johan janssens will forget to write what he really ought to write in one of his columns.

## ONE-UPMANSHIP

*When oscarke was with ondine, she goaded him into thinking that his mother only thought of her own interest, that she'd had this villa built but didn't pay the builders, that she was selfish and begrudged her son a girl friend . . . and besides, look at your father, he's got to try and find elsewhere what he doesn't find at home . . . I think that what your mother's got between her legs is made of wood, otherwise it's not possible . . . not surprising if your father looks for a plump girl who can give him a bit of pleasure where he likes it. Oscarke listened to her with throttled heart; it was the 1st time he heard anyone talk like this about his parents and he did realize that people can't live without That, but his parents weren't people, they were gods . . . and now they toppled from their pedestals but this still didn't make them into humans, they became fallen gods . . . he felt faint when this picture—his father with a plump girl—came before his eyes. Ondine realized that she'd been too hasty: however much she longed to be married, to get away from home and to create a new world in her own house, it was put off, from day to day: oscarke never had anything positive to say. It would go on like this till she became furious and as she was thinking this she was already busy getting furious: there's nothing but deceit and lies around me, it's got to change . . . change in this sense that no longer shall I be deceived and lied to, but the others . . . my days are frittered away and I say little more than: oh, well . . . let things be . . . I'll leave the old gate hanging from the old post and I sink away in a state of mind I damn well don't understand myself. But now all that's finished! And for the hundredth time she burst out in fury. What she lacked was self control . . . in order to achieve anything she should have been more steadfast, more patient, more faithful to her ideal. But she wasn't. Everything in her went up and down like waves. In the evening she wrote a letter and as she was writing, it became as clear as crystal that she should have been at the head of a big concern, of a trading company with business abroad for instance, for which push and courage are needed and in which one is forced to trample petty bourgeois principles in the dust. First she wrote to brussels that proof had been found . . . showing that valeer had fraudulently appropriated the money. She threatened with the police, with god, with everything of which small folk are frightened to death. And then she wrote a letter to the schatts; first she thought of using the old, well-tried excuse that she was pregnant and HAD to marry oscar, but she rejected this romantic rubbish, especially because the old grey cat was capable of sending a doctor to examine her. And she was afraid of doctors who might examine her. No, she remained clear and businesslike in this letter: the files had been completed and would be sent to court: she hoped an agreement could still be reached, in which case the 23rd of june would be held as the final date, signed, yours faithfully, ondine bosmans. And as she drew a resolute line under her name she resembled the old ondine of her youth: the one who had enough faith to move mountains. She looked at the sheets of paper spread out on the table: that was that, and now she was ready to tackle something else, at once. But she received a letter from oscar's mother in return . . . it was obvious that both of them, ondine and mrs schatt, were cut from the same wood . . . they stood face to face, not as water and fire, but as 2 fires, flaring up against one another. Age had blunted mrs schatt's sharpest edges, but had made her all the more cunning. Her sentences twisted like adders, began sweetly and ended in wrath. Oh, you cat, thought ondine. She'd been shrewd enough to address the letter to mr carolus bosmans, builder and carpenter; that, as had been agreed, she would commence payment, to the extent that circumstances would permit, but that at present circumstances prevented payment from being commenced . . . and she respectfully asked if the date, which she assumed 'he' hadn't decided upon, could be deferred to a later to be specified date. And then there was a second letter enclosed in the first one, in pencil, addressed to ondine, that she'd sue her because of her having depraved children over by the railway. It was signed: mrs schatt. But in such a way that it could have been anyone's name, even that of ondine herself. Her best trick followed in a postscript: which she had made him sign: also signed by me, oscar. There it was, in 'a frightened, childish handwriting . . . ondine laughed hysterically; she went upstairs to the attic and put the letter in the tin where she'd once kept the 1000 francs.*

## REYNARD'S ADULTERY

With the iron cooking pot rammed down on his head, squashing his ears, isengrinus didn't know where he was, and after that kick on his behind he didn't know which way he was rolling . . . I must be a dirty bishop, he thought, whirling round and round . . . but fortunately a big oak tree appeared in his path and collided with the cooking pot. The pot broke, isengrinus fell on his back and hundreds of thousands of stars shone in the sky. He picked up the pieces and walked back with pain in his heart, with blind fury in his head, but unfortunately only with plans for a revenge which couldn't be carried out. However, he hadn't come.to the end of his disasters yet, because on the way home his wife hersinde came to meet him in chapel road . . . wringing her hands with much hullabaloo, rolling her eyes. And what she told him, with a voice choking with tears, and then again smiling and winking, with ribbons to embellish it and with pins to tear his skin, boiled down more or less to this: how can I tell you what happened, isengrinus, your fine nephew reynard came to our house and relieved himself in the children's bed. He doesn't like our children, he says they all take after their father who's a greedy pig and a dressed-up monkey . . . and although I must admit that there's some truth in it, isengrinus, I didn't agree with him . . . but I did have to agree with him that the children don't resemble me at all, they've got none of my thrift, nor of my diligence, not to mention beauty, because I don't want to be vain, like other women . . . but when he'd done that and the children began to call for me and I got out of bed . . . because you know, a woman has always got something the matter with her, if it's not the children it's some illness or other . . . my motherly heart bled, but he jumped out of the door and how could I get him back? Could I run after him, with my varicose veins and my back-ache, and anyway, he was already out in the road, shouting that I was trying to assault him. So I stayed and shouted after him . . . maybe you'll say that I must have invited him back, but that's not true . . . it's true that I invited him to come, but that was only to give him a thrashing . . . and he came and I pretended to be scared and ran upstairs meaning to drop the trapdoor on his head so that he'd roll down the stairs and break his legs . . . oh, I wish it had happened like that but what do you think happened instead? . . . that fox was too quick again, as you never are, isengrinus; I was just about to push the trapdoor down but he was already upstairs, beside me, beside the bed in our room where the wax flowers from our wedding day are still hanging on the wall, covered with years of dust . . . And then, my dear, dear isengrinus, while you'd forgotten me, while you were heavens knows where, and I was without a strong arm to protect me—hersinde wept, wept with much noise—I ran away, I wanted to escape round the bed, but I got stuck between the bed and the chimney piece because of my plumpness and the narrow space. And reynard, did he come after you? . . . the wolf groaned hoarsely. Hersinde nodded her head and wept, she looked up at isengrinus, who was enraged, who stood there with one eye nailed shut and his tongue tied and with the pieces of the iron cooking pot still in his hands. He stared at the fragments and all he managed to say was: if you glue these bits together you get a cooking pot, but if you glue the bits of your story together, hersinde, you get a soup which not even the devil will eat.

## WE'LL WAIT AND SEE

On this glorious easter day you really ought to have gone for a walk in the fields, to enjoy the sun and the blossoming fruit trees which van gogh painted . . . but along the road from your house to the fields they've built cheap working class dwellings . . . 120,000 francs a piece, with the doors already splitting although they've only just been put on their hinges, with miserable windows and miserable floors and with only 2 little corner fireplaces, one in the front room and one in the kitchen. They've been built in terraces of 4, side by side like numbered soldiers or unemployed men in a queue. And instead of walking further and enjoying the sun and the blossoming fruit trees, which van gogh painted, you go back home, wondering what kind of a civilization this is? You push the front door open and see a letter from tippetotje:

I don't know if you've been wondering of late what kind of a civilization we live in, but I have, and I can give you the answer by means of a story: I'm at the moment painting in brussels, at the avenue de avenueren, I'm doing the portrait of somebody who's a bit small, a bit fat, a bit insignificant . . . a co-director of a little factory called LOPAJE where they make trimmings and braid to sew on children's clothes. He's asked me to paint his wife and daughter too, all in oil on canvas. And when I was painting the insignificant portrait of his insignificant daughter, she told me of their insignificant life . . . my dad earned some money in the war . . . that's to say, we already had some money, but he met a sculptor during the war . . . someone who doesn't sculpt any more because he's got something the matter with his hand, some injury . . . so this sculptor met my dad and said: you've got some money, you join in with me, I know of something that will bring in quite a lot. So they started business together and it did bring in quite a lot. But then they met a 3rd person, someone who used to keep an underwear shop but later became a nazi and who knocked fortunes out of the ground. Then the war was over and they had to do business in quite a different way; they decided to start a factory together, LOPAJE, because my dad's called louis and the sculptor paul and the other jef. Actually, only the sculptor and my dad run the factory, because the other one, jef, was so terribly rich, he only put his money in and nothing else. To tell you the truth, it's only that sculptor with his hand who runs the factory, because my dad sits in the office all right but he doesn't know anything about business the way it's done these days. He can only do business and make money the way it used to be in the war. Because, and this is between us, do you know how they run their business now? . . . at a loss! . . . since my dad has been in this factory he's lost a quarter of what he made in the war . . . do you call that business? And now, the whole thing is going to the . . . I mean it's going downhill; jef collapsed and was dead on the spot, dead as a doornail, and his cousin wants all the money back which is still in the factory, I mean the three quarters that are left. I said to my dad, you'd better take out your three quarters as well . . . the sculptor with his hand will have to see how to manage on his own; we'd rather wait and see.

This is how I, tippetotje, conclude my letter about the LOPAJE factory at the avenue de avenueren in brussels . . . I only want to underline something which that daughter put forward as her philosophy of life, with an ugly grin: when the ship sinks, the rats leave. And again, I want to underline her last words: we shall wait and see. That's the authentic image of our civilization, wait and see, because it's more profitable to do business when there's a war.

## ONDINE LETS HERSELF BE NAILED TO THE BROOM

*Evening fell, and of course ondine needn't go to the broom bushes, because oscarke wouldn't be allowed to go out so late; god knows, maybe the old grey mouse had sent him to bed without his supper, like a child. She cursed at this dog's shit bourgeoisie . . . the people of termuren, for all their slavish stupidity, were a hundred times better. She went to see the girls with whom she used to be at school: maria and liza, and listened to the litany of their daily worries. Liza only had a few stumps of teeth left, although she was still so young, and maria had become as blind as a bat. Maria happened to be sitting by the stove at liza's when ondine called and asked who is that? Isn't it vapeur's ondine? She had breasts that sagged down to her stomach, an awful sight. Oh, they were grey and wilted, these girls, and swore bloody hell and goddammit at the drop of a hat, and at another drop of a hat they lit candles and prayed to saint antony for his help . . . because they were frightened of the one they called our lord; he belonged to the rich. They laughed at things that weren't worth laughing at. They were, no, ondine couldn't find a word to describe what exactly they were like. She preferred to go to her uncle's café, and played peck-a-bird with the menfolk of these termuren women . . . she smoked a cigarette and these men had never seen such a thing: they thought she was a whore, a bitch . . . they would have murdered their own wife for this, but liked it in another woman: they almost had a fight over who was allowed to walk home with ondine in the dark evening. She didn't mind . . . not out of love, or lust, but only to see how the poor of termuren did it. We'll play for it, she said . . . there was a sour smile round her mouth, when she saw how their heavy, calloused hands trembled as they threw the darts. It was the mason of the filature . . . whose wife had been in hospital for weeks and who'd been in bed without a woman all that time . . . he fought tooth and nail to win: he walked home with ondine, silent, clumsy, boorish . . . and she asked him all about his wife, had he got to know her amongst the cotton bales, in the mill loft . . . and how he managed now, all by himself in bed. She had to wrench his sullen answers from his lips . . . a yes and a no . . . and meanwhile they'd arrived at her parents' house and he looked at the opening on her dress, wringing his sweating hands. Come along, said ondine. She went back with him into the dark, she led him to the old spot where she'd grown up . . . where she'd got to know happiness and grief, in turns, where a miracle had been done to her, but where she had also shat on the world, in fury and misery, and where she'd made oscarke crawl on top of her. She laughed and pretended elation, but in her there twisted the adder of the awareness that there was something wrong: am I not a coward, really? Would I dare start a fight with that old grey mouse? She persuaded herself that she would. And nailed to the railway bank by this man, feeling his rough breath on her mouth and neck, she decided to wait till oscarke came back of his own accord. If he wants to possess me like this mason of the mill possesses me, he'll have to fight for it.*

## BLUES FOR YESTERDAY

It's one of those glorious evenings of which there used to be so many; your friends-heroes have made your house their own . . . the poet and weekly journalist johan janssens had turned the radio on to listen to that dreary spoken journal and msieu colson of the ministry is about to wring its neck and put a new record on the turntable. While the music master and tolfpoets are constructing a caricature of the world together, the one with a certain labored seriousness, the other rather scoffingly, maria, child of nature, bedecked with ribbons and bows, demonstrates the latest novelty in fashion to the pretty lucette. Meanwhile kramiek is standing in your pantry, stuffing himself. *While this is all going on, you ask them whether they've read the last piece about ondine . . . how she let herself be nailed to the broom . . . and everyone falls silent because no one has read it. They're still your friends and your heroes but not one of them reads about ondine any more.* Trying to save the situation somewhat, the music master says that there is indeed no longer any interest in art and other spiritual things: everybody flies in airplanes or drives a car or a scooter, everyone moves at top speed, as if it's their duty always to be 100 miles further than where they are . . . and when you rush along at 100 miles per hour you can no longer understand people like . . . like . . . and he sees a buddha sitting on your mantelpiece: like that man there, he says. Kramiek, who's come out of the pantry, says with his mouth full: always faster and faster. In the old days it used to be great fun for the children in the street to watch the boozers trying to get home, swaying and tottering, flopping down and falling asleep on the pavement . . . but now these same boozers drive around in cars and they first knock down the frightened street-urchins before going to sleep somewhere with their car crashed into a tree or a wall. I saw an accident like that yesterday, says maria, the child of nature; three men, all of them sozzled, first they knocked down a girl on a bicycle and then they crashed into another car so that their own car turned over three times and broke its axle . . . and these three sots got out and didn't even have a scratch, our lord is on the side of the drunks; they crept out of what was left of their car and one of them said: let's put it back straight and drive on. In the old days it was only country yokels who used to get into fights and there'd be a few broken arms and legs and a lot of trampled grass . . . says msieu colson of the ministry, holding his new gramophone record in both hands, a record of louis armstrong . . . but now it's one half of the world against the other half and there are millions of dead, and cities are turned into scorched deserts. In the old days somebody like me invented a pistol by accident, says tolfpoets with a grin, but now people like me do sums and calculations to split the atom . . . naturally, all their calculations are faulty and their results wrong . . . but this wrong result, the atom bomb, remains with us all the same. The pretty lucette butts in: last week I went to see mrs tiddylomba, the wife of the chief engineer at the labor, and she'd just had her living room papered with flowered wallpaper—and when it was done she almost cried: look, how awful it is; I don't like flowered wallpaper! She prefers plain, but why does she ask for it then, only to cry her eyes out when the job's done. She doesn't want to look at it, so she jumps into her husband's car and tears off, flies off, at 100 miles an hour or more.

When silence has returned the buddha is still sitting on the corner of the mantelpiece and msieu colson of the ministry says: now I'll let you hear my latest acquisition: louis armstrong singing: blues for yesterday.

## MEDICAL EXAMINATION

It's the 1st of may . . . and johan janssens, poet and journalist, reads with satisfaction what we have gained so far, in the struggle for a better existence . . . we have, he reads in the paper, obtained vocational guidance and medical examination.

Yes, says the music master, that's right, we've got medical examinations . . . now let me tell you the story of my colleague, who's been in teaching for the last 4 years or so, and he's thinking of getting a loan to buy himself a little house where he's going to live with his little wife who's soon going to give him a little schoolteacher. Well now, this colleague of mine had to go into hiding during the occupation, but immediately after the liberation he became a soldier . . . after a medical examination which showed he was very suitable. And after his military service he went into teaching; he got a temporary appointment. And he's been in temporary employment for the last four years now. But now he's got to have a medical examination before his post can become permanent and now they look doubtful; it seems his heart isn't altogether normal. Now I wonder whether it wouldn't be the right thing to do to examine whether my colleague got this 'not altogether normal heart' in the army, or during the 4 years in his temporary teaching post. And if indeed that's where he got this 'not altogether normal heart', ought they then simply to give him a kick up his behind and leave him to his fate? His fate: thrown out, with a mortgage, soon with a little ex-teacher to look after, fighting for his bitter existence all by himself and maybe starting up a little business. When the music master has finished, no one gets a chance to get angry, because tolfpoets starts blurting out something, tolfpoets, who doesn't take our civilization seriously and who's always cracking jokes about it: the doctors told me too that my heart isn't altogether normal. But they said they knew people who'd won the marathon with a heart like mine. What does that prove? It proves that science knows nothing; they look at ten thousand hearts and draw a conclusion: these are the most commonly found hearts and so they're normal. But I often wonder whether everyone hasn't got a heart best suited to his own constitution: look at that teacher who was suited to be a soldier but not to get a permanent appointment . . . and look at the man who didn't have a normal heart and who yet won the marathon.

Naturally, everybody laughs at tolfpoets' little joke, but soon enough they're all serious again, when msieu colson of the ministry adds: in the ministry there's one department where nobody likes to get stuck, because the work there is extremely demanding on one's nerves and one's stamina and one's power of concentration. There are girls there who start off young and fresh like flowers and they work there for a few years like overstrung wires and then, because excessive strain always affects something specific, one after the other they get trouble with their stomach or trouble with their heart and they look like withered cut flowers. And only then do they have their medical examination to see if they can be given a permanent appointment and all those wilted flowers are chucked on the rubbish heap: you're not in good health and not suited for this work. So they're squeezed like lemons and wrung out like floorcloths and then they're flung out into the street, when the medical examination shows that they're not suitable. Let me tell you about an old office clerk who's been working in the ministry for over 30 years, but always as a temporary clerk . . . for 30 years he's been temporary and for 30 years he's been waiting for his permanent appointment . . . and then comes the medical examination showing that he's got something the matter with him, maybe also a heart that isn't altogether normal . . . and he's therefore unmasked as if he were a bandit or a swindler: for 30 years he's been working in the ministry and now he has the temerity to have something the matter with him; to have a disease. So he's not appointed, that'll teach him. But . . . he's allowed to stay on as a temporary clerk. He's allowed to stay till he gets the retirement pension of a 'mere temporary clerk' who was unmasked as a sick man by medical examination. And so they'll be able to punish him by not paying him the higher pension of permanent clerks, and he will have no right to certain advantages to which others have a right: haha! we've caught a little sucker, a little sick sucker in a trap!

Kramiek has listened to it all and now tells us something of what happens in the factory behind the 1st dirty houses where he's a clerk; there'd been an error in the building plan which meant that a number of girls had to keep running up and down the stairs every 2 minutes, put down their work and run down the stairs and up again . . . and a few of these girls became exhausted and had a breakdown; and it happened just as with that colleague of the music master's: the medical examination only came later and showed that these girls weren't suited to running up and down the stairs all the time, so they were put on work where they earn less . . . because you see, they say to these girls: you're not suited, you're ill and weak and so it's only fair that you shouldn't earn as much as the others.

Johan janssens puts down the paper, the special 1st of may issue which announces with cynical and painful bitterness that we have obtained the right of medical examination.

## MAYBUGS

It always rains and rains in your books, they say . . . but can you help it? Look at it, it's may and it's raining and it goes on raining. You remember the may evenings of your youth, when it was so wonderful and quiet, with flowering broom and flowering jasmine and girls coming home from benediction . . . tolfpoets, too, remembers those past may evenings, and looking at the rain beating against the window pane he says: we can't go and catch maybugs tonight. Everybody smiles. *But can you let your heroine say such things? Can you make ondine say to oscarke: we can't go and catch maybugs over by the broom tonight?*

It's raining and in french rain isn't very different from tears . . . il pleut and il pleure . . . so it rains in your books and it weeps in your heart . . . your sister jeanneke is dead and lies out there in the rain and your mother goes about the house while it rains on her face . . . and furthermore, she's angry with you . . . angry because you're still alive and your sister jeanneke is dead. But can you do anything about it? Can you help it, that it rains in may, that it rains in your books and that your sister jeanneke is dead? That she wasn't yet 25 years old and is already dead? Your mother goes about her empty, silent, desolate house and is angry with you . . . she hardly speaks and is only happy—no, not happy, but it consoles her—she's only consoled if somebody tells her that so and so is dead too. Only the dead can console her. But can I console her, I who am alive? Can I simply go and die, in order to console her? Your mother is angry with you and says afterwards to others: he comes in and sees I'm crying and he says: are you crying again? . . . you see, it makes me angry with him, because he ought to know I *can't* forget our jeanneke. Or she says: he comes in and sees I'm crying and asks: why are you crying?

. . . you see, it makes me angry with him because how could he have forgotten that I cry because of our jeanneke? Or she says: he comes in and sees I'm crying and he asks Nothing . . . you see, that makes me angry, because if a dog whines for its young, surely you ask why he's crying, but nobody asks me anything. You hardly know any more what to say or ask or not say. Because your mother is really angry because you're still alive . . . she's angry when you're silent and she's angry when you speak . . . she's angry when you come to the house and get in the way and look at her tears . . . and she's angry when you stay away and leave her alone with her grief. It's may and it's raining . . . it rains in my books and it weeps in my heart . . . but can I brush it aside by saying to my mother: we can't go catching maybugs tonight?

## BECAUSE I'M NO MARCUS AURELIUS

All I can do now, says the music master with brave determination . . . all I can do now is to face my pupils with the fact that the world, or rather our civilization, is approaching its end . . . and to show them in the histories of declining civilizations which men stayed on the sinking ships like dying captains: I gave them the wonderful example of marcus aurelius who reigned over a dying rome . . . and who managed to delay its death for more than 50 years by sheer will-power and intelligence. There, too, the rot attacked what was most beautiful, everything of value began to stink, then, too, there was immense chaos, cynicism, unrest and despair . . . there too the best minds went astray on the paths of gospels, theosophies, spiritualisms, existentialisms and personalisms . . . but he alone stood firm as the captain of the sinking ship, watching the rats flee . . . he conducted conversations with himself, sorting and sifting and trying to see clarity in the chaos. And who knows what the music master might have gone on to say if johan janssens, poet and weekly journalist, hadn't interrupted him: now, after two thousand years, the clouds of spiritual dust have settled and we see clarity in the chaos of dying rome . . . we see that the best in it was attacked by the dreadful disease which is with us again now: the spiritual plague, spiritual decomposition. We see that in the midst of the disorder marcus aurelius was the captain of the sinking ship and that the rising Christian religion was the new faith which was going to move mountains—was going to, but after toiling for 2000 years it left them standing. And now? How about now? Who is the captain in the bow of the sinking ship, who are the deserting rats? Don't we take the captain for a rat who's abandoning his ship? And the deterioration of everything beautiful and noble—the Beautiful and the Sublime, as dostoievsky once wrote with capital letters—everything beautiful and sublime decays and stinks even worse than what was already repulsive at the beginning of creation. Personalism and existentialism and theosophy and spiritualism and neofascism spring up overnight like mushrooms . . . communism and socialism and reaction and capital and labor struggle against each other, biting their own toes thinking it's their opponent's toes . . . and what is still part of the changing civilization and what is already part of the coming new civilization? Is a new civilization going to come at all? I don't know, because I'm no marcus aurelius. I'm only johan janssens, the weekly journalist.

## OVERSENSITIVITY

Just imagine this! exclaims poet and weekly journalist johan janssens furiously . . . just imagine this! And when he sits down it looks as if he doesn't quite know himself what he's been imagining because he's incapable of expressing his anger coherently. Of course, he continues, less excitedly, of course there will probably always and everywhere be sentimental people but the way He exaggerates sentimentality, it's too much for me . . . I met poet johan brams and he tells me that since recently he's been having scarlet red ultra-marxist sympathies . . . first he explains to me that although he still writes in the socialist press he'd much rather write in the ultra-marxist press, but that well . . . er . . . well, he's got a wife and child and he's got worries in his head . . . and anyway, he's got a job he can't afford to lose. When he's finished telling me all this with lots of frills and ribbons, with flowers and with barbed wire, he reproaches me that I still write in the pinkish red socialist papers and no longer for the ultra-scarlet ones. And he ended with scorn: so you're really nothing but a hack, he said. I, johan janssens, poet and weekly journalist, I, a hack! To my face he said I was a hack but I sup-pose that behind my back he said that I was a whore writing for money. You imagine that! Johan janssens suddenly starts to roar, so that you give a start and upset your inkwell. You imagine . . . because a hack, what does that mean? . . . weren't the cathedral builders hack builders, was goya not a hack painter, was Shakespeare not a hack actor, was dostoievsky not a hack novelist? But what really makes me so livid is this: so he's got so-called ultra-red sympathies and he says he dreams of art in the service of the community, where the writer no longer takes up his pen to write down beautiful things but on the contrary, Puts His Pen At The Service . . . that's what he says, but at the same time he can't stand it that we're fed up and can't be bothered, for the time being, to write fat books which nobody reads anyway and which moreover don't bring any grist to the mill . . . and it galls him that instead we sharpen our quills in order to earn our bread in the weekly press and say what we think . . . In order to shut johan janssens up at last, you ask: what did you say to shut him up, johan janssens? He says: I told him that writing for a living is as honorable a craft as any other craft . . . not the way of writing, nor the paper for which one writes, but what one writes is what matters . . . and I also showed him that all this talk of a whore who gets paid, is sentimentality because if you work you must be paid, some are even paid to represent the people, and others to serve and praise god . . .

But oh, dear me, johan janssens has hardly finished, and he's hardly gone out of the door, when . . . sentimental more sentimental most sentimental . . . he hurtles down from the superlative, head over heels, into something much worse: because there at the wall of the labor a sentimental dog story is being enacted: a very small dog smells at the hind legs of a very large bitch, and naturally, he wants to show his dog's devotion and do his dog's duty, but he only prods about a bit at her hind legs . . . and she calmly walks on as if nothing was happening . . . he watches her go, baffled and sad, as she disappears round the corner of the labor. Johan janssens remains silent and looks at you, and you look at johan janssens from the doorway, and both your angry moods change into endless pity, into grief, into boundless sentimentality.

## OSCARKE'S FLOWER

*Ondine waited for days on end, but oscarke didn't come . . . often she had to suppress the desire to take her golden bracelet and her sunshade and go and look for him. She told herself it would be a sign from god: if he came they'd get married . . . if he didn't come, then . . . well . . . What do I care, after all, she thought. But one afternoon in may, when it was drizzling, their front door opened and there he was. He'd been up for conscription and had to go and draw lots, whether or not to be a soldier, and the other termuren boys had overtaken him in chapel road. He was slouching along dolefully, although he'd drawn a good number and wouldn't have to be a soldier . . . the others had flowers in their caps and still sang of leopold, vivat leopold, he can come and kiss our arse . . . although leopold was dead and another king had come in his place . . . but in termuren no one had noticed. One of them took a flower from his cap and stuck it on oscarke's oldfashioned hat . . . they went in at Christ's and played peck-a-bird. Oscarke, who hardly knew what beer was, soon felt the floor sliding away from under his feet . . . an immense sadness came over him, a drunk's sadness, a universal sentimentality . . . he sobbed and told the others what he felt; they weren't listening but this didn't prevent him from displaying all his insoluble problems like a shopkeeper setting out his wares. With the paper flower in his hat he staggered off and when he arrived at ondine's house he entered, without thinking. In a haze he saw himself standing in this strange kitchen and he asked: oscarke, how is it you dare come here? . . . Yes, I dare, I'm oscarke, I dare do everything. Ondine laughed, harshly, mercilessly in her triumph, because he's come to her . . . she also laughed at the flower in his hat and asked if he was going to be a soldier. No, he said. Oh, the fool . . . why have you got a flower in your hat then? He looked at her with muddy eyes, he no longer knew what a flower was, or a hat, or oscar, or ondine: the world reeled before his eyes; he saw a swaying ondine, pulling the flower from his hat and putting it somewhere else . . . he heard her call: look, this is where you should put it! He looked, and at first to his astonishment, then to his deep, deep shame, he saw she'd stuck the flower in his fly. At the same time he heard a braying laugh, and turning round he saw, for the first time, zulma, sitting by the window . . . she pointed with her thin finger, as if to explain to herself that he was wearing a flower in his fly, and when her eyes followed her finger, and discovered the flower, she bared her whole toothless mouth in laughter. Oscarke watched this crazy scene and felt the world heaving more and more under his feet . . . he heard ondine calling something, he saw her grey eyes shooting fire, and then noticed her hands which became swarming things without a name . . . she was probably telling him why he should put that flower THERE and he tried to reflect on it . . . he blathered: certainly, that's the truth. But if she'd been saying the opposite of what she was probably saying, he would have had to agree with her just the same, that she was speaking the truth. All these possible truths were hammering in his head. Yes, that's the truth . . . and nodding his head in agreement he suddenly began to vomit all over the floor . . . ondine hurried for a glass of water and pushed him in a corner by the stove, where he fell asleep at once. Later she sent him home . . . she watched him go from the door and felt happy, without knowing why . . . she wanted to call something cheerful to him as he was walking away in the may drizzle and she blurted out: we won't be going to catch maybugs tonight.*

## THE HISTORY OF GODMOTHER WANNE

I suppose you know chapel road like your trouser pocket, someone says to you. You start talking about your parents and your grandparents and your great-great-grandparents, who all left their footprints in the dust and the mud of chapel road . . . only your godmother wanne, she wasn't actually from chapel road, she was from way beyond termuren, from back in the fields where the peasant still stoops over his fallow land . . . she was 12, godmother wanne, when she started work at the filature, and got to know godfather sooi, who pushed her on her back like it behooved a man of chapel road in those days . . . and when they got married, he had to cross the fields to her house on foot, but he'd forgotten the letter from the priest, so he had to go back and fetch it. He had his wedding shoes on and as he had never worn shoes in his life, always clogs, his feet hurt him cruelly . . . he sat down by the path in the field, with his feet in the brook which winds on to behind the castle . . . he sat there and stayed . . . meanwhile godmother wanne was waiting and waiting . . . finally her brother came to see where the bridegroom was, and found godfather sooi with his bare feet in the brook; hey sooi, aren't you coming? Godfather sooi answered: you know, it's lucky you come to look for me, because I'd never have come of my own accord. So godfather sooi took his bride to chapel road . . . to one of the 7 cottages by the level crossing, they've been pulled down since . . . and it turned out that godmother wanne, who'd worked at the filature ever since she was 12, couldn't read or write, count or do sums, cook or wash, laugh or cry; she couldn't put coal on the fire and was no use in bed either; she said she was ill and had something the matter with her stomach . . . with my stommick, she said . . . she sat huddled in a worn old armchair and never left it . . . godfather sooi became the cobbler of chapel road and sat hammering the leather in the back kitchen, he came to look at the fire in good time and cooked for the two of them—it was always chops at noon, and in the evening a sandwich with a little salt sprinkled on it—he washed and scrubbed and dusted and cleaned the windows . . . bring children into the world all by himself he couldn't do, of course, but otherwise he might have managed even that . . . occasionally he got sozzled and he was sorry he wasn't married to marie from the café. Godmother wanne, however, sat in her chair and had something the matter with her stommick, *she gazed out and broodingly watched a leaf fluttering from a tree,* and she knew exactly who had and who hadn't gone past the house during the day . . . she had no desires, no wishes, no hate and no love, no pity and no humor, and she was angry with the socialist band because it made too much noise: all that noise in our chapel road, she said. Only in her last years she began to listen, on Sunday afternoons, if she could hear the ice-cream man's whistle, and she'd buy herself a 50 centime cone . . . later, with time and competition, there were 3 and even 4 ice-cream vendors passing through chapel road, but godmother wanne didn't want any ice-cream from them: it must be a 50 centime cone from the ice-cream man with the pock-marked face, she said. She'd wait the whole sunday afternoon for that pock-marked ice-cream vendor; and look, here comes a miracle peeping round the corner: suddenly this pock-marked ice-cream vendor died and on the same day, at the same hour, godmother wanne, who'd always been waiting for him, died too; they lie side by side in termuren cemetery; he with his pock-marked face and she with her stommick . . . but he can no longer sell her any 50 centime cones . . . actually, those cones have been costing 5 francs for a long time now.

And talking about her stommick . . . she did indeed have something wrong with her stommick, because when she was dying, suffering the most frightful pain, doctor goethals dropped in one day . . . purely and simply out of friendship for godfather sooi who repaired his shoes . . . he looked at godmother wanne and said: cancer. It was the 1st time this cruel word had ever been spoken in chapel road. Cancer, what horrible thing was that?

## I WOULD HAVE GIVEN YOU A CHILD

*So this was god's sign, and ondine must no longer hesitate . . . the next day she went to the schatts' house and rang . . . she was carrying her sunshade like a weapon, determined to lash out at anyone who might thwart her. But to her astonishment the door was opened by a spare little man with a goatee . . . this must be mr schatt! . . . she had to smile at it, that this shriveled creature, this goat, this office stool, was a tyrant in his own house and for the rest didn't understand anything that went on in life, whose only interest it was to crawl under some skirt or other. As if he was nothing but a dog . . . or rather, a billygoat . . . ha! she stood there laughing in the open door because he'd stuck the symbol of a goat on his chin. For the rest he was supposed to be a good encyclicalist. He couldn't make her out, why should she be standing at the door, laughing . . . he thought of That again, he tried to look right through her clothes, between her thighs. It was really a bit ondine's own fault. After all, somewhere deep inside her she felt very much a woman and she wanted to know whether his desire went out to her . . . whether she could still be compared with the girls from the town . . . He closed the door so that they were locked in the empty, chilly corridor together . . . he muttered a few words and came closer, so that she was almost pressed against the double doors, to the living room. His hand was already reaching for her skirt, but she checked him with her cool, grey eyes: pride rose in her, the awareness that she could do what she liked with him made her drunk. She made up her mind to exploit this and to lay down the law to him. She asked for oscar . . . and if the grey mouse had dared enter the hall, ondine would have laughed at her, she would have undressed, down to her bare skin in front of this goat here. The old man was surprised she asked for oscar . . . it was obvious that he knew nothing, absolutely nothing, of what went on in his own house. With a shrill, squealing parrot's voice he called: oscar! . . . and straightaway oscar appeared from behind the living room door, as if he'd been eavesdropping all the time. He looked at the floor and drew figures on the mat with his foot, not daring to speak to her. No, he was hardly likely to conquer her heart by storm . . . but at this moment she wasn't thinking of these details, she didn't weigh up whether it was worth her while carrying on with her struggles beside him . . . she only thought of getting her stubborn way. And besides: it was his very awkwardness that endeared him to her . . . whenever a man had crossed her path and had started to sniff at her like a dog, she'd thought: another one that's going to lift his hind leg. Only oscar, in his childlike naivety, had touched a more tender string; he had talked of his dreams, and how difficult it was to cut a mouth in stone, how one had to struggle in order to make it smile . . . and he had only thought of love when she'd asked, at last, come on, love me a bit. She saw all this again, as he was drawing figures on the doormat with his foot . . . she took his arm and led him outside . . . but a certain shame prevented her from going in the direction of termuren, to the broom where last week she'd let herself be nailed to the railway bank by the mason from the mill . . . no they went towards the town. She made him hold her arm, because she wanted to show to the town, to the world, that she was coming, with him . . . that she'd preferred his childlikeness to their coarseness and cunning. She asked him, what about marrying, and he turned away his head in embarrassment. Don't you like me any more, she asked . . . and he nodded, still looking away.*

*She laughed and pinched his arm. This whole conversation, without her being able to look into his eyes, did her such a lot of good that she could have asked him the most outrageous questions, only to see him nodding and shaking his head. They walked along the waterside, past factories, past the station; they went through a street of patricians' houses, and unconsciously she slowed down and looked around: this is where she should have been living. She pointed at a house with a big upstairs window: that would be a nice studio for you, she said . . . and the fact that she thought of a thing like that made him almost ill with happiness . . . he became excited and talked feverishly of big statues, of a rider on horseback.*

*Ondine told him of a dream, long ago, that she hung from a horse's mane and how beautiful it would be to sculpt a naked girl in stone, large as life, with her back against the side of a rearing horse. He stood still and looked her deep in the eyes: and then, sadly, he shook his head; no, it would be no good, it was too great, a thing like that. Teach me. said ondine, teach me how to sculpt and I'll make it. You should have been a man, said oscarke . . . and she stood still, in surprise . . . suddenly she felt strangely cold . . .*

*But she shook off this peculiar feeling and turned it into a joke: then you should have been a girl, she said, I would have organized you! They both laughed at the idea. I can just see myself, pregnant, said oscarke . . . and looked down, in shame.*

## WHERE IS REYNARD?

The next evening tolfpoets asks casually: where's your reynard, johan janssens? Johan janssens throttles the spoken radio journal so that it's silenced, and says: I've written so much about reynard that I'm almost turning into a reynard myself . . . look how I cut our life's work to pieces and sell them to the papers . . . a piece here and a piece there so that I think: soon they'll see through it and realize I'm nothing but a swindler. But it's the only modern way to write a life's work and earn your bread with it at the same time . . . dostoievsky used to write his novels as miscellanies and the papers paid him per week or per month . . . but I cut mine into columns, into bits and pieces, so that to the world . . . that is, to the very small world which is still interested in literature, it becomes a kind of crossword puzzle . . . a secret code to which we alone possess the key. Johan janssens halts, we see his reynard-smile change, fade and vanish. But, he says, but, deep down inside me I still doubt whether I really am a reynard, I fear I'm much more of an isengrinus who wants to grasp all and therefore always loses all . . . because I have the cheek to kick everybody's shins in these columns and yet to make them pay me . . . one day they'll see through the game. Because you see, suddenly all writers and artists are being drummed up who are of the opinion that they should Put Their Pens At The Service . . . supposedly in order to see What Can Be Done For These Artists, but really to use them for the umpteenth time and then, having used them, to give them a kick in their arse. I'm not going, in the first place because I can manage by myself and secondly because I have no wish to be a servant being exploited by a master . . . I want to unite in order to conquer something for myself and other artists, through proper trade union channels . . . but I don't want to unite in order to serve as a dressed up monkey. At this congress there were also artists from holland who want to put their pens at the service, but who don't want to have anything to do with johan janssens himself because, well, johan janssens, you know, in holland they don't care much for him. Finally, the case of the ultra-marxist daily was brought up at the congress: we, flemish men of letters and intellectuals have no use for this paper, they say, and the non-flemish-speaking chief editor, who hasn't understood at all what the flemish intellectuals were complaining about, makes a speech in which he says that intellectuals and artists should all read this paper, because every-thing they ought to know is in it. Furthermore it was said that artists are given complete freedom, but that they should preferably paint the unemployed, for instance, dropping dead at the factory gate . . . and all the editors present, including the sports editor and the editor of broken arms and legs, applauded . . . and all alone at the back of the room sat a lonely artist, weighing the world on the tip of his paint brush; he listened to it all, got up and left . . .

While johan janssens is telling us all this, his 10 year old son jo has come in, to tell his father to come home . . . he's listened attentively to his father and says: maybe that painter was unemployed. Everybody laughs, but johan janssens, who wanted to be a reynard, doesn't laugh.

## STRIKING EXPRESSIONS

Maybe that painter was unemployed, haha! Tolfpoets laughs his 2 golden teeth bare, and talks and talks of all sorts of things and incidents and occasions when someone he knows found an apt word to show up a situation comically . . . in my own way I'm a poet and a writer too, he says, because I've carefully written down all these jokes and anecdotes, funny sayings and striking expressions . . . in the evenings I sometimes read them out to myself, and they often make me laugh, especially if there are some I didn't know yet—like the fool who sent himself a letter and didn't know what was in it; he only knew the next day when the postman delivered it—and if I may, let me remind you of a few striking expressions:

the music master, noticing that his wife has twisted her hair in a knot at the back of her head: lucette, you're wearing your head behind your head. My wife maria: he was as drunk as shit. Kramiek: let's form a circle, the two of us. Again the music master: I who have misunderstood so many books already. Our writer, boon: he crept through the eye of a needle, but from the wrong side. Again the music master when johan janssens' son jo announced that he wanted to join the 'concord' football club: we're in a team too, aren't we, lucette, only ours is called discord. The wife of boon, our writer: a doctor's wife can never fall ill. Msieu colson of the ministry: my wife has got grey hair from living in a villa . . .

Tolfpoets wants to go on reading from his book of striking expressions, but the music master says: tolfpoets, you must keep that book carefully . . . my mother has got the handlebar of a very old bike in the attic, and she keeps that carefully too.

## ONDINE ON THE WRONG TRACK

*Coming back from their walk, between the town of the 2 mills and termuren, ondine and oscarke turned into a narrow alley . . . it wound along the back of the 1st dirty houses behind the labor and consisted only of a high, blind wall and the tall, overgrown hedge of a farm, which had incongruously remained in existence in the town of the 2 mills . . . it was dusk there in the middle of the day and there was such a foul smell it was as if half the town came here at night to relieve themselves. She stood by the hedge, looked at him and waited . . . but no, it didn't occur to him to touch her; it made her happy. Again she began to hammer on always the same nail: that his mother wouldn't let him be a sculptor, so that finally he began to see that it was better to let his mother stew in her own juice, that it was partly her fault if his father sought consolation elsewhere. And still hidden in the hedge she asked did he know that his father had tried to get under her skirt: did you know he put his hand under my skirt, in the hall? Don't talk about it, begged oscarke . . . he pulled her by the hand like a frightened child as if to get her away as fast as possible from that dark crevice between the blind wall and the overgrown hedge. From this dark alley you came to the 1st dirty houses behind the labor; children were fighting there, men sat in the doorways on their behinds, and there were as many as 4 cafés . . . the people of the 1st dirty houses looked at ondine and oscarke and their mocking eyes said: we know what you were up to in the hedge. Then came sunday and on their way to town they saw the river and the filature, strangely deserted . . . on a barge a woman was nursing her child at the breast and ondine made oscarke look at it: she had the strange wish to show him, in this woman, her own nature, her own femininity . . . She pressed his hand and whispered it must be wonderful to sculpt something like that: one day you'll have a live model, one day you won't even have to leave our home to sculpt it straight from nature. The thought that he himself might have a child, a son, excited him . . . he said how wonderful it would be to see the best of her and him united in their children . . . he was as romantic as could be, and listening to him you'd almost believe that babies come out of cabbages. But for some reason ondine no longer answered . . . he turned to her in surprise and saw she was looking at the other side of the road. What was there to be seen? Nothing; there wasn't a soul there, only the poor, drab office of the young socialist party; justice and freedom . . . squeezed between the walls of a brewery and a glucose factory. It was also a shop with the sign: co-operative. Oh, it looked poor, it looked as if it barely managed to keep going, with the small savings of devoted workers. He didn't understand why she should be staring at it, in dumb silence . . . he didn't know that to her the things of today were wiped out, at this moment, and that she stood again at the fountain of her youth . . . that she saw once again that she had left the main road in life and had got on to a wrong track; it seemed to her that this co-operative had only come into being through her fault, through her lack of will. He pressed her arm, like she always did to him, and she turned to him in surprise . . . swear to me, she said, that you'll never in your life mix with these people. He almost laughed at her solemn face, but the tears which choked her voice checked him.*

## THE CHINA SHOP

When isengrinus heard that reynard had deceived him with his wife, he dropped the pieces of the cooking pot from his weary hands as if they were the fragments of his scattering world . . . but after that hopeless gesture the emptiness of the Void—or rather, of his unheard-of stupidity—flashed before his frightened eyes, so that he quickly closed them and burst out in angry curses instead. He looked at everyone in turn, explaining his case, wringing his hands and gnashing his teeth. And although they all sniggered at the stupid wolf, they listened politely, commiserating profusely, but for the rest they quietly went their own way. He tried to persuade them to go on a new pilgrimage, to king noble, because he was convinced that noble alone could bring about a solution . . . he insisted that they'd all go . . . but as soon as they'd gathered around noble the king started complaining about his illness—interrupted by nobeline who stated officially that every house has its problems . . . at your house it's this, but at ours it's even thisser . . . There you are, interrupted the wolf rudely, that's just why I . . . you . . . well, that's why I summoned all the others. And flinging his story of reynard and hersinde at their feet, he added: if only I'd been able to get that stupid cooking pot off my head a bit more quickly, I might have caught them in the act. Well, answered noble, I must say I don't care much for such stories, it's just as with death: you today and me tomorrow, and we can't have a court case about it because everybody will be able to tell . . . or rather conceal . . . something of the same kind. What do you mean, called the bull, who stood at the back, suppose that red thief, the swindler, the cunning bastard, had played the same trick on my wife? I'd have got hold of him, I'd have broken his back, I'd have ground him to pulp, I'd have thrown the stinking mess in the toilet. Another murder, grinned grimbear, the badger, the only one who was remotely related to reynard. No one could help laughing at the tone in which grimbear said this. Let's have a look at this china shop, he said: you, isengrinus, say that reynard nailed your wife between bed and mantelpiece, but did you see or hear anything to prove what happened. Did blood flow, was she robbed of anything, was the house damaged or even a chair broken? If I heard properly there was only mention of a broken cooking pot. My dear wolf, you only make trouble for yourself and pile shame on the head of your poor hersinde, who, believe me, isn't present here of her own desire. That's true, said hersinde softly, I told him often enough that I couldn't remember myself what happened between me and reynard, or how it all went exactly . . . and wherever I go reynard remains the hero and isengrinus the dupe, and I the fool who far more than my innocence couldn't keep my secret. johan janssens.

## I SHALL DO MY DUTY

*Have you told them about our marriage now, asked ondine in a dull, flat voice. Yes, said oscar, although it was a lie; the truth was that at this moment he made the firm resolution to talk about it. Ondine was excited, she tried to draw him out about everything the old mouse had said . . . he answered very little, because he was a poor liar. They walked back past the patrician's house with the big upstairs window, doctor goethals' house . . . and ondine pointed out to him the freestone ornamentation under the windows: look, she said. He looked and didn't understand. They're a woman's breasts, she said. And looking at those stone breasts he wondered why she should always be drawing his attention to Those things . . . yesterday that woman on the barge, and now these ornaments; he said nothing and was worried. She coaxed him along chapel road to the 1st dirty houses and to the dark alley at the back, and it became to him something like sunday mass: always the same, leaving him indifferent.*

*But now that he'd talked of their marriage at home, ondine began to hurry things: she went to brussels for her 1000 francs but she didn't get them just like that, she was given 100 francs and next month they'd see again . . . it was a thin time for traders, people were much too thrifty and all they sold was the odd sugar bun to a child. She didn't see valeer, he was in the café on the corner, playing cards, said their cousin . . . and suddenly a thought opened up before ondine like an abyss: she wanted to see valeer in his small daily doings: she went to the corner and saw him playing cards behind the window, or rather watching the players and meddling in their game unasked. It was . . . it was . . . life went on at termuren and at forest, and in brussels, and in any other dump no matter where. Everywhere was a small bit of life, blind and poor . . . and she knew that he would, at this moment, have been sitting in her uncle's café at termuren, meddling in the card game, if she hadn't chased him away. Something very powerful in her, the age-old urge to discover the secrets of life, wanted to push her through that door, to ask him if he was happy now . . . but an equally strong power in her, the blind fear of finding out the secrets of life, kept her in check . . . she hesitated and looked around, she ran past the shop and hurried straight to the tram stop; 100 francs, that was her entire treasure. Treasure, schat. She couldn't help laughing. On the way back she looked out of the train window but the landscape didn't interest her: a cow and another cow, a farm yard and another, dirtier, farm yard and in order to kill time she began to take stock of all her belongings, on a piece of paper: 100 francs from her cousin, plus a golden bracelet which she might turn into money . . . maybe she could pinch a few things at home . . . she would tell oscarke, too, to keep his eyes open. And as she was writing it all down, something occurred to her, a diabolical idea at which she giggled in advance. It made her impatient, she stuck her head out of the window and tapped her feet crossly when the train lingered at some village station. At last she arrived at chapel road and rang at the schatts'. But there was only his mother. Ondine looked at her with a contemptuous smile and asked for . . . for oscar . . . god, suppose she mentioned that diabolical thought she'd had earlier on, in the train, and said that she'd really come for the old man, for the goat with his beard. The mouse invited her to come into the bare, cheerless living room . . . there was still no fire, although it rained and rained these may days . . . and she began to talk of the marriage at once: I won't mention it that you've turned my oscar's head . . . I don't know how . . . because he doesn't need a wife, he's got his mother . . . but if it had to be that she was going to be robbed of her son, she'd have to make one thing clear to ondine: I can't give him anything because we haven't got Anything, we haven't got any money! She threw it out, triumphantly . . . at last she could be pleased at not having any money. But putting her petty bourgeois housewife's mask back on her face, she added soberly and with dignity: but for the rest I will do my duty.*

## THERE ARE SOME WHO DO THEIR DUTY!

At last we've got a day with some sun . . . it's still a bit chilly and windy, but it's not too bad . . . and you go for a walk in the fields behind termuren, with the whole crowd. Far from termuren, far from chapel road, you think wouldn't it be nice to live here, in a little cottage . . . you could throw out the whole caboodle of chickens and rabbits, stick a big window here, put a door in there, and you live cheaply, beautifully, and moreover, you'd be far from this ill-starred world. Someone who doesn't think about politics could lead a peaceful life here, agrees johan janssens. Someone who doesn't care about the end of the world could live happily here, adds the music master. You stand still and look around as if you're already living here and you take a deep breath . . . deep and free. Johan janssens understands your silent happiness . . . your provisional happiness, because who knows whether you'll even find a cottage for sale, and whether you can afford it if it is for sale and who knows whether you wouldn't even miss the world and chapel road. Johan janssens understands your provisional little bit of happiness and says suddenly, out of the blue: when I ask myself what's worth anything in life then there's only my son jo's sense of humor—he's 10—he has his own life, without listening to me or to my advice . . . his own life full of fantasy and sparkling imagination and scathing wit: an approaching car is a wild animal storming towards you, he says. He compares the headlights with eyes and the bumpers with grinning teeth. When he comes for a walk with me he tells me about a book he's reading where there's talk of bears . . . and while we're chatting about this we meet a schoolmate of his, with glasses . . . look, there's another bear, he says, but it's one with glasses. It's my wife's sense of humor, when she was still a young girl and had a carefree laugh . . . the humor and the carefree laugh which charmed and seduced me, in those days, but which she has lost now.

But msieu colson of the ministry, who was a few feet ahead of us, turns round at once and says: what's the matter with you all: you want to buy a cottage in the country and not care about the world and chapel road . . . you want to escape from the world and shirk your duty . . . like johan janssens' wife shirks her duty by leaving her laugh and her humor behind her . . . and then when you write about somebody who actually does do his duty, you're cynical: *look at that grey mouse, saying triumphantly that there was no money, that she'd send oscarke out without a shirt on his back if he was going to get married . . . but that for the rest she'd do her duty. I wonder what there was left for her to show her duty with . . . Nothing, there was nothing left, so her words were only a phrase . . . an empty, lugubrious, hollow phrase.* And yet there are people who do their duty, who are steadfast like rocks and go on doing their duty: did I ever tell you about the girl in the ministry whose job it is to sort out the ministerial paperwork concerning the people who're going to be decorated? Well, when somebody's going to be decorated, that means a lot of work in the ministry . . . papers, forms, etc . . . and all those people who've made fortunes during the war and who're now going to be decorated, rush to this girl at the ministry and beg her to hurry up with those forms . . . and they've got a plain envelope in their hand, you can guess what's inside it . . . and the girl at the ministry says: I will do my duty; and she does her duty: she tucks away the papers and forms somewhere very deep, very far, in an inaccessible place . . . which means that the decorations too, have been tucked away deep, far, and inaccessible. I saw her in the lift yesterday and I took my hat off right down to the floor.

## THE CHINA SHOP CONTINUED

Hersinde trembled over her whole body and whereas one moment fever or shame made her cheeks blush, the next moment beads of cold sweat stood on her temples. Amongst all these people she was more conscious than ever of her sharp nose and her thin lips—how often had reynard teased her that she was a greedy vixen? But she sighed and said: grimbear is right, I'd be much happier if the father of my children would come to an agreement with reynard, although jesus and all his saints may be my witnesses that nothing worth mentioning has happened between me and reynard, and although I'd like to say to all those who were present at our wedding 10 years ago . . . so many of them that there was no room to put an egg down . . . that never in all that time have I done anything that even the most pious nun would need to confess: I will submit to the hot iron and the cold water ordeal for this . . . and besides, reynard is no more to me than a thistle, only relished by donkeys. Hersinde had hardly come to the end of her sentence when carcofas clapped his hands and put his glasses, which had fallen off, back on his nose: hersinde's words fill me with immense joy, and if I've understood her well, I must conclude that isengrinus may well be right to be angry, if he saw through the cracks in the cooking pot that reynard was deceiving him . . . but I must also conclude that hersinde wasn't wrong in virtuous asinine soul . . . oh, may it please god that my jenny-ass were as faithful and wise as you, hersinde; we know that things always go wrong in the world, that people nod their head when they ought to be shaking it . . . and besides, she spoke of lord jesus, that proves much more to me than any other evidence . . . if our friend the wolf were to have the misfortune to die, I'm sure she wouldn't turn up with a new husband right away, while the whole country would still be mourning poor isengrinus' death. Carcofas the donkey wiped his glasses and when he glanced around he noticed that everybody was looking very upset and that they were all staring at the king and his new nobeline . . . because the king himself had only very recently remarried. Carcofas understood, and crossed himself, thinking the devil must have been sitting on his tongue. Even sweet hersinde was white with rage and her sour lips were tight like a knife. In the general hush the rabbit asked for silence, scraped his vocal cords and gave a splendid summing up: first there was isengrinus, saying that there was something the matter in his house, then grimbear saying that nothing that was broken could be mended, then hersinde, swearing her innocence by lord jesus, and finally carcofas, who'd concluded very sensibly that maybe the one was right without the other necessarily being wrong . . . now we only need to summon reynard and listen to his explanation . . . if he dare come and give a demonstration of what happened . . . the reconstruction of the crime, as it is called—and if we are then able to conclude that indeed it wasn't worth the trouble, we can proclaim general peace . . . I have finished. johan janssens.

## ONDINE IN THE CAFÉ AT THE 1ST DIRTY HOUSES

*As soon as ondine and oscarke had started on their walk, ondine wanted to carry out her diabolical plan: she sent oscarke round the block: I've got an errand to do, wait for me down in the alley. Oscarke went . . . and she hurried into the town of the 2 mills, straight to the bank, which was just closing. Oscar's father came out and she looked at him with eyes which achilles derenancourt and even his spiritualist brother norbert hadn't been able to resist, when she was young. I'm going to get married to your son, she said, but we haven't got any money . . . now you could help us by giving us one month's salary. And he, the fool, the hot-blooded ass, was at once willing . . . he wanted to take her to a place where they could discuss things at leisure, and he mentioned a private house in a street which sounded familiar to ondine . . . she went with him because she wanted to know where it was, because her curiosity for these things would probably never cool off. But as they arrived at the door, she looked up . . . goodness, it was the same house where she and ludovic gourmonprez . . . and she left him standing by the door, with the excuse that his son was waiting for her . . . she smiled and looked him deep in the eyes once more, as she'd done earlier on, fobbing him off, making a promise and yet not a promise for another day. When is pay day? And when he confessed that it wasn't pay day till next week, she said: see you next week then, here at this door. His face began to burn and he gave her a trembling hand . . . She left him and hurried to the alley . . . oscar wasn't there . . . she walked all over the town and finally found him in front of doctor goethals' house, gazing at the big window, lost in dreams. Of course they couldn't go and live there . . . how could we go in and tell that doctor to buzz off. The scorn in her words wounded him. I don't think we'll ever have a house at all, oscar said sadly. But on the way back they passed the café at the 1st dirty houses—or rather, they passed the old-fashioned inn which would later become the café at the 1st dirty houses—and she suggested that they go in and have a beer. The woman came to serve them, wearing torn black combinations, with wet hair in a bun at the back of her head . . . ondine in her perplexity asked for a room instead of beer. It was oscar's father's fault, who'd made that dirty proposal to her to go to a room together . . . and she said to oscar: it's because of all that house-hunting. I get a room mixed up with a glass of beer. A room, said the slut in her worn combinations—or did they not wear combinations in those days, wasn't it a torn slip instead?—A room, she said . . . I've got a room, but do you want it for a couple of hours or would you want to live there? She invited ondine to follow her, up a worn, broken staircase, amongst the whining of children and the smell of stewed cabbage . . . oscarke peeped into one or two open doors and stared into an unknown world . . . meanwhile the woman had entered a door somewhere with ondine, he didn't know which one . . . he stayed on the stairs and waited, staring at this unfamiliar world, almost crying. Ondine stood in a tiny room and the horror of poverty clutched at her throat . . . she thought . . . no, she couldn't think*

*. . . she couldn't Think . . . but she remembered in shame her dreams of big rooms and parlors, she remembered also oscar's dreams of a studio with bright light. She called oscar and asked him what he thought of it . . . he looked round the pitiful little box room and nodded hesitantly. To tell the truth, he had hardly entered and he already loved that room . . . because it was so small . . . because it might be warm and cozy: he would be able to work there at their dream—mother and child—which he was already modelling in his mind. But ondine couldn't accept it so easily . . . that bed, for instance, to have to lie in a bed in which other people had slept. That bed, she said. Oh well, it's only till we've found something better, oscarke replied with her own words. But she knew better.*

## WHEN WILL REYNARD'S REPUBLIC COME?

You see, you should never lure me so far away from termuren, says johan janssens . . . and in his eyes there is still something of the perplexity that people feel when they've crossed a wobbly plank across a deep ravine. You should never entice me to live in the country, in a peasant cottage . . . be-cause the very thought has turned my head, so that now I loathe my daily journey to brussels: first in the morning, I have to fight for a scat on the train, then I have to read all the world news in the morning papers . . . news which isn't news about a world which isn't a world . . . and when I get to north station I have to struggle for a place on the tram and only then can I start on my thankless daily task: to show the world that it isn't a world, but a machine rushing down into an abyss . . . I realize that one day I shall have to hurry, or else the machine, instead of being stopped by me, will roll right over me and my columns, heading for the abyss. My thankless task: to take people's heads off their bodies to make them look at their own stupid faces . . . and again I realize that one day I'll have to hurry or else those same people will take my head off, but they will do it literally, they'll behead me. Meanwhile your cottage glimmers in front of my eyes where you can live cheaply, beautifully, safely . . . and suddenly the perplexity of people crossing a ravine overpowers me and I curse you for having made me think of that safe far-away cottage. Be-cause you see, while I'm taking a stand every day again, proclaiming my opinion from the rooftops and flinging the truth into the face of the world . . . while I've been doing this there's suddenly a letter from doctor pascalius prostituaan and he writes that I ought to have the courage to take a more positive stand: your articles are sometimes against the encyclicalists and libertines and then against the pink socialists or the ultra-scarlet socialists, you daren't take a stand for any of them. But doctor pascalius prostituaan doesn't see that day after day I do most certainly take a stand: my own stand, my own malpertus from where I incite them with all possible means in order that they . . . like my reynard . . . may proclaim the republic of the free, the honest, the believers in Nothing.

## THE LATE MR GOD

As I was writing one of my latest papers . . . says poet and weekly journalist johan janssens . . . I evoked a hero who in my opinion belongs to the republic of the free believers-in-nothing and I wrote this about him:

from the shelf marked: 'avant-garde' a little book stares at you reproachfully, contemptuously, like an accusation or like god's threatening finger: avant nous le deluge, par Stanislas woelixsz. You, Stanislas woelixsz, who didn't expect the great universal confusion to come after us, but on the contrary, just before us and around us . . . you, Stanislas woelixsz, who because of this mistake were irrevocably classified as an avant-gardist by the old bookseller . . . you, Stanislas woelixsz, permit me to state a few things about you: to start off with: you have twice been to my house, the 1st time in the war, with a suitcase full of money, to pay the people who were in hiding . . . you almost forgot the suitcase . . . and the 2nd time with a suitcase full of poetry, avant nous le deluge, par Stanislas woelixsz; and you read from it, swaying rhythmically in your chair like a jew reading the bible, maybe you were hoping to sell a few copies . . . you never let the suitcase out of your sight, for a moment, because the printer hadn't been paid for these copies yet. And you also read from a novel—a failure, but still, a novel, with a lovely title: the late mr god. Talking of novels, in the first place you weren't the person to write a novel, you were far more the kind of person about whom someone else ought to write a novel; even your parents, they came here as refugees from somewhere far away in russia, out of fear for the bolshevists, only to see their son grow up into a bolshy, reading de lautréamont and lenin and sade, all mixed up and in 1 breath. You've been a spiritualist and you've studied biology and you've written surrealist things and what kind of a hopeless hotchpotch your mind is only the late mr god knows: a hopeless image of our hopeless times. But all right, in the war you were a partisan, you suffered hunger and want and fear, and after the liberation you were allowed to carry a musket from the days of maria theresia . . . because it couldn't be big and old-fashioned enough, your gun, and it couldn't make enough noise . . . it wasn't supposed to kill or wound anyone, your gun, it only needed to look impressive, and crack, and go pop, and show everyone quite clearly that Stanislas woelixsz had lived through terrors and had survived, that he existed spiritualistically and biologically and bolshevistically and that his future novels would not be to be sneezed at. Alas . . . they say in funeral orations . . . alas, it wasn't for nothing that you'd been on the road in weather and wind and night, as a partisan, it wasn't for nothing that you slept with your maria theresia musket on the floorboards in the farm loft, it wasn't in vain that you left your job with the fellow travelers in the attic room . . . you, poor penniless russian and partisan, spiritualist and biologist, and friend of the soviets, you came down from the dusty attic, and downstairs on the costly carpets, you ignored the wealthy fellow travelers . . . also it wasn't for nothing that you went into hiding, as the youngest office boy in a large insurance company: you made the shattering discovery that tuberculosis was eating your lungs. Avant nous le deluge, and now you are in Switzerland at the expense of your mother who works a bit harder and maybe eats a bit less, and at the expense of a few friends who made a collection for the benefit of . . . yes, how do you think they put it? . . . for the benefit of the late mr Stanislas woelixsz? Never mind, Stanislas woelixsz, console yourself in Switzerland, your musket and your faith may have gone by the board, but your collection of verse goes on grinning at us in the second hand bookshop, from the avant-garde shelf. And what more can a man wish for in life, than the knowledge that he, perhaps by mistake, belongs to the avant-garde, the peak, the republic of the free?

You see, says johan janssens, this is what I wrote as a greeting to someone I thought would have applauded the republic of the free and the believers-in-nothing . . . but my column appeared and it rained protest letters in the editor's office and in my own house in chapel road. Letters from his mother asking whether I wasn't ashamed, telling her that she ought to work harder and eat less . . . and I got letters from all his friends and acquaintances asking me if I wasn't ashamed, making fun of the tragic case of their friend Stanislas woelixsz, and making it known to all the world firstly that he had That disease, and secondly that he had carried a musket whereas in fact it was a mauser . . . and I got letters from goodness knows whom else and finally I got a letter from Stanislas woelixsz in which he said that he took the whole thing as a joke . . . a more or less misplaced joke, calling him already the late mr Stanislas woelixsz. And I, johan janssens, run through my list of people whom I consider worthy of belonging to the republic and I see with dismay how few they are.

## THE WOODEN MOUSE

*So the following week ondine stood outside the closed house waiting for oscar's father . . . the thought of going in there with him was far from her mind . . . but to take the money and then say that his son had found out everything and wanted to drown himself . . . that he . . . it was easy to find a reason—1 reason! to find 1000 reasons. She worked herself up, looking for more and more reasons; she scorned herself for her disgusting cowardice: what a petty-minded woman she was becoming . . . where had the time gone when god would have allowed her even to commit a murder? Oscar's father came, with the money . . . she went with him, upstairs; she got undressed. She stood in her slip which she had already undone at the shoulders, she only needed to let it slip . . . she held it up, with her hands against her breast, and still he saw nothing of her nakedness. She waited. She didn't know for what. She only waited, dumb and silent. But suddenly she began to cover him with reproaches, telling him that he was a whores' goat leading a whores' goat's life . . . keep your money, you stinking goat . . . choke in it, squander it on your whores. Then she reeled off all sorts of things that existed in life outside a woman's skirts: art and science, and heroism and struggle and pure love and duty-before-all-else . . . and . . . but what did he know or understand of all this? . . . life to you is this, here—look, look at it! And then, maybe for the 1st time in his life, he turned away, he turned his head away and threw his month's salary at her feet. Take the money and be happy with our oscar, he said. She took the money and stared at him for a long time. She tried to fathom him. If I wasn't ondine, I mean if I wasn't who I am, I'd think you were a nice person, she said. She added a great deal more, that maybe it wasn't his fault, only the old mouse's. This moved him so much that he began to explain haltingly that he would do anything to help them . . . I'll find the money and give it to you. He kept shaking his head, repeating: that grey mouse . . . yes, it's the truth . . . but do you know, it isn't only a grey mouse, it's also a wooden mouse. And he laughed scoffingly, a bitterly cynical, horrible laugh.*

## THE KING'S FAITHFUL SERVANT

Carcofas the donkey's words were still floating in the air and they were all gazing at these words, dumbfounded, till finally the badger saved the situation somewhat by suggesting that they summon reynard himself . . . at that very moment, as if it was a punch and judy show at the peasant fair, they heard a rustling noise in the wings and reynard emerged, strangely attired with a string of old shoes round his neck. With a gesture of: I know I'm putting my foot in it, he carefully put the old shoes down so that the holes in the worn soles and the nails in the gaping mouth lay staring at noble and his nobeline and all the other animals. He greeted them and said: I've come from far and I'm a bit late; I've just heard with mixed feelings that there is a charge against me—here he glanced briefly, with a slight inclination of his head, at that incomprehensible witch hersinde—a charge concerning certain unnameable things . . . forgive me that I cannot name them . . . because my heart fails to understand and my mind fails to comprehend that a lady, who allows the apples to be stolen from the garden of eden, should confess this to her husband afterwards. When I look around I see only mild feelings and great understanding: the donkey and the sheep, the owl, the monkey and the goat, and all the other honorable animals; I can confess to them that neither in my uncle's isengrinus' thrifty wife, nor in me, can the slightest trace of guilt be found, because nothing has happened between her and me . . . and if it had, the fault would lie with isengrinus himself, who had left his wife and children and was looking for adventures on the highway; he wanted to become bishop of houblon and walked about with a cooking pot on his head. Having said this, reynard pointed theatrically at the old shoes and said he'd had quite different, far more serious worries on his mind: when you were all fussing about your own trivial affairs, I thought about affairs of general interest, and of the illness of the world . . . I wondered what illness it might be from which our king and all the world are suffering—because that's the main question: in order to cure someone we should first know what he's suffering from—and on my long journeys I wore out many shoes, and wherever I went I saw the same: masters and leaders suffering from the same illness, which I therefore diagnose as: king's disease. The cause of this disease is that kings, masters and leaders, are no ordinary people but are raised above all treason . . . and from this I conclude that in order to escape from this illness one should live like the commonest people: for instance, if noble wrapped himself in isengrinus' skin, he would attain the health and appetite of a wolf. Although . . . and here reynard grinned . . . although he would have to take a medicine lest he should, together with his appetite, also acquire his stupidity. As soon as isengrinus heard the first syllable of his name, he started hurrying off . . . not even looking for hersinde; he pushed and elbowed to get out of the circle before anyone could catch him. In his blind haste he knocked off carcofas' glasses, which broke. Carcofas grabbed him by the shoulder and started shouting at him: you ass of a wolf, you'll pay for my glasses; and instead of escaping as fast as he could, the wolf committed the error of serving carcofas with a retort, so that he was seized and skinned and had to leave without a skin on his naked body. johan janssens.

## THE MISFIRED PRODUCT

Now it's may and it's raining, but johan janssens and the music master, followed by tolfpoets and kramiek, walk along the road which leads to the faraway fields beyond termuren . . . because they've had enough of it, they want to live far from the world in a little peasant cottage. Never mind if it's pissing down, says tolfpoets, we'll seek and we'll find. Johan janssens pinches his nose and says: I went to see the world of art yesterday, to write a review for the cultural page . . . I saw the whole tragi-comical pseudo world of artists as if it was for the last time: those pipes and long hair and their artistically displayed bohemian misery . . . very chic misery, actually, very artistic misery . . . danse triste de granados . . . it was quite disgusting to see them trailing after my journalistic behind hoping for a favorable notice . . . they know nothing about art, they always confuse it with craft; they think craft is art: a corpse that topples over when you so much as point at it, but a corpse which is technically correct, technically okay. And the music master, with the mud of the country lanes on his feet, adds: anyone with ears and eyes can hear and see everywhere that man is an inferior being . . . whatever he does, it's useless; too small, too imperfect, it's always only *as if it* is something . . . man is an inferior being, a misfired product of the earth, unable to embrace and comprehend enough . . . his height of 5 ft 9 is too little and he hasn't got enough brains under his flat skull. He uses his little brain to commit stupidities, to camouflage himself, to make himself look bigger than he really is, more important, more heroic, more courageous, wiser . . . and especially, richer. Msieu colson of the ministry, who's lagging behind, calls after them: and the rare people who are really People, live like exotic flowers on a compost heap . . . like orchids on rotting tree-trunks . . . they live there and bloom, but they can't change the existing facts because they themselves are rooted in the rotting mess . . . they are its products . . . children of decay, an error, a cynical whim of nature which occasionally allows a lovely flower to come out of the stinking mess. The last in the row is kramiek who's also got to shove his oar in to show he's there and has something to say: last week they showed a nudist film in the small town of the 2 mills which had been accidentally overlooked by the town council and so they hadn't been able to forbid it . . . it was an appeal to go and live somewhere on a farm, like adam and eve . . . and all the people who like to get their kicks on the sly, went to see that film, after dusk, with their collars pulled up and an old cap pushed down over their eyes . . . so as not to be recognized . . . and the next day, coming back from holy mass, they said: such smutty films shouldn't be allowed, good heavens, the way they went about, all in their naked flesh! And one person asked another: have you seen it then? So the second one, replied, if he thought he couldn't have been seen: no, I only have it from hearsay. And if he thought he might have been seen: yes, but only to see how far they'd dare go with their smuttiness.

## THE JOKE OF THE CROSS OF BRAVERY

Tolfpoets gets forgotten . . . because in your search for a farmer's cottage in the rain and wind of may . . . and in reply to everything the others have been saying about the smallness of man, tolfpoets comes up with a bit of yarn too: the day before yesterday somebody was decorated, the old mason from the labor, he got a 1st class cross because of some heroic deed . . . and when they handed him the decoration they asked him: how did you suddenly, at the critical moment, find the courage for that deed of heroism? And the mason answered: oh well, you know, when you're sozzled . . . He goes home with his 1st class cross and of course he visits a couple of bars on the way and when he finally comes home to his family they all crowd around him and want to see that cross . . . he's a bit tipsy again and searches in all his pockets, but it isn't there.

## A WEDDING OF QUARRELS AND VEXATIONS

*Ondine started to make such haste with the preparations for the marriage that it startled both vapeur and the schatts. Things had to be paid for, just when vapeur had to pay his first instalment of interest to the timber yard . . . it was an enormous sum which gave him an even bigger fright than the marriage; if he was going to have to fork out a sum like that every 6 months, he wouldn't know what to do. It was no good putting his trust in god, god was too great, god was heaven and earth and science and all people together. But he kept his troubles from ondine, he suffered in silence, he carried his bitterness in his heart without uttering a word . . . and whether he didn't want her to know what the situation was, or whether he took pleasure in nurturing his self-torment, he simply said that he hadn't got any money for the wedding. Ondine said that she didn't have any either . . . they stood facing each other and it was strange to see on both their mouths a little smile, stemming from the same source, from the same family trait, yet with quite different expressions, because of their so different attitudes to life: Oscarke also got his share of the general pain and torment, he too had to go to his mother now and then, asking for money to pay for this and that . . . the mouse asked in surprise: what's this? . . . only to make her son miserable. She shook her head and said she had no money for such things . . . but his father, who was a bit of a scoundrel and a judas, asked what she did with his money then: you never pay in the shops, you live in a villa without paying off, we hardly eat and you don't buy any fuel either, and now that the boy is getting married you want to throw him out without a shirt on his back . . . you must be hiding the money under a floorboard or somewhere. She turned pale, she almost fell from her perch, because it was the truth, she did hide what little money there was in the loft . . . if he got to know about it, he'd soon pinch half of it and squander it on his whores. Oscarke looked from one to the other, not knowing whom to believe. It was an odd wedding—a wedding of quarrels and vexations, and ondine, who'd ordered meat and flowers and pastry and carpets in the church, had asked for the bills to be sent to the schatts. At first she'd intended to let both sides pay half, but after all, the one was her father, and she hated the mouse too much: it isn't a mouse, I was wrong, it's a rat, she thought, a rat which ought to be kicked to death. And she arranged for the service to be held a little nearer noon, so that it would be more expensive. It was strange, but as you saw them walking up the carpeted aisle; oscar at his mother's arm and ondine at her father's, all smiling . . . a rigid smile, it is true, a posed smile . . . it was a wedding like 1000 others. Only zulma behaved a bid oddly in church . . . but even valeer, who was witness for ondine, looked as normal as the priest himself. The party, if it could be called a party, passed in silence. They sat at trestle tables in vapeur's work shed, divided into 2 factions: the bosmans and the schatts. They took the meat and hid it, the mouse's reticule was crammed full of cakes and valeer stuffed away bottles of liquor in a corner full of wood shavings. There were only 2 who took no notice of anything: ondine and her father-in-law; they sat in a corner, flattering each other as if each one feared that the other might let out something. She regretted that when they were in that room together she'd taken sides with all that is Beautiful and Sublime in the world . . . she should have been smarter, she ought to have milked him dry altogether. How are things now with . . . with . . . mr achilles derenancourt, she asked, gasping a little as she asked it; she pressed two fingers on the throbbing vein in her neck. Oscarke's father told her, whispering, and demanding eternal silence, that mr achilles derenancourt always had to have new blood around him, ever younger, ever more luscious . . . at the moment he'd got a little girl who was still at school in pont street . . . and do you know where he found her? In that house by the station where she was available after school . . . he'd taken her away with him and had written an article about moral decline and now he went to bed with her himself. Ondine saw in his eyes the regret of his small dog's soul . . . regret because he hadn't been able to take that child from the brothel. But he saw in ondine's eyes regret too . . . regret . . . ondine cut short his thoughts and suddenly asked rudely: why was it that he thought of nothing else but to live under a woman's skirts . . . while oscar, on the contrary . . . oscar . . . She looked at him significantly. He smiled pityingly: wait and see, maybe oscar has got a little of his mother's fish blood . . . but you know, I myself was seventeen before I got a taste for it . . . you'll find he'll make up for it one day. Thereupon ondine stood up and smoothed down her skirts: you're a dirty old man, she said. She called oscarke, and left them all sitting there.*

## CANCER

You see, you've just uttered your immense pity for that misfired product: man . . . for that bit of mildew: man . . . for that bit of cancer, physical and spiritual cancer, which is man . . . you have just uttered your immense pity for him, thinking: we're getting towards the end of our book and we must make sure we display a certain amount of pity . . . so now you've just remembered to display your immense pity, and you happen to walk to the town of the 2 mills with your father who says: have you ever noticed that all those pro-germans from back in the war really have german faces? The words fall on your heart and mind like a bucket of cold water, because it's true: if you look at those who were to some degree affected with this spiritual cancer, you see that they've all got to some degree the same physiognomy . . . and that it can't therefore be their fault if they thought and felt with hearts and minds like concentration camps. So you arrive at the shattering thought that maybe there's no question of Crime because everybody acts according to what he thinks is best, and that this is determined by the construction of his brains, by his heart and his kidneys, by hormones and glands . . . and that therefore there may well be specific kinds of people, each kind acting according to what he thinks best. As you're tormenting yourself with this thought, which may be wrong, you stare at johan janssens' son—10 years old—and you wonder to what kind of race he belongs . . . probably to the same race as his father, the race which wants to embrace the whole world in endless mercy . . . but therefore also the race that's always being knocked about, pushed in a corner and crushed underfoot, which gets locked up in concentration camps and trampled on by pushers and go-getters. Angrily, you feel like boxing yourself on the ears, you run to a gunshop and buy johan janssens' son an air gun with lead pellets: here, take this, learn to shoot like the best of them. And soon enough he's back in your garden, trembling lips and an unfathomable strangeness in his eyes, in his hand a dead sparrow. You can't describe it, because emotion heaves through your pen in waves: he's proud, showing you that dead sparrow . . . proud, because he can shoot so well . . . but he bursts out in passionate tears because it was a sweet little creature which he shot down and which now lies dead in his hand. Dear little sparrow, knocked down by me, just like that . . . We went back to that garden together and buried the dear little sparrow. But look, over there behind the other gardens, in the garden of the derenancourts' castle, their son stalks about with a much more expensive airgun, one that can be set at automatic . . . rouf-rouf—20 slugs . . . and with this he riddles the sparrows, all the sparrows he sees. There you stand, you and johan janssens' son, who's 10 . . . with your immense pity, ready to be massacred for ever and ever in all eternity amen, by those who do not have immense pity. And best of all, you mustn't show them that you're filled with immense pity for them, because that really would make them feel triumphant . . . and moreover, you mustn't write that basically there may be different human races, because then they'd take advantage of your opinion at once and look upon their own race as the Highest race, the race which has the right to crush johan janssens' son under its heel.

## IN THE ROOM OVER THE CAFÉ

*Vapeur didn't see his daughter leaving for good . . . he was drunkenly blathering his world language . . . he sang; he sang his grief away and he sang in order to get enough courage to start on that gutter tomorrow . . . he'd have to start on it, because he needed the money to pay the next 6 months' interest. Ondine and oscarke walked down chapel road in the dark, to their room in the café by the 1st dirty houses . . . they heard footsteps behind them . . . mouse-footsteps . . . it was his mother, returning to her unpaid villa all alone and weeping, calling to oscar in the dark. It was like a symbol: his mother calling and ondine pulling him along by the arm. They slipped into their room and at last got into bed together . . . oscarke fell asleep at once, beside the warmth of her body . . . but ondine lay awake, she pressed her thighs together and dared not let the sheet touch her cheek; it was the bed in which strangers had slept. On the wall above the little corner fireplace she noticed a crucifix . . . she saw it moving. But although she had threatened all and sundry with god and his hellish punishments, the days in which she had believed in miracles had gone long ago . . . she stood on the bed and looked carefully at the crucifix . . . it was really moving . . . she took it from the nail and saw a teeming swarm of bugs. A chair and a bed in which she daren't sleep, plus a crucifix moving with bugs, so that's what she had acquired in life, after all her fighting, all her desperate struggles to make something of her youth. She had imagined marriage as . . . as something different . . . as something in a faraway future which would change everything, which would at last bring about what she had always longed for. She had longed for something, for a change in this stupid termuren life . . . the change had come, but it wasn't exactly an improvement. Oscar could talk about stone and marble . . . and as ondine suddenly discovered in self-mockery: about hard and cold . . . but practically, he wasn't worth a cent to her . . . oh yes, she'd known it, she'd wanted just this . . . but to be honest, he had turned her head too, after all, with one thing and another: wasn't he going to be famous? Yes, he was, but he simply sat on the edge of the bed—because she was sitting on the only chair—waiting for noon, for dinner time. They didn't even have a stove to cook on, they had no wood no coal scuttle no potatoes no bread . . . and oscarke suddenly realized that he was married and that he . . . but no, he almost certainly didn't realize anything, he simply waited to see what ondine was going to say about it.*

## THE OLD HUNCHBACK'S NOVEL

The old hunchback meets you in chapel road, he stops, because I want to have a word with you, he says: I hear you've written a story about our chapel road and that you now want to leave us and live in a cottage in the country; well now, your life's all wrong, just as your story is bound to be all wrong as well . . . living in a cottage far from the world is no life . . . and a book about chapel road is no book . . . if I were to write a book it would be like this: it's something very old which my late mother told me when I was a child: a poor but beautiful girl is orphaned and the workhouse sends her to be fostered with a farmer, as they used to do, and she grows up and becomes even more beautiful than she was before, and the son of the notary or the burgomaster fell in love with her but he's got to go and study at the youniversity, to be a doctor, and he becomes a doctor and he marries a rich lady and the beautiful girl has a child from him and is held in contempt by everyone and she gives her child away at the convent, she puts it on a plank and the plank moves away and she's lost her child forever, maybe she sheds a tear or two, and goes outside, and then begins her life as a poor but beautiful fallen girl; later she gets The Disease and she's got to go to hospital and she's going to die and at her death bed are the priest and the doctor and the doctor is her lover, he can tell from the ring which he put on her finger long ago, and he asks what happened to our child and she replies that she left it at the convent of the sisters of saint dromedary, and the priest says: I'm your son because I'm the child that was left in the convent of the sisters of saint dromedary. Here the hunchback stops and looks at you, because this is the novel he would write; of course, a bit spun out and padded to make it longer, he says. You see? that dying woman who was a poor but beautiful girl, and at her death bed the doctor and the priest who should have been her husband and her son . . . that would have been a proper book, but your book won't be a proper book, there'll be nothing in it about life *AS IT REALLY IS.*

**LOUIS PAUL BOON** (1912-1979) started out as a house painter but went on to become the author of a large and rich oeuvre spanning several genres: from the compelling historical epics he composed later in life to his sharp, witty work as a newspaper columnist and his tongue-in-cheek, scabrous novels. Boon is one of the most important writers of Flemish literature in the twentieth century, a keen observer of society, the individual and the interplay between them.

**ADRIENNE DIXON** is a translator of Dutch and Flemish literature.

**CHAD W. POST** is the founder and publisher of Open Letter Books, the editorial director of Dalkey Archive Press, and founder of the Translation Database, the Best Translated Book Awards, multiple literary podcasts (Two Month Review, Three Percent), and the Three Percent website.

www.ingramcontent.com/pod-product-compliance
Lightning Source LLC
Jackson TN
JSHW080933100925
90244JS00001B/1
* 9 7 8 1 6 2 8 9 7 5 1 9 2 *